ENDPOINT

- BOOK 1: DAY ZERO -

J.W. GRIFFIN

JWGRIFFIN.US

Cover design, illustration & interior formatting:
Mark Thomas / Coverness.com

"And so in this sense of the words,
this exitus mortis, the issues of death,
is liberatio in morte, a deliverance in death..."
John Donne - 'Death's Duel'

LOST OASIS

"As a dark shadow grows long across
our galaxy, I know what I must
embrace, what I must become."
-Ryan McBain

In the darkened crew compartment, caramel skin glowed from reflected light off a data tablet. Long and lithe—measuring six feet in height—Khattara Uldago Eschala of House Menduvalli sat alone with her legs folded under her. The rightful heir of Centauri was tall by human standards, but childhood events had made her shorter than the average female from her home world. She was, in many ways, a contrast of convention. Although born of royal lineage, she looked away from it. Early on, her honor and her innocence had been stripped away. In their place, a trial by fire had fanned the spark of a warrior of legend. The hand found the hilt, but a bitter stone of betrayal remained and rattled through her heart.

She resisted much, not the least of which was any attachment to others. Fierce and unyielding, she had learned to conceal feelings and bury need. She was labeled "difficult"—no one dared tread on her, save one improbable fool. Now she sat separated by time and space from that same improbable fool—the one who had grown so precious. Her eyes—dark brown with brilliant violet edges—danced across the language on the screen. Her fingertips came momentarily to her lips, then moved down, toying with an Earth falcon amulet.

She traced around golden wings that arced up to cradle a light blue headstone. Although it appeared like a priceless artifact from the pharaohs of old, the secret power it possessed was far more valuable. But in this moment, she wasn't thinking of the value or the power. As her hand came to rest over her upper heart, she was thinking about the one who had given her the jeweled pendant.

"Virginia, I'm not sure about this."

"What is the source of your hesitation?"

"I'm just not sure I should be reading this."

"Before I was assigned to you, the commander transferred a complete archive into my database. You have access to all libraries, records, and technology. This includes his personal journal. Ryan was very specific about your authorization level in a crisis contingency scenario."

"Would you categorize our situation as such?"

"It is logical to acknowledge that our return is not certain. I have authorized access to his personal records and will translate into your native language."

Eschala thought for a moment. "There's so much I want to know, but first I need to know about the Daerk attack. Can you take me to that segment of his personal record?"

"I am accessing it now. Portions of it appear to have been modified recently."

Personal Record
CDR M. Ryan McBain
Date: Day Zero Endpoint

Day Zero began as a routine of routines, which looking back now should have been sufficient foreshadowing. I was outside on a vanilla EVA supervising automated drones. They were repairing exterior shield panels on Hadley's orbital station. Riveting work, if you'll excuse the pun. Being assigned to my brother's post was a penance associated with the recent events that had clipped my wings. I'd gone from fleet command to robot command, and I wasn't wearing humility particularly well. There was also a certain post-traumatic edginess that wept forward into the mundane daily activities of my work. I was a tiger in a small cage. The fight with Hadley the night before hadn't helped matters. I was a grown man, and he was still treating me like his little brother. What I needed was a little encouragement and support. Instead, I got some kind of half-baked lecture on responsibility, focus, and sacrifice. I'd largely ignored earlier needling comments, but when he stepped up on his soapbox, I snapped.

I leaned back in my chair, and we stared at each other for several seconds. I think I said something about "cheap talk from safe sidelines," and I asked him how many lives *his focus* had recently saved. The smoldering discourse had flared full blown, fanned in no small part by the whiskey, into a childish spat. His provocation, as always, was well played. Strafing down on target, he responded that he was too busy constantly saving his *misfit little brother*. I tipped my glass to swallow the last of it and felt the burn going down. With meticulous care, I placed the empty shot glass on the table and straightened my jacket. As our eyes met, I bolted up and dove across the table. I tackled his smug little face right over the back of his chair. I do feel badly for Station Safety & Security. 3S was called in to break up a bar fight, but upon arrival, they discovered the ruckus was between the station chief and its top military commander. They honestly didn't know what to do. It certainly wasn't our most professional moment.

Working the next morning—outside both the station and his oppressive regime—felt good. He'd left me a video message before our shift that was one of those "I'm sorry..." messages that progressed with twisted logic into "...but you made me do it." I remember thinking it was so typical. The only redeeming part of it was seeing the blossoming shiner that he'd have to explain all day. I replayed the message twice on mute; it was glorious. I so yearned for the end of that post. I wanted to get away—away from my life, from my family, from everything. I should have been more careful what I wished for. The stinging anguish over how we left it has never diminished over the years. I'd give anything if I could go back.

At 10:07 local station time, I was wrestling with a stuck panel caught on a crate when a thousand flashes signaled the entry of an armada—a massive armada. My head turned and had scarcely cocked in confusion when the silhouettes and symbols registered in my memory. Twice before I'd seen these ships. Before my eyes could grow large, the space erupted in a blinding flash of fire. Orbital platforms were hit first. There was a blast. As it turned out, the panel in my hand shielded me from most of the fire into our station. I don't know how long I was unconscious. My eyes opened to an even greater nightmare.

Jagged and twisted debris floated everywhere. Our station, and my brother with it, was just gone. The aggressors had moved lower in orbit and were now bombarding the planet surface. I could see solid beams of light firing off hundreds of ships and converging through dozens of consolidating devices. The confluence from each formed a single concentrated cutting beam. Far lower, flashes and explosions marked the points where they struck the surface, slicing deep across the planet.

Suddenly, a massive octahedron-shaped vessel eclipsed the Sun. I saw it clearly as it passed over for what seemed like several seconds. It was different from the legion of cruisers and frigates surrounding the planet. Its charcoal color had a dull, matte finish, and it soaked up all light that touched it. There were no seams, portals, or markings on its perfectly smooth surface. I watched the ghastly specter silently sail past. I couldn't take my eyes away from it; looking upon it felt like diving headlong with open mouth into a fountain of dread. Smaller frigate class ships buzzed around it in escort as it moved off toward the Sun.

Earth forces were immediately overwhelmed with the power and numbers of the attackers. A few ships from Fleet jumped in, but they were instantly bathed in a frenzy of fire. I could hear automated distress signals on frequency for a few moments before they were dashed into oblivion. More flashes announced the arrival of perhaps a hundred more ships in the aggressor fleet. The new arrivals were fatter and had a bottom concave focusing shape. These undersides were firing luminous, bluish-purple spherical objects. Hundreds of these sparkling projectiles rained down on every corner of the planet. Where each landed, there was a momentary blinding flash. There were so many that it looked like a bank of flashes from paparazzi. Even from orbit, I could see a warping distortion at the point of impact; the surface rippled, and a mushroom cloud rose off each. Massive planetary fractures and fissures were now visible between the growing clouds of debris.

The slicing beams and bombardment were literally pulling up, twisting, and skinning the planet. Our species had never seen an energy display of this magnitude. The atmosphere rapidly grew murky as the offensive continued to pulverize and chew up the crust of our Earth. After several minutes of bombardment, an angry orange cauldron of planetary mantle churned up through a continuous dirty brown debris cloud. The assault began to eject massive orange and yellow segments of mantle, hurling them away into space. The bombers moved further out into orbit to avoid the planetary spatter. Waves of coordinated fire on opposite sides of the planet pitched and chipped larger segments of mass into space.

As the dark minions worked feverishly to eradicate all trace of humanity, the one driving them in the massive black ship took position very near our Sun. The octahedron hinged open into two hollow pyramids, exposing a central core of brilliant light that looked like a small purple star. From my position at that time, I could only see a giant cyclone, which started pulling in the Sun's corona. As it continued to pull and strip off Her fiery glow, She diminished first in luminescence and then in size. I was witness to an evil harvest as the dark ship slowly swallowed our star. I watched as Her glow flickered and faded. I strained to see any trace of Her, but She was gone. Her light and Her song were taken, just like billions of my people below. The dark ship hinged closed and vanished.

In less than an hour, it was done. The minion ships flashed away just as they'd come. All that remained was debris and dust veiled by darkness. I looked around, struggling to comprehend what I was desperate to deny. There was no light where our Sun was supposed to be. Our home planet had been scatter shot into the cosmos, as had our moon with all her colonies. My brother, my aunts, and billions of other lives on the surface had all been snuffed out. It was a perfect ambush by minions streaming from the seam of an evil void. In a single assault, the darkness had executed a nearly perfect genocide of our species—all save one.

They left me floating away like space garbage. As the level of adrenaline in my bloodstream diminished, I became aware of a physical biting. During the initial volley, I had been peppered by shrapnel from the blast that destroyed our station. The outer layers of my helmet visor had cracked, and an incessant chiming in my ear indicated critically low oxygen levels from a leak. Under the damaged suit, my body was battered and badly broken.

A piercing pain in my shoulder nearly overcame me when I tried to reach across and cover the suit breach in my upper arm. I panted as I struggled to look left, right, above, and below. There was so much death and destruction; my thoughts spiraled faster and tighter into an apex of dread. Heart pounding, I struggled and thrashed for the breach.

For several minutes, I tried but could not reach it. Pain and fatigue overwhelmed me. Dizzy and nauseous, I gazed at the space where my planet—my beautiful blue marble—should have been. I strained my eyes, doubting that the Earth, with all her people, could really have been destroyed. But everything I'd ever known was gone, and my life was leaking out into the vacuum of space.

In that moment, the inevitable registered in me: *death… imminent*. I closed my eyes and just tried to breathe. So many faces and moments washed past. After a time, everything became very quiet, except for the chiming, and I let it be in the background. As my mind drifted, the coldness of space permeated through me. It was surprisingly peaceful.

As I diminished, I could feel a presence and then a warmth. There was a blinding brightness, and all at once I could feel my mother come upon me. The pain was gone, and being in her presence was joyous. Her fierce rocking embrace surrounded me. I could smell her and feel the fuzziness of her favorite sweater on my cheek. Serenity wrapped around me like a warm blanket. My silent lips mouthed, *Mom!* I reached to her, and she whispered into my soul. I think of those words when I get low. A thousand times I've replayed them:

"Brave boy, I love you so. The path ahead is rocky and steep. Draw strength. The flame of your candle will suffer the winds of a long and starless night. Face into it with courage. Know that all things with beginnings have an end. No power can ever forever divide us. Have faith. If you reach, you will find my hand."

I felt a rush and a separation from her. I reached for her hand, and suddenly there were excited voices and noises. Through the gurgle of blood in my lungs I cried out, "Mom!" I regained consciousness in freakish pain on the medical table of a Paavi ship. A kind hand assuaged my restless thrashing. Fear and confusion wept from my eyes, and I laid there a tangled mess. Helpless, I could only watch as the hands of an alien surgeon worked frantically and methodically to save me. Every so often, those surgeon's hands would pause their purposeful urgency to softly touch my cheek.

In her eyes, I saw something. It was immeasurable love. That brilliant woman was my Paavi mother, and on that day in her saving hands, I was reborn. Though I didn't yet understand the soft murmur of her words as she tended to me, I felt the message like a chord of truth reverberating through the hollows of my soul. I regained consciousness many times over the next few weeks, and each time I woke, I met those encouraging eyes. I had no idea what would happen next, but the healing power in her gaze eclipsed the terror and buffered the loss.

The Darkness came so close, but hope slipped through its fumbling clutches. And so, I was laid down at the base of the mountain. Narrow, thin, and fragile was the beginning of the path for the Arm Behind the Goddess. The climb ahead was relentless. Setbacks were a howling wind continually trying to blow me down. For most of the journey, my only companions were haunting memories that followed me all too closely. Often in each waking hour, I invoked the mantra of my life: "Eyes forward; keep moving forward. Don't stop; keep moving, just keep moving."

Higher along, several trails converged near the apex, and I would meet other survivors in the climb. Our paths joined, and these rebels became family. One such raven-haired warrior of legend would redeem me in ways I couldn't have imagined. Over the past two centuries, victory over the dark armies has demanded ghastly acts I never thought myself capable of. I've waded so far into the evil ether that I've forgotten where I came from. Adoption of another culture to obscure my origin, close alliances with alien species, and becoming a guardian for beings I originally sought to destroy have blurred the lines. Nothing is clear anymore and I realize I've been drifting, lost in a vast gray sea. The beauty that is my perfect half defines the light, and in recent days, it was she who revived my humanity. A Centauri brought me back to earth. For this and for her, I am eternally grateful. As a dark shadow grows long across our galaxy, I know what I must embrace, what I must become. But I have no resolve to afflict her with this presence. In the most selfish moment of my life, I have blocked her from continuing on. Goddess forgive me; this I've done that the love of my life would survive.

Eschala read the last words of the entry over and over. Her mouth was slightly open, and her head shook gently. She looked to the side as the light of the tablet dimmed. Clutching it tightly in her arms, she lay down and closed her eyes. "I shall take a moment before I return to this."

"Understood. We are at best possible speed back to the fringes."

ROUGH DAY

"MY PEOPLE EXCEL AT CREATIVE THINKING
AND TAKE AN OATH. THAT MEANS HOLDING
THE LINE, EVEN IF IT CUTS THROUGH
YOU."

—GENERAL LUND

Many years earlier...

The side access door to the Military Command briefing room nearly came off its hinges. The Command Guard normally took care of opening doorways and access entries, but events everywhere this day were happening at an accelerated rate. The supreme commander of Earth's aligned military bowled through the entry as his attachés struggled to keep up.

If there was a physical die stamp for creating military leaders, Major General Aiden Keim would fit it. The SC's chest and torso were like a large barrel. The legs below it were spindly little things that moved the man much like small whirling propellers attached to a large ship. This wasn't to say his movements were at all graceful. Over many years in the field, he had racked up countless injuries. Now fused joins and scar tissue all moved together in a gait like a lumbering foxtrot. Heredity and stress had both ganged up on him over the years. Light brown and thinning hair dusted his forehead. The only remaining evidence of the thick curly mane of his youth was framed in pictures. Weathered lines ran deep across his face like a road map that chronicled the stress canyons throughout his career. But the roughness of his face gave way to kind eyes.

Although he was a fair and thoughtful man, the twinkle in his eyes was the glint from a sharp, business-like edge. It took a certain will to knowingly send young people to their demise, and the general was very good at his job, although the guilt stayed with him. Even the bourbon couldn't quell the voices in the silence of the deep of night. Today's events were enough to cause the SC, as well as many others, to spree later in a vain attempt to drown out the memory.

He'd barreled fully into the room before a startled Command Guard shouted, "atten*TION! Supreme commander!*"

Everyone lurched up as the SC came to stand at the head of the table. He nodded as everyone sat—everyone but him. He leaned forward on both hands and scowled sourly across the room. "President's taking credit in the press for successfully repelling the Khrylic invasion. But make no mistake, the smile is for the media, and she's making a very different face at me. So, let me make this very, very clear: We need to understand how Khrylic forces electronically defeated our defense net across the entire system, did so without alarm, disabled integrated battle systems fleet-wide, massed in near space undetected, launched a planetary-scale invasion unopposed, and somehow," he said, waving a hand in the air and raising his voice, "have been miraculously repelled...with, with..." he shook his head, "some sort of dumb luck?" An uncomfortable quiet smothered the room. "I need answers. How'd this happen? And where the hell are they now?"

The brightest eyes from leaders across the Unified Forces of Earth all looked down. There was restless shifting and a muffled cough. The eyes of the supreme commander searched the room for some spark of information, some data point that could reverse his dire sense of the situation. A fan motor from a projector display changed speed, and the subtlety of the noise only served to highlight the deafening silence. The inner ring at the table lay low and quiet.

Looking out further into the secondary seats lining the room and the two rows of seating in the back gallery, the SC hoped to meet bright eyes, but he found no relief.

A man seated in the back of the room did, in fact, have answers. His head was also down, but he stared at the floor for very different reasons. Rings of shock washed through him as an incalculable loss racked down to his core. Languishing there, he sat alone in a room full of others.

The SC grimaced. "Don't everyone speak at once," he said, and looking to his immediate right, "Dana, how the hell'd they breach your grid?"

General Dana Bencix looked up through thin-framed glasses. A soft-spoken, small statured woman of Krio descent, her knowledge and words wielded great power and influence with the SC. Many years earlier, after surviving a blast that nearly took both her legs, then Major Bencix had continued to fire on approaching hostile forces. Although her logistics group wasn't supposed to take fire on the front line, the younger Bencix found herself caught in the midst of a flanking force.

There were flashes of heat and oppressive pressure from a barrage of explosions. The booming of automatic rifle fire echoed and rang out so close. Rounds whizzed through the air, plinking and thudding as they landed all around. Urgent voices shouted, edgy with panic. One voice, however, was a tether of sanity in the face of mortal calamity. Cooled by logic and utility, Bencix's even voice directed resources over her shoulder between bursts of return fire.

Rifle barrel pivoting dramatically, her rounds purchased additional seconds for her people. Wood splinters and dirt ricocheted around her from enemy fire. She turned her head, squinting, but the debris was merely an annoyance. She was undeterred. Her relentless fire suppressed the advance long enough for her men and women to converge and retreat.

The other side escalated in response, and the blast was deafening. She was aware of her own body in flight. Bencix regained awareness as she looked down at her lowered rifle barrel, its strap tangled around her wrist. A stinging pain shot through her lungs as she took normal breaths. A body was crumpled under her, and she could see the legs pointed out and upward.

Her staff scrambled around her, and she couldn't hear what they were saying. As her body lurched, dragged backwards by her collar, she realized that the legs crumpled under her were in fact her own, if barely. She looked up just in time to see an enemy round glance through the shoulder of her sergeant. Looking back toward the onslaught, her left eye squinted gently. Resolve percolated just beneath her glossy stare.

Clumsy paws racked her rifle, and defiant to the last, she raised the barrel again. The enemy was very close and now advancing in the open. Firing quickly, she shot four of them before the remainder of the enemy dropped again for cover. She continued to fire while being dragged away by the collar of a smoldering vest. The major's barrel only quieted when she succumbed to her injuries.

She woke some time later in a hospital and faced an even greater challenge: to soldier again with a missing leg. For days she wept quietly, looking down at the emptiness on the bed, where she could still feel the leg that should have been there. There was unimaginable pain in her recovery. She made it her business to become an expert at standing back up.

She regained mobility and sued to stay in the service. Through all the hearings that exposed the intimate details of her physical fitness, one officer stood with her. He was the one who had sent her on that mission, and he was the one she woke to in the hospital. His words echoed for a lifetime in her mind, confronting her doubts. "*Dana, this ain't hard. This ain't nothin! You wanna know what hard is? Hard is shooting four enemy combatants after having your legs blown to hell. Hard is laying down suppressing fire in low visibility from all the smoke coming off your own burning flak vest. What could you possibly face that's harder than that? Huh? You're a giant! Don't you ever forget where you come from. That's an order.*"

He was then, just as he was now, her commanding officer. Bencix was part of the supreme commander's inner circle. Their history, in addition to countless records still held to that day on encryption cyphers at the War College, had made her the best candidate for chief of electronic warfare.

After clearing her throat, she responded quietly. "Apparently, they used sub-routines in a number of maintenance programs to plant segments of inert code. These fragments appeared more like code dust after various system events or compilations. Over a period of many months, these fragments represented enough data to form an active routine. The code fragments alone didn't pose a threat or raise any flags, but when all the elements coalesced via an unknown catalyst program, the components compiled into an active virus."

"The intruder spawned inside our firewalls. Our systems detected it, but as our defenses hunted the virus, it was quickly able to move through internals until it found the source system for our anti-virus protocols. Once there, we believe it decompiled into many smaller fragments and indicated a false kill of itself. Our defense systems registered and labeled the remaining data fragments as benign or neutral. One such fragment passively shut down our defense networks for what was classed as an extended maintenance window. When the window elapsed beyond our timing limits, the system initiated a module restart. The restart isolated the trigger indicators for network status that the code subsequently flipped again, spoofing the trigger mechanisms."

The SC squinted sourly at the chief for a long second. "Dumb it down for me, Dana. You sayin' some kind of secondary virus tricked our systems into thinking the net was on when in fact our entire defense grid was down?"

"Yes, sir. That would be an accurate statement."

"General, when you return to your people, I want you to impress upon them the significance of determining specifically how this happened. More importantly, let them know their very survival depends on preventing it from happening again, because it does. This cannot happen again. Are we clear?"

"Crystal, sir."

"Can anyone tell me what the hell did work?"

The languishing man in the back heard a voice say, "Sir, we're your dumb luck." Only a moment later did he realize it was his own voice.

The SC's head snapped like a hawk. "Who said that?"

Clearing his throat and speaking louder now, the man replied, "General Richard Lund, Sir, skipper ED4."

Craning his head, the SC boomed, "Make a hole for the Marine!"

General Lund rose on tingling, unsteady legs. Upon standing, he realized that he couldn't feel his toes. He pulled his dress jacket down and straight. The heavy wool material felt strange, and he realized that his fingertips were also tingling numb. He was acutely aware of his dull steps touching the floor as he navigated carefully toward the front. Two higher ranking generals moved aside so he could approach the big table.

The SC instantly recognized the face. Not just who the man was, but the state of the man. The wide-eyed and far-away look was haunting. The SC had too much familiarity with the kind of empty eyes that came as a result of loss— great loss. He'd already been briefed that smaller defense forces were the only groups to mount attacks, and he knew in general terms that there had been a heavy toll. Here was a sharp sting of sacrifice amidst extraordinary heroism.

General Lund's eyes confirmed the briefing data. The SC looked at the approaching general with a small, tight smile because in that moment, he had a face to represent the group that, despite overwhelming odds, had squared off and ultimately defeated a far superior force. With an appreciation welling up within him, he stepped away from his chair and motioned to it. Quietly, he said, "Right here if you will, Rich. Save the planet, and you get the big seat. Please, sit here."

General Lund moved down the length of the table and plopped down into the leader's chair. He perched on the front edge and momentarily thought that the chair, much like the world, was rather large around him. The SC turned around and sat on the edge of the table with his back to the rest of the room. Looking down to the side at the general, he asked, still quietly, "So, your guys launched in what, short-range small raiders?"

"Affirmative. The Wing is comprised of single pilot, heavily armed kestrels."

The SC nodded. "kestrels, those are like...fifty-year-old ships?"

"The mark IX's are approaching twenty-five years on the frames, but they have upgraded power plants, modern threat management systems, and current fleet weaponry, including short-range nuclear payloads. They're classed as quasi-automated. Many systems are manual, and the ship's been hardened with mechanical switches. Automation aside, it would appear that human intervention was the key in this engagement."

The SC nodded again. "Which bases and groups engaged?"

"Everything. The remaining thirteen active squadrons launched from orbital and Terran-based positions to address the threat. The attack came during a shift change cycle, so everything space worthy went out. All my people went. All of them."

Lund swallowed, and after a short pause, he continued. "One of our patrols initially discovered an anomaly that ultimately uncovered the network breach. After the call, several crews jumped in and located and identified multiple enemy vessels approaching the Earth. We took fire and determined that the armada was a hostile planetary invasion force. Subsequently, we targeted and engaged the remainder of our forces against prioritized enemy assets."

The SC tightened one cheek. "How'd they do against the Khrylic advance?"

General Lund shook his head gently and looked down at the table.

The SC nodded. "Heavy losses?"

With eyes wide as a galaxy, Lund looked off, nodding gently.

"Can you brief us on what happened?"

Ryan was nearing the end of a scheduled ten-hour patrol trip that had extended into a twelfth hour. The trip route included several passes around Mars Station and a perimeter cruise of the system edge defense sensors, or SEDS, located along more than twelve percent of the solar system's quadrants. All equipment was functioning, and the only challenge was trying to stay awake at the midpoint. Near his shift's end, Ryan stole a moment to look beyond the sensor edges, out into deep space. He stared, wide-eyed, into the endless expanse.

Without realizing it, Ryan raised his hands from the controls and up toward the glass. The vastness pulled at him. Inside the horizon of the mind's eye, an ocean of possibilities extended ahead. A flashing system monitor broke through the intoxication, and he split his gaze between the console and the view outward.

Unlike most of his colleagues, Ryan looked for excuses to stay out on the edges for prolonged periods. He was reminded of the same feeling from his youth. So many nights, he would gaze into the high desert sky. Breathing the cold, crisp air, he'd take the entire sky in one field. With arms extended, his fingertips would reach for the stars. His eyes would close slowly, and the chill of winter gales would blow straight through him. He'd feel himself expand out, enmeshed into the very fabric of the galaxy. Inevitably, the call of a distant coyote would return him. Looking above, he'd imagine the destination of the commercial craft rocketing across the sky. It didn't really matter where it was going, so long as it was anywhere else. The future was always better over the next horizon.

The corner of Ryan's mouth curled upward at the memory. That kid had dreamt of the seat he now occupied. Shifting in his seat to fight numbness, he lamented not having imagined a slightly larger cabin in his childhood dreams.

While gently flexing his legs for the sake of circulation, his left hand checked off status in a report tablet, noting everything as situation normal. While his right hand stowed the tablet and other loose gear, his left simultaneously entered coordinates for his approach plot back home. Ryan's head repositioned slightly as his arms awkwardly crossed over each other several times, blocking his view. As he made the turn for home, he looked back one last time toward deep space.

A powerful and irrational thought of unknown aggressors invaded his mind. He tried to quiet the voice of random paranoia before it could grow roots in his consciousness. It wasn't quite a vision—more a piercing sense of attack forces streaming out of the ether. The sharpness of the invading thought was disturbing, and he tried to write it off as patrol fatigue. A glance at the clock confirmed that he'd been on post now for twelve point five hours.

In the turn for home, he spotted a point of light. Over the next few minutes, as he returned in the rotation, the point expanded. He was in love with a certain approach vantage, where the white dot grew into a bright blue smudge. Looking out a few minutes later, he marveled at the big blue beauty as he inserted into orbit. He took a deep breath as he gazed, and the corners of his mouth crept upward.

On his descent, the thought of invaders rattled him again. This time, it was even more powerful and urgent. As he made his approach, he tried to push the thought from his mind. Glancing outside, he saw puffs of clouds scattered below over the central Pacific Ocean. Coming down lower into the troposphere, he buffeted through coastal turbulence. As he repositioned the ship nose high for landing, he could see the pad grow larger through the monitors.

He felt the bump as the ship made contact with the ground. Shielded, old-school rocker switches clacked loudly as he shut down engines and avionics. He closed his eyes, turned his head toward the warming sun, and took his hands from the controls for several seconds. Sitting there, he relished a moment of zero movement. Like a fistful of rocks pitched into a quiet pool, the comfort shattered with another fleeting thought of invaders. He fidgeted, antsy in his seat as ground service automates started pulling his ship into the hangar.

Deck Officer Zelda "Zeek" Darden watched as her favorite machine crept into the hangar. As was her custom, she was the first to greet him. "Welcome back, chief. How'd she do?"

"Hey. What's our defense status?"

"Uh, good I think. Weren't you just out there?"

"Yeah, I guess. Sure. Yeah, but check it for me anyway, the status since I left?"

Zeek's eyebrows pinched together. "Sure; I can check it. Any particular thing I should be looking for?"

He paused, ringing his closed eyes with thumb and index finger. "Nawh," he said. "Just tired, I suppose. Never mind, Zeek. Disregard. How you doin'?"

"Sure thing and doing just fine, sir." She reached out as he handed her his helmet. As she set it on the ramp beside her, she thought, *They're stringing these patrols out too far. Our pilots are paranoid about defense before they've even left the cockpit.* She tried to reassure him with a question she knew the answer to. "Hey, who's your relief?"

"Atlas52."

Zeek pretended to look over a list on her tablet. "Ah, right. Tigertail."

"Affirmative." He caught a glance at her tablet. He could see it wasn't displaying a roster. Ryan smiled at her benevolent wit and pulled his gloves off.

Zeek rummaged behind him to secure the ejection seat and remote survival system. "Can I ask a personal question?"

"Shoot."

"Have you ever thought that call sign was derogatory?"

"What? No." Ryan turned his head and talked over his shoulder to her. "You know the story behind it, don't you?"

"Negative."

"Really? I never told you that story?"

Zeek shook her head. "No."

"Well, years ago, on a training hop for advanced flight maneuvers and evasive tactics, Lieutenant Commander Anshra's flight instructor lost his lunch. They were set up on a course into and around the asteroid belt, 'cept Anshra decided to mod weapons out for more engines. They were going so fast that they hit the bio barrier six or seven times in turns and nearly overstressed the ship. Instructor said the entire flight was like holding on to a tiger's tail."

Zeek chuckled. "That's crazy."

"Yeah. He passed Anshra on without so much as another flight, and the name stuck."

"Sir?"

"The ride. It was like holding on to a tiger's tail. You know, the call sign... Tigertail."

"Oh, right."

"Know who the instructor was?"

"No. Who?"

"General Lund himself. To this day when he's not lookin', we leave sick sacks on his desk."

Zeek laughed, "Lt. Commander Anshra's a great pilot."

"Yes; she is. Although I was initially convinced of her intent to kill me, she's the best instructor I ever had. Jeeval stuck her neck out for me when I wasn't very deserving."

"I'm sure all's well under Tigertail's watch."

"Yeah, suppose you're right."

"Help you outta there, sir?"

"Nawh; I'm good. Thanks though."

Zeek walked down the ladder, chuckling at the story. Although she knew Anshra was perhaps their best interceptor pilot, she was thankful to be assigned to the chief. She knew if she needed anything, he would relentlessly pursue it. This included times when he used "creative sourcing" to barter with other service groups for required parts. And once, when a new technician inadvertently caused a coolant leak that destroyed components of several internal systems, the chief took the reprimand, claiming the issue was cockpit related.

Zeek remembered overhearing the verbal abuse the chief took through the walls in her office. "Why is your command the one continually demanding my presence? We're under increased scrutiny, and you represent half of the screwups in our wing. Get your house in order before you burn us all down! Are we clear, soldier?!"

The general hollered so loud next door that she noticed the pictures in her own office swinging crooked. A few minutes after he stormed away, she quietly appeared in the chief's doorway. He barely looked up from the paperwork on his desk and said quietly, "Well, that should pretty much cover maintenance mishaps. See to it, would ya, Zeek, that it doesn't happen again?" With wide eyes, she could only squeak back a "Yes, sir." Zeek was even harder on her folks because of what they'd done to the chief.

A few months later, at The Sandbox base lounge, Ryan was "holding court" at the ping-pong table. As was his custom, he would hold a paddle in each hand and play two opponents at the same time. No team had ever been able to win a game against him. The betting was still surprisingly lively, and Ryan even allowed his opponents to "purchase points." All Ryan's proceeds were deposited into the "kitty," which was a very large Japanese maneki-neko piggy bank. When it grew to a large enough sum, the funds were used to throw a party for the entire group.

Zeek was the treasurer in charge of the kitty. She asked, in light of the recent violation, if Ryan wanted the proceeds this time for his "retirement fund." He laughed and took a sip of his beer. "Nawh, Zeek. We're good. Know how you lose flight status? Go get yourself promoted."

He continued nodding emphatically. "Good performance, good evaluations, and bammo, next thing you know you're sent off to be a cadet at the Military College. That leads to a commission, promotions, and a fancy desk. Thus begins the death of your flight career. So, in a way, one of your grease monkeys helped prevent just such a tragic turn of events. Also, I figured you'd go crazy on your staff on account of me getting dinged. I knew they'd learn I took a bullet for them, and it would further galvanize team loyalty. And I remember you told me earlier the guy who did it, Mr. Goodwrench, was a keeper. I didn't want to see him get ruined over one stupid mistake. God knows I wouldn't be here if we had that rule. Plus, if he busted out, you'd have to pick up someone else that maybe wasn't a keeper. And you can bet Mr. Goodwrench and anyone he ever influences will not repeat the same mistake. Yep, I rest easy knowin' I'll always have the best kept ship in the Wing. The way I figure it, everyone got something. Lastly, I was raised by my aunts, so I grew up with multiple 'mothers.' Gettin' hollered at was just part of a normal day."

Zeek smiled at the memory as she stepped down off the hangar ramp. The chief was the best commanding officer she'd ever had.

Grunting and swinging out dull legs, Ryan made a lumbering roll out of the cockpit to all fours on the side platform. Slowly standing tall for the first time in hours, he stretched backward and felt the tingle of blood returning to his crinkled limbs. As he came down the ramp, he spied Zeek talking to a technician under the aft section of the ship. Grimacing again, he changed direction and walked back toward her.

"Hey. I changed my mind. Can you check defense stats for me?"

"Sure thing; we're just gettin' her plugged in." Zeek held up old-fashioned braids of cables in both hands and nodded toward the ship. "Is it OK to check with you in a few minutes when I get back to a console?"

"Yeah. OK. It should take me a few to rack. I'll wait to crash until you call."

Sensing the underlying message, Zeek nodded. "I won't forget, sir."

Ryan nodded as he shuffled away for the tram transport.

A few minutes later, when Zeek was back at her terminal, she was mumbling about paranoid pilots while click-clacking on the keyboard to pull live stats on the defense grid. Her freckled red brow furrowed, and her head cocked as she scanned the screen. Her butt raised up off the stool, and she strained forward, looking into the monitor. Typing at an accelerated rate, she waved off an incoming question from a technician and focused on the display. Typing even faster and squinting at the screen, she mumbled, "What the hell?!"

"Rhydel64, still up, sir?"

Ryan was headed across in the tram toward base housing. Having Zeek address him by his call sign caused him to immediately reverse the cab's direction back toward the hangar. "Whaddya got, Zeek?"

"Sir, Atlas52 currently en route to a grid anomaly."

"Anomaly? Where?"

"Just about where you ended your patrol. She actually just called on your sensor logs for comparison."

"Christ, on my way. Get me back up there, Zeek."

"Yes, sir. There's something else too; hold on." She yelled in the background, "YO!" and followed with a cat whistle. "Yeah, get'r ready, she's goin' back out!" Ryan could hear warbling in the background from her hand partially covering the microphone, and then her voice again booming, "No, as in right now! Quick turn. Mooove it people!" There was a pause, and then in a soft, pleasant voice, she addressed Ryan. "Chief, still with me?"

Ryan chuckled at the change. Zeek stood barely five foot one, but the voice and bearing of the Montana redhead made her seem eight feet tall. Being the youngest and only girl of six, she wasn't afraid to mix it up. She was also precise, organized, and thoughtful, and she oozed common sense, but god help the person who either broke her ship or borrowed her tools without asking.

"Yeah; I'm here, Zeek. Was there somethin' else?"

"Oh yeah, Grid's running a PRM17-34."

"A what?"

"It's a maintenance routine."

"Not following, Zeek."

"It's offline."

"What's offline?"

"The defense grid, sir."

"What part?"

"All of it."

"All of it?"

"Affirmative; the whole lot."

"That's not possible."

"I know, but that's what it says. Satellites, recon drones, remote weapons platforms, lunar missile batteries, projectile platforms, sensor bars, arrays, the whole lot of it."

"How long?"

"'Bout an hour ago, and estimates back online in six hours."

"Is it in alarm status? "

"No."

"My god, hasn't anyone noticed?"

"It's showing telemetry, but it's like some kind of loop with prior data. I had to actually drill down into a couple devices to see that they were offline. I sent in a ticket, but who knows when they'll pick it up," Zeek said. She continued in a nervous, low tone, "Chief, this is some kind of drill, right?"

"No, Zeek. They'd never take the entire system offline."

"How's this possible?"

"Don't know, but spread the word. Get it to everyone."

General Lund placed a perfectly temped cup of tea in the optimal spot on his desk and sat down. He carefully rotated the cup in the saucer to align the handle at a forty-five degree angle with the desk edge. Surveying the surface, he verified the alignment and space between each object. There was some old school paperwork just inside the right corner, which sat neatly completed well before the deadline. Three tablets were lined up in proper sequence based upon the level of completion of the reports contained within. One held complete logs, and the second was processing information he'd just filed. With the proper tea, he would begin his work on the third. If he held this pace, he would be out of the office on time for an early start to an orderly evening. The world within his sphere of influence was well oiled and tuned. When he had his cup raised mid sip, the transmission broke the peace.

"Cap, Rhydel64."

Lund grimaced and set the cup haphazardly into its saucer. "This is Cap; you sound clear. Where are you?"

"Hangar hairpin."

"McBain, I'm in the middle of something right now—"

"General, defense grid's offline, whole damn thing. Running some kind of six-hour maintenance routine, and there's fake telemetry spoofing the monitors. If you drill down to the devices, you can see they're offline. Sir, it's a breach. Atlas52 is investigating some kind of gravity anomaly out near SEDS. I think she stumbled into some kind of invasion force."

Ryan could hear the clicking of keys on the workstation behind the general's desk. He listened intently after a few seconds of silence.

"What? This can't be right. Fleet just chirped out a notice that there's some kind of system issue that's locking up integrated systems. Sweet Jesus! I can't believe what I'm reading. This is awful coincidental. I need more data. I need more eyes! Who's energized, and what's your status?"

"My DO is notifying Command and all the other crews. I'm outbound t-minus moments."

"Command is chiming me; I need to get with them."

About fifteen seconds later, piped in through the tram speaker, Ryan heard tri-toned emergency chimes

DING-DIN-DING

followed by an audio recording of a pleasant female voice: "Attention. Attention. Citizens of Earth, this is a planetary alert…"

DING-DIN-DING

◊ ◊ ◊

The chimes and urgency took Ryan back to a different place so many years ago. With her thick Delhi accent, then Lieutenant Jeeval Anshra transmitted, "Those chimes are ringing as sounds simulating my cannons cutting your hull to pieces. Why will you not apply what I know you surely have learned from me? Specialist Ryan, you are flunking out of this cockpit. If you cannot repel a single ship-to-ship contact, how can you be a pursuit defender? Hmm? Our home, our Earth depends on your skill and cunning. There is no cunning here."

"I understand, ma'am. It's just—"

"What? What is it just?"

"This is cardboard and rigid. Would you ever mount such a clumsy attack like this?"

"Why are you caring how I engage?! Your one job is to repel my approach as you've been instructed, not critique the method of the attack."

"I understand, master instructor, but this is like memorizing some kind of weird dance instead of mounting an actual defense."

"Cadet, you are my most difficult student, and my patience has evaporated away completely. Where are you going with all this?"

"Come at me like you would really attack. No rules, just real life."

"You'd not survive it. You cannot defend a simple approach."

"Let me try. If I fail, I'll make space in this seat for someone capable and deserving. Try to attack me at point," Ryan paused, typing in a coordinate, "… point designated WASHOUT. I'm loading the coordinates in now."

Anshra looked down and saw the location in her nav computer. "Ahh, the Kuiper Belt is my old friend. You'd be wiser to make your bed elsewhere."

"Perhaps, but then we'll both know either way."

A few minutes later, she tried to jump him coming out of a dense section of the asteroid belt. He instantly countered directly into the field with maximum acceleration. As objects blurred past, Ryan felt a strange sensation of being loosed away from the cockpit. Things became quiet and simple. Gone was the voice message from his brother just before launch that he should surrender this "incessant dream of space flight" as it was "simply just beyond your capacity." In fact, gone were all the voices, problems, doubts, and decisions. It was as if the tremendous speed allowed him to fly out of the garbled cloud of ground-based trouble. Ryan was completely in the present moment. The speed and fear of impacting an asteroid tipped him more fully into a familiar cognizance. This high zone was far clearer, far easier. There was a comfort on this edge because left or right was do or die. Life and death in this plane was Boolean.

His mind accelerated past the challenge of traversing the dense field of objects and reached further out, tracking Lt. Anshra. So many things around him were happening at great speed, and in those compressed moments, Ryan's consciousness expanded into a harmony with everything. His presence stretched and became like jeweled movements powering some kind of quantum clock. He could see what was happening around him, feel what was going to happen next, and exert the influence of change. A goofy smile settled over his face.

"You should being careful in here; these here are not soft."

"Nor am I, ma'am. I know where you are. Can you see me?"

Anshra traversed the field and recorded ion trails to sniff out Ryan's location. She was somewhat shocked and altogether curious at this turn of potential in him. Tones rang out announcing that Ryan had her targeted. She took evasive action, twisting wildly while accelerating through the field. No simulated or live pursuer had ever been able to keep up with her for more than thirty seconds in the field. Ryan held pursuit for a minute and a half. He'd very nearly locked weapons on her several times. She continued to accelerate and evade deeper into the field. When she was satisfied that she'd lost him, she slowed and began hunting him. She heard tones once more and broke away again.

"Impressive. You've not yet killed yourself."

"Master instructor, I'm focused on a kill, but it isn't mine."

"I see you back there." She nodded with great excitement. Adrenaline aided her as she split her attention between her own navigation and instructing. "Good! Good speed, but watch where the density in the asteroid field increases—many there are grouped and drifting. Those gaps can get close.

Anticipate my turns around wider openings. Now, try this one."

She dropped electronic and optical counter measures. A blinding flash obfuscated Atlas52's hard turn, followed by acceleration and several more evasive maneuvers. A quick glance at her situation management system, or SMS, indicated no sign of him behind her, and she smiled.

"Are you there still lurking?" There was radio silence. A wide field scan indicated multiple metallic objects in the field behind her. She circled around to inspect. As she was coming closer to what appeared as crash debris, she heard a simulator tone indicating she'd been virtually "killed."

"What! How?"

Ryan chuckled through the coms. "Proximity mines."

"So, you destroyed the instructor that returned to check your well-being?"

"No, I destroyed the aggressor that returned to ensure my destruction."

"Hmm. Clever…and slippery. Very slippery."

"Ma'am, would you say that was more realistic?"

"I would say I did not like being fooled and killed. But that would be alongside the point. You shall have the 'kill.' More importantly, we may have just been breaking through. You don't learn with the standard rules do you, hmm? I'm not sure what to make of this. It's outside the standard teaching process."

Anshra took a long breath, grimaced, and closed her eyes tightly. "If I put out my neck and teach you, you mustn't be a leaky, rusty bucket. You must capture each and every word I am telling you. Do you fully understand this?"

"Yes, ma'am. I absolutely will."

"OK then. I believe we've had a good day, and it was certainly more fun than others. I'm not sure how I'm going to catalog this. It does not fit into any record or unit. And I'm sure there will be many raised noses at my loss."

"I think you mean raised eyebrows."

"Yes, yes. Whatever it is."

Jeeval camped out in front of Lund's office early the next morning. She was just over five feet in height, and with a stone in her pocket, she weighed one hundred five pounds. Gray streaks highlighted raven hair that was parted in the middle and bundled tightly behind. Sparkling dark brown eyes were framed by a time-weathered face. Her eyebrows were thin, with a pronounced arc that raised higher at the finish. The narrow ridge of her nose sat above a small mouth with full lips. Lines around her lips gave way to high red cheeks. She perched neatly on the front edge of the reception chair. Lund's admin glanced up and noted how the lieutenant sat completely motionless. She caught herself pondering how Jeeval's appearance belied the age noted in her personnel folder. While sitting patiently, the lieutenant kept a smart watch for their commanding officer. She had no appointment, but she would not be denied. She popped up at first sight of him and followed closely into his office. As he was hanging his jacket, he turned to her.

"Lieutenant Anshra, you're his third instructor." Lund paused for a moment and looked to her. "Jeeval, he's nearly flunked the class. Now you want me to authorize a non-standard training program for him? What makes this cadet so special? And why'd you take him anyway?" Lund moved across to his desk and sat down.

Jeeval pivoted around and stood facing him at the foot of his desk with both hands clasped in front of her. "Because I saw something. Sometimes the gifted children are the most difficult. Do you remember the day I asked to take his training jacket?"

"Yes. It surprised me. I was just about to bounce him."

"I knew, but that very morning, I had just picked up a delicious pastry when I heard a commotion and children screaming. I looked up and out the shop window. It was just in time to see Ryan leaping off the street with a small child held forward and high in his hands. The vehicle passed just behind him and struck a lamp post further down. I watched as he patted the child's head, turned, and ran down to render aid to the driver."

"Yeah, I remember that, a while ago on the Broadcast. Old guy driving on manual and had a heart attack, almost drove over a class of preschoolers. Some guy saved a child; that was McBain? They were looking for him."

"Yes; I know. Later, I told him about the broadcast and the search for the 'hero.' He asked if I knew of the child's well-being. I asked if he planned to identify himself. His response was that he didn't watch Broadcast and saw no point. He did not believe doing the right thing defined a hero. But if they were going to call it that, he said an anonymous hero was more powerful because it allowed everyone to imagine themselves doing the right thing. I asked him why he held the child out in front of him. It was then that he said the most important thing. He said he held the child out and high in order to throw the child clear if he thought the vehicle was going to strike him. And that is why I chose him."

Jeeval jabbed her index finger at Ryan's training folder for emphasis. "He is a protector." She wagged her finger. "This is not something you teach; it is something you are. It is also why you should let me, your most seasoned instructor, have this opportunity to try something different. I believe he may well become one of your best."

Lund set his glasses down on the desk, exhaled audibly, and rubbed his eyes.

Before he could respond, she added quietly, "And yesterday, he beat me in the Kuiper Belt."

Lund's eyes shot open, and he looked up through his brows at her. Pursing her lips, she nodded back. Lund took a deep breath. "Do you think you can do this without further taxing the group's time and taking resources away from other cadets?"

"Yes. And what's more, we may develop teaching improvements that can be applied to the program."

"Write this up, and I'll approve it. I don't know why I'm going to, but I will. Please do it quickly before I change my mind."

Jeeval nodded and turned with haste toward the door. Before she could exit, Lund asked, "You got jumped in an asteroid belt? You?"

Without turning back, she groused, "I'll not be talking about this."

He smiled, shaking his head as the door closed behind her.

Six months later, just outside the system on a training sortie, they picked up a distress signal from a cargo ship.

Ryan picked up the raw stats. "SMS says she's Paavi with sixty-four souls on board."

Anshra huffed. "Why are they here? Paavi are unremitting pacifists and carry no weapons for defense. It's rare to find their species in the open. They should not be being stopped out here." Both kestrels streaked in formation past the bow of the vessel and arced around it.

"She looks to be OK from out here. I've hailed them." Ryan looked down at the message response. "I don't think it was planned; they just answered. They've got a core leak and need to vent before making repairs. They've declared an emergency and are requesting our help."

"I am not at all happy about this. A thousand bad things live out here. No, I'm not happy. Not at all. This is a big target. Please tell me friendly assets are near and can come here presently."

"Nearest Fleet wing is about fifty minutes away. Signaling them now. With transit times, they're probably over an hour out. Ma'am, what kind of defenders don't answer a distress call?"

"The kind that are in training!" Anshra said, raising her voice. "The kind that have only sixteen weeks of operational experience flying in kestrels, and just the kind that could become a second distress signal! I am not happy with this situation."

They flew along for a few seconds before Anshra broke the silence. "We shall circle this inoperative ship as you desire. Let us hope they've not left a long trail attracting pirates."

Anshra transmitted an audio signal to them. "Transport ship Aihl Rhydel, we are an Earth Force patrol. We will circle on post while you effect repairs. A wing of Earth ships is en route and will be here presently. Do you require special assistance?"

The response transmission was scratchy. "Jyes, Eart ship. Tank you. Making repairing very quick. Tank you for guard. We careful holding refugees from Lahmaard colony."

Ryan and Anshra split apart to run a standard two-ship short patrol around opposite quadrants of the vessel. While on station, Ryan intuitively reprogramed a series of lightspeed micro jumps around the Paavi ship and back to Anshra's wing. He created four color-coded quadrants around her ship that his nav system continually plotted based on her position.

Two pirate fighters entered nearly on top of Anshra, with projectile weapons firing as they came into normal space. They bathed Anshra's kestrel in fire, and she took damage to her core, starboard engine, and cockpit. The ship decompressed, and consoles popped and arced before going dark. Remarkably, neither Anshra nor her protective suit were hit directly, but her ship began to pitch and roll off axis. Pawing through the buzz in her head, she saw debris floating by outside her cockpit.

Ryan saw her engines go down and used the pirate's vector to calculate a trajectory, placing himself in the quadrant just on the other side of Anshra's ship. Timing was everything; if he initiated a jump too soon, he would end up right in front of the enemy ships. There was also the very real possibility he would physically jump into one of their ships. But if his timing was correct, he would jump in immediately behind both. No one would be prepared to defend against such a move.

Anshra could see the pirate ships rapidly moving away from her. Just before she looked away, there was a flash behind them. Ryan jumped nearly on top of them, and collision alarms sounded on all three ships. Before they could react, Ryan's index finger pulled hard on the firing hammer atop his flight controls. It wasn't like the simulations, and he noted that the trigger was heavy up to a point where it gave way easily. Projectile fire erupted from his barrels. The hum from it, the subtle vibrations, and the tracer rounds dancing around a frantic target were strangely pleasing to him. The second pirate fired a missile before jumping away. He tagged and tracked that missile while continuing to fire on the first.

Ryan's mind was a duality of emotion and logic, swirling like an angry cauldron of oil and water. He felt an expanding rage that anyone would dare threaten or harm *his* Anshra. The other sense was cold and emotionless as the depthless black eyes of a great white shark circling for the kill. Before his target could jump, he anticipated the next evasive maneuver, positioned to lead it, and let his rounds tear through the engine section.

Tango Delta! Ryan instantly broke away hard toward the torpedo fired by the second pirate. It had circled around and was headed toward Anshra. She'd caught a glimpse of the faint blue eclipsed glow from the missile's engine. As it grew, so did her eyes. Anshra was praying for the gods to take her to peace when flashes off her port side destroyed the missile. Ryan had used the same quadrant program to jump back. She watched him streak past and turn hard toward the second aggressor. Reinvigorated, Anshra struggled to get her com system operational. Quickly flipping switches to redirect emergency power, she restored SMS and synced with Ryan's systems. Her coms came back online, and she keyed her mic. "There is a second pirate ship."

"Well, that's helpful. Thought you were taking a nap. You OK?"

"I'm alive but disabled. You should leave this place now in one piece."

"What, and leave you? Negative."

"What if it was an order?"

"Court martial me later."

"It will not matter if you are dead."

"Stop talking to me." Ryan turned head on with the second fighter, and an audible tone indicated potential collision. The second fighter veered away, and Ryan countered a pursuit angle. In response, the aggressor turned back head on. Ryan strained forward into his harness, mumbling, "*That's the spirit!*"

Anshra saw their trajectory, and concern pulled her brows together. "You're flying straight into him."

"Again, not helpful." Ryan quickly programmed one of his missiles to arm but not fire its engine.

"You're going to smash your nose with his."

Ryan ignored her, his focus locked on the approaching ship. The pirate ship began firing projectile weapons, and anger pushed Ryan harder forward into his harness. Rage seared through him. "*You. Will. Not. Survive!*" He slipped and skidded the kestrel violently left and right to avoid most of the fire. An imminent collision alarm sounded loudly as they closed in on each other. Ryan released the missile less than a second before both ships nearly flew through one another. Just after they passed, he remotely detonated the missile. The second pirate ship was destroyed.

Breaking hard again, Ryan accelerated toward the first disabled pirate fighter. It had managed to fire missiles at the Paavi cargo ship. Two sparrows were barely a ship's length from the Paavi bridge when Ryan hosed them down and destroyed the missiles with projectile fire. The remaining inert fragments peppered and pinged over the transport ship's hull. Turning back toward the pirate fighter, he aimed and fired, strafing repeatedly into its cockpit. With both pirates destroyed, he maneuvered back to Anshra.

"How you doin'?"

"I'm OK, thanks to you. Your trick with the missile was slippery, very slippery. Tell me, where do you learn such slippery things?"

"I read a lot, but mostly from practice in the simulator."

A flash announced the arrival of the pirate mothership. Jeeval keyed her mic, "Ryan, that is a big ship. You cannot beat it alone without missiles. You must retreat now!"

He took a deep breath. Thoughts floated up from the deepest recesses of his mind. There was a certain peace now from feelings that had long tasked him. *One that's already lost in exchange for many others.* Ryan nodded, and a small smile crept onto his face. With a "release" vector plotted, he transmitted, "Negative. There's one missile we have that'll stop it." He turned and accelerated toward the pirate base ship.

Anshra cocked her head. "What are you intending? It is wrong to kill yourself."

"Nawh, this is about the math. Think of it more as a trade. There are sixty-four souls on that Paavi ship. One for sixty-five is an acceptable return."

"Do not do this. Our forces are coming here momentarily."

"No time. Lieutenant Anshra, maahir, thank you for believing in me. I think I would have been a good defender."

"You are a good defender."

33

Ryan accelerated to near light speed, making a final transmission, "Remember me on my birthday."

Collision alarms sounded. The pirate ship erupted with a hail of defensive projectile rounds as Ryan flew toward the command bridge, corkscrewing down. He thought of the front row view of their demise. He paused for a moment, nodding before something compelled his hands and arms to move in a blur. As the pirate ship grew large in his field, he cut the main engines and rapidly spun around, pointing his cockpit in the opposite direction.

Having oriented away from the pirates, he screamed as he punched down through a clear protective cover and into a large red ejection button. The seat fired at the last possible moment and into the leading edge of the explosion. The timing was so close that Anshra didn't see him eject. With the bridge destroyed, the pirate weapons ceased firing, and the enemy ship went dark.

Anshra bowed her head for a few seconds. Still looking down, she pressed the button to transmit externally. "On guard, mayday, mayday, mayday. Atlas52 declaring emergency. We've been attacked by pirates. I'm disabled on station and I have lost...my wingman is killed. Require immediate assistance. Encoding location on guard, mayday, mayday, mayday, Atlast52."

Five minutes later and without any transmission, the repaired Paavi ship flashed away into light speed.

Anshra gazed at the dead and drifting pirate ship while ticking off the beads of her charm and chanting a Vedic prayer:

Asatho Maa Sad Gamaya. (From untruth lead us to truth)
Thamaso Maa Jyothir Gamaya. (From darkness lead us to light)
Mrithyur Maa Amritham Gamaya. (From death lead us to immortality)
Om Shanti, Shanti, Shanti. (Om peace, peace, peace)
Ryan, Shanti, Shanti, Shanti. (Peace, peace, peace)

Her chanting was interrupted seven minutes later, when another pirate ship entered nearby. Thirty seconds later, Earth Force Cutter Winston S. Churchill entered and instantly rained fire on the second mother ship. The second pirate quickly jumped away.

"Atlas52, this is UEF Churchill, we have your location and will retrieve you momentarily. We're also picking up another very weak distress beacon."

◊   ◊   ◊

Ryan woke with a start in a hospital bed, looking up at Colonel Lund. "Am I in trouble?"

Everyone in the room laughed. "No son, not at all," Lund replied. "You did good; real good. Rest easy. But before you do, I have something here for you. First, we have to resolve a little administrative problem you've created for me. You see, I have something here that can't be awarded to a cadet." He held up a medal in his hand. "So, we had a little change of heart. This particular Merit of Valor won't be awarded to the cadet as it stands."

The colonel put it back in a box and tucked the box under his armpit. He fumbled around in his coat pocket, grabbing something small. "Allow me to clarify. I will be presenting this award instead to a flight wing officer." Lund raised his eyebrows. "But you seem to be out of uniform." He bent over and grasped the collar of Ryan's hospital gown. "You know, we take this sort of thing very seriously. I'm willing to overlook it this time, but in the future *Flight Officer* McBain, I expect you to show appropriate pride in the uniform." The colonel pinned a winged flight wing officer rank insignia to Ryan's hospital gown and then stood tall, smiling and winking at him.

The colonel's attaché stood behind. "AttenTION!"

Ryan looked at the five others in the room saluting as the colonel spoke. "Very well, then. For service above and beyond the call of duty, for selflessly putting yourself between harm and those we're sworn to protect, and for demonstrating the very best qualities of Earth Defense Force Four, I hereby award *Flight Wing Officer* Mitchell Ryan McBain this award for merit."

He took the medal out of the box again and pinned it to the pocket on Ryan's hospital gown. Rising back up, the colonel saluted. Ryan looked around the room at Anshra and his Aunt Virginia staring forward, both smiling with pride through their salute.

As Anshra was leaving, she leaned down and said in a loud whisper, "You must get well enough to climb the ladder to the cockpit." She gently poked him in the chest. "Officer and medal aside, you should not be thinking this will save you from the rest of my training. This is just the beginning, Flight Officer McBain."

He smiled widely. "Yes, ma'am."

DING-DIN-DING

"Attention, citizens of Earth, this is a planetary alert. Planetary alert, Earth Defense Forces are now at State 2. Earth Defense Forces now at State 2. This is not an exercise. Make ready."

DING-DIN-DING

"EDF activate; we are at State 2."

Hearing the recording somehow made it more real and grounded him in the urgency of the present moment. He stared at the tram doors, willing them to open. As he came to a stop at the hangar platform, the immediate noise and bustle of the deck was welcome. Ryan was sailing across a cloud of adrenaline, and he could barely feel his legs touching the deck as he traversed the hangar. Then he saw her.

The kestrel sat just as she had for hundreds of sorties, but today, she looked different. She was sleek and black skinned, with the figures 99264 adorning her tail. She had never once failed him. The human stood, facing the machine, and as he gazed at her, he smiled. Combined, the ship and the man were something altogether different. They were a raptor's shriek coming through the Sun's glare. Today, there was a job, one they were built for and potentially their last. Zeek's approach returned him to the moment.

Ryan beamed like an approving coach from the bench. "Zeek! Nice work spotting the fake telemetry in the maintenance routine. You may have just tipped it in our favor."

"Sir, I was going to say the same to you. How'd you know?"

"Same intuition that caused you to drill down into the defense grid. We are ED4. We question; it's what we do. Here and now is just more compelling evidence that we make a great team." He smiled again at her.

Zeek briefed him as they walked briskly toward the cockpit stairs. "I got you a couple EMP pods on board. I swapped the cargo bay for the special payload mounts we been workin' on."

"Zelda, you're the best DO in the fleet." He turned to her at the base of the stairs. "You really are; it's been my pleasure."

His use of her real name and those words nearly stopped her heart. With a shaky voice, she snapped back, "Don't talk like that! You uh, take care of my ship...Sir."

Smiling, Ryan reached his hand out to shake Zeek's. When she grasped it, he pulled her into a quick hug. As they separated, Zeek saw a depthless pool in Ryan's eyes and tried to mask her concern. She stepped back to the base of the ladder and stood sharply at attention. With her eyes forward, she saluted crisply. Ryan smiled warmly, climbed the ladder, and nodded as she followed up behind him. "Behave yourself while I'm out. No more parties in the hangar. Don't think I don't know what you guys do in here while I'm out on patrol."

She smiled widely as she scrambled up the stairs. After giving the ship a once over inspection, Zeek tossed him his helmet. Her small frame teetered way over the side of the cockpit, and she was a blur of arms and elbows clicking and flipping switches. She was the only human he'd ever trust to prep and initiate the startup sequence. Around the blur of her movements, Ryan secured his helmet and pulled his gloves on. After scissoring between his fingers to pull them tight, he verified an airtight suit environment.

"Preflight and engine start checklist complete, sir." After she cross checked his harness, he saw Zeek continue without pause to fire the ignition sequence.

"Hey, crazy woman, get out of here, or you'll be fried bacon." As she turned, he grabbed her shoulder, stopping her momentarily. "Thanks again, Zeek."

She punched him pretty hard in the arm and yelled, "Board's green. Godspeed, chief; give'm hell!" She started to depart, but suddenly spun around and lunged behind Ryan, grabbing a "remove before flight" red tag attached to a safety pin that enabled his ejection seat. After quickly sliding down and against her personal Zen of order, Zeek awkwardly hucked the cockpit ladder into the middle of the hangar floor. Looking back, she nodded at him before turning away.

Ryan watched as she waved her arms wildly overhead, running and yelling at everyone to evacuate the hangar. As the canopy came down, the outside noise was muffled, and he could now hear the whine of the old-school gyro instruments spooling up. Reactors were online, and mains were ready for primary start. Ionic fields were solid, there were no breaches, and power showed availability beyond one hundred thirty-four percent. The hardened inertial navigation systems spooled into the green, the sensors were warm, and the coms were still set to departure frequency.

Glancing out, Ryan saw Zeek pulling the heavy radiation door closed. Just before it shut, he saw her salute with the signal that the hangar was cleared for starting transorbital engines. He saluted back, crisply snapping with emphasis.

Buffeting through waves of growing anxiety, he rubbed his palm up and down his thigh. He mumbled aloud, "Quick, quick, we gotta go; come on, sugar." Most humans have two primal instincts: fight or take flight. But ED4 pilots have a third hybrid sense. They're anxious nearly beyond their own skin to take flight, but only to put the fight out as far from the nest as possible.

Ryan glanced at multiple engine and powerplant gauges displaying numbers increasing in a blur too fast to read. Words and feelings passed through his consciousness.

Vulnerable.

Late.

Go.

Quick.

Go!

Several needles on gauges started to rise from the white and into the green arc. Quickly running through the departure checklist, he tripped the platform switch that slow rolled the ship out to a reinforced pad. Ryan was struck with an odd feeling. His hands and arms were moving inside the cockpit in preparation for launch, but it was as if he was watching from a third party's perspective. With a split focus, his body was doing what he'd practiced and perfected in so many thousands of repetitions. At the same time, he felt hollow watching, and he wondered if this was what a person felt at life's end. *Is this what's coming?* It was more odd than upsetting. He dwelled on feelings of rage, and it blunted the edge of his fear. *Death imminent.*

The sense of finality passed through him, and he welcomed the respite. And yet, in the far reaches of his mind, there was the smallest tug of sadness. It was as if there was something more, something larger that he was meant for. As he reached the outside launch pad, the moment of reflection evaporated, and a hawkish focus returned him fully to the moment.

On his flight management screen, he plotted a vertical ascent with a skip jump from lower orbit. Such jumps created a massive shock wave of disturbance and were not authorized under normal circumstances.

Ryan keyed the mic and transmitted externally, "Los Angeles Departure, Rhydel64, departing Swift Station Two One, request Traffic Clear, emergency orbital insertion via sectors 576 and 578. I'll be skip jumping near point...uh, VELVET. EDF State Two."

The audio response was scratchy and crackling, "Rhydel64, Los Angeles Departure, clear to depart as requested, break, VirginAir Fifteen Thirty, PanPacific Two Three, Traffic Alert, recommend traffic collision avoidance resolution for emergency vectors, uploading your traffic now, break. All Los Angeles area traffic, be advised Earthforce kestrel will be making vertical transition via sectors 576 and 578, break. Rhydel64, SoCal Center and Orbital Control report your designated traffic path above is clear of craft, debris, and platforms. Clear to orbit as requested."

"Thanks, keep an eye on things for me while I'm out."

"Godspeed, Rhydel64."

Ryan felt the ship rumble as it spooled to life. The vibration gave him comfort as he punched in coordinates for intersections in low orbit that would serve as his point of jump entry. He was antsy, sipping from a geyser of fomented anxiety. *Come on; come on, sugar. Let's get to it!*

Running his hands across the knobs and switches in a familiar and linear flow, he confirmed that the ship was configured for departure. He pressed his butt down into his still warm seat and focused on the familiar feel. His nose tingled as if he had just been boxed in the face, and he was desperately trying to combat the growing anxiety for the unknown happenings above. Drunk with a growing realization that this was really happening, his mind momentarily focused away. As he glanced outside, he was captured by the beauty of the surrounding grass and weed infested drainage field. Without looking away from the beautiful green, his hands began the memorized process to activate the primary engines.

His eyes were still captivated by the vivid colors outside; it was as if he was seeing such a thing for the first time. Recent rain had nurtured temporarily brilliant shades of green. The chatter on the radio, the increase in noise from his ship, the present danger, all momentarily faded into the background while his eyes drank in the beauty of the good Earth.

Now hovering externally, he reoriented the vessel's nose upward and repositioned the cockpit for high Gs. Core reactors were spooling up and generating progressively larger pressure waves. Shrill and piercing reverberations emanated from oscillating turbulent eddies as they sheared across each other. Still gawking out and down to the side, he watched the vivid green foliage sway in waves off his exhaust. *Bright. Beautiful. Home.*

The flight management system made a pleasant two-toned chime like a door bell that indicated departure core power was now available. The chime connected like a hard-wired reflex through his subconscious and out to his thumb. All disparate corners of thought and perception folded inward to one focus, and from the core of his soul, a powerful voice boomed, *Protect!* With it, his head snapped skyward as his thumb twitched, depressing a small button on the stick that engaged the primary engines.

The kestrel class defender bolted skyward like a stallion from the gate. With a howling roar that rattled windows for miles, Ryan was pinned into his seat. Through the growing well of gravity, a pleasant female system voice indicated it was now providing pure oxygen. From the ground, his exhaust looked like a long, white, twisted rope snaking upward into the sky. The bouncing and force of acceleration quelled the fires of anxiety within him. Ryan felt a visceral sense of the pent up, pure power released off the engines, and his symbiosis with the ship smoothed his tension away. New pilots would have diminished capacity under the heavy G forces, but like many other experienced defenders, Ryan was accustomed. Having been the diligent pupil of the Speed Master herself, it was his intent to push the limits further.

With growing speed, Ryan welcomed the transformation. His helmet visor darkened, and the outer layer mirrored. No longer a man and a machine, speed alloyed them into one. Now they were Rhydel64—an instrument, an agent, a force, a weapon. Like the mythical guardians of Egypt long ago, Rhydel64 animated into a relentless predator, brought to life and awoken by the approach of beings that would do harm.

Coming through ten thousand feet, Rhydel64 powered up to thirty-five percent. Ryan looked to the side as he skewered through scattered cloud decks perpendicular to his vantage, and the layers fell rapidly beneath him. Looking through his helmet HUD rearview back toward the planet, he could see many enhanced icons at stations scattered around the globe that represented dozens of other defenders preparing to launch. He knew the beings behind each symbol. His ED4 family represented an extraordinary field of strengths and specialties. Their avatars gave him strength in community, both figuratively and literally. These exceptional pilots came from all walks of life and every corner of the planet. The diversity of this group was a proverbial viper's den of trouble for any aggressor force.

Looking back skyward, he saw icons representing the commercial traffic originally vectored away from his path. Clear of their paths and green across the board, he increased output to fifty percent and strained at the additional acceleration force. As the remainder of the grid came on line, it showed tens of other EDF ships now preparing to launch toward the anomaly. Looking outside, he could see the atmosphere thinning at the horizon. As the deep blue grew anemic and faded to black, he thought of his aunts. They were all down there. As Earth fell away, he looked back, almost like a child through the rear window of a car departing from grandmother's house.

Ryan had always sought communion and community, but he'd never felt it. The early loss of his parents and the subsequent shuffling among aunts had never allowed him to feel at home in any one place. He always felt much more connected to Earth from orbit. Now as the nose pointed into the growing darkness, he couldn't help the thought that he was headed back to his parents. A flash on his display indicated point VELVET, and without hesitation, he skipped away.

Coming out of light speed and entering a lunar orbit, he transmitted, "Rhydel64 is sabers and angels."

Atlas52 responded, "I'd have known you'd be the first."

Ryan smiled at the voice and her quirky expressions. "Sounds like I missed something back there."

"You missed nothing, young man; you did just fine. The anomaly I've discovered came after you passed."

"I'll be on your wing in moments."

The general transmitted from Earth. "Atlas52, this is Cap. What do you have?"

"The data is conflicting. I have something pulling serious gravity but no spectral contact. Something very large here is not wanting to be seen."

"Start a standard grid on the fringe; I'm trying to focus Edge devices to provide you a vector. You've got angels inbound."

"How many?"

"Everything and everyone. Bull10 and Taco29, best speed to Sector 8382."

Rhydel64 closed in on a platform in lunar orbit. The special payload mount Zeek had referred to was a quick change external mount they were testing. Zeek had supply drops on the platform that would top off the fuel and energy the skip jump had taken. Docking with the lunar post, Ryan keyed secure internal coms. "Zeek, you on?"

"Yep. Good telemetry, clean departure, nice skip. All systems green."

"Have they restored anything on the grid?"

"Nada; they're working on it."

"So, we don't have an integrated battle system?"

"Negative."

Ryan looked up and around as he thought for a moment. "Hey, can you get SEDS in a diagnostic routine to take wide spectrum electromagnetic readings?"

"Uh...what exactly did you have in mind?"

"EM pulse energy in the center of the gravity distortion. They're probably not masking the entire spectrum. If we could get a non-visual shadow recorded on some frequency, we might know what we're dealing with. Can you capture those readings?"

"Yeah, I could configure a basic program to read and relay signals back to Earth. I could load raw data and theoretically reconstruct a three-dimensional representation from the shadows." She quickly added, "But how you gonna drop an EM charge though? All our probes and missile batteries are offline."

"I'll take care of that; just get ready to take those readings."

After a thirty-second resupply, Rhydel64 was again at full stores and full power. Ryan engaged maximum power back toward Earth.

"OrCon, Rhydel64 lunar inbound for a sling toward Sector 8382."

"Rhydel64, OrCon, I have your route path, there are no conflicts in or near; proceed as requested."

Ryan slung into high orbit over Earth, and gravity dramatically increased his speed. The speed and angular acceleration pushed him into his seat for several seconds. He grunted and breathed hard under the stress until his flight management system indicated critical speed. Then, using minimal energy, he nudged the ship into faster than light speed toward Sector 8382.

A few minutes later, he emerged. Augmenting power to one hundred fifteen percent, he adjusted fire control for high-powered, close-range bursts. He could feel a presence like a draft passing through a pitch-dark room, and the hair on his neck stood high. Thieves were inside his house. Watching and waiting, they could target him, but he could not see them. Ryan pursed his lips as a fire within grew quickly. He half shook his head and mumbled, "Unacceptable." The effort to expose them involved terrible risk, but if successful, it would potentially turn the tables. The moment ran parallel to every narrow margin of his life.

A vehicle accident had taken his parents when he was a child. As far back as he could remember, an unquenchable anger had been ever present inside him. Mere millimeters under the surface, the fire neither dimmed nor diminished. As Ryan grew up, the ugliness of it was left unchecked and often flared hot. There were several significant events at school, and a few resulted in expulsions. Countless social workers tried in vain to extinguish it. No one knew how to handle *Mr. Hyde.* As a consequence of each outburst, Ryan and Hadley were passed down to the next aunt.

More than once, he'd overheard comments about the "troubled brother." Once while waiting on the other side of the principal's door, he overheard an administrator comment, "Why's one so well spoken while the other's such a terrorist?"

One night, Hadley lay on the lower bunk and kicked the bottom of Ryan's bed. "Because of you we have to move *again.* It's always you! I liked this school. I have friends here. You ruined it...*loser.*"

In an episode a few days earlier, Ryan had watched from a short distance as several older boys surrounded Hadley during recess. He couldn't hear what was said, but his brother's body language indicated distress. Children on the swings next to Ryan noticed he was no longer responding to them. His focus was on the situation unraveling around his older brother. He rose abruptly and walked with purpose toward Hadley. As he approached, he saw the lead bully shove his older brother down.

Time seemed to slow as Hadley's body rolled backward in the inertia of the fall. The older brother's face crinkled. He held up an arm in surrender, and fear wept from his eyes. Ryan squinted as an inferno violently spiraled upward within him. He bolted forward and jumped abruptly, striking the boy in the back of the head with the heel of his fist. The concussive blow knocked the bully down and out. After landing, Ryan scooped up a handful of gravel. As he turned and stood, he threw the gravel at the remaining older boys. In the seam of shock, Ryan rushed into them, punching one boy in the crotch. He attempted to gouge the eyes of another. The largest boy grabbed him from behind and hoisted him upward. Ryan violently pitched his skull backward into the softer bones of the other boy's nose. The two remaining boys fled as Ryan let loose a piercing, primal scream. Ryan turned and kicked at one boy, who was already writhing on the ground. The playground attendant tackled Ryan and dragged him away.

Ryan found himself sitting in the car in front of the school with skinned knuckles and a swollen eye. He was waiting for aunty to come out of the office. He looked up as an ambulance pulled away and saw Belle approaching. She was the last aunt they'd been passed to and barely an adult herself. Although the youngest of the aunts, she possessed a natural ability with children.

Belle was frequently mistaken for a younger copy of Ryan's mother, Emmy. Twelve years separated the sisters, but they shared the same dark brown eyes and rosy, round cheeks. Belle's black, straight hair swept down just barely above her right brow. Although Emmy's hair was light brown in color, the two shared the same style. One of Belle's favorite pictures of Emmy was a black-and-white that hung in her studio. It was a close up of the two smiling and very near laughing while cheek-to-cheek. They wore matching, heavy knit stocking caps and stood in front of a white background. Belle had taken the picture as a self-portrait assignment while pursuing her art degree. She named the piece "mirror me" and hung a larger print of it in an exhibit. Emmy was Belle's greatest fan and a good sport to family comments about Belle's more youthful resemblance. Kindness in spirit was another overlap. Their likeness was deeper because Belle also shared her oldest sister's sense of care for others. While the other sisters were standoffish and introverted, Belle's warmth was immediate. She had a special connection to Ryan and was his fiercest advocate.

Belle got into the car and they sat in silence, both staring straight ahead. As Ryan languished in the moment, Belle sat with her gloved hands on the clutch in her lap. Although he felt badly, he thought himself properly braced for sharp words. He was accustomed. But instead, aunty looked at him, smiled, and gently swept his bangs from his eye.

"You know, anger is a powerful emotion," she said. "In the right setting and focus, it can be quite beautiful. Don't ever be ashamed for what you feel or who you are. You are perfect. Don't let anyone ever tell you different."

The little ruffian started bawling. Kind and gentle words had so easily unlocked a bunker of emotions. He babbled a nearly incoherent apology for being "such a bad boy." Aunty Belle instantly snatched him tightly in her arms and countered, "Nonsense!" The power of her words released from him a feeling of defect; they were the headwaters of self-acceptance.

A few weeks later, the shadow of tragedy was once again cast over the family. At the crossroads of fate, Ryan was sent down a path to a military school. The brothers were separated, and the physical distance deepened the divide between them. Ryan survived many lessons beyond the initial hazing. He embraced the fire within and learned to channel it. He discovered he could draw other emotions, like fear, into a cauldron of rage. He used this ability to eclipse all else, making it possible for him to face terrors that caused others to cower.

Bobbing and battered through life's churning sea, he discovered that vigilance and tactical leverage were vital to survival. Following the rules only favored the inertia of those with an advantage.

The freckled little blond boy from the playground was gone, and the bullies today were coming for his planet. Over the years since, he'd sharpened into an EarthForce defender. A worn ED4 patch adorned his shoulder, and his hair was peppered with gray. On this day, he was part of the line blocking an invisible enemy, and their presence here would not stand. Today, the fury was powerful and beautiful.

Initial patrols narrowed the area of the gravity distortion. The risk he had in mind to reveal them flanked the rules. No reasonable person would jump into the middle of an obscured enemy armada to touch off an EMP probe. Although the blast of energy would paint an electromagnetic shadow of every ship out there, a collision jumping into an enemy ship was likely. It was a move that no cloaked enemy would ever expect.

Ryan inhaled deeply and nodded before mumbling, "*Audentes fortuna iuvat.*" Pyres of the past lit his path forward. He touched the jump accelerator and put the ship into light speed.

He emerged between two massive cruisers that had a blurred visual appearance, almost like they were sailing across a desert mirage. Touching the screen again, he simultaneously dropped a buoy and jumped again to what appeared to be the center point of the fleet. Heavy cruiser defensive fire bathed his prior position an instant after he jumped. Before they could fire again, the buoy erupted, producing a heavy electro-magnetic disturbance. As advertised, it painted a super accurate shadow picture of the lead enemy forces in the attack. EDF had a matrix of targets now.

Cap on Earth mumbled at his console, "Sweet Jesus," as silhouettes from hundreds of aggressor ships appeared on his display. The significance of the numbers started to resonate with him. Seeing the icons on his screen heightened the urgency. Amidst the numbing reality of the force's size, he couldn't help smiling at the icon that continued jumping through the enemy fleet, ruining the secret of their numbers.

Ryan wasn't done; he jumped into the center of the largest reading. A support ship was headed right toward him, and radiation from the next EMP nearly melted off their communication equipment. Earth registered a shadow behind the support ship that defied belief. It appeared to be one massive ship, but recon analysts quickly discounted it as either a shadow anomaly or a formation of six or seven cruiser class ships in the read.

Ryan saw better with his own eyes. Just before jumping, he saw its shadow.

Now with raw telemetry indicating the boundary of the group of enemy ships, he plotted seven jumps around the edge of the armada. Using multiple jump engines, he was able to enter, drop a probe, and jump before taking fire. On his next hop, his proximity system sounded a collision alarm with the largest ship. The second he saw it close up, the Goliath size of the beast took his breath away. He was close enough now to see through the blur, and there was a landing bay on the far side. Ryan estimated that it was wide enough to hangar several cruiser-sized vessels. This ship was large enough to be called an orbital station. He jumped just as a massive wave of defensive fire flashed nearly upon him. The fire he drew and the probe he dropped were able to provide a clear silhouette of the beast to Earth. There was little doubt that this was a planetary invasion force.

Over the next few minutes, Earth Force fired several manually reprogrammed missile volleys toward the armada. These missiles were massive planet-to-system rockets with nuclear payloads. Once in orbit, they malfunctioned. Four redirected back, hitting disabled Earth Force cruisers that were drifting in orbit around the planet. The aggressors still had unknown access to defensive systems and were able to hack missile guidance. Any ship or projectile with central defensive system control was vulnerable.

Ryan monitored the distress calls; one cruiser was hit badly enough to force evacuation of personnel down to the surface. An idea hit him, and he scrambled a channel back toward Earth.

"Zeek, what's the status of the kestrels from the 145th and 92nd?" he asked, referencing two recently decommissioned squadrons.

"They're pickin' and pulling from them off Saturn station. Why?"

"How many still have engines?"

"Dunno. I'll check. What do you have in mind?" Ryan could hear staccato keystrokes as she queried status.

"Honestly, I was thinking we could take missiles from our blotto platforms and mount them on surplus kestrels. We manually arm them and then lead those unmanned ships into advancing forces. If we time it, we can overload the power cores as the missiles detonate."

"That would be a hell of an explosion. How are you going to direct their flight path?"

"Don't worry about that yet. Are the damn loaders and maintenance bots caught up in this virus thing?"

"Checking. OK, so we have fourteen ships with engines and cores, and they appear to be flight ready." Ryan could hear more clicking on her keyboard. "And ironically, it seems the maintenance drones are not caught up in the maintenance virus."

"Can you start a program to have the drones scavenge missiles for me?"

"I'm already on it. "

"I'm headed to Saturn now."

The bots started prepping the ships with missile loads and detached them from their moorings.

"Chief, if you're thinking about the automated program on the kestrels, it isn't a combat program. It's just a simple follow program for dock and hangar work. We don't have integrated systems, so we can't pilot them remotely."

"That's why we need a rabbit."

"A what?"

"A rabbit, something they chase right into our targets."

"What are you gonna program to fly that close?"

"No programming, Zeek; I'm the rabbit." There was a long pause as Zeek frowned off into space. Ryan continued, "Can you give me manual control of missile detonation? Get those engines spooled over a hundred thirty percent when they come out of light. Have them jump right on the coordinates; the worse that could happen is there's a collision."

Zeek shook her head. "Chief, you're going to have to be nearly on top of the enemy vessels. You won't last long inside the sphere of defensive fire coming off cruisers and frigates. You'll be cut in two before the drones can emerge."

"Right, let's cut the interval down. Say, four seconds behind me. The first one's critical. That should soften the target up and give me more holes in their defensive grid."

"Chief, sir, don't do this."

Ryan took a quick breath. "Zeek, the bastards are at our door. We're out of options. This'll work. I have the best bird in the fleet, and I won't loiter. Standby one."

Ryan recorded a message in Khrylic and broadcast on an open frequency. "Khrylic forces, you violate treaty. Leave immediately. If you remain, death imminent."

"Chief, I've got four of the kestrel's ready to go."

"Good, keep working; we're gonna need them all. Keep in mind that we may be able to fall back to hard coding a coordinate location. If we can disable enemy propulsion and maneuvering, we won't need a rabbit."

General Lund transmitted from Earth, "Attention ED4: A mass has separated from the main battle group, and it's headed toward Earth. Looks like an advanced battle group. Probably two or three cruisers or a couple

49

destroyers. Likely they're coming in to recon and destroy our offline platforms. The defense grid is still down. ED4 holds the line!"

Ryan could hear chatter as multiple ED4 ships engaged just outside the asteroid belt. With growing anxiety, he could hear the names of casualties. He mumbled, "We're losing," then transmitted, "Zeek, hold on the kestrels, I'm going over to join the engagement near Ceres."

Ryan hopped to the front line and discovered one of the aggressors had taken damage, but both were continuing toward Earth. "Rhydel64 on post and I'm glowin'. Anyone over here fast enough to cause a scene?"

Atlas52 smiled in her cockpit. "How much time you need?"

"How about a full second?"

Jeeval raised one eyebrow. "You are going to be needing some speed to escape that blast."

"Yeah, good thing I was well trained."

Jeeval smiled widely. "I'm ready. Call the engagement and advise when weapons are away."

"I'm in position. If you would, ma'am, please cause a scene!"

Jeeval jumped in nearly on top of the damaged cruiser. Twisting wildly at full speed, she was barely a ship's length from the enemy. She wasn't firing but directing all focus and energy toward speed.

"I'm entering; prepare to jump." Ryan jumped nearly into the cruiser as Jeeval was holding their fire, raking across the aft section. "Two seconds; fly Atlas!" Jeeval jumped away as the nuclear tipped missile came off the rack of Ryan's ship. He depressed the button to jump away at light speed a tenth of a second before impact. The proximity and speed were too much to defend against. The warhead impacted just under the bridge section. A large flash signaled the impact and vaporized the enemy's command section. The ship's lights flickered, and it pitched off axis. Gasses jetted in flames from the exposed sections.

Ryan came out of light speed. "Status on target?"

Bull10 responded, "Nailed it! Helluva shot, Rhy; she's down. Focus fire on remaining target."

Jeeval nodded. "Nice timing, Rhydel64. Perhaps there's a moment here on the remaining target for a strafing sombrero."

"Yes, ma'am. Let's soften her up."

Several kestrels setup on strafing runs. Their rounds were released too far out to cause much damage, but they provided a focus for defensive fire. Ryan and Jeeval set up their runs just behind the others and timed approaches so that they converged on each other at forty-five-degree angles on target. The speed and proximity to the cruiser allowed them to disable several defensive firing positions over several runs.

"What do you think? Are they soft?" Ryan transmitted.

Jeeval responded, "Negative. We need a few more runs."

Ryan nodded quickly. "I think we're good. And we're short on time. It's sombrero time!"

"Not yet; she's still in the game."

"Oh, there's blood in the water, and I'm quicker. I'm going for it; everyone scatter, scatter, scatter!"

Rhydel64 circled the ship in tighter and tighter spirals. With increasing speed, he braided down on the command section. His flight system was not automated. On manual, he dynamically plotted his course around multiple axes of the ship while simultaneously firing back. The idea was to braid down while accelerating and hit critical speed for light just as the nuke hit the hull. Coordination and timing were critical. Atlas52 and Rhydel64 held the Intercommand Earth Force record for successful kills with this maneuver during planetary wargames. As Ryan spiraled down on the ship like he was dancing around a sombrero, Jeeval entered out of light speed, close in on a direct line course for the bridge section.

The weapons' bay was open, and three tiny LEDs illuminated as the nuclear device went active. As the torpedo slid off the rack, Jeeval transmitted, "Jump, jump, jump!" and both kestrels punched away.

Cap smiled from Earth. "Nice shot, Atlas. Good work, people. We've got additional targets that look to be flanking around for a lunar orbit. Fall back, intercept; hold the planet!"

Ryan transmitted back to Earth, "Cap, Rhydel64, I've got something."

"Go ahead."

"A way to force augment. With missiles strapped to automated kestrels from the 145th and 92nd, we could drone up our fleet. We set them to follow, overload their cores, fly into the aggressors, close in, and manually detonate the missiles. Should cause the cores to breach."

"Sounds like suicide."

"Only if you're still there when they detonate. I don't plan on it."

"Authorized. You have what you need?"

"I've got the drones but need another rabbit and everyone to clear out."

Jeeval quickly butted in, "Cap, Atlas52, I've always fancied having long ears."

"Approved. All ED4 forces fallback to high Earth orbit and avoid crossfire with the advancing group. Atlas52 and Rhydel64, proceed."

As Ryan was typing into his SMS, he transmitted, "Atlas52, pick your poison."

"I am designating targets as Alpha1 and Alpha2. I'll take Alpha1; you focus on Alpha2."

"Roger that; I have Alpha2. Two drone kestrels inbound, thirty-seven seconds, one homing on each of us."

"Rhydel64, today slippery and fast."

"Yes, ma'am."

Ryan's nostrils flared as he drank in a long, deep breath. The reaction time required for escape on this maneuver would approach the limits of human response. He closed his eyes momentarily, gathering himself. Half cocking his head and nodding, he opened his eyes and jumped at the target.

As he emerged, what Ryan saw outside caused his core muscles to tighten. He leaned slightly forward in his restraints as the enemy vessel filled his entire field of view. Collision alarms wailed loudly. As he decelerated rapidly from near light speed down toward the enemy ship, a maelstrom of defensive fire streamed upward at him. Glowing rounds converged and cut through his deceleration path. While avoiding the majority of it, he was forced to fly through a couple of linear streams.

Lights and alarms lit on the console, indicating that several critical systems had been hit and damaged. He came down to within a half ship's length of flying into the destroyer. Nearly blacking out in the turn, he traversed the massive ship's length barely ten feet above their hull!

Ryan saw a flash, and he knew without taking his eyes off the destroyer that an overloading drone kestrel was tumbling down toward him. *One one-thousand.* Ryan accelerated to maximum toward the edge in an effort to put the Khrylic destroyer between himself and the drone chasing him. *Two one-thousand.* Weapons, nav, life support, and all energy were redirected to the engines. *Three one-thousand.* At this speed, he pushed over the edge of the ship, clearing the drone's line of sight but exposing himself to enemy weapons fire. His thumb twitched, depressing a button that detonated the missile attached to the drone.

There was a blinding flash as the core detonated on the other side of the destroyer. While the enemy ship was between him and the explosion, massive amounts of debris from the destroyer exploded outward and peppered his kestrel. The collisions caused him to spin away, and damage alarms piled up on his combat management system.

"*Arrogant bastards were running compressed!*" Ryan mumbled. Most combat ships closed compartments and decompressed non-essential areas when there was a possibility of a combat breach. "Hey, Zeek, they cracked like a walnut. I've got shrapnel damage; can you help me clear some of these?"

Zeek was monitoring remotely and had already started working through the ship's alarms. "Chief, core shielding's damaged. I'm making adjustments, but it will hinder your speed."

Ryan thought for a moment. "Negative; amplify the core."

"Chief, with the core shield damage, you're already taking near lethal doses of radiation."

"Amplify it, Zeek; I'm dead quicker without speed. How many rads and how long can I function with it?"

"At max, probably…ten minutes."

"Proceed, amplify. All this'll be done in two."

Lund was also monitoring from Earth. "Rhydel64, Cap, good shot; Alpha2 destroyed."

Ryan keyed his com. "Status Alpha1, status Atlas52?"

◊ ◊ ◊

Three weeks earlier on leave, Ryan had pulled up the worn wooden latch on an ancient hardwood gate. Inside it was a hidden treasure of foliage and the front of Anshra's house in a New Delhi suburb. Beyond the flowers and the dark wooden porch was an open room rich in colors. The home was bright and smelled of spices and incense. Ryan stood in the open front doorway, "Hello? Commander Anshra? Jeeval?"

"Ah, Ryan!" Jeeval rounded the corner with her arms raised outward toward him. She was wearing a long-sleeved angrakha style kurta. The long tunic was a brilliant orange-red with a short, standup collar. A sporadic pattern of gold lotus floral paisleys spread over the silk. A long chain of golden elephants marched down the edge of the garment's long flap, which tied closed on her left side. The bottom of the dress ran below her knees, with high slits on each side that flapped up to hip level. She wore white silk pants beneath and simple, black flat slippers. Seeing her casual appearance out of combat uniform was both strange and pleasing to Ryan. She glided over and gave him a warm hug. As she pulled back, her wrinkled hand gently reached up and patted his cheek. "You are well, yes? We are making most delicious things. Come, come." She turned toward the kitchen and motioned for him to follow.

Ryan noted many children in a room they passed as they walked toward the back of the house. She stooped and noted the projects that each child was working on. Patting some on the head, she spoke in Hindi to them. Her tone was such that Ryan knew she was encouraging them. One child asked a question, and she looked at her combat watch, held up a finger, and responded.

Ryan smiled. "These are all yours?"

Anshra smiled widely. "Yes. Today, many are here. You've not seen so many here?"

Ryan shook his head.

Jeeval pressed her hands together and bowed in a prayer gesture. "A great blessing. I now have fourteen grandchildren and great-grandchildren. Eight are here today." As they entered the kitchen, she turned to stiff-limbed Ryan. "Don't be such a soldier," she said, shaking his shoulder gently. "Put down your rifle for a minute. You are in the warmth of my home, yes?" She motioned for him to take a seat.

"Yes, ma'am." Ryan smiled widely and sat down. His nose tingled with strong scents of cardamom, pistachio, and saffron.

Anshra was up fidgeting with cleanup around a kitchen counter. "I was surprised pleasantly to get your message. What news?" She met his eyes. "You are troubled?"

Ryan spoke softly. "When were you going to tell me?"

"Tell of what?"

"Jeeval, I know. You're quitting."

"To speak of retirement in such a way makes it sound badly. To my knowledge, I have not died. You and I are still close. You will still come to see an old woman, yes?"

"Of course. It's just..." Ryan trailed off.

Anshra smiled and cocked her head at him. "You know, all things with beginnings will have endings before starting again with another beginning. This is the natural order." She came over and lightly grasped his shoulder. Looking down at him, she asked "What of you, Ryan? What is your plan after ED4?"

He looked at her while thinking hard, and the lines in his face betrayed an internal twinge.

"Ryan, you have accepted that they're dismantling the Wing? The winds of change are blowing toward us from the horizon. You and I have been doing this now for many, many years. Everyone always says," she waved her arms in the air, "'Oh change, goddess save us! Change is suffering.' Well, change can be a good thing. You need to get out. Live a little. Do something different. Stop chasing ghosts."

Ryan quickly looked up to her.

She paused, then she spoke to him again, softly this time. "You should seek love. Yes, find a nice girl." She poked his shoulder with her finger. "Settle down, have little ones, have a family. Huh?"

A smile cracked his stone face, and Ryan chuckled while fidgeting with the silverware on the table. "You know I don't have too good of luck with family."

"Then maybe you could go back to school. Surely you could go to the Academy and gain a commission."

"That's quiet work."

"I am quiet?"

"No, ma'am, I guess not. I just don't—"

"You don't like controls. You don't like rules."

"I follow the rules now."

Jeeval squinted. "Really?"

Ryan nodded. "Really. I think we can say those days are behind me."

"Then who is this person I've been hearing rumors about, the one that has been increasingly hand-flying in combat simulations?"

Ryan glanced quickly toward her.

"Your look cannot deny what I have uncovered."

"You hacked my logs?"

"I used to be your instructor."

Ryan took a deep breath. "You are still my teacher, and you're not an old woman."

Jeeval smiled warmly. "Why have you been practicing combat maneuvers with manual controls?"

"Just an experiment."

She narrowed her eyes and leaned toward him. "And?"

"I was practicing in the simulator. I guess it really just started as recreation."

Anshra raised an eyebrow and one corner of her mouth.

Ryan noted her impatience and continued. "After a while, I got good at it. Really good at it." He looked at her with a twinkle of mischief in his eyes. "And now I'm better than the programmed automates."

Anshra's brows scrunched down into a single tight brow. "How can this be?"

"I don't know. You ever play dodge ball?"

Anshra nodded. "I know of this game."

"When I was little, I could track inbound balls, catch them with one arm, target and simultaneously return fire with my other arm. I was the dodge ball king in my school."

Anshra chuckled.

Ryan continued. "I've always been able to do more than one thing at a time. They tested me and told me I was abnormal."

"Abnormal; yes, this certain truth is known." Anshra winked and smiled at him.

"So, I have this feeling when I do both. Hard to explain, but when I relax and focus on that feeling, I can fly and fight at the same time."

Anshra was quiet for a moment as she tucked a recipe card into a small wooden box. She looked at Ryan and smiled. "You feel released when you do both."

Ryan's eyes grew wide as Anshra continued. "Yes; as you suspect, I can do this too—a little, but not as well."

"The asteroid field?" Ryan blurted out.

Anshra smiled. "Yes; that was manually flown."

Ryan slapped the table. "I knew it!"

"But I can't fly and target at the same moment. That requires split focus and greater speed."

Ryan spun a rupee coin that had been left on the table, watching it arc across the surface. "I don't know how, but I guess I can do both faster than a computer."

"Faster than the onboard system?"

Smiling, he stopped the coin and nodded.

"This is extraordinary, Ryan. Have you told anyone?"

"Reported what? That I'm breaking combat protocol? Uh, no."

"I suppose that would not go favorably. And in these matters, you have some experience, yes?" She winked at him.

"No; wouldn't go well, especially now that I'm losing my go-to person." He looked up to Anshra.

She spoke quietly while wiping the counter. "My last sortie will be in a few weeks."

"What! So soon?"

"Yes, Ryan."

"There's so much more. It's just, you're the best...in our history. I just thought—"

"Thought that if we kept running sorties that they might forget and let us continue? Hmm? Ryan, have you seen the kestrels out at Saturn station? They're dismantling them. It's happening. No, my work here is done."

She looked at her watch and moved toward the stove. Opening the oven door, she pulled a metal sheet from it. With spatula in hand, she slid a warm plate of nankhatai shortbread cookies onto the table in front of him. "Have one. I know you, and you cannot resist a smile when eating my mithai." She smiled widely and put another plate of yellow peda in front of him. "It will all be OK; you will see."

"What will you do now?" Ryan asked quietly.

Before she could answer, calamity burst from the hallway as the children rushed into the kitchen, all howling for a treat.

"All right! All right! Calm down! Each one of you shall have a treat if you are polite. Ryan asked politely." She emphatically motioned with an open hand toward Ryan. "And see how he is eating a treat now?"

All the children looked at him and shouted, nearly in unison. "Hello, Ryan!"

With no less than three children clinging to each of her legs and smiling up at her, she looked back to Ryan. "I will be teaching kindergarten."

Ryan nodded and smiled at something that was so obvious. "From kestrels to kindergarten. Well, OK then." They both laughed loudly and smiled at each other.

More children rushed in and surrounded her. Ryan watched as they dragged her into another room to work on some macaroni art project. As he watched her from the doorway, it struck him how perfectly logical it was that she would teach the young ones.

◊ ◊ ◊

Ryan's fingers worked feverishly to clear alarms. He keyed the mic and transmitted again. "Atlas52 status? Status Atlas52?"

There was a pause as the frequency went silent. Ryan looked over to ensure his com was still operational. Before he could query again, Cap responded. "Atlas52 KIA. Disabled on approach and the drone detonated right on top of her. Aggressor Alpha1 damaged but still in the fight."

Ryan's fingers stopped moving, and his head shot up. He squinted his eyes closed, his scalp tightened, and his chest felt tight. He drank in a seemingly never-ending breath of air, and his head shook as if with a palsy. Holding his breath for a moment, he opened his eyes. Exhaling, he whispered, "Goodbye, Jeeval." He could almost hear her voice in his head. "*Ryan, clear your head. Fight! Fight as I taught you! Hold the line!*"

He keyed the mic again. "Acknowledged, Rhydel64 has Alpha1." No one on frequency challenged him.

"Comin' back 'round. Zeek, it's a destroyer, and they've probably decompressed now. Send four drones staggered inbound on two-second intervals. I need a twenty-second callout on the first's ETA from Saturn Station. Stage the next one from Jupiter orbit. Send the last two from solar orbit."

Zeek mumbled out loud at her console, "*This is madness.*" Then, transmitting to Ryan, "Where you gonna take cover when they all hit?"

"I'll figure something out. As god's my witness, these bastards don't cross the line."

Ryan cleared all the major alarms and deactivated the radiation protocols. This afforded power increases but created lethal exposure levels. He punched a syringe loaded with an antiradiation injection through his suit's medical port. He barked into the mic, "Where'r my drones?"

"Two minutes."

"Call out when we're thirty seconds." Ryan plotted a short light hop that would put him five hundred yards off the aggressor's stern. This was inside the accuracy variance and could very well have jumped him into the Khrylic destroyer. He spooled power up to begin a cascading overflow.

He imagined his mother smiling and reaching out for him. The first drone came in from Saturn and was cut down far enough out to cause little damage. The second from Jupiter landed nearer, followed closely by the first drone from the Sun. Ryan detonated them nearly simultaneously. In the momentary blindness from the blasts, the second Sun drone was missed, as well as Ryan, who had traversed very near to the bridge section.

"*Swallow this!*" He initiated detonation a millisecond before clearing the back side of the ship. The last drone was a direct hit on the bridge, and the massive explosion broke the destroyer apart. Ryan escaped the energy from the bridge strike but flew through the remains of the Jupiter drone. His ship was pelted and violently displaced. The blast knocked him momentarily unconscious. Groggy, with his nose stinging, he struggled to restart the ship as he tumbled toward one of the destroyer's larger engine fragments. The debris was flashing with arcs of plasma and jetting burning gas. Ryan was pawing through radiation fatigue as the light from the burning fragment caused his cockpit to glow brighter.

Redirecting energy at the last moment, he restored emergency power, maneuvered with thrusters, and narrowly escaped impact with the animated debris.

He tried twice to restart the main core. On the third attempt, he mumbled aloud, "Come on sweetie..." The coaxing was successful. *That a girl. Stay with me sweetheart; just a little longer. We're almost home.*

The SC looked down, meeting General Lund's eyes. "So, it was one of your guys that used improvised EM pulses to create a shadow picture of the enemy fleet?"

"That's affirmative. From it we determined their armada size. With our defense network offline, we were concerned about losing the planet. So, we engaged the initial battle groups in an effort to buy more time. Their cruisers and frigates created a perimeter sporting heavy defensive fire. We might as well have been shooting spit wads at their shielding. After just two engagements, we'd suffered heavy losses. The enemy fleet began to advance en mass and unchecked. There was a quick field conference between the remaining squad leaders. We knew our fleet and automated defense forces were still unavailable, and it would be several more minutes before the Defense Net came back online. There was good evidence that the largest Khrylic vessel was a flag ship, and she carried ground forces purposed for the surface capture of our planet. Although we'd lost the majority of our Wing at this point in the battle, my squad leaders regrouped the remaining forces with the intent to assault and destroy the Khrylic flag ship. It was an incredibly bold idea under the circumstances, and for that reason, unexpected by the enemy. My teams capitalized on a moment of combat confusion. In a ruse, one of my commanders slipped through their defenses and successfully made it onto the flight deck."

"Who was it and how'd she or he do it?"

"It was a he, Master Chief Ryan McBain."

The SC chuckled, "McBain? Figures. I know his aunt, Virginia Battle. She's my command general that runs Special Forces. Can only imagine how big a pain in the ass he must be."

"He's one of my best." Lund paused, looking down at a notification on his tablet. "I've just learned we have telemetry and video off his transponder."

The general looked to a staffer in the gallery, "Please load it now."

All heads turned to the screen behind and watched the footage from the vantage of the front of Ryan's ship. Flashes of photon energy made the audience squint. A voice from the table asked, "Can we dim the flashes?"

The SC piped up, "Negative! I want to see exactly as he did."

"Sir, we're piping in the audio."

"Atlas52, status?"

"Bought it assaulting Alpha1 destroyer."

"Bull10 status?"

"KIA, delta frigate."

"Rhydel64, you're in charge. Whadda we do?"

"Something different. Unexpected...slippery." Ryan jabbed a stim and more antiradiation medication into his medical port and struggled to speak through the burning sensation. "OK, here's the plan. All remaining forces, converge near me. Focus fire on target designation Kilo7."

"Got it, but that's a minor support ship."

"Yeah, let's hope we can disable it. I'm going to mount what's left of her. We're going deep. Target designation Zulu1. It's the largest ship I've ever seen and likely full of forces purposed for an Earth invasion. It's a good bet that she's also the command ship. We take her out and it ruins their parade. This is how we save Earth; this is how we save our home."

"Uh, you want us to attack that thing?"

"No, I want you to attack me."

After several seconds of silence on frequency, "Say again?"

"I'm going to mount Kilo7," Ryan was clicking keys in background, "and hopefully a good transponder. 'member that hack we were briefed on for Khrylic transponders a few weeks ago? I'm going to squawk Kilo7 requesting emergency cover. Then I'm gonna fly coupled to her onto Zulu1's flight deck while you fire on me for effect."

"Uh, Rhydel64, are you—"

"I'm gonna fly her onto Zulu1's flight deck and then I'm gonna detonate my core." There were another few seconds of silence. Ryan stopped typing and continued on. "Guys, we were dead the moment they entered the system. I'm glowing with exposure, and I've only got a few minutes. This is the only way I know. If we're goin' down, whaddya say we take as many of those bastards with us as we can?"

There were a few seconds of silence on frequency. "Well, I guess I'll never have to smell Plinker's stinky feet again."

"Hell, why not. I'm in. Goddamn it. Let's do it."

"Ten minutes...ten lousy minutes from a cold one. They couldn't have waited just thirty more minutes? I'd rather have done this drunk."

"Jesus, I just thought of something. If we're successful, they're probably gonna name some educational facility after Carrots."

Carrots piped up. "Hope it's an all-girls school!"

Ryan smiled bitterly at the banter. "Roger that. From beginning unto the end, with blood and bone—"

Everyone in unison recited the credo. "—the sons and daughters of Terra forge the line. Inerasable, defiant, through us no harm shall pass."

Ryan spoke the challenge. "Custodes lineae—"

Multiple in unison, "—et telluris protectores Terra!"

"Protegas planetae, protegas domum!"

"Oh, hell yeah!"

Ryan, "One planet...one force...ED4...to the last we stand!"

Multiple in unison, "hurRAHHH!!!"

The telemetry showed a few minutes of transition to the leading edge of the Khrylic fleet. The audio piped in with flashes of fire from other ships.

"Coming in high on Kilo7; we need to break her back."

"I got you; have you got an angle on the engines?"

"Got it; low yield should disable her—sparrows away! Three seconds, cover, cover, cover!"

There was a flash as a low yield nuclear detonation severely damaged the aft section of Kilo7.

"Nice!"

"Comin' 'round for the bridge shot—wait for it...and," an electrical static sound, "you're done." There were more flashes as several ships crisscrossed while firing at the command deck.

"On a forty-five, right behind you..."

"Good shot; I'm laying in on your six."

Heavy fire pierced the bridge and shielding. The compartment was compromised, and debris escaped into open space.

"Let's hope she's still transponding with the rest of the fleet."

Ryan typed into his communication system, "Yeah! We're golden; she's still transmitting. I'm coupling now to a few hard points. Hacking in and broadcasting a request for assistance. We're transmitting! Give me a four-second head start to get this franken-pig moving. Jump at near-light toward Zulu1...to uh, intersection designation HOLO. Fire on me. Make it look good, but you know, not too good."

"Rhydel64...Ryan, make it count."

"Roger that."

The group traversed a little further toward the massive orbital ship designated Zulu1.

"Rhydel64 roll over so I can fire on Kilo7...I'm firing."

"Zulu1's lazing us for range!"

"She's ignoring Kilo7."

With a sarcastic deflated intonation, "Oh good, she's attacking us..."

Ryan, "Just a little closer...this had better be a flight deck...it's been a privilege!"

Before he'd finished his sentence, all ships escorting and firing on Rhydel64 had been cut down.

Telemetry showed Ryan set his power core to cascade into an overload. Rhydel64 broke free of Kilo7 at the last and accelerated again. Several defensive beams crossed in front, some hitting the ship as she entered the flight deck. The camera jostled as the ship collided with the deck. There was a scratchy sound from the cockpit microphone almost like a wheeze from Ryan. "Stupid bastards...told...you...death...imminent."

The ship configuration bar on the screen showed core overload status as Ryan clumsily pawed at the interface to activate all mining charges for a five-second delay. Khrylic personnel on the flight deck scrambled away from view. The screen split showed a console camera of Zeek monitoring remotely. Her red eyebrows had scrunched together into one. The ejection seat safety pin was still in her back pocket, and she looked ahead at the monitor with great concern. Shaking her head, she lost her composure and screamed, "Eject! eject! Goddamn it! Eject now!"

She slammed her hand down repeatedly on a button that would remotely fire the ejection pod. Back in Ryan's frame, there was a bright flash, and then, in the bottom corner of the screen, a curly-cue stream off the small chemical propellant rocket on Ryan's escape pod. Several parked enemy ships passed through the narrow field of view as the rescue pod streaked through the hangar and out toward the far exit.

Just as the camera showed the pod making a right turn past the deck entry and aft toward the engine section, there was another massive flash. The camera showed momentary static from the force of the blast. As the escape pod traversed the aft engine section, multiple additional large explosions blurred the screen. The blasts propelled large pieces of debris that overtook the camera's field of view and drifted out, jetting burning gasses into space. The only remaining audio was a high-pitched, double chirping noise in concert with a red strobe off the pod. In the corner of the frame, a motionless gloved hand drifted into the field of view and hung lifeless in space.

General Lund broke the silence in the room. "There's uh, several more minutes as the pod drifts on before he's picked up by automates from the medical frigate Astoria. For reasons only known to god, McBain's still alive—barely."

The video cut to black, and Lund continued. "We think the core explosion started a chain reaction with other internal agents. I don't think they ever expected to take fire from inside the flight deck. The assessment that the massive Khrylic vessel carried command assets and ground forces required for invasion appears to have been correct, as her destruction caused the remainder of the enemy fleet to bug out. "

The SC raised his eyebrows. "He flew his own ship into the flight deck and detonated it?"

"Affirmative." A pin dropping in the room would have caused a sonic boom. Lund continued, "For anyone unfamiliar, entry to ED4 is volunteer. We scrub applicants for certain suitability requirements."

A mumble from the audience broke the silence, "More like behavioral issues."

"NO!" General Lund boomed out across a sea of brass in the room. Then, more quietly, "My people excel at creative thinking and take an oath. That means holding the line, even if it cuts through you. In the very midst of being deactivated due to some misguided perception of human fallibility, we were the defiant line that remained at muster to defend our home, our planet, our species."

Lund raised his voice. "Machines and automation did nothing here. Boots in cockpits saved this room!" As silence descended over the group, Lund looked up to the SC. He spoke in barely a whisper. "But the entire Wing, one hundred fourteen of the finest..." his eyes grew wide, and he cocked his head. "Lost them, I lost all of them."

The admiral nodded and mumbled, "They saved the planet." He rubbed his eyes. "Their names, I want to know them. I want them known by all." He glanced around the room and pointed at the screen. "In their memory, you will all personally ensure this never happens again."

He looked back to General Lund. "I want to be involved in communications with the families. They should know the sacrifices of their loved ones literally saved the planet. It won't bring them back, but they should be proud."

Lund shook his head and spoke quietly to the Admiral. "Very few...most... had no family. Part of the suitability. We were the family."

"Right. Absolutely. These were our brothers and sisters. I want to talk to that chief of yours as soon as he wakes. I have a special forces major general to call. I need to tell her that her nephew's still alive, even if just barely. It will be the only good call I get to make today."

BITTER TIN

*"...Why am I still here? It's a mistake;
this is all a mistake."*
—Ryan

Ryan woke to the wail of alarms. It was dark, and he struggled to see clearly. As the haze lifted, he realized the sounds were not coming from his cockpit. He was laying down as machines rang out, indicating his return from the dead. His shoulder felt pinned, and a terrific pain wove through his entire body. He felt a rhythmic, stinging sensation with each breath. He tried to swallow and gagged. There was large tube going down his throat, and a machine was forcing air into his lungs. He gagged again slightly and tried to relax. He was alone in the dim glow of the room, and his eyes darted back and forth as his senses sharpened. Tubes and wires were coming off him from everywhere. He couldn't move, and the sense of pain was increasing by the moment.

A small, white remote was woven by its cord around the bed railing. Thrashing for the call button, he couldn't quite get his hand to reach far enough to grab the device. Struggling with greater effort, he could only manage to flop his arm at it. His hand would hit it, but his grasping motion was too slow. Focusing intently, he tried to close his hand. He was telling it to close, but even with concentration, he couldn't close it completely. The rhythmic beeps measuring his heart rate raced faster than twice per second as his mind slipped to the precipice of panic. At that moment, a nurse rounded the corner to his room and caught sight of him struggling. She turned back toward the hallway and shouted, "Verified, bona fide, he's awake again!"

She came quickly to his bedside and silenced the alarms. She put one hand on his forearm and leaned closer to his face. "Mr. McBain, my name is Nurse Darcy. Can you hear me?"

Ryan tried to nod and winced from the pain. Instead, he snatched her forearm. Time and adrenaline were improving his motor skills. He looked at his hand grasping her arm and squeezed. She smiled and patted his hand. "Good! You have some strength."

His eyes were wide and locked on her.

"Sugar, you got yourself banged up pretty bad, and you're in a hospital. You don't know me, but I've been taking care of you on and off for many days. You're gonna be OK. I need you to try your best to relax, OK? I can see you're pretty wound up. I'm gonna get this tube out, and we'll get you fixed up, but I need you to relax for a minute while I work. Can you help me? Can you do that for me? Just blink once for yes."

Ryan closed his eyes emphatically.

She continued her work. "You've been in and out for days. I swapped shifts for tonight. I just had a feeling you might finally come out of it. It's gonna be OK. You're OK. Hang in there with me, darlin'."

She continued to fuss around the bed, working on him and talking to him. Ryan was distracted by her voice. It was familiar and soothing. His eyes surveyed the small room. A door on the far side appeared to lead to a bathroom. The floor and walls were a light, bland color. It had older fixtures, and there was nothing to indicate it was a military hospital.

She came closer again. Leaning over the bed, she asked, "Hey, you a poker player?"

Ryan looked at her for a moment and then closed his eyes emphatically.

"Good. You should know that we have some winnings to spend when you get better. There was a pool on you ever waking up. I knew you were a fighter. I've been doing this for a long time, and sometimes you can just tell, you know? Well anyway, as the days stretched out, your odds, well, let's just say Nurse Darcy knows when to double down."

She was adjusting the bed and glanced back to him. "Oh, I know folks are gonna howl and say I knew something and cheated—they always do. Well, no matter, you showed them. Only seems fair that we split the winnings, don't you think?" She looked back to his eyes, "You still with me, sugar?"

Ryan blinked once.

She gushed, "Wonderful, then it's a date." She stopped for a moment and smiled at him. It made sense that Darcy had a particular interest in and concern for Ryan. The compass needle in her heart had always led directly to the strays. Twice divorced at fifty-eight, her soft spot for the hard cases had left scars on her heart and crow's feet around her eyes. There were still many males in her life, but the five strays now living with her were rescues of the K-9 kind.

She stood at average height, clad in purple scrubs. Her curly, light brown hair was pulled back neatly with a costume jewelry brooch. Bright purple readers hung below her neck by a flowered Croakie. Her nails were short and colorless due to her sense of professional practicality. She wore no rings. Her strong hands betrayed a historical love for the sun with freckles and spots. Quick in her walk, she was always moving. Her level of action, along with an addiction to yoga, were the primary reasons why her friends would describe her as skinny. Darcy would always correct them, preferring to describe herself as fit rather than underweight.

As she looked on at him, several other nurses, doctors, and technicians rounded the corner. Ryan squinted as the lights came on.

Two hours later, he was sitting up and feeling a bruise over his sternum when he breathed deeply. Darcy came through the doorway with a plastic tumbler and rattled its contents. "Ice chips for you."

"Oh, Darcy, please. I'm so thirsty. I haven't had anything to eat or drink in weeks. Even POWs get water!"

"Whoa there, mister! You can't be that ornery with me, least not yet. We haven't known each other that long. Besides, a couple hours ago you couldn't even talk, let alone drink something."

"I had a tube in my throat."

She set the ice down and raised her eyebrows, "I may have liked it better when you couldn't speak." She winked at him and then inspected his IV. "The surgeon should be in shortly. She can clear you for light food and fluids. 'Til then, it's ice chips. You don't realize what you've been through. You need to slow down a little." She repositioned the pillows behind his back. "On a pain scale of one to ten, how's the shoulder feel?"

"It goes from numb to sharp pains when I try to move it."

She put her hand gently on it. "Give it some time. It's going to take some patience and some work. It was barely attached when you first came in. For several days, we weren't sure if we'd have to amputate. That wasn't even the biggest part of all this. You had so much radiation in your system that we all had to wear shielding around you. Probably a good thing that you nearly suffocated in space; it slowed down your brain injury and also the radiation. Somehow, luck doesn't adequately describe when, how, and what happened here."

Ryan was quiet for a moment.

She cocked her head. "Anything else I can do for you, other than the water?"

He was looking down when he spoke softly in an even tone. "Who else survived?" When she didn't answer, his eyes rose up and met hers.

She looked away and fidgeted with his bedding, "Oh, well, I don't really have those answers for you."

"Please don't lie to me."

She stopped and looked back to him. "Mr. McBain—"

"Ryan. I'm Ryan. Please tell me what you know, Darcy."

With a taut smile, she put her hand over his. "Ryan, it's not my place. Others will be along soon, and all your questions will be answered. Just a little more patience, and someone will be in here for you."

He turned and looked out the window as she quietly left the room. What she wouldn't say confirmed what he already knew. They were gone—all of them. He'd hoped that even just a few others might have survived or been picked up. He sat and stewed, replaying the entire battle. The moment when he'd lost Jeeval physically jarred him. He winced as he replayed it over and over. His focus shifted to the reality of losing her. So many thoughts raced through his mind.

He panted and snatched the bed railing. His eyes searched the room for any detail or distraction, but the room was quiet and sterile. He was alone, left to rankle. His mind snagged on the oddity of so many things that just no longer existed. And the consequences, big and small, of what had just happened hit him like shrapnel from an explosion. The Tuesday poker game, helping Alister move this weekend, and he hadn't called the bakery back to clarify the spelling of Jeeval's name for her retirement cake.

Before he could settle on the insignificance of icing, waves of emotion crashed over him and swept him over into a churning ocean of grief. All these things were now pointless. There was nothing, just nothing. All his brothers and sisters were gone. It was instant, and it was final.

He pinched his eyes tightly, softly shook his head, and mumbled, "No... no...no." He panted again and swatted the bed with an open palm. The jostling caused a bolt of pain in his bad shoulder. His eyes shot open, and the walls of the room felt too close. He looked around wildly and caught sight of the tube in his arm. He followed it up to the IV and thought about the tether of fluid that had kept him alive. Washing his hand over his face, he mumbled in anguish, "So many. So many better lost. Why am I still here? It's a mistake; this is all a mistake."

He reached down and felt the momentary sting as he yanked out the IV. He swung his legs over the side of the bed and pursed his lips. The room was spinning, and he paused, waiting for it to settle. Then, in one movement, he stood and braced himself with his good arm. He took a breath and gingerly stepped toward the end of the bed, but his knees buckled, and he dipped down. With clenched teeth, he pulled himself back up and took a few more breaths. Standing felt better than waiting.

Letting go of the bed rail, he steadied himself for the walk across the room to a cubby with drawers. The next tiny steps were better, and he was able to make the crossing. Bracing himself alongside the counter, he was able to slide open the top drawer. To his relief, he found pants and a shirt. He saw stars and slowed, weathering through a few moments of nausea. Draping his clothes over his good shoulder, he turned around and spotted the side chair next to the bathroom doorway. His eyes plotted all the brace points leading to it.

Shuffling slowly and deliberately, he reached the seat with a light head. After draping the shirt and pants over the chair arm, he positioned himself just in front of the seat. He needed to sit, and with his good hand, he started gathering his hospital gown up. When he had most of it pulled up to his waist, he gingerly sat down in the seat, naked from the waist down. Ryan amused himself with the thought of being discovered at this moment in time.

He dropped his pants on the floor and pushed them around with his feet to correctly position the legs. He put his feet into the legs and bent down to pull them up. He made it halfway down before he croaked from a flash of pain through his shoulder. Retreating back upright, he breathed through it for a few seconds. With a different approach, he alternately wiggled his legs to work as much of the pant legs as possible up toward his knees. The pain in his shoulder was still pronounced, but moving slower mitigated the sharpness. He sat for a moment with the waist of his britches around his knees and caught his breath. He reached down with his good arm, grasping the waist, and in one movement, he stood up while holding it. The pants came up as he rose, and he fought dizziness for a few seconds. When it subsided, he mumbled curse words at the difficulty of closing zippers and fastening buttons with a single hand.

Covered in a glaze of sweat, he sat back down and breathed. Just putting on pants had nearly exhausted him. He still had to remove the goofy gown and pull a shirt over his head. For the next five minutes, he maneuvered the gown around to remove the last of it from his injured shoulder. Several times he heard steps in the hallway, but no one had yet discovered him. Grasping his shirt, he slid the arm over the bad shoulder first. Pulling it over his head nearly caused him to pass out. He maintained his focus on breathing and sat fully clothed, gathering his strength. As he stood up, the door swung open. Darcy had returned with the surgeon.

Before the doctor could speak, Darcy was on Ryan's arm. "What in god's name are you doing out of bed?!"

"You're busy, and this place is, you know, for sick people. I'm good—good to go."

"I'm Dr. Clarkston. You're taking over my job by discharging yourself. You don't want to get me fired, do you?" She spoke softly and with a lack of intonation in her voice. It wasn't altogether monotone, but she was able to ask an edgy question without conveying a sense of anger or irritation. The effect caused Ryan to accept the question with sincerity and pause.

Darcy was altogether shocked at the doctor's response. Perpetually grumpy, Clarkston was generally cuddlesome as a pufferfish. On more than one occasion, Darcy had apologized to patients for the surgeon's abrasive bedside manner.

As Darcy held onto Ryan, the surgeon drew his focus back inside by moving to the center of the room. Dr. Clarkson was less than average height, and Ryan guessed—based on the gray peeking through the part in her short hair and the lines around her eyes—that she was in her late forties. She was neither skinny nor overweight, and her manner reminded him of Aunt Enid; she stood relatively still with her hands in the large pockets of her white coat. When she did remove her hand, Ryan saw she had a modest and worn wedding band on her ring finger.

Ryan looked to Dr. Clarkson. "I'm sorry, ma'am—doctor. I'm not trying to be any trouble. I just need to get somewhere."

"Really? Where? Where do you need to be?"

Ryan just looked at her. She smiled back and without looking down added, "Certainly won't get far without shoes."

Ryan looked down and then to Darcy. "I suppose you wouldn't direct me to my shoes, would you?"

Darcy emphatically shook her head.

Dr. Clarkston tilted her head. "Would you sit on the bed for a minute so I can at least give you some information before you leave?"

He looked at her and thought about the offer. She added, "A medical debrief."

Ryan nodded, and with Darcy's assistance, he shuffled back to the bed. Dr. Clarkston ignored Darcy's pained look and pulled a rolling tray over, retrieving a small pad of paper from her coat pocket. She spoke with perfect clarity and volume. She explained to Ryan the extent of his injuries and specifically how badly his shoulder was damaged. She sketched out a rather good diagram of the muscles that comprise the shoulder and arm. She identified the ones that had been severed and others that had been destroyed. As she spoke, Ryan thought Dr. Clarkston's eyes seemed larger than average and noted how she paused to scan his face for any sign of confusion. He learned that they had dispatched him to this civilian research hospital because she was an expert in an emerging field of nanomuscular augmentation. Ryan had her repeat it twice.

Dr. Clarkston chuckled and nodded. "It's OK; this is an emerging field. If this wasn't my thing, I wouldn't have any idea what it is either. Basically, we're using organic tissues interwoven with synthetics. In your case, augmented tissue was interwoven with nanotubes. Your particular nanotubes were imbued with certain zeolites: charcoal, germanium, and some others."

Ryan's head nodded slightly at each word. The doctor paused and smiled. "We rebuilt your arm with some of your own repurposed muscle, along with materials that provide greater strength and resiliency. But more importantly for you, we laced in chemical compounds that bond with ionizing radiation and scavenge cells already damaged by radiation."

"So, this means, what, I glow in the dark and have superpower strength?"

She chuckled. "Sorry, afraid not, at least not in revision one. The compounds are still present, but they were most active when you came in here already 'glowing in the dark.' The nanotubes will allow greater resiliency to muscle strain or potential damage."

"So, you're saying the next time I catch my arm ejecting, it won't nearly rip off? Terrific."

"No. Actually, I'm saying that your recovery should be quicker, and the transplanted tissue will be less likely to tear as you recover. That's assuming you recognize the second chance you've been given and realize how fragile your shoulder is right now. It's not gonna be easy. There will be a lot of physical therapy and continuing medications. You have to plan for and commit to your recovery." She paused for a moment. "Darcy, would you be kind enough to get Mr. McBain a tumbler of water? You do have time for some water?" she asked, looking back at Ryan.

Ryan nodded.

As Darcy left the room, Dr. Clarkston fluffed the pillows and motioned to Ryan. "You could lean back a little while we talk and rest that shoulder." Again, Ryan nodded, and the doctor helped him swing his legs back onto the bed.

"Darcy said you were ornery. Usually she reserves that term to describe me, behind my back, with the other nurses."

"Guess I'm taking your job again."

"I suppose." She looked off.

Ryan caught the look. "Forgive me, doc, but your eyes look like I feel."

Her face was slightly puffy, her posture slightly rigid. The left corner of her mouth tightened into a bitter smile. She pulled a laminated picture from her pocket. It was a soldier. "My kid brother. The day this picture was taken, he was so proud. We were all proud." She chuckled. "Well, I was nervous but also proud."

"What happened?"

"He was an extraordinary soldier. He was a warrior—born that way. But aside from his size, he was kind and gentle, sort of a sensitive giant. I'd introduce him as my 'little brother,' and people would laugh. I always thought he was invincible. He was a 'glass half full' kind of person. Nothing could stop him. That in mind, it didn't surprise me one day when he lived through something that many others didn't."

She pulled a top cover blanket over Ryan and spoke more softly. "But something did happen to him. He was injured; we just couldn't see it. I knew he was struggling, but I didn't know the extent. He lost his way down into a very dark place, and one night a few years back we, uh, we lost him."

She sniffed and shook her head. "So, then you came into my OR, and I did my job. I put you back together. Just after, I was briefed on what happened to bring you here. It reminded me. I went to my office, still in my scrubs, and I shut the door and I just cried and cried again. I said I wasn't going to do that anymore, but I did."

She patted his hand and nodded her head. "As your doctor, I'm advising you: Don't rush back somewhere into things and try to smooth this over by moving on. It doesn't work that way; it doesn't heal that way. You have to talk to people. You have injuries I can't see or fix, but they can still be just as life threatening."

Darcy wheeled around the corner through the doorway with a large plastic tumbler. Dr. Clarkston stood abruptly, sniffed, and wiped her nose. She quickly drew two shots from the pump of an antibacterial bottle on the counter and washed her hands together. To Darcy it was a natural medical process, but Ryan could see a raw angst in the washing motion of her hands. The doctor pulled a stethoscope from her coat pocket. Ryan's eyes followed hers closely, but she did not look at him. Without turning around, Dr. Clarkston asked, "Did you reach him earlier?"

Darcy set the tumbler down next to the bed as she spoke. "Yes, doctor. I called just after he woke. He's on his way."

Ryan's eyes narrowed. "Who'd you call?"

Dr. Clarkston put her stethoscope back around her neck. "Your commanding officer. He asked to be informed the minute you woke, as did your aunts and your brother." She looked around, and Darcy nodded her head, adding, "Also on their way."

Ryan took a deeper breath. Dr. Clarkston put her hand gently on his chest. "You're surrounded by people only interested in supporting you. You did something amazing for the planet; let some on the planet do something in return. Rest easy, soldier. Rest here. And don't drink too much of this; just a few sips. You don't want to vomit with that shoulder."

Ryan nodded his head. He noticed the lines around her eyes and could sense a depth of concern from within them. Her hand was in her lab coat pocket, and she looked at him for a few seconds. "Soldier, you know how to follow orders?"

Ryan nodded again.

"Good. Then follow doctor's orders. No more escape plans, OK?" She looked to Darcy. "We'll see about getting you on some light solid foods." Looking back to Ryan, "What do you say?"

"I'll stay, but I'm not wearing the damn gown."

Dr. Clarkston smiled and spun around. "I'll let you negotiate that out with Darcy."

Ryan caught the nurse's eyes. "Am I gonna have any more trouble with you?" Darcy asked him.

"No, ma'am," he replied, smiling back. "But could you tell me where my shoes are?"

Darcy raised her eyebrows. "They are well secured. Now, I have other patients, and your food is coming. Stay in your bed, and behave yourself. I don't want to catch you out of it again."

A week and a half later, Ryan was discharged. Darcy, along with most of the floor staff, came in to see him off. He was transferred to a recuperative clinic near San Diego, where he stayed for a few weeks before he could procure a ride up to his former Swift Station. He was shocked at the front gate security, or lack thereof. Several horn blasts summoned an overweight guard in a golf cart. In just a matter of weeks, the base had become a ghost town.

He opened the street side door to the hangar, and the front reception desk was gone. The only evidence that something had formerly been there were stains and depressions on the carpet. Wires hung from broken wall plates. Grotesque holes remained where the squadron shield and symbols once hung proudly.

There were scraps of paper and debris on the stairs. The names on the offices had been stripped off. Rounding the corner to his old office, Ryan saw five banker boxes stacked perfectly and equally between the walls. His office had been packed up with such organizational perfection that Ryan's eyes began to water. Only one person could have done it with such care. Although she had been reassigned to Greenland, he could still feel her presence.

He removed the top from one of the boxes and discovered something wrapped in white tissue paper. Unraveling it, he discovered it was the maneki-neko kitty bank. Under it was a ping-pong paddle that had been signed by everyone in the group. Ryan stared at it for a few minutes before he returned it to the box. He carefully returned everything as he had found it and slowly walked backwards out of his office into the hallway. He wandered in a daze down further toward the hangar floor.

As he came through the main fire door, he was dismayed to see that the big hangar door had been left open. Birds had taken refuge there, and the floor looked like that of a bird cage. The giant round cavern was empty. No technicians, no tools, and no big bird. Ryan had a flashback to the very last time he had stood in nearly the same spot looking toward his kestrel. Back then, he'd contemplated death, not realizing how alive he was in that moment. Now he stood here, scratched by death and desperate for the life he had once had. He coughed and sputtered on the ashes of his former life. He could feel his heart race unbounded, when a familiar voice brought him back. "Did you forget where you parked your ship?"

Ryan smiled and spun around. He saluted, "General, seems as though we've misplaced the entire squadron."

General Lund, now retired, was in street clothes. He had on white sneakers with black calf-high dress socks. He was wearing a pair of checkered pattern walking shorts, complete with a white belt and a bright blue golf shirt. Completing the ensemble was a Greek fisherman's cap that nearly caused Ryan to laugh out loud. Lund looked up and around the hangar, nodding.

"Your DO would have kittens if she saw the place."

Ryan chuckled. "Yes, sir; I believe you're correct."

"How's the shoulder coming along?"

"Better. I have pretty good range of movement. We're gonna start working on strength therapy next week."

Lund nodded. "Can I give you a lift back? I'd like to meet the poor bastards who have to work with you."

Ryan squinted at the General. "Which one?"

Lund cocked his head at Ryan. "Come again?"

"Which one of my aunts put you on watch?"

Lund smiled. "I think we're all in sync."

Back at the facility, Ryan gave the general a tour and introduced him to several of his therapists. Once they were back in Ryan's room, the general fidgeted with some papers. "You should know they're gonna pin a medal on you."

Ryan huffed and looked down. "Stupid. Doesn't change anything. Doesn't bring anyone back."

"Negative, the proper response is 'thank you, sir.'"

Ryan nodded. "Respectfully, sir, we're way past that. This was the worst day of our lives, the worst day in ED4 history. It's a perversion and an abomination to throw some kind of medal party. It's disrespectful."

The general pursed his lips and spoke in a hushed whisper, "Square yourself, soldier." Then, looking around the room as if searching for words in the ether, he said "You have to recalibrate. On this day the line held. Tragic? Hell yes, but on the day that everything went wrong, ED4 didn't. We were the ones that held the line. No, I've been thinking about this. That's not our worst day. Our best laid down their lives to hold the planet, and you will honor their sacrifice. You will honor the line. You will honor it by taking the medal. If not for yourself, for them. You take the tin."

"I get a medal because a bunch of my family died. It's wrong; it's all wrong." Ryan plopped down and put his head in his hands, "I should have found them first. It should have been me, not Jeeval. I was tired, and I knew there was something wrong, but didn't and couldn't..." He opened his mouth, but no words came out. The center of his core was so tight that it ached, and he labored to breathe. Starting again, he said, "I should, and I...I uh, missed. And now...they're gone. They're just all gone."

A quiet hung over his words, and the General spoke softly. "You did everything that anyone could do and more. Discovering them forty minutes sooner wouldn't have changed the outcome for Atlas52. Would Jeeval have thought to mount a disabled enemy skiff and fly onto the hangar deck of their flag ship?"

"Maybe."

"Bullshit! She was good, but she wasn't crazy like you. She herself made those remarks in your evals. You were there for a reason, and she knew it. Think about that."

After a moment of silence, Ryan spoke in a quiet voice. "Then why am I still here?"

"What?"

"Why am I still alive? Why'd I survive? Seriously, why me? I wasn't the best or the smartest or the model example to carry on. I shouldn't be here. This is some kind of sick joke, either that or a horrible nightmare." He popped up and threw a duffel across the room.

"You're getting a medal, and you need to get a hold of yourself. If Jeeval were here, what would she council? You know they'll be there in spirit. Don't you dare disrespect them. Stand tall, stand proud, and take it for them."

Ryan looked off. "Please don't make me do this. Give it to someone else."

"It's out of my hands. You're the one."

"You mean the only one left."

Two days later in a grand hall, Ryan stood on a stage like a statue. Over a thousand dignitaries attended the ceremony. Ryan was in formal dress and stood crisp and shiny and broken. He said nothing. His throat was tight like dry leather. One by one, the names were called out. Their faces were fresh in his mind, his head was buzzing, and he felt dizzy. So many names, all gone. His mind flashed to memories of each person, but the call to attention snapped him painfully back to the present moment. He remained stoic with tired, heavy eyes. The fire off the salute caused him to noticeably jump three times, wincing at each sound. It was as if imaginary rounds were tearing through him.

The later hours alone were the hardest. Ryan couldn't sit still in the quiet. His mind filled the vacuum, and he swore he heard sounds from the battle. He would pace for hours and often wander the streets in the dead of night. The bottle drowned out the feelings for a short period, but invariably he would wake with a dull cheek. Opening his eyes to the cold hard tiles stretched out in front of him, he would crawl across the bathroom floor to the basin. His body tensed to a point where he feared it would turn completely to stone. Standing rigid, he would labor to breath and try desperately to relax. The memories and feelings had hold of him like the jaws of a bear.

The following week, Ryan sat with his shirt off in a rundown single-story shop. A motor hummed from the machine in the hand of a man seated next to him. The man was glancing at a list of numbers and wiping away excess ink from Ryan's upper arm. One by one, the service numbers of those close to him were memorialized on his upper arm. Lt. Commander Jeeval Anshra, friend and mentor, was the first. Every year thereafter on her birthday, he would say her name aloud and toast her memory.

Getting through the medal ceremony was just the beginning. For the next few weeks, his orders were to attend several defense department events. He was the wrong brother for speaking to crowds and standing in the spotlight. Everyone seemed to know him and had great interest in talking about the attack. The barrage of questions was relentless.

Hadley was assigned to travel with him. Although Ryan was supportive of the tour, he just wanted some space from that day. Unfortunately, it was all that everyone wanted to talk about.

Two weeks in, he was scheduled to meet with a local city group at a high school. There were banners and even a parade that day in his honor. While mingling through the crowd at an evening reception before the formal speaking event, he answered the same question five times in less than ten minutes. A few minutes later, Hadley looked at his watch and surveyed the room. Ryan had slipped away. Searching outside, he found him by a drinking fountain in a deserted hallway.

"Hey, it's show time, bro. We're looking for you."

Ryan raised his hand. "I just needed a minute to catch my breath."

Hadley's eyebrows bunched together. "Catch your breath? Are you sick?"

"Nah, just get a little wound up sometimes when people start running around."

"Well, then let's get going. Pull it together, bro, and let's go."

"I just sometimes don't want to talk about this and keep going through it. Is that asking too much?"

"Mitch, why you doing this right now? Get it together and let's go, OK?"

Ryan looked down and nodded. Hadley calling him by first name was a reminder of family and a comfort. Looking at his older brother, he remembered the good times before they were separated, before they drifted. Few knew that Hadley's polished public face started very differently. He carried a lisp for many years. In particular, he had difficulties saying the letter "R" and instead enunciated the sound of the letter "W." As such, he called his younger brother "Wyan." One afternoon riding home on the school bus, some boys bullied Hadley for his impediment. Ryan used his shoe as a weapon and hit one of the boys in the face with the heel. The brothers found themselves walking the remainder of the way home. In an effort to console his older brother, Ryan told Hadley to call him by his first name. From that point forward, it stuck.

Ryan stood in the empty hallway with cow eyes as Hadley approached. The older brother put his arm around Ryan and gently squeezed his neck. "Mitch, what's gotten into you? I mean, this is great. You're a hero, and everyone loves you. You could get a free dinner anywhere on Earth right now. You could probably even run for president."

Ryan rolled his eyes wide and toward his brother. Hadley held up his hands. "I'm kidding. But you have to admit it isn't a bad idea. I could be your vice president. Yep, the McBain brothers runnin' the show."

Ryan shook his head as Hadley gently shook his brother's shoulder.

◊ ◊ ◊

A few weeks later during a broadcast event, Ryan was asked about being a hero. "I'm not. Everyone keeps saying that. I just did my job. That's all I did. The heroes were the ones who didn't come back. They made the ultimate sacrifice."

"You're talking about your comrades who didn't survive?"

"Yes."

"You're far too humble. Your actions and your skill took out the Khrylic base ship. The others just, well, fell short."

Ryan stood up and started pulling the microphone off his collar.

"What are you doing?"

"Interview's over. You know what?" Ryan snarled, leaning toward her. "You're an idiot. You have no idea."

Later that evening, Ryan received a call. The voice on the line said to hold for a call from the president. After being patched through, he learned that the president had been watching that interview. The words from the planetary leader were kind and thoughtful. As it turned out, she too was a veteran, and in her youth, she had some experience with combat trauma. At one point, she asked Ryan what he wanted. Without hesitation, he answered, "Out."

◊   ◊   ◊

There were three solid knocks at his hotel door. Ryan opened the door to Hadley in the hallway holding a half-crumpled piece of paper. "You had to go and ruin it, didn't you? What the hell was the thing on the broadcast? At the very least you had a book deal. Jesus, Mitch, they probably would've made a damn movie about you. Why did you fire the publicist I lined up for you? What are you doing, buddy?"

"I don't do books and I don't do talks. I fly and defend our space. That's what I do."

Hadley shook his head and put his hand to his forehead. "Did! You did fly in space. All that is gone, remember? You never think ahead. All this was your future!"

"No, bro; it was yours. I'm out. I'm headed back to California tomorrow first thing."

Ryan bummed around for several weeks before General Lund finally caught up with him.

"So, you're going to hang it all up and walk away?"

"Guess so."

"A quitter, then."

"Yeah, whatever. I quit. I'm done; there's nothing left."

"You're wrong. You're letting grief stand in the way. There's a lot more."

"You quit too."

"I retired; it's different. This isn't about me. Chief, Ryan, don't let it end like this."

"What do you want from me, general? It's over. I just don't have anything."

"So, you're going to go out and do something else, like teach kindergarten?" Ryan's head snapped toward Lund. "That's not you, and we both know it. This is what you do. If you don't believe me, then maybe you'll listen to someone else."

The general pulled out a tablet and read from the screen. "Let's see, candidate McBain...ah, here, '...*the cadet possesses a raw energy and character trait as a natural protector. He seems to go out of his way to find trouble, sneak up on it, and blindside it in a defiant attempt to protect the defenseless. If he can learn to focus and control his tendency to throw himself wildly into the frays, and assuming he survives this despite himself, he may well season into one of the best officers in our command forces...*' blah, blah, date, and signed Lt. Jeeval Anshra."

Ryan stared off out the window.

"That was back then, but there's more. The president herself wrote a letter on your behalf, just as I did. That probably won't mean as much as the third recommendation. This was dated three days before the attack." Looking back at his tablet again, Lund read, "'*I'm filled with joy thinking about the opportunity to make this recommendation. I had the privilege to extend my hand in training this young person. Over the years since, his passion forged a path to the apex of excellence in our ranks. It's been my great fortune to witness the birth of greatness. He's truly no idea where his abilities could take him. In our work together, he's grown into a co-collaborator as well as a dear friend. Looking at his service record, there is a preponderance of evidence to support what I already know from personal knowledge of this candidate. His determination and the depth of his character would reflect the very best of what we strive for in the endeavor of this institution.*' Blah, blah, blah... Whew, Anshra sure could lay it on thick."

Lund's eyes met Ryan's. "So, here's the deal. She was a really smart lady, and she had 'character radar.' She knew about these sorts of things. You knew at one point I was gonna bounce you out of the program, didn't you?"

Ryan smiled. "Yeah, that was fair. Don't know why you kept me so long."

"Simple: Jeeval. You popped up on her radar. She said sometimes the most gifted are the most difficult." He chuckled and raised his eyebrows while handing Ryan an envelope. "Don't ever stop proving her right. You said once that you wouldn't let me down. Don't let her down—that one I'm holding you to."

Ryan opened the envelope and quickly read the front page. He flipped the pages quickly and discovered the general had orchestrated an appointment to the Military Academy.

"Why?"

"Because you're a pain the ass, and there's more. If you don't believe yourself or me, listen to Jeeval. Go and represent, and don't screw it up!"

"I don't know what to say."

"Well, that would be a first."

GET AWAY

THERE WAS A NARROW PATH, AND TIME WAS OF THE ESSENCE. IF HE WAS WRONG, HE'D HAVE SOME EXPLAINING TO DO. IF HE WAS RIGHT, IT MIGHT COST TWO LIVES INSTEAD OF ONE...

"I'm sorry, Sir, but I can't give you a pass on this. I hope you know how much I... how much we...all of us appreciate what you did."

The words floated through Ryan's light head as his nostrils flared to pull in more air. With his cheek still mashed onto the floor, he closed his eyes as tight as he could and held a deep breath.

The medical technician reached out with his hand. "Help you up?"

"Nawh, thanks. I'm good." Ryan rolled around, sat up, and rubbed his shoulder.

"I hope you understand. The physical standards are for your protection as well as others."

Ryan nodded. "I get it. I'm just not there yet."

"I wish I had better options for you. God knows the Academy and the rest of us wouldn't be here now if it wasn't—"

Ryan raised his hand and waved quickly in protest. "I'm not looking for special treatment."

The front foyer of the six-story medical complex was a wall of windows.

Each floor ended in a balcony overlooking the front atrium. Ryan walked out into the bright daylight of a large central courtyard shared by various other Academy structures. He stopped walking when he recognized General Lund. He was sitting on a bench and looked up from his newspaper. Smirking and shaking his head, Ryan walked toward his former commander.

"You know, for a retired guy, you sure do get around."

Lund stood up and quickly folded his paper. "I take it by the look on your face that you didn't pass the physical."

Ryan shook his head and looked away.

General Lund looked at his eyes. "You still in?"

Ryan shrugged. "I guess. I'm still in PT, and I go to fish bowl interrogation every week."

Lund smiled. Ryan referred to his mental therapy as a fish bowl interrogation because so many mental health professionals had been assigned to his case. One-on-one therapy for Ryan meant being in a room with a two-way mirror.

The general reached out and touched his shoulder. "Still having difficulties getting along with others?"

Ryan smiled and met the general's eyes.

Lund patted his shoulder and continued. "I think you just need to get out a little. You need a job."

Ryan squinted and leaned in closer to the general. Lund raised his palms up. "I'm not promising anything—"

"Does it have to do with flight?"

"Now don't get excited. I'm not even sure you'll pass the psych evaluation. You know, you could try to cooperate every once in a while. That would go a long way toward getting you released."

"I'll do it."

Lund smiled again. "Do what?"

With wide eyes, Ryan nodded emphatically. "Both. Whatever. I'll do whatever it takes to get back up, to get back in it."

Lund squinted back, nodding slightly and surveying Ryan. "OK. I'll make some calls."

A week later, Ryan woke to his communicator chiming.

"Yeah?"

"Were you asleep? You're not going soft on me, are you? It's 0630 for crying out loud."

"General?" Ryan fumbled with the device, nearly dropping it, and swung his legs down to the floor. "General, that you?" He squinted at the screen through the sleep in his eyes and put the device back to his ear.

"Hope you didn't put your flight bag up in a yard sale."

Ryan stood quickly, put his free hand on his forehead, and tensed his body. "Wha…oh please don't be kidding with me, sir."

"I had to talk fast and call in some favors, but it's legit. Before you get too excited, there're a couple conditions."

"Oh?"

"You take your current therapy team with you. I was advised that's non-negotiable."

Ryan winced, squinted his eyes shut, and looked up, exasperated. " 'K. What else?"

"It's a government research program that's already well underway. You have a great deal of catching up to do."

Ryan nodded emphatically. "YES. I'll do it."

The General chuckled. "You don't even know what it is yet." There was a pause, and Lund broke the silence. "Still there?"

"So, what is it?" Ryan asked quietly.

"They're trying to generate a new type of energy wave behind an advanced and much faster propulsion system." Before Lund even finished his sentence, Ryan pumped his fist in the air. He'd read up on several research projects since their original conversation, and this was the one he was most interested in. Among other aspects, it involved a tour in deep space. He could get away, far, far away from all the stares and comments. He'd go faster than any human and perhaps achieve breakaway speed from the gravity of the past. The opportunity to move forward and once again be relevant drew a large goofy smile to his face. He interrupted the general. "Yes, sir. I'll do it."

"Hold on. There've been some complications. I had to take this to the president, and she wasn't exactly thrilled at the idea of risking Earth's hero in a test pilot program. See, they recently lost their lead pilot in an accident—"

"Yes, sir; I know. I read up on it. I think he made some critical mistakes. The science behind this tech is good—real good. I can get behind it."

On the other end of the connection, Lund smiled and shook his head. "Do me a favor?"

"Sir?"

"Be careful. I'm not kiddin' around. Some of this stuff reads like monkey in a capsule business. They're running lean and quick on some of these research programs. Exercise mindful caution."

"I will. I promise." Ryan looked to a rucksack standing tall and full by the front door. "When can I start?"

"Get yourself together, and I'll have paperwork in order sometime next week. Officially you will be on loan to this program. Pack your shorts, you're not going to believe—"

Ryan began nodding rapidly. "I know, they repurposed our old Swift Station. It's a sign. General, this was supposed to happen. Thank you, sir. I can't express that sufficiently. I won't let you down."

The general nodded and smiled as the com link ended.

The car dropped Ryan at the front gate. He set his rucksack down and took off his sunglasses. He closed his eyes and turned his head up toward the sun. The gentle breeze smelled of the Pacific. His heart warmed like the sun on his skin. The base was teeming with staff, and four sizable MPs guarded the front gate. As he approached, they took notice of him. "Halt! State your business. This is a restricted area."

"It certainly is." Ryan's oversized smile garnered suspicion from all four. The lead carefully inspected Ryan's paperwork.

"Just want to say that I appreciate the care you fellas take on this point of entry."

The MPs responded with piercing stares.

"You shoulda seen the guy on guard here after ED4 deactivated." Ryan looked up and past the gate at the complex ahead. "Warms my heart to see this place full of life again."

One of the MPs' eyes lit up. "Holy crap, I know you. Hey, this is the guy!" He snapped his fingers. The others looked at Ryan. "This is the chief, Chief McBain."

The lead MP looking at his paperwork nodded. "Yeah, so? How'd you know?"

"Because, this is the McBain from the Khrylic attack. He's that McBain."

One of the three others immediately stood tall and saluted. Ryan saw the wide eyes of the lead MP as he spoke. "I'm sorry, sir. I didn't know. They don't tell us—"

Ryan shook his head. "It's OK. Just another soldier, and glad to be back."

"Sir, do you need a lift? Where are you headed?"

"I'm not a 'sir.' Chief or Ryan will do just fine." Ryan glanced up. Halfway across the grounds, an oversized golf cart with three technicians dressed in white coats was tearing toward the gate. "I think my ride approaches." Ryan recognized them and shook his head.

"Hey, any chance you'd tase these guys comin' toward us in that golf cart?"

One of the MPs immediately unholstered his taser and turned. "Which guys? Those guys a problem? We could detain them, chief."

Ryan smiled. "Nawh, not necessary. Stand down." He passed through the entry and turned back to them with a tipping salute. "But thank you for the moment in my imagination."

The cart pulled up, and Ryan threw his duffle into the back. "Chief, have you waited long? Are you OK? How are you feeling? You look distressed. Would you like an anti-anxiety?"

"Nice to see you boys too. I am fine. If this is going to work, you're gonna have to change your approach. No one wants a lead test pilot who's constantly being checked for mental fitness. Whaddya say we just assume that I've still got all my marbles and work outward from that point?"

"Sir, we're here to ensure you adjust to your new environment."

Ryan put his sunglasses back on and smiled. "No, gentlemen. This time I'm the one who will be ensuring you adjust here. This is my home. This is my element. You should know this."

"We were concerned this might trigger memories that—"

Ryan shook his head. "Nope. All good memories here."

"We're only trying to help."

"I know." Ryan surveyed the three of them. "Which one of you is in charge? You, Gleim, Dr. Gleim is it?" For many weeks, they'd engaged in the same room, but for Ryan, it was like they were opposite poles on a magnet. Whatever they said or did, he looked the other way. A byproduct of this resistance was avoiding names or any personal connection.

The front passenger nodded. "You can call me Irwin if you'd prefer."

"Irwin? Seriously, your name is Irwin? I'll call you Dr. G." Ryan sat in the cart and looked at the smaller man next to him. "What's your story? You the one on the other side of the mirror watching me?"

The man had a sick look on his face. Ryan chuckled. "Oh, come on now. You put me in a room with a four-by-eight-foot mirror and don't think I know it's a viewing blind? Aren't you guys supposed to be the smart ones?"

The smaller man responded softly. "I am Dr. Sanjay, and I am newly joining this team."

Ryan looked to the back of the head of the man directly in front of him. "You driving, you moonlight as a golf cart driver or you also part of this project?"

"Unless you want me to start a battery of memory tests, you should remember we met before at the lab."

"Oh, I remember. You were pretending to be another patient in the waiting room and tried to strike up a conversation with me."

The driver smiled. "How'd you know?"

"You smelled like a scientist."

They drove for a few seconds before Dr. Sanjay sniffed at his own jacket.

The driver momentarily looked back over his shoulder. "You remember my name?"

"Kendal, was it? Or was that your fictional patient name?"

"No memory tests needed. While it's true I wasn't actually a patient, Kendal's my real name."

"Just Kendal, or is there a Dr. somewhere in there?"

"Not yet. I'm post graduate, working on my PhD in a research project under Dr. Gleim."

"Ah, I see. So there's still some hope for you."

Kendal smiled and shook his head. "Isn't your aunt also a scientist?"

Ryan tipped his head. "Ah then, so also a researcher. Gold star for you, Mr. Kendal."

Dr. Gleim looked at Kendal with a questioning expression. "When I was working on my master's at the University of Chicago, Dr. Enid Ardiel was faculty in my peer review circle. She used to tell us stories about raising a couple of ruckus nephews. Which were you, chief, the young politician or the one who blew things up?" Kendal smiled and glanced at Dr. Gleim.

Ryan stared ahead as if he hadn't heard the question.

Nervous concern bubbled from Dr. Sanjay as he broke the silence. "You, you've a background in politics?"

Ryan turned and tilted his head down, looking over his mirrored glasses and through his brows at Dr. Sanjay. He said nothing to him. Like Dr. Sanjay's eyebrows, they moved up and down the base corridors in silence for several minutes.

Ryan took off his glasses and leaned forward. "So, Dr. G, I suspect there is a round of new tests to complete before I'm signed off for flight authorization?"

Dr. Gleim nodded. Ryan continued. "How long'l these tests take?"

Dr. Sanjay piped up. "I have estimated the required time necessary based upon the rate of progress from your prior testing, the scope of the new testing, and some other variables regarding the schedule of our visits."

"And?"

"We should have all testing completed in nine months."

Ryan stared through him.

He continued nervously. "Give or take a month."

"Guys, that will preclude my ability to participate in this program."

Dr. Gleim turned in his seat and faced Ryan. "This was precisely my concern and the reason I was not in favor of your assignment here."

"What if I provided you several hours of access each day and fully cooperated?"

"Cooperation would help."

The cart came to a stop, and Kendal spoke. "This is building Charlie—"

"Guys, I know this is Charlie. I lived here, remember? Let's start our sessions tonight. I'll see all three of you at The Sandbox at 1900 hours." Ryan grabbed his ruck and disappeared through a side door.

Dr. Sanjay leaned forward. "What is a sand box? This is where children make pretend villages, yes?"

As Kendal pulled away, he replied, "Castles, you mean pretend sand castles. But I think it's use here is the name of a bar on base. I believe it's on the beach. I suspect the chief is going to attempt to inebriate us and gather data on our methods."

Dr. Gleim nodded his head. "That in of itself is a kind of participation. So, I guess that's progress."

Kendal chuckled and raised his eyebrows as they pulled away.

Ryan opened the door to his old quarters. With a familiar squeak, the door swung half open. He swallowed dry and hard and stepped inside. The last time he'd been here was the morning of the attack. Contorting around the edge as the door swung closed, Ryan stepped back and leaned against it. His eyes moved around the room for several seconds. Although the room was empty, memories rushed out like a wave of banshees and swept him back to that morning.

He looked down to the side, remembering the bag of laundry he'd set by the door. Looking up, he saw the box of sand dollars he'd collected for Anshra on the kitchen bar. There was an empty pizza box on the coffee table that he hadn't had time to take out. There was a remote he picked up off the floor and a lone boot he'd set beside the door. He'd left a mug and bowl on the counter as he scrambled against the clock to make his shift. It played so clear and vivid in his mind. The Ryan in that past didn't know what was in motion just beyond.

An aching came upon him, gripping him and causing him to bend at the waist. As he returned to the present moment, there was a stinging in his shoulder, and he realized his fist was still tensed around the strap of his rucksack. He forced himself to let go and set it down. He took one step forward and reached back around for his bag. Picking it back up, he mumbled, "This is silly."

He stepped through the single bedroom, bathroom, and main area of his quarters as if he was a new tenant sizing the place up. He stood motionless in the middle of the room for several minutes before a knock at the door caused him to jump. Opening the door revealed a large man with a clipboard.

"Master Chief Mitchell Ryan McBain?" The man was wearing a grimy gray jumpsuit and finally looked up, nodding toward him. "You McBain?"

"Yeah."

"Great. We got your personal effects." The man turned his head and yelled down the hall. "Yeah, down here! This is the one."

Ryan opened the door wide as two other taller skinny men brought in a well-worn leather arm chair. Ryan smiled at it. A few minutes later, the men produced a large box. The large man shoved the clipboard toward Ryan. "Sign here, please."

Ryan looked at the box and then back to the large man. "This isn't all of it. There's a second chair, a bed, other boxes?"

The man looked over his clipboard and flipped to a page. "Says here this is it."

"Where's the rest of my stuff?"

"Don't know what to tell you, man; this is all that made it." He produced a ballpoint pen from behind his ear and scribbled on a crumpled packing slip, then handed it to Ryan. "Here; call this number. They can help track down the rest of your stuff. Probably just stuck somewhere between here and there, you know?"

Two hours of hold music and run-arounds later, Ryan set the phone down. He turned around, surveying the chair and opened box. "Well, I guess we're the survivors." He thought for a few moments and then called down to the front gate. "Yeah, this is Chief McBain. You guys let me in a bit ago. Yeah, that's right. No, I'm good; well, mostly good. There's something you could help me with. Do you know where I could score a cot? If I go to Procurement, you know it'll take weeks. Yeah, I know, it's crazy. So, do you have any idea where I could borrow one? Really? Nawh, I don't care if it says cellblock. That's actually fantastic! Yeah, now's great; I'm here. Hey, you guys are the best. I'm headed over to The Sandbox in a couple hours if you guys are off. First round's on me. Cool. Maybe see you there, and thanks again."

At exactly 1900 hours, the three behavioral scientists arrived at The Sandbox. The roof of the building was faux grass, and large tiki torches lined the walkway around to the side entrance. They wandered down the path looking like tourists from a brochure. All three wore round cotton hats with narrow brims, tucked in T-shirts, pressed shorts with a dress belt, black calf-high socks, and white sneakers. Tentatively, they climbed the wood steps and entered The Sandbox.

The building had a central bar and barely any walls. The windows were all open, and each had a woven shade rolled up above it. Several of the painted wooden pillars had various types of art and old pictures of the base. There were multiple TVs mounted up high in the corners, displaying everything from football to surfing. The seating was wicker-style patio furniture topped with faded red, white, or blue cotton cushions. The ocean was mere steps away, and the breeze off it was perfectly refreshing.

Ryan was gathered at the bar with four others, one an off-duty MP from earlier at the main gate. They roared with laughter as Ryan finished a story. He was pointing down at a small-framed picture on the bar in front of the group. The bartender grabbed the framed portrait of a certain flight officer of Indian descent. He turned around, stepped up, and placed it high on a shelf behind the bar with several other pictures. Ryan raised his glass toward it, and the others followed. He said loudly, "Janmadin kee shubhakaamanaen!"

After the toast, he caught sight of the approaching behavioralists. Stepping toward them, he said cheerfully, "Ahh! Gentlemen, welcome to The Sandbox!

Please, come in." Ryan looked to the bartender. "A round for my friends here." They noticed Ryan was wearing flip-flops, board shorts, and a stretched tank top. His dress was consistent with that of the other patrons. With a quick wink, he introduced them as "mission specialists and team members from *way up north*."

After a few minutes, Ryan looked to Kendal. "OK, you guys are standing so close to each other that you look funny. Relax. When was the last time you just went out and relaxed?"

The three of them looked at each other, and Dr. Sanjay shrugged his shoulders.

"Seriously, you guys don't go out? And you were sent to certify my behavioral health?" Ryan took a swig of his beer. "Now I'm actually a little more concerned about you." Ryan noticed Dr. Sanjay staring at his shoulder. "What?"

Dr. Sanjay jumped a little. "Oh, I'm sorry. I've just never seen…" he waved at Ryan's shoulder.

"My scar. Oh, right, real bugger isn't it?" Ryan pulled his tank to the side and traced the scar lines. "Although, I have to admit that Clarkston did a great job; some of the lines you can't see anymore. The damage has nearly vanished, at least on the surface. But I can still feel it inside at times, especially when it's cold."

Dr. Sanjay nodded with excitement. "Nanotube technology; it's fascinating. I read the material in this nanomuscular augmentation contains compounds that can absorb radiation. It's also incredibly strong."

"Yeah, and I can punch through brick walls."

"Really?"

"No. But you're right, it does still have radiation blocking materials in it. What do you think? Should we go test it?"

The three scientists all stared at Ryan. "My god, you guys don't go out, and you have zero sense of humor. There's so much work ahead of me. This assignment will be good for you. You may have been assigned to me, but I think there may be a higher purpose at work here." Ryan clinked his bottle to Dr. Sanjay's root beer. He jumped, and they both laughed.

Kendal discretely noted the numbers tattooed on Ryan's arm. Looking back to the bar, he surveyed the portraits in the small pictures on the high shelf.

The following week, Dr. Sanjay was working with Ryan in a session, when he paused and queried, "Why do you fidget so?"

"I don't know. I just can't sit here endlessly."

"How did this go with Dr. Ardiel when you were growing up?"

Ryan smiled and looked at Sanjay for a few seconds. "OK, I'll grant access to that data, but not here."

Sanjay tilted his head. "At The Sandbox?"

"No, I think we need to next level this a bit. You're good for it. Do you surf?"

Dr. Sanjay shook his head.

"Perfect. I'll teach you. We're going surfing. While we're in the surf, you can ask me anything. Nothing's off limits." He looked past Sanjay at the mirror. "That goes for you too in there, or both, or whoever's in there." Ryan looked back at Sanjay. "What do you think? Any question fair game, huh? How badly do you want this data, and what are you prepared to do in order to help your patient?"

"Would this require bathing into the ocean when there are strong waves present?"

Ryan laughed out loud. "That's generally the place and circumstances for surfing, yes. Ocean and waves."

"I'm not a very strong swimmer."

Ryan leaned closer toward him and said, with a piercing stare, "I would never let anything happen to you."

As it turned out, Mr. Kendal was something of a surfer, and the three of them began having daily "sessions" at sunrise. One morning, Kendal and Ryan were sitting upright on their boards, watching Dr. Sanjay try to catch a wave just ahead of them. Sanjay peeled off his board to the side just after standing. Ryan yelled, "That was close, doc! You gotta look up. Just look straight ahead, and stop looking down." Then, turning back to Kendal, "Hey, how is it that a master's student of behavioral sciences was in a class taught by a brain surgeon and chemist?"

"Your aunt's involved in a segment of chemistry that overlaps with behavioral sciences. Her more recent work on neural triggering mechanisms and the chemistry behind them is ground breaking. Have you kept up with her?"

"Sure, a little. Don't always get back to see her as often as I should. We don't talk medicine when I do, though." There was a long pause before Ryan continued. "You know she raised me, don't you?"

Mr. Kendal nodded. "And that would explain why she's sent me a number of requests for medical information about you that I cannot disclose. She's obviously very concerned for you. As a personal favor to me, would you please call her? And I don't mean a conference call with your other aunts. She told me about that. Jesus, really? A conference bridge?"

"Hey, that's not completely fair. I wanted to tell them all at once that I was OK. You have any idea what would have happened if I'd called one before the others?" Both of them looked up as Sanjay wobbled on his feet, riding away from them. Ryan screamed loudly, "Yeaaahh! Well done, Sanjay! Mr. Kendal, I think we may have just had a breakthrough."

The working environment evolved into a far better collaboration. Upon the patient's urging, the two-way mirror was replaced with a transparent window, and filming sessions occurred with the recorder in the same room. The exchange of data allowed Ryan to learn that their area of expertise was not just behavioral but applied behavior science with a focus on flight. That in turn became the point of common ground. The testing shifted from behavioral health to operational flight fitness and flight efficiency.

One afternoon, Ryan was in a flight simulator working with Kendal. The simulator was configured such that Ryan was seated in an exact replica of the research ship's cockpit while Kendal was just behind him in a control room. From the control console, Kendal could load and modify the parameters of the simulation, as well as simulate emergencies.

On this particular exercise, Ryan was working on a flight profile that required a dynamic navigational path through debris and disturbances. Basically, it meant that he was constantly plotting and replotting his course, all while piloting manually. This wasn't an unusual exercise, except that right in the middle of this sortie, the left display panel came off and into his lap. Someone had done some recent work and improperly refastened the component. Kendal heard Ryan giggle and looked up.

"Huh. Little problem here."

"What's going on?" Kendal rose up and could see that Ryan was holding the now dark control panel with his left hand and continuing to fly with his right. "Do you want to abort or pause?"

"Nawh, should be a good challenge."

Kendal watched as Ryan flew the simulator and simultaneously retrieved a tool from his bag behind his seat. He was able to reattach a cable and a safety screw to the panel back. Kendal cocked his head at the spectacle in front of him and had a hunch. Before Ryan could complete the work, Kendal caused a failure in the primary coolant on the starboard engine. The engine shut down and the simulated flight began to pitch off axis.

Ryan looked over his shoulder. "You jerk."

"Abort or fly the profile." Kendal watched intently and chewed on his fingernails. Ryan was working with the flight problem and resolving the coolant. While he was doing so, Kendal quickly programmed a solar storm approaching. He watched Ryan, thinking to himself, "*He won't see it; it's not possible.*" To survive the simulation, Ryan would need to not only see it but also calculate an evasive course closer down to a nearby planetoid to escape the main front of the radiation.

Ryan grumbled more, noticing the approaching wave of destructive energy. Kendal shook his head and mumbled, "This isn't reasonable." Looking down, he pressed a few more buttons that created a fire in the main engine room.

Ryan groused over his shoulder, "Really!?"

The researcher stood with furrowed brow and watched. At a couple of points, Ryan's hands seemed to get in each other's way. He was a blur of movement addressing all the problems simultaneously. He addressed each and all without any calculable delay. In other words, he was able to perceive, react and resolve each challenge simultaneously. Kendal recorded the entire event without knowing exactly what to label it.

As he exited the simulation, Ryan mumbled "devious bastard" toward Kendal. Standards and practices for the simulator called for no more than two emergencies in one instance. Ryan thought the researcher was just being particularly malevolent to simulate so many concurrent failures while he was repairing broken equipment. Kendal shrugged at Ryan and did his best to hide his astonishment at the display.

Two days later, the excited researcher tracked down Dr. Gleim in a passageway. Gleim held up his hand. "Yes, yes. I received your voicemail. But I'm currently late for a meeting, and your message left me a little confused."

Kendal stepped ahead and blocked the doctor's path. "He can perform parallel tasks without any cognitive delay."

"What are you saying? He's switching very quickly or task prioritizing? This is not uncommon."

"No. I'm saying that he's truly able to do two things in the same cognitive instance."

"That's not reasonable."

"I know, I know. That's what I thought too, but I witnessed it. Then, I prepared a couple more simple tests. While he was doing this, I monitored his brain activity. I could measure two distinct energy patterns at the same time. He has a duality of presence."

"A what?"

"I call it a duality of presence. It's like he can cognitively split himself."

"That's going to be difficult to prove."

Excitement animated Kendal's nodding head, and he spoke more quickly. "There's more. I don't think he's unique."

"You've lost me."

"I started wondering about his survival in the Khrylic attack. What if you had this ability in a combat environment? Wouldn't that give you an advantage? So, I went over his flight records again. You remember we found that automation anomaly on his kestrel during the Khrylic attack?"

Gleim shook his head. "I'm still not following."

Kendal took a breath and started again more slowly. "Remember, we found what we thought was a sensor glitch that indicated McBain had disabled automated flight in favor of manually flying?"

"Yes, I remember now."

"So, I loaded his flight profile and the kestrel combat management system into our simulator. I don't know why we didn't think to do it before. Anyway, you'll never guess."

Gleim leaned in toward Kendal. "Have automated systems had difficulty repeating the profile?"

Kendal spoke in a lower, hushed tone. "The computer has yet to survive in over a thousand attempts."

Gleim's eyebrows pinched together, and he cocked his head. "Are you saying he was flying manually faster than an automated system?"

Kendal nodded. "And he wasn't alone. So, what are the odds of an automated flight sensor glitch on ninety percent of the kestrels that lived up to the last ten minutes of the engagement?"

Gleim's eyes grew wide. "What you're saying is hard to believe and harder to prove."

"It would be if none of them had survived. But one did. We would need enough evidence to coordinate a study."

"You think you can get McBain to agree to such a study?"

"He might if he understood the number of lives that could be saved with this knowledge."

"We should speak of this further. Please write up a brief, and be in my office first thing tomorrow. We can decide best how to pursue this research."

Being back home was therapeutic for Ryan, but there was a certain restlessness that was growing stronger with time. For many nights, in what was becoming a pattern, Ryan had difficulty sleeping. Certain images kept returning to him. They weren't violent or gruesome, just simple images that created a sense of dread. The difficulties edged their way into his waking moments. The first happened in the hangar.

Ryan was standing near a test bench with two technicians testing some emulation profiles for the research ship. A worker started opening the large hangar door, which caught the corner of Ryan's eye. Instantly his mind flashed to vivid imagery from the past. He replayed a memory of an ED4 crewman opening the main hangar door for a launch scramble in his kestrel. Everyone was racing to address the unknown threat above. Just like it was in that moment, Ryan's heart raced.

"Chief, are you OK?"

Ryan turned back. "Oh, uh, yeah." He looked back at the opening door. "What are they...do they have to?"

The other technicians looked toward the low growl of the door rollers. "They're just opening the doors up to get some fresh air."

Ryan head shook as if struck by a palsy. "Yeah, but it's opening."

The technicians looked at each other in confusion. "Chief, are you OK? You were mid-sentence."

Ryan's head snapped back to them. "Oh, uh, what was I saying?"

"You said you'd found a bug in the program and were just about to explain it when you trailed off."

Ryan's hand went over his heart, and they noticed his face was pale. He leaned on the counter for a moment. "I uh, just, I...winded...I need a minute. Be right back."

They watched as he walked erratically away and snatched the railing of the stairs that led to the old hangar control booth.

"That's darn odd. Should we call someone?"

"I don't know."

A few seconds later, another test pilot, Gerardo Couve, walked up. "You seen McBain? His presence is requested in Design Ops."

One of the technicians motioned to the metal staircase that hugged the inside wall of the cavernous circular hangar. "He went up there."

Gerardo's brows scrunched together. "Hangar Control is deco'd. You guys using it for some kind of storage?"

"No. One minute the chief was talking, and the next he staggered off saying he needed a minute. We were honestly wondering if we should call for Medical."

Gerardo looked at the staircase and held up his finger. "I'll just go check on him."

He found Ryan sitting on the floor in the dusty control room. "Hey man, you OK?"

"Yeah, weird, something came over me. I got really dizzy and I just needed a minute."

"You need me to get Medical?"

"No. I'm good. Must have been something I ate earlier." Ryan grasped Gerardo's hand and he pulled him up.

"You sure you're OK?"

"Yeah, thanks. I'm fine now."

A few days later, Ryan shot up out of bed and gasped for air. It was almost like he'd forgotten to breath for a few moments. His heart was pounding through his chest wall, the same way it had in the hangar incident. A few days later, he had an issue with a data terminal. The clicking sound of the keyboard triggered anxiety, and the system would not move quickly from screen to screen. The slowness in response to his typing caused his heart to race. He had to sit for a few minutes with his head between his knees.

Ryan blocked out a few days of leave on the project calendar. Dr. Sanjay was taking the same time off and asked about Ryan's destination. Ryan responded, "Out." Dr. Sanjay asked again about his specific destination. With piercing eyes, Ryan responded, "Visiting family."

As Ryan disembarked the shuttle, the air in Palam, India hit him. The humidity was stifling, even for this time of year. Ryan wandered around what seemed to be a never-ending terminal. It was enormous, and there were thousands of people milling about in different directions. A few passengers late for a flight ran past, and a porter yelled across the terminal. The bustle and the noise triggered his anxiety. Ryan's heart started pounding, and his eyes grew wider as the spectacle took him back to another place in time. His mind saw and heard technicians racing across the hangar floor, preparing his kestrel for departure on the day of the attack.

He had started calling them his "little episodes." They hit at unpredictable times, and he wasn't able to control his reactions. Though he wouldn't admit their existence, the fishbowl team had advised him not to panic if he ever felt symptoms like this. They suggested he close his eyes and focus on a place where he felt safe and calm. For Ryan, this was a waterfall above a swimming hole in his youth.

While the hordes in the airport terminal navigated past, the tall man stood motionless in the middle path with his eyes closed. As Ryan felt his heart rate lowering, he heard a gentle voice behind him in the crowd. Turning around and opening his eyes, he saw Anshra Jeeval's widow, Pari. She was a smaller woman, much smaller than he. There were lines under her eyes, and she looked pale. Ryan rushed to her and abandoned a formal greeting for a more western bear hug. He may even have raised her feet off the ground.

Pari smiled up at him and studied his face. She gently grabbed his shoulder, "I trust your trip mattered simply?"

Ryan smiled back, knowing what she meant. "Yes. How've you been, Pari?"

She looked down. "Not as well as I should."

Ryan put his arm around her, and she looked to him. "And you?"

"I feel a void, and I find myself searching it. I know that's not the right path, but nonetheless, I struggle."

She squeezed him. "This way for our transport."

"Is it cooler here than normal?"

"Yes, and we have just passed through our rains, I hope."

"I brought some tools for that patio of yours."

"Ryan, you do not need to do this."

He looked down, "I know, but we sorta talked about this design and the tiles and went to get them, and I just feel like it's my duty to finish what she..." His voice trailed off.

Pari understood. "You were working on this together. I think it would be good for you to complete what you and Jeeval had started. I'm not sure I ever liked the design to begin with. After many discussions, Jeeval was so dedicated to this project. Now, I find myself waiting with great anticipation to see it done and the beauty that it will surely be. I am also thankful that you are here with us for the celebration. There will be other family here, as you know."

Ryan smiled. "I was hoping for all the grandchildren to be here yelling and making a commotion."

Pari smiled. "Yes; the grandchildren and great-grandchildren will all come. They're all worried about me, I think. They believe the poor old woman will be shriveling away all alone." She smiled as they both chuckled out loud.

For the next couple of days, Ryan worked with a crew to prepare the surface of the back patio for the mosaic design he would lay into it. It was a pattern Jeeval had designed. As he studied the drawing, Ryan looked off, smiling. He remembered how he'd complained for weeks about her dragging him "to the far reaches of the planet" for certain color and materials of tile. There were endless swatches. Jeeval would hold each up and ask which Ryan liked best. He smiled widely, thinking about how she would always pick the opposite of his choice.

Ryan's face froze stoically, remembering his complaint to her that the project would be "the death of him." Just before the attack, they had finally procured and amassed everything needed. Ryan returned to the present moment and inspected the compacted sand and border stones. It was time to lay Jeeval's pattern.

Several times a day, Pari would peek out of the back doorway to see the progress. She brought water out on a break. "This is starting to look truly wonderful. May I ask, how is your shoulder?"

Ryan massaged it momentarily. "It's better. It doesn't hurt all the time, but I can still feel it. I don't want it to go away completely. Is that weird?"

He looked down, and Pari put her hand on his. "Soon, Diwali will be upon us. Do you think your work here will be complete?"

Ryan nodded. She looked up at him. "It is difficult, but we must move forward." Ryan nodded again as she rose and returned inside.

Two days later, Ryan was in his formal, olive-green dress uniform on the finished patio. The evening was cooler, and in the twilight, his dress shoes scuffed traces of sand around the mosaic. Many Anshra family members were in the residence, and in the case of the young ones, tearing through it. Dozens of unlit red lanterns were staged at the ready in the back courtyard. Perhaps a hundred jaipuri haat brass kuber deepak oil lamps were lit in and around the house and in the back. A shrine of Ganesh sat outside on the far end surrounded by five lotus petals that held bright red candles. Little boys in white dress shirts and girls in pretty sarees chased one another, screaming as they rushed in and out of the large, open French doorway. Pari came outside and put her hand on Ryan's shoulder. "Are you well?"

He nodded. "Sometimes yelling and movement in low light makes me a little anxious. I just needed a moment." One of Jeeval and Pari's grown daughters, Abala, approached with a platter. She offered them a festival sweet.

"My katli is not as good as—" She stopped talking abruptly and looked up. Ryan looked to her and smiled.

"Your maji is here, you know, and I can just hear her saying 'nonsense' to that comment." Ryan took a bite and nodded his head. "This is delicious; this is fantastic. Jeeval was so very proud of you. I hope you know that." He jumped noticeably when fireworks went off nearby.

Pari held his upper arm. "Perhaps you would come inside. We will have the children run outside or play a quieter game inside for now. Come in."

The next morning, Ryan was on his knees folding clothes into his bag. Pari came in and sat quietly behind him. Sensing something was on her mind, he spoke over his shoulder. "What's up?"

"Last night when I released my lantern, I let go of something I wanted to admit to you."

Ryan turned around toward her.

Looking down to the floor, she spoke softly. "I was so terribly bitter at the military service." She paused and looked up to Ryan's eyes. "I was bitter at you. I wanted more time with her. She was always talking about your adventures, and it made me jealous. I did not realize until she was gone that I was jealous of her time with you. I had wanted to grow old," she chuckled, "I guess I should say grow older with her. Just as I thought we would finally be together more, she was taken away. And it was you who was with her at the end, not me. That pebble has rubbed raw in the sandal of my heart for months. It is now gone. I am sorry I felt this way toward you."

Ryan took a big breath and sat back on his haunches. "She and I were taking on two vessels, big ships. These were battle cruisers, destroyers with far superior firepower. In a real sense, it was crazy. But they were coming for us, for this, for you, for Earth. We split up and I wasn't..." Ryan paused and looked up. Pari's face tightened into a small pained smile, and she cocked her head.

Ryan took a choppy breath and started again. "The flash subsided, and she was just gone. Where she was one moment she was no longer. And I had to move. I couldn't even stop to recognize that my friend, my mentor was gone. I just put it out of my mind and pushed ahead."

Ryan looked at Pari, and his head shook gently. With difficulty, he continued. "Pari, it should have been me. I shouldn't be here. This is a mistake. Jeeval should be here with you now. I am so sorry. This is all a mistake."

Ryan was still sitting back on his knees when Pari came quickly upon him. She reached out and felt the hair on his head between her fingers. She spoke in a hushed tone down toward his ear. "All these things have come to pass for a reason. You must believe this. You are meant for something else in this body. Apparently, the physical universe is not yet done with you."

Ryan nodded and chuckled. "Pari, you should know too that while she was with me, all she talked about was you. She nearly nagged me to death about helping her make that back patio perfect and to your liking. She even warned me that it might involve making it more than once if you didn't like the first version." Ryan smiled through wet eyes at the memory. He looked up to her. "You meant everything to her, Pari."

Pari started to cry and pulled him close. "Thank you, Ryan. Thank you. I pray Jeeval and I will find each other again many times. I do think we will be together again. There is a path for us. If I believe that, then I can be alone here for a time."

On the transport home, Ryan tried to put the stream of images from Diwali out of his mind. The sea of red lanterns was both beautiful and painful. That night, the Anshra family had huddled closely around Pari. His attention was split between Pari and the lantern he had released. It floated up and away into the night. As it disappeared from sight, he noticed he was standing off alone in the darkness. The thought caused his head to shake as if he was trying to shoo a fly from his brow. He pulled out a tablet that contained his program manuals and directed his attention to reviewing project information. In the coming week, they would move into a new phase of flight readiness tests.

Morning twilight sparked a warm glow inside Ryan's quarters. Below the paned kitchen window, there was already a morning bustle of activity in the street. A new dawn was coming quickly. Under piles of flight manuals and mission profile documents, Ryan lay in the leather recliner. He stirred, and several binders tumbled to the floor as he sat up. With fingertips rubbing tired eyes, he thought about the profile today.

He and two others would be flying live simulations in low solar orbit. Several small sparrow class reconnaissance craft had been repurposed to simulate the flight profile of the new propulsion prototype ship, the United Earth Alliance, or UEA Tereshkova. Although an additional flight computer on the sparrows was programmed to emulate the handling and flight systems of the Tereshkova, the similarities ended there. The sparrows were very small tandem seat craft with a tubular shape that looked more like a mid-stage in a heavy lift rocket. The Tereshkova on the other hand had slightly larger mass than a destroyer class vessel, and she was a beauty of automation. Her systems, as well as her lines, were breathtaking.

The sparrows were full of mechanical rocker switches, and crews joked about having analog gauges. Emulation equipment was haphazardly installed, and there were visible wires where some of the interfaces were mounted. In briefing the junior flight officers the night before, Ryan provided a moment of levity by handing out diapers, rolls of duct tape, and bailing wire for their flight kits.

Aside from the test craft, another potential hazard was the Sun. The mission involved a close slingshot around Earth's central star. She was ramping up into Her solar maximum and very active. As such, Research Command was monitoring several spots near the solar equator. Although solar forecasters were typically very accurate in predicting prominences and coronal ejections, Ryan thought it poor judgment to attempt flight in the current year. However, the original project timeline had been delayed, and the remaining budget was such that the flights had to continue.

It wasn't surprising that four hours into the flight profile, they received an alert of an emerging prominence. Ryan was flying lead in call sign "Wave One" when the alert came to abort any and all near-solar flight profiles. Ryan was powering away from the Sun when Wave Two, piloted by Gerardo Couve, transmitted. "I think I just flew through...uh, yeah, I've got spots."

The cockpits had been hastily equipped with low-tech radiation placards. The material in the center of these placards would spot dark and eventually turn black if they were exposed to higher levels of radiation.

Ryan responded, "How bad?"

"Not bad; just a few dots. I saw a flicker on my main display. Whatever it was didn't show on the alert."

Ryan rolled his lips together and shook his head. "That's it; I'm calling it."

"I'm OK. It was just a trace amount."

"Understood, but remember, we're not flying in hardened or shielded equipment. This is a total strip down and diagnostic when we get back, so let's not take any chances out here."

"Roger that, Wave One; I'm in the turn for home. Sorry."

Several minutes later, Wave Three had already fired her deceleration and landing boosters when the last two entered orbit. Ryan saw a momentary contrail streak ahead of him from Wave Two as it descended down further into the atmosphere. He could almost see Gerardo ahead of him. Ryan heard a few seconds of static, which he wouldn't realize until later was the first indication of trouble.

Command broke the silence. "Wave One, Command, do you have eyes on Wave Two?"

"Negative contact; he's just a bit ahead of me." Ryan thought for a moment and transmitted again. "Why do you ask?"

"It's probably just a glitch, but we lost telemetry from him."

Ryan heard static again and strained to make out someone speaking in it. "Wave Two, is that you? Say again, Wave Two."

There was a long pause before Command broke the silence. "Wave One, we're still dark on Wave Two. He may have had…standby one."

Anxiety coursed through Ryan's veins, and urgency raised the hair on the back of his neck. Sparrow landings were manually flown, but Ryan reactivated the automation system that emulated the Tereshkova. He rapidly typed an automated routine to fire retro thrusters. He estimated the weight of two ships and calculated using a rule of thumb for necessary thrust and associated fuel. His fingers danced and tapped as he created additional automation for an emergency parachute deployment. He looked up as he heard more static. Ryan transmitted, "Command, are you receiving this static?"

"Negative. What are you hearing?"

Ryan ignored the question and instead shot back, "Wave Two should have fired for deceleration by now; are you seeing that?"

There was a long pause before they answered. "Telemetry has no firing, but we think we may have spotted her on the scope. Transmitting the position now."

Ryan sat tall as his eyes widened. He quickly touched the screen in two locations of the arcing streak just ahead. He used those two points in conjunction with Telemetry's last position echo to project Wave Two's likely trajectory. He sat like a cat waving its tail on a picket fence, ready to pounce. There was a narrow path, and time was of the essence. If he was wrong, he'd have some explaining to do. If he was right, it might cost two lives instead of one.

He programmed a rollover arcing maneuver that would vector him diving downward. The radio erupted in chatter between confused command center groups. For Ryan, the path was clear. His left eye squinted as he depressed a button engaging maximum emergency propulsion. The rockets fired and pinned Ryan in his seat. Five seconds into the burn, Wave One rolled over and arced downward. He grunted and strained through additional G forces. Ryan yelled over the roar of the rockets, and his voice vacillated from the G forces. "I need to know where he is. Find him; find him now, please."

"Wave One, say again—whoa, why are you accelerating?"

The ship was buffeting from the thrust, and terra firma was looming larger ahead. Ryan strained looking forward. He was in an accelerated dive toward Earth. His heart was pounding as fear jumped out from the shadows. Recognizing the signs, he focused on fury. At that very moment, flames burst around the ship as it caught fire in the atmosphere. The buffeting of the flames outside helped Ryan clean his mind and galvanize his cunning.

The mission commander stood next to the lead communication officer. "What's happening?"

"We've lost communication with Wave Two, and we haven't seen her deceleration burn. Wave One is accelerating downward in what we believe is an attempt to intercept."

The wide-eyed commander motioned rapidly toward the communication officer's headset. "Tell him to stop that pursuit." He leaned forward, talking directly into the microphone. "Wave One, Ryan, this is mission commander. Cease and desist all rescue activity. I repeat, stand down. Do you copy?"

There was no reply, and the telemetry board showed Ryan continuing to accelerate.

Ryan broke the silence. "Discipline me later, but for now, why ruin a perfectly good burn? Sure would appreciate it if you guys could give me an updated location on Wave Two."

All eyes in Command looked to the mission commander. He shook his head for a moment and then barked out, "Give it to him!"

Ryan cut engines, and his sparrow continued the accelerated descent through the upper atmosphere. As he surfed breakers across a sea of fire, a strange comfort came upon him. This moment was an opportunity for the universe to correct what was wrong. Flames diminished off the forward portal as Wave Two appeared and grew larger. Ryan engaged the automated routine and fired deceleration thrusters. He nearly lost consciousness and strained to focus on the other ship. With the burn complete, they were falling in formation.

Ryan thought he could see Gerardo through the portal. The static was stronger now, and he could clearly hear Gerardo. "Stupid bastard; you're gonna get yourself killed."

Command could only hear Ryan transmit, "Shut up and cooperate. Why's everyone so difficult? Extend docking guide arm."

All eyes were on the trajectory board back at mission control. "They're coming through forty-five thousand…forty now."

The mission commander stood perfectly rigid, looking up at the telemetry.

The two ships bumped into each other, and Ryan gently fired positioning thrusters again to catch Gerardo, who had started pitching off axis. Ryan mumbled, "Oh, come on now. Almost gotcha."

He saw the portal docking green lock light at the same moment he saw the ground proximity warning. They'd fallen below ten thousand feet, and Ryan smashed down on the automated deceleration routine. Wave One's computer was now directing the systems for both craft and their rockets fired at maximum. The first five seconds were unbearable, followed by the next five seconds of diminishing consciousness. The last five seconds were a haze before the ships fired apart. They tumbled momentarily as massive emergency parachutes deployed from each. A second or two before impact, Ryan's skids automatically deployed, and he bounced hard on first contact.

The Command center was a silent hush of anxiety. The board showed that both craft were down. Through crackling audio, they could hear Ryan giggling, "I got him." Everyone cheered as the mission commander bowed his head, took a deep breath, and plopped down in a seat. CapCom put his hand on his shoulder, smiling widely as he broadcast, "Wave One, report status."

"Ha ha, hey, let's not do that again, or maybe we should. Wave One down hard off skid and Wave Two soft landed nearby."

Ryan heard Gerardo through a scratchy com. "Soft landed? Call that soft? I'm maybe gonna need a little assistance here."

Ryan relayed, "Cap, I have transmission from Wave Two, he's requesting assistance."

There was another collective roar in the Command center.

"Roger that; stay put, we're coming to you."

Ryan shook his head and tried to blink away a blur in the corner of his eye. He removed his flight helmet and touched the back of his head. Peering out the portal, he knew they were hundreds of miles from the intended landing zone and probably somewhere on the border between California and Arizona. Ryan punched down on the emergency hatch release. The explosive bolts made him wonder if this was what it sounded like inside a shaken beer bottle when the cap was removed. Stumbling on his first few steps, he could see the parachute from Wave Two about a mile away in the desert.

Mission commander looked at CapCom. "He's getting out of his ship, isn't he?"

CapCom nodded.

The commander shook his head and raised his palm. "If I told him to get out, do you think he would have stayed put?"

CapCom transmitted again. "Wave One, stay put, Ryan, we have assets in motion. They'll be with you shortly."

CapCom looked at his screen and back to the mission commander. "We've got an evac chopper coming out of Yuma. ETA twenty-two minutes."

Ryan plodded along under the baking sun and fought an increasing sensation of vertigo. Standing at the base of Wave Two, Ryan could see that Gerardo's emergency skids had not deployed. His sparrow had hit harder and also come to rest on its side. With the remaining propellant, it was a small miracle it hadn't exploded. Clamoring over the rocks and up to the craft's cockpit section, Ryan peered in at Gerardo. He was crumpled on the cabin floor and motionless. Ryan pried the emergency latch mechanism out and stood to the side. Yanking down on it, the door blasted by him, landing several feet away on the desert floor. Waving smoke and dust with his arm, Ryan mumbled, "Yeah, way worse on the outside." He peered in at Gerardo and saw blood on the cabin floor. As he climbed in, he asked, "Hey bud, why you out of your seat?"

Gerardo responded in a breathy whisper. "Manually extended...docking arm...thanks for coming...better not alone."

Ryan gently rolled him over and saw the large piece of jagged metal impaled into his lower right abdomen. "You got yourself a bit of a snag there."

Gerardo was gently holding his side. "You think?"

"Don't you worry about it. Chopper's inbound. They'll have you fixed up in no time. Just keep yourself calm."

"After just now, I'm calm...very...very calm." Gerardo brought his gloved hand up slowly and grabbed Ryan's. Panting, he said, "Tell Ashlynn...love her...sorry."

Ryan shook his head. "Nawh, tell her yourself." Ryan quickly removed his flight gloves and used his hand to apply pressure around the wound.

Gerardo winced and labored to speak. "Glad back uncharred...not imbedded...some crater...easier...this way."

"Gerardo, you're gonna be fine. Hang in there. Have faith. It's gonna be OK."

"Ask something?"

"Shoot."

"What'd feel...drifting...after Khrylic?"

Ryan looked up. "I didn't feel until later. I was out like a light and woke up in a hospital bed."

"Rude awakening...think were dead?"

"Yeah, sometimes Gerardo, even to this day."

"Like today?"

"No, right now, for the moment, I feel very alive, not unlike you my friend. You're alive. Hang in there with me. Hey, you hear the one about the horse that went into the bar? Bartender says to him, 'why the long face?'"

Gerardo's eyes squinted as he smiled and grasped Ryan's hand.

"Then this dung beetle comes in and says to the two of them, 'is this stool taken?'"

Gerardo tucked his chin down. "Your jokes...kill me before metal does."

Ryan's head lifted and turned to the side. "Hey, you hear that? Evac inbound. Hear that? They're coming, Gerardo." Ryan squeezed his hand and kept talking to him while the noise grew louder.

As the medical crew worked to extract Gerardo, Ryan stood outside with wide-eyes and tightly clutched his helmet. Gerardo had lost a great deal of blood, and the medics were scrambling to stabilize him. There was an edge and urgency to their voices. Ryan looked down and saw that there was blood on his hands and streaked across the white glossy surface of his helmet. He watched as a lifeless arm dangled over the side of an emerging stretcher. Implications of the event hit him in waves, and he was overcome with nausea. His helmet dropped to the ground as he leaned forward, bracing with hands on his knees. The stubble of Death's cheek had once again brushed across the back of his neck and passed over him.

On the ride back in the helicopter, one of the medics noted a palsy coming in waves over Ryan. A heated blanket had slipped off his shoulder, and he was transfixed by the bustle of work going on around the injured pilot. Repositioning the cover around him, the medic gently waggled his shoulder. Bending down closer to Ryan, he shouted over the noise, "It's OK. You're gonna be OK."

Ryan's wide eyes left Gerardo and darted to the medic. Racing with panic, Ryan snatched his arm. With his other hand, he pointed toward Gerardo. Shaking his head, he said, "Shouldn't be. Not him." Ryan released the medics arm and patted his chest. "It should be me. Take me. Not him. Please!"

The medic grabbed Ryan's arm and nodded. "It's gonna be OK. We've got you. We've got you both." He re-examined Ryan and noted asymmetrical dilation of his pupils. He held on to Ryan, and for the remainder of the flight, the two looked on at other medics swarming over Gerardo.

Ryan didn't see Gerardo again after they landed. He was whisked away to surgery while they directed Ryan to an examining room in the ER. The smell, the fixtures, and the counters were like those in every other emergency room on the planet. People were milling about everywhere, and he felt very alone. Ryan's blood pressure mirrored his skyrocketing anxiety. He lasted about ten seconds before nurses found him staggering and panting in the hallway.

"Sir, are you OK?"

Ryan nodded and waved his hand in the air.

"Then we need you back in your room. Someone will be in to see you shortly."

With his helmet still under his arm, Ryan shook his head quickly. His eyes darted around. "I'm sorry," he said, motioning toward the room. "I...I can't. Don't put me in there." The lead nurse approached to clean up the situation and clear the hallway. Before she could speak, Ryan's sincerity softened her crusty, cranky exterior.

"It's OK. I'm gonna take care of you," she said. "Nobody is going to make you." She gently touched his arm, then spoke in a lower voice, "Well, we can't very well have you wandering around in the hallway." Looking over her shoulder, she saw a gurney temporarily parked along the wall. "Here," she motioned toward it. "You can lay here. I'll be over there at a station or moving between rooms. You'll be able to see me the whole time, OK?"

Ryan nodded. She helped him up and started to take his helmet, but Ryan held it steadfast. "I, I'm gonna need that."

She smiled back. "There's been an accident. You've been in a crash. You're not going to need that just now."

Holding his helmet firmly, Ryan looked to her with dull eyes.

"Let's just put it at the end here so you can lay back." Ryan loosened his grip, and she moved it down to the foot of the bed. "Do you remember hitting your head at all?"

Ryan looked to her from the corner of his eye. "I was just in a crash."

She chuckled. "That's true." Glancing at his forehead, she noted, "You've got a pretty good bump going here. No more walking around until we can check this a little closer. You can stay out here if you promise me not to get up."

She broke protocol and allowed Ryan to stay in the hallway. After tests cleared him, Ryan talked fast to negotiate a release that night.

Seven exhausting hours later, Ryan dropped his flight bag just inside the door of his quarters. He had managed through this incident with only two bandages: one on his forehead and another in the crook of his arm, where they'd taken what felt like a gallon of blood. He ripped the cotton ball and bandage from his arm and leaned over the kitchen sink.

Earlier moments from the free fall chasing Wave Two flashed vividly in his mind. He turned on the water and focused on the sound. The stain of Gerardo's blood was still on his hands. Ryan lathered dish soap thick and felt it squish between his fingers. No matter how hard he tried, the red seemed to shine through again and again as he rinsed under the water.

Images of the Khrylic battle invaded his thoughts as he stood fidgeting and washing and washing at the basin. He hummed and twitched his head sideways in order to cast off the memories, but wave upon wave of them rushed through him, and he began to shake and shudder. He was spiraling further into bad waters when his chiming communicator caused him to jump.

"Nguh." He sniffed loudly. "Cinch up." With a mostly dry hand, he raised the device to his ear. "This' McBain." He nodded his head. "That's great news. Prognosis is full recovery, then?" Ryan grabbed a dish towel to dry his hands. He turned and crossed into the main room. "Well, that's to be expected. When did he get out? Is he awake yet?" Ryan spun around and plopped into his easy chair. "Are Ashlynn and the kids there yet?" Ryan nodded again. "Great news. Thank you, sir, for letting me know."

He looked up at the ceiling in the darkened room. "I will. No, I'm fine. Just a bump on the head. I'm AOK. Super good." He shifted in his seat and retrieved a remote he'd sat on. "Sure thing; I will. See you in the morning. Thank you, sir." Ryan terminated the call and winced from a phantom shooting pain in his shoulder. He leaned back in the recliner while rubbing it. With the dish towel still on his lap, he was overcome with exhaustion and passed out.

Some weeks later, Ryan entered the main administrative building on the base. Walking up to a group of people waiting in the hallway, he sidled up behind a man leaning on a cane. Before the man could notice him, he leaned forward and whispered in his ear. "Hey big boy, you wanna go for a ride later in a spaceship?"

Gerardo smiled and turned his head. "Hey there, chief. I think my flight days are behind me now."

Ryan looked past him at the pretty lady holding his hand. "Hi, Ashlynn. How are you guys?"

She instantly crossed past her husband, wrapped her free arm around Ryan's neck, pulled him into a quick hug, and then kissed his cheek. "Mitchell Ryan, it's good to see you." she looked back into her husband's eyes. "I think we're making real progress."

Gerardo nodded and raised his eyebrows. "I've recently regained complete control of my incoming and outgoing biological functions, so what more could a guy want?"

Ryan winced. "Oh, wow, that's a little too much good info."

They all chuckled as Gerardo shifted his weight slowly, pivoting toward Ryan. "Hey, when does the PT get better?"

Ryan smiled. "It will get better. Just about the time you think you'll never be strong again, it starts happening. Then one day, they kick you loose." Ryan winked at Ashlynn. "Then he's not going to know what to do with himself, and you need to be ready with a big list of projects."

Gerardo motioned like he was going to hit Ryan with his cane. "Buddy, hey, what are you doing to me? She already has a mile-long list of honey-do's. Come to think of it, no wonder I haven't progressed further."

Ashlynn smiled and pulled on her husband's arm. "I'm just so thankful to still have him to nag." She looked to Ryan, choking up and teary eyed, "Words just can't express—"

Gerardo squeezed his wife. "Yeah, nice to be here to complain. Thank you for what you—"

Ryan recoiled with a raised hand. "Nope, not that big a deal, and you would have done it for me."

Gerardo smiled. "It is a big deal, Ryan. You saved my life. I still don't fully understand how you put it all together so fast. So, no then, I don't think I could have done it for you. I'm just really thankful that I had someone behind me who was really good on the stick and half insane."

Ryan smiled and nodded. Gerardo leaned closer to him and whispered quietly, "Your skill aside, be careful. There are failure profiles that even you might not be able to fly out of. They're running fast and thin on this thing. You know what I'm talking about—"

"I'm OK."

"I know. I'm just saying, be careful. Question everything."

Ryan nodded. "I hope the accident review in a few minutes here will shed some light on all this. I have a feeling that things are going to move forward with a greater margin of safety."

Indeed, the inquiry board determined that the source of the crash was ultimately related to time and money. The chain of events leading up to the radiation exposure was identified. Components were not accurately tested and integrated on Wave Two. There were gaping holes in process and communication with the departments in charge of solar weather and forecasting. Backup systems were not fully tested or checked. Basically, it was only a matter of time before something like this occurred. A focus on results, lack of proper funding, complacency toward the dangers, and an overaggressive timeline had pushed crews and resources into an unacceptable risk area. The report contained hundreds of pages, and the summary presentation of findings took more than two hours.

Later that evening, Ryan was on his single surviving recliner when his communication device chimed. The calling source display merely indicated "POE." With cocked head, he answered. The voice was familiar, but he didn't initially place it. He nearly jumped out of his seat when the voice identified herself as the Earth president.

"Thank you, Madam President. Yes, I'm fine. It was a bit of a scrape, but I think we have it under—" Ryan sat up listening. "Yes, ma'am, I understand, but the risks are worth the benefits of this technology. I strongly urge you to reconsider. The program and this propulsion could have a profound impact on our planet, perhaps even save us." Ryan chuckled. "No, ma'am, I don't think this is the same kind of planet saving, but thank you. I just think better oversight would ensure the success of this mission." Ryan nodded. "Yes actually, I did have someone in mind, but he's not gonna like it."

A week later, Ryan was sitting in a golf cart by the main gate as General Lund exited a local transport. Ryan smiled as he cleared the front gate. "General, I trust your trip was uneventful."

"You and I have different ideas about the definition of 'retired.'"

Ryan smiled as he pulled away. "That we do, sir. That we do. It's good to see you."

Lund grimaced and put his hand on Ryan's shoulder.

◊   ◊   ◊

The accident caused a six-month delay in the project timeline. The pause allowed sufficient time for Ryan's concussion to heal and for him to regain flight status. It also provided time for Mr. Kendal to pursue his side project around the duality of presence. Following his research, he pulled the DNA records of all the pilots who had survived up to the last ten minutes of the Khrylic engagement. He ran an analysis that looked for any areas outside of basic traits where there was commonality. He stared at the data wide-eyed for ten minutes. The next morning, he was in Dr. Gleim's office.

"You look as though you haven't slept."

"I haven't. You're not gonna believe what I found. There's a very specific pattern of genetic mutations in common among the ED4 pilots who survived up to the last ten minutes of the attack. This segment of proteins is big, and it's complex. I'm going to need help to completely analyze it. And it doesn't appear anywhere else. I searched millions of other records in several databases, and there are no other examples. So, this appears to be a fairly recent drift. This is evidence that the trait we're talking about is a genetic anomaly. This is huge, and I'm not sure what we do with this information. What if we could engineer something like this? Can you imagine?"

Within a week, the trio had applied for a study grant. It was picked up immediately. Three weeks later, Ryan stormed into Dr. Gleim's new office holding up a piece of paper. "I'm reassigned to a new research project? Are you kidding me? I didn't agree to this. Then I find out someone went to visit my flight partner's widow, used my name, said they were working with me, and asked her all kinds of upsetting questions. I don't know what you guys are up to, but how dare you bother her. How dare you! You will not make contact with Pari Anshra again. Is that understood? I don't know what this is all about, but count me out."

Ryan pointed down, "I'm in this *here*." He motioned his palm back and forth. "You and me, we're done. This propulsion mission is the greater good." Ryan crumpled up the orders and threw them in the round file as he stormed out.

General Lund was just sitting down to a perfect cup of tea when his communicator chimed. Looking down, he could see it was Ryan. Setting the tea down before he could take the first sip, he answered the call. Ryan was so animated that Lund had to hold the device away from his ear. A few calls later, the president intervened with an executive order stating "...no such testing would be done on survivors or family of survivors." The DNA mapping was cataloged "top secret" and archived into obscurity.

DIVA OF LIGHT

IN THAT INSTANT, SHE RECOGNIZED HIM
AND SMILED UPON HIM. HE WAS CAPTURED
BY THE GRACE OF THE LIGHT...

A gentle ocean breeze danced through Ryan's hair. He sat in the early morning glow, surveying the expanse. The mighty Pacific growled and hushed in a constant cadence. The sea stretched beyond oblivion to a place where all things connected to the heavens. Much like deep space, the endless expanse pulled at him. His eyes danced back and forth, marveling at the infinite facets. From a distance, it appeared uniform and smooth, but a closer look revealed a churning chaos moving and spilling over in every direction at once. When channeled and focused, the sea was unstoppable.

Ryan closed his eyes, listened to the washing of the surf, and drank in a deep breath. Like countless sailors dating back to ancient times, he laid down his wish upon its shore. A seagull floating overhead squawked at him. Looking up, he spoke playfully to it. "Yeah, I know; time to fly."

Today marked the culmination of the Earth-based segment of the research project. This would be his last day on the planet for some time, and more importantly, it would be the last day he would reside on this base. He stood, dusted the sand from his seat, and turned for one more glimpse at the expanse, mumbling to himself, "This...this I will miss." Turning back toward the growing glow behind the base buildings, he made his way back to quarters.

There was time for a quick bite before catching the shuttle up to the orbital station, where the mighty Tereshkova was moored. She would be home in the coming months as he set sail into deep space.

Five days later found Ryan pinned in his seat, calling out stats of the accelerating research craft. Waves of thrust reverberated through Ryan's shaky voice over the radio. "Power steady coming through thirty-four percent; reactors are green, five healthy engines, full power available."

The Tereshkova was an energy pump and channel of propulsion. The vessel was nearly all engines; neither her hull nor her purpose were cluttered with weapons. For those who heard the whisper of the heavens and felt the siren's call, the Tereshkova represented the purity of discovery.

Ryan's eyes danced around several management consoles, and he barked under G forces into the coms. "We're in the lane. Approaching the next power step. She's raring to go!"

The Sun radiated through the forward view portal, and Ryan marveled anew at Her size. Life on Earth started from and was sustained by the big round fireball. Although it was massive and inhospitable, he smiled as he faced the source of Earth's light. Chuckling in thought, he transmitted, "Regarding those course calculations, I have good news to report: The Sun is in fact filling the forward portal. She's a beautiful light!"

"Roger that, Tereshkova. Say the word, and we'll send up some sunscreen."

Chuckling, Ryan replied, "Roger that."

"Tereshkova, I'm showing you're less than a minute from ELOS." ELOS was short for "eclipsing loss of signal." The flight path would take the Tereshkova close enough to the star that signals from the ship would be drowned out by the Sun's radiation. Methods for relaying a signal close to a star were known, but the research project was limited in resources. A formal plea for military relay assistance in this flight segment was still being processed through a thicket of bureaucracy. The decision was made to forge ahead without it.

Ryan nodded. "Acknowledged. I'm boosting signal strength to maximum for telemetry. Hopefully you can get some of it here and there."

"We'll be monitoring your trajectory and reestablish coms when you emerge on the other side. Safe travels, Ryan, and Godspeed!"

"Roger that, Gerardo. Ah, shoot; I forgot something."

Many brows furrowed in the command center, and ears leaned toward the transmission.

"Understand you are missing something? Do you need to abort?"

"Negative. It's something I forgot to ask earlier. Hate to put you on the spot, Gerardo, but would you check in on General Lund for me while I'm gone? I think he gets a little bored in his retirement." Ryan smiled widely, knowing General Lund was monitoring.

"The general wishes to convey 'you're welcome.'"

As he began his final descent path and increased power, two-way communication with Earth Command was lost. Two minutes into the full power envelope, a slight tremor rattled a tablet on the main control console. Ryan tilted his head and looked up wide-eyed as he felt a vibration move up the length of the ship. Every good captain becomes an expert in rattles and vibrations, especially the wrong kinds.

A split moment later, the control console lit up like a carnival. Ryan's scan was interrupted by a solid lurch forward that felt like a nudge from a bumper car. It was an ominous indicator; the force required to displace a ship of this mass would be significant. Before Ryan could focus on the stream of alarms, the impact from a second explosion much nearer to the control deck threw him forward, slamming his head into the console. An audible master caution alarm provided confirmation of catastrophic failure, and all secondary compartment doors automatically began to close.

Ryan felt a piercing pain in his shoulder as the ship began to pitch off axis, tumbling down nearer to the surface of the Sun. The engines were still at full power; automated systems designed to bring them offline had failed. Ryan's fingers were a blur as he tapped quickly on the screen, trying to clear out the alarms and regain control. Images of ships exploding in the Khrylic attack invaded his thoughts.

He struggled for focus as his pulse rose and he hissed, "Not now!" He reached over his head and pulled down on a red T-shaped handle that was supposed to manually cut several systems that would shut down the engines. Instead, the effort produced another series of explosions.

Back at Command, several technicians received data fragments from the Tereshkova's telemetry. Many eyes grew wide scanning the information, and there was a sudden explosion of chatter.

"...we're way off course; she's too low..."

"...primary propulsion is beyond max limits..."

"...I've got nothing on core readings..."

"...Cap, we've apparently had a major event..."

A hush fell over the center after the initial reports came in. The mission commander was standing near the chief communication's officer when he overheard the solar weather officer. "What the hell?" She flipped through three different displays before looking up. "There's a massive coronal hole rotating around. I've never seen one this big. Where the hell'd this come from? It wasn't there a minute ago. I don't understand."

Before the mission commander could comment, the chief of flight ops approached with his headset unplugged. "Sir, we have primary echoes that indicate the ship's in at least three large pieces. We're getting an automated emergency beacon from her. I'm afraid we've had a catastrophic failure."

The primary engines finally cut out, and the pleasant hum that had started the mission was now replaced with more tremors, groans, and rattles. Through the forward view portal, the light from the Sun rose and set at an increasing rate. Ryan struggled and fought the tumble with the positioning thrusters that remained operational in the forward sections. An image of Anshra's kestrel tumbling down into the Khrylic destroyer flashed through his mind. His heart raced as he mumbled, "No, no don't."

With intuition and by the seat of his pants, he manually fired positioning thrusters to slow the rotation. Doing so created further orbital decay. The ship rolled slowly over to a stop, with the view portal facing directly toward the star. The explosions and proximity had drawn a presence to the flight deck. She saw him. The "She" in this case was our Sun, and a glance from Her was far more than a human look. Her light shone down into the very fiber of his being.

In that instant, She recognized him and smiled upon him. He was captured by the grace of the light and felt a serene quiet. While components overloaded and exploded around him, he could smell something fragrant like roses. The ship had sheared into three large sections that were now streaking in tandem across the solar sky. Primary fuel cells in the center section exploded violently and snapped Ryan back to his memories of the Khrylic attack.

Wide eyed, he lifted his shaking hands from the controls. He saw more visions of explosions as his mind replayed the deaths of his ED4 family. His voice was like the sound of a creaking door as he moaned, "Nooo."

More explosions caused a stream of debris to brightly shoot out forward and ahead. The streamers caught his attention. As he focused on the objects, he saw that they were actually several kestrels traveling off ahead. He shook his head and blinked his eyes. Before he could discount what he was seeing, he heard the chatter of familiar voices on frequency.

Again, shaking his head, he couldn't believe what he recognized just outside. Their service numbers were freshly memorialized on his shoulder; the voices and ships were his brothers and sisters.

He transmitted, "ED4, on guard, on guard! How do you read?" They continued to speak but did not acknowledge or respond to him. Ryan giggled with joy on frequency. "Bam, Rockjaw, Carrots, look at you guys right there! Can you hear me? Please respond."

At that moment, another kestrel traversed across the Tereshkova's bow, so close that Ryan could nearly touch it. He could see her pilot in the cockpit and transmitted. "Tigertail! I'm here! Jeeval!"

The transmission was scratchy, "Ryan? What are you doing? You should not be here; you're not authorized."

"Jeeval! Ah gods, I've missed you. I don't understand how."

The ships were all traversing quickly down toward the surface of the Sun. Without logic or reason, Ryan fired positioning thrusters to follow them down.

"Ryan, you cannot follow us here. Many things lie ahead for you there."

As their ships streaked further ahead, Ryan's face buckled and pinched together. "Please don't go. I've been so lost."

Another blast just behind the bridge section coated the portal window with burnt propellant ash and obscured his view. Ryan screamed into the mic, "Jeeval! Are you there? Jeeval, don't go!"

Her voice was further off and scratchier. "Ryan, I will always be in the strongest corners of your heart. If you look, that is where I will be. Tell Pari—" Ryan strained to hear her faint words. "—tell Pari I miss her touch, but I am at peace, veiled in a red shawl."

Ryan called out over and over without response. They were gone—again. His heart ached hollow and puckered in pain. Flames raged and buffeted the remains of the Tereshkova as he sat alone, shaking. The ship was braiding down well below gravitational limits. Over the roar, Ryan panted and looked all around the smoke-filled cabin. Loud groans were punctuated by popping noises and the screech of metal on metal. Fear and anguish comingled. There, in that moment, in the trough of despair, something extraordinary filled the divot.

The Sun began to sing. Loud and clear, the star song brushed across his soul like velvet to the cheek. He bathed in the notes, clung to them. Just then, fire burned the propellant ash off the forward portal, and the love of the light cast through. Straining to see his blinking control console, Ryan saw a flashing message. It was from Anshra. "Ryan, listen to Her with your heart. She will guide you to your future. You must rise Ryan. Rise!"

The ship continued to groan under the increased gravity, and some of the remaining compartments in the forward section started imploding. Engulfed in flames and so close to the Sun, it was difficult to ascertain the correct trajectory away from Her. Ryan craned his neck to search around the glare coming through the window. While moving his head, he discovered resonance differences in the tone of Her song when facing different directions. He didn't understand it, but somehow he knew that the changes in the resonation were a guide to steer him away from the fiery depths.

He closed his eyes, took a deep breath, and let go. He began to tap the console, firing positioning thrusters to turn the ship based on the guidance from Her notes. The speed that resulted from turning toward the Sun earlier had provided sufficient velocity to escape orbit. As he arced down very near the surface, She created a cradle, allowing him to pass through safely. Although he couldn't see it as he traveled across, he could feel Her face. Her presence was emotionally overwhelming, and Ryan struggled to concentrate. He focused on the notes of Her song. He continued to tap on the console as She sang, and tears cascaded over his cheeks.

A short time passed, and the pressure diminished as he traveled up from the depths. Knowing he had slingshot away from Her at high speed, he rotated around, facing Her voice, and fired everything that remained for braking. As the propellant for the small thrusters was exhausted, Ryan's head rolled like a loose bowling ball atop his shoulders, and his body slumped over the console.

Every being in the Command center was pawing and slogging through a quicksand of shock. A primary echo from an object caught the attention of one of the telemetry officers.

"Sir, are you seeing this?"

"What do you have?"

"It looks like...it can't be. There, look! That's definitely a power signature."

"What?"

"Sir, this spectral is consistent with chemical retros firing. The energy signature is very weak, but there's a mass. It's small, but whatever it is, it's coming from our same trajectory. And it's definitely slowing down."

"Track that object; don't lose it! There's only one reason why something on that trajectory would be slowing down. Notify Evac to intercept that object."

Ryan's eyes opened to Nurse Darcy. He started to speak and cleared his throat. She turned and came to his bedside as he spoke in barely a whisper, "How much we win this time?"

She smiled widely, put her hand on his shoulder, and pressed the call button on his bed. "Well, least I don't have to tell ya where ya are."

As other nurses streamed into the room, Ryan smiled back to her. "Radiation?"

She nodded. "Darlin, you have some strange affinity for the stuff like I've never seen. I'm not accustomed to repeat customers."

"You sayin' I have an irradiation addiction?"

"That or a ship crashing problem."

"Maybe I just need a better way to see my favorite nurse." Ryan looked around inside the critical care room. "I hate this place. I really do."

She gently patted his shoulder.

Aunt Enid and Aunt Evie were in the hospital waiting room. Both cried out with joy and relief when Darcy told them. Enid struggled through teary eyes to send a message to her sister and Hadley that Ryan had regained consciousness. Shortly after, Ryan was transferred to his own room, and they were there waiting when he was wheeled in.

Enid spoke first. "Oh, my boy! So good to see you awake and alive. You gave us quite a scare."

Aunt Evie was gently holding Ryan's arm and added, "Again."

Ryan smiled warmly seeing them both. The familial resemblance aside, they both wore their customary short-sleeved dresses with top buttons in the front. The collars were short and crisp. Although the colors and patterns were different, they shopped from the same earth-toned palette. Ryan couldn't remember a time when he'd seen either of them with a dress that didn't span below mid-shin in length. This style was the preferred uniform, even in the cold of winter. They both were fond of long-sleeved, button-down sweaters. As a child, Ryan would sometimes imagine their arms to be his mother's; she was also fond of fine knit fuzzy sweaters.

Over the years, Evie's chestnut hair had faded out, and gone were the days of Aunt Enid's nearly black tresses. Both had the same customary hair style, but now pure white hair was pulled back neatly into a high bun. The exact length was unknown to Ryan; he'd never once seen them with their hair down. All the aunts shared the same round face, rosy cheeks, and thin lips.

There were cross glances from the hospital staff as *Dr.* Enid Ardiel snatched Ryan's chart and began to study it.

Evie split her attention between her nephew and sister when she asked, "Are you OK?"

Ryan looked to Aunt Enid, who was flipping back and forth between pages in his chart.

"Looks like you're remarkably well, considering. You've been exposed to near lethal levels of radiation again. That's not good, but your high-tech fancy arm there is doing its job. Is it tingling?"

Ryan nodded. "Like you cannot imagine. It's a burning sensation, like a burning itch that I just can't scratch."

"Well good. That means it's working."

Evie looked at Ryan. "Honey, what happened? Do you remember?"

Ryan looked at her for a moment before he began. "There was a rumble and alarms and then some kind of failure. The engines didn't automatically cut out, and I think the ship broke up."

Both aunts looked stoically at him before Evie spoke. "I'm sure they will determine the root source. Virginia and I will put our eyes on it."

The three surviving sisters may have lacked the capacity to express love toward one another, but they more than made up for it with an ability to team up. In Ryan's lifetime, he had witnessed them band together and pull from interdisciplinary elements woven through their collective areas of expertise. In time, he'd come to appreciate that the three expressed love in actions and work on behalf of each other. Now sitting in front of him were two white-haired ladies, one examining his health chart and the other—an electrical engineer—already making plans to scour the accident report.

Ryan continued sheepishly. "There's something else. I'm not sure how to explain it."

Enid's eyebrows scrunched together. "Something with the ship?"

"No. It was the Sun. I wasn't alone."

"Who was there with you?"

"I don't know exactly how to describe it, except to say that it was love. She sang to me, and I saw ED4."

Darcy was still loitering in the room pretending to be doing something.

With eyebrows as high as they could travel, she piped up. "Well, as you can see, he's quite tired and needs his rest. I'm going to ask that we leave and give him some time to rest."

As Evie and Enid shuffled out of the room, Evie asked rather loudly, "Did he just say he found a girlfriend during the accident? You sure they checked his head?"

After shutting the door behind them, Darcy returned and adjusted some pillows behind Ryan. "Is your shoulder comfortable?"

Ryan watched her eyes. "Think I'm crazy?"

Darcy stopped moving and looked at him. "Can't imagine how much crazy I've seen here. Sometimes I think I've lost it. So, it's hard to say. I do know that you were in an environment and circumstances that were very taxing."

Ryan nodded. "So it's nuts then."

Darcy smiled and dimmed the lights as she pulled the door closed behind her.

The next day, two men entered his room unannounced. One was shorter and paunchy in the middle, while the taller one was more svelte. Ryan guessed Mr. Tall was probably in his fifties, and he had the rough-lined face typical of a smoker or a drinker. The shorter one was fifteen years junior and had a full, round face. Both were wearing unremarkable blazers and slacks. Mr. Junior had a pad of paper and was fidgeting with a recording device. The taller one was looking intently at Ryan.

Ryan squinted and slightly cocked his head. "The investigators."

Mr. Tall identified himself as Agent Korbrandt and flashed his badge. Mr. Akers fumbled in his jacket and finally produced a shinier badge. The men were from the EarthGov Accounting Office.

"We're here to interview you about the events leading up to and surrounding the loss of the UEA Tereshkova. The science vessel represented a sizable government investment, and our interest is to determine how and why she was lost."

Ryan read Agent Korbrandt almost immediately. "I'm sure you're also investigating because it almost took a human life." Ryan waved his hand.

"Yes. Of course."

Akers placed the recording device in front of Ryan. "Standard procedure requires us to record this interview. Can you uh, state your name and rank for the record?"

"Sure. Why are you so nervous, Agent Akers?"

Korbrandt shot his junior partner a sharp look. Aker's lips twitched for a moment. "Not nervous, no sir. This is just a standard interview."

Ryan looked at him for a few moments before glancing at Korbrandt's flat stare. "I am Master Chief Mitchell Ryan McBain, service number one seven, one alpha, eight niner, three delta. Can you tell me what happened?"

Korbrandt spoke up and did most of the talking from then on. "Actually, we were hoping you'd tell us what happened. There are some inconsistencies that we're trying to clear up."

"Inconsistencies? What inconsistencies?"

"OK, chief. I think we can cut to it. Did you feel you were well and competent to fly that day?"

"Of course I did. We were a few minutes from engaging the wave device when the ship just came apart. There was no warning, and the emergency systems did not engage. Instead of asking me what I had for breakfast or what I see in ink blots, can you guys tell me why the ship folded in two?"

Korbrandt and Ryan stared at each other for a few seconds before the agent broke the silence. "We know where the structural failure occurred. We've also recovered the data recorders and other monitors from the wreckage."

"Great, so you can pinpoint the source then."

"Well, see that's the interesting thing." Ryan's eyes narrowed, and he craned forward as Korbrandt spoke again. "We have recordings of cockpit audio."

Ryan shook his head slightly. "So?"

"Who were you talking to during the event?"

Ryan's eyes grew wide. Korbrandt pulled another device from his jacket and set it on the tray in front of Ryan. He pressed a button, and Ryan could hear his own voice. He was talking to ED4, except there was no audio from Anshra on the recording; it was only Ryan's voice.

As the recording ended, Korbrandt retrieved the device. "So, you can only imagine we were a little startled to hear the pilot of the Tereshkova talking to dead pilots in the middle of this event. We started wondering if you had run the emergency checklist procedures during the emergency. Then we started wondering if you followed standard procedures before the emergency. Could the event have been caused by distraction? Could the loss have been mitigated by a better response? Can you understand why we might have these questions?"

Ryan pursed his lips and looked at Korbrandt. The senior agent tilted his head and leaned forward. In a softer tone, he continued. "You know, we're going to go all through this thing. If you have anything you wanna tell us, it would be better now than later. You have a history that includes saving the planet, and while doing so you lost a lot of good people. You recently survived another accident. I think there was a great deal on your mind."

Ryan continued to look through Korbrandt. "I have nothing to add to my initial report. There's nothing to hide and nothing further to tell you. I would like you to leave now so I can rest." He pressed the nurse call button.

"Chief, you were under a great deal of stress, I get it. You can make this a lot easier on yourself if you cooperate with us here and now."

Ryan became visibly distressed. "I didn't screw up. You guys weren't there. You don't understand."

Darcy came through the door and saw Ryan's face.

"What don't we understand? Tell us."

Darcy snapped into mother-bear-nurse mode. "Who are you people? What are you doing in here with my patient?"

Agent Akers jumped up and flashed his credentials, but Korbrandt moved closer. "Talk to me, chief."

"I would like you to leave now," Ryan repeated.

Darcy boomed, "That's it, you're harming my patient. Up! Up, both of you, out. Now!" She shepherded both men out of the room and followed them down past the nurse station.

"The door is at the end of the hallway." She turned to another nurse at a station and said, within earshot of the retreating agents, "Make sure security knows these gentlemen need to check in first before they're allowed up on this floor again. They're not authorized to enter patient rooms without consent."

Both agents were in the stairwell when Akers spoke first. "I got the recording in the room, but I'm not sure what it's worth. He didn't admit to anything."

Korbrandt spoke back over his shoulder in response. "Yeah, we really don't need it. We have him talking out loud to dead people."

"Poor bastard. I mean, with what he's gone through."

"Don't feel too badly. Part of being captain in command is knowing your own mental health and limitations. He took a research vehicle out when he was unfit for duty."

"But maybe he was fine, and then there was some kind of trigger. Maybe he misunderstood some other transmission."

"Maybe. Who knows what he heard. We did catch all that singing in the other audio channel. But it really doesn't matter what the source was; he never should've been there in that cockpit."

"Hey, speaking of that, did you ever source identify that singing?"

"Negative, but that gal sure could sing, huh? I'm not an opera guy, but those pipes even made the hair on my neck stand up."

"Yeah, well I am an opera guy, and I've never heard anything like it. I'm not even sure what language it's in. I'm going to rip a copy of it when we get back."

Darcy came back into Ryan's room. "You OK, darlin'?"

"I don't know. I think I may have lost my mind. It was so real. I swear I didn't screw up, but I did hear them. Do you believe in spirits?"

"Just because you heard something doesn't make you nuts."

Ryan's communication device buzzed with an incoming video call, and he could see it was Pari. Ryan cocked his head and put his finger tips over his lips before answering.

"Ryan, it pleases me so to see you. How is your well-being?"

"Uh…well, my body's better. The food is awful though. I think that's how they motivate patients to heal up and leave." Darcy winked at him as she was leaving the room.

"I saw the launch live, and I felt the horror that everyone did, but there was more for me." Pari's voice trailed off quietly.

Ryan shifted in his bed and responded quietly, "Oh, what's that?"

She stared at Ryan until he asked if she was still there. She nodded, "I'm still here." She wiped her nose with a tissue before continuing, "I was very upset at the thought you were lost, but fairly quickly, I felt a joy for you. A joy that you were released and reunited with your chosen family."

Ryan nodded and wiped his eye with the back of his hand. "Pari, there's something else going on. I'm having a hard time explaining it. I don't know what to do, and I'm not sure how to talk about it."

"What is it? A feeling? You are safe telling with me."

Ryan shook his head. "No, it was something I saw and something I heard. It's also about you, Pari. Do you believe in spirits?"

Pari felt a knot in her throat, and her heart pounded as she forced herself to nod.

"I saw her, Pari. She spoke to me."

Pari shook her head and looked away with tears in her eyes.

"I don't want to upset you, and I'm not sure I haven't lost my mind, but she gave me a message for you." Pari looked back to the camera as he continued. "She told me to tell you she missed your touch and that she was at peace. And there was another part I didn't understand. She said something about a red hat. No, it was a shawl. She said she was veiled in a red shawl. Does that mean anything to you?"

Pari's head lowered, and a silence hung on the call. She sniffled and shook her head. "I am sorry, Ryan. I'm not well. I must disconnect."

Later the next day, the frail woman stood in the doorway of his hospital room. Darcy stood next to her and knocked on the door frame, "OK for a visitor?"

Ryan opened his eyes, looked up, and nodded. "Pari, you're here." As Pari entered the room, Darcy pulled the door closed behind her. Standing apart from Ryan in the middle of the room, she spoke quietly. "A few weeks after she was lost, I had imagery in my sleep." She looked askance at Ryan.

He nodded. "A dream?"

"Yes, a dream. She came to me while I slept. It was so very vivid." She paused for a moment and smiled. "We spoke of many things, and I wept that it was all a fiction of my mind. She said love was no illusion. She also spoke that I would have to embrace the present to move us to the future. She told me there would be two moments that would allow me to move past. I protested. I did not want to let go, but she said I would have to in order for us to be together again." Pari sniffled and wiped her nose with a handkerchief. "Daiwa was the first event for me. I could feel myself let go."

Ryan listened quietly, and in the silence asked, "And the second?"

"I asked in my dream how I would know the experience was true. She said the second event would be the sign."

Ryan felt the difficulty and the loss in her voice. He motioned to the bed. "Please, Pari, come. Sit next to me."

As she sat on the edge of his bed, he took her small weathered hand and surrounded it with both of his. She looked into his eyes. "Ryan, she told me that she would be veiled in a red shawl and that I would know in time what that meant."

Ryan's eyes were wide, and he put his forehead down on her hand. She could see his labored breathing and tenderly ran her other hand through his hair. Both of them sat for a time together before she stood and straightened her coat. In a cracked voice, she said, "This is the last time we are together. I am old, and my final days will be at home. You must also move forward, and this is why I traveled one last time to give you this message."

Ryan nodded. "Thank you, Pari. When you speak to her next, tell her I said thank you."

Pari nodded, reached to squeeze his hand, pulled away, and quietly left the room. After she left, Ryan looked outside through high windows, smiling widely at the clouds passing by above. With taut cheeks, he mumbled, "Goodbye, Jeeval."

Nine months later, Ryan stood perfectly motionless, looking off through floor-to-ceiling bay windows. Outside, a frothy Pacific Ocean churned as the wind whistled around the edges of the building. Off in the expanse, Ryan could see the storm was starting to break. The display light on his communicator timed out and went dark as he held it down in his hand. The call had been a courtesy notification of the final report from the accident review board.

He'd been cleared of all charges in the loss of the UEA Tereshkova. Medical experts had testified that the concussive blow he had sustained as his head made contact with the control console as a result of the explosion should have rendered him unconscious. It was their professional opinion that any hallucinations Ryan experienced were caused by the accident and not the other way around. A hollow logic told him that he should have been relieved and ecstatic with the board's findings.

Stepping outside onto the deck, he leaned on the weathered railing and faced into the wind. As it continued to howl, he closed his eyes and felt the gales pass right through him. He'd walked down the fence line separating this world from the other side. In the boundary between life and death, he had felt an indescribable connection. Those he saw, the reunion with Jeeval, and the presence of the Sun had felt so very real. In those brief moments, he had felt a peace. The logic and the possibility that the experience was somehow manufactured caused him to bristle.

As gusts buffeted through him, he felt warmth in recalling his communion with the perfect beauty of the Sun. Just then, Her light shone through an opening and raised a smile on his face. A vibration in his hand indicated an incoming communication. Ryan looked down and saw that the call was from the admissions department at the Military Academy.

RESCUE

THE AIR ON THE FLIGHT DECK HUNG STAGNANT LIKE DEATH. I FELT THE HAIR ON MY NECK STAND TALL, AND THE WORLD SUDDENLY BECAME VERY QUIET.

Eshala shot up in bed, and her eyes surveyed the room. Her distressed expression was replaced with a grimace as the Centauri warrior brought her hand to her forehead.

"Good morning, Eschala."

Sleepy-eyed, she swung her legs down to the floor and glanced at the time. "Is it really that late? Why didn't you wake me, Virginia?"

"You were in a deep sleep cycle. Such periods are essential for regeneration and repair. Considering the accident, it was prudent to give you additional time."

Eschala smiled at a memory: the first time she had heard Ryan's intelligent life companion, Violet, she had been taking after Ryan over the coms. Eschala had asked if the voice was his mother. Virginia had assumed the same role for her. She gingerly touched the back of her neck when Virginia spoke again. "The skin treatments have nearly healed the burn. I am very sorry about your hair."

Eschala smiled. "It's alright. Long hair isn't always combat convenient. I'll have better respect for plasma conduits in the future. We're very nearly back to the fringes, and I feel like we need to take extra precautions."

"Agreed. Can I ask a personal query?"

"Yes, go ahead."

"You still bare a tattooed slave mark. For what reason did you keep it?"

Eschala lifted her arm and looked at the mark on her upper shoulder. She looked up and thought for a moment. "I guess just after I was rescued, I had intended to remove it. But when I came home, no one knew what to do with me. Most of the planet thought I was dead and couldn't have imagined where I'd been. Most completely avoided me because they didn't know what to say."

She shook her head. "So here I was, a young person with a traumatic experience, and no one would talk about it with me. Everyone around me pretended it didn't happen, and it was never brought up in conversation. I walked around for years wearing long sleeves and thinking there was something wrong with me. My uncle was the only one brave enough to ask me to talk about what had happened."

"Is that your uncle the king?"

Eschala shook her head. "No. There were few words between the king and me. It was my other uncle, Bayhden. I was able talk with him about things that I couldn't discuss with Mother. I don't know why. Maybe it was because he reminded me of Father. Maybe a little because I didn't want to burden my mother with it. When my father was killed, and I disappeared, she sort of lost her mind. So, it was Uncle Bayhden who taught me how to fight, well I should say, fight more effectively with structure and discipline. He was also the one who intervened and helped me get my muscular mods as a young-ager." She flexed her arm muscles, smiling at the memory, then looked at the tattoo again. "Then I reached a point where I made this mark my own. It frightened people and stopped them from speaking with me. I also wore it in a kind of defiance. It symbolized a past that I was no longer ashamed of. And now...now, I keep it to serve as a reminder."

"I do not understand. Do you want to be reminded of the experience?"

"No. It reminds me there were Centauri who knew what happened to me and did nothing. It reminds me to be careful of who I trust. It also reminds me that I'm a fighter, a survivor. Its appearance puts me further into the present moment and the force that I am."

"Is that why you cut your hair?"

"I cut my hair because half of it caught on fire!"

"You could have trimmed it up and kept thirty-four percent more of it than what you elected to discard."

Eschala thought for a moment and ran a hand through her pixie cut. "Maybe, Virginia. Perhaps deep down it was symbolic and an acknowledgement of the situation we now face."

"May I ask a different personal query?"

"Go ahead."

"In your regenerative cycle, you were speaking, and you said Ryan's name. You have enunciated his partial or full name three hundred and eighty-seven times in the same manner in the recent months. Do you regularly have projections of him during your regenerative cycle?"

Eschala smiled. "Are you asking me if I dream about Ryan?"

"Yes."

She nodded. "I do. We have a connection that he doesn't understand. Last night was different though. It felt different, and I'm very fearful something's happened. It feels like it may be something with the Daerk. Can you show me again the entry in Ryan's personal journal where he first encountered the Daerk?"

Personal Record
LCDR M. Ryan McBain
Date: Three and a half years post-graduation from the Military Academy

---

Nine rescue boats, including mine, converged on the small, innocuous looking ice planet. Intel showed concentrated satellite coverage, but we expected light resistance for a commerce outpost of this size. We had no idea what kind of maelstrom we were headed into. The dwarf-sized planet, as it turned out, was one massive military outpost and a security holding area. The satellites were all military. The defense systems were highly evolved and developed for a full scale planetary siege. The mission basically amounted to suicide.

Lieutenant Commander Ragnvald Djarvstrom entered upper orbit in Evac Boat 077, about two hundred thirty miles ahead of us. The vessel was exactly on time and precisely at the assigned point of entry, not at all surprising considering her captain.

Ragnvald, aka "Ragn," and I went through the academy together. We met taking the same session of Initial Flight Systems. I was near failing the orbital navigation segment of the class when I asked him for help. He met me at the lab, and he ran through my math. Try after try, I couldn't get my satellite entry simulation to nest into orbit. I'd either skip it off the atmosphere or ram it straight into the planet. I had just cratered another when, out of frustration, I said something about being too dumb to operate in space.

Ragn sat motionless and didn't respond. He was grossly absorbed, looking over a printout of my formula. Freezing the simulation, I turned around and looked at him. The furrow of his brow relaxed, the corners of his lips curled into a smile, and he looked over his reading glasses at me. "Oh, you're an idiot for sure, but not at orbital math. Look here." He showed me where my dyslexia had caused the trouble. I was reversing values in a key formula. He suggested I make a song or a phrase out of the formula to keep it straight. It was simple genius.

He rode shotgun with me on a number of simulations until we were sure that I had it right. He believed in me when the lab TAs either didn't have the time or the confidence. I aced the final sim, which allowed me to pass the class, just barely. We became fast friends and subsequently housemates. A few years later, I repaid the favor when he lost his hold in a rock climbing accident.

Every chance we could, we'd challenge our endurance and savor the adrenaline. We were addicted to climbing. On this particular day, his harness was tethered to another friend's. Unbeknownst to them, the rock face had damaged their safety rope. Djarvstrom fell about fifteen feet when the rope went taut momentarily and snapped. He fell about forty feet, bouncing like a rag doll off the cliff edges down to a small ledge. My climbing partner and I saw the whole thing from the top.

While my partner was freaking out, something clicked inside me. I hustled a rope over the edge. My partner asked what I was doing as I clipped the rope to my harness. I turned, speaking calmly and clearly to him. "Call right now for medivac from the top here. Can you make that call please? Be right back."

Raising my eyebrows and smiling, I dove off facedown toward Ragn. Poor bastard Swede regained consciousness just as I was flying down upon him like a spider. His eyes opened with a start, and he raised one hand up. He winced and looked around. Before he could say anything, I was crouched next to him. "Hey bud, you still with us? Try not to move. How do you feel?"

He replied in a hoarse whisper, "I just fell down a mountain, you ass."

"Well, at least your mouth still works. Can you feel your legs?"

"No. Wait. Yes, I can feel."

"Which parts hurt?"

"Everything. I just fell down a mountain, you ass."

"Well, at least your mouth still works."

"Why do you keep saying that?"

"OK, memory good. You're coherent."

"Stop with me. I think I've died. I barely open my eyes, and I see you falling straight down on top of me. Now I'm thinking I've gone to hell."

"Hate to disappoint, but the hell has yet to come, my friend. It's getting late, and we've gotta get you outta here. If your spine is still in one piece, then it's going to happen over my back, which is gonna hurt like a bitch."

"You are kidding? You are not kidding. I never thought I would hope for a broken neck."

"Up is better than going down, unless you can climb yourself out of here."

I checked his neck and then rolled him on his side to check his back.

Ragn wheezed. "Uuhhhhh... I hate you."

"I know, buddy."

A quick assessment revealed broken ribs, likely concussion, and a broken femur. No neck or spinal injury. I laid down on my side and backed up against his chest, speaking to him over my shoulder. "Put your arms over my shoulders and prepare yourself." A few clicks confirmed the connection between his harness and mine.

He groaned and then panted in pain after moving. Holding his arms over my shoulders, I sat up in one swift moment, pulling him up with me.

"Oh jessss."

"Almost there; we're going to stand. Try not to put weight on that left leg."

He grunted as we stood. I'm sure the ribs were excruciating with weight on them. I stood hunched over with him on my back and verified that his harness was clipped to mine.

He was breathing fast but shallow. "I'm either going to pass out or vomit."

"To the side, please. Hurl to the side."

"I really hate you."

With Ragn dangling on my back, I swung out laterally across the rock face to a far less vertical adjacent slope. I was able to stand and lean forward, carrying Ragn on my back. With the lesser grade slope, I could switch left and right in the climb while standing. Two climbers above pulled as I walked up the face, with Ragn wincing in pain at every step.

"You walk like a rhinoceros. Why couldn't a ballet dancer have rescued me?"

"Oh, you still awake back there? I thought you were taking a nap."

"No man could sleep bouncing like this. I think my kidneys have now additionally been injured."

"Hey, good, cheap rescue help is hard to come by."

"I suppose I should thank you for coming down and bringing me up."

"Yes, that would be appropriate."

"I should, but I'm not."

"Well, that's OK," I said, laboring in step. "I should tell you, that redhead you like so much, the one from the gym, what's her name?"

"Celeste?"

"Yeah, Celeste. She asked me out."

"Wha, she asked you? You're lying."

"I wasn't going to mention it, but since we could both die doing this, I thought you should know."

"She asked you...you?"

"Yep!"

"I should have thrown up on you." He paused for few seconds. "What did you tell her?"

"I told her I already had plans this weekend to hang out with my friends. So here I am instead, dragging your sorry, whiny ass up the side of this cliff."

"You know you're an idiot."

"Yeah...I know."

An emergency medical team had already arrived and were waiting when we reached the top. After I set him down gently on a board, they took over his first aid.

"His pulse is thready, and he's in shock. We need to get a move on."

Ragn pinched his eyebrows together. "Do they not know I can hear them?"

"Dunno, suppose you could already be unconscious and imagining this whole thing?"

"Yes, but it would be far more pleasant."

In unison we both said, *"Rescued by a ballerina!"*

He smiled back, and as they were picking him up he said, almost inaudibly, "Thank you."

"Behave yourself. Maybe you'll meet a cute nurse."

Later in the hospital, Ragn told me half flippantly that he thought I should go into Evac Corps. The thought rolled around in my head, and it's my earliest memory of a turn down the path that would shape the trajectory of my life.

We both ended up taking it as a summer elective after our third year. Ragn was a genius in the classroom, but it was a real struggle for him to earn the basic evac merit. As it turned out, I happened to be naturally suited to the endeavor. The group commander pulled me aside and asked me if I had plans after graduating. I shrugged, and he asked me to consider a tour with them.

"I know your history. That's not to say this is some kind of entitlement. What it means is that we recognize in your performance a certain ability to keep your cool. It's easier in our experience when you've had practice in near-death situations. But I must caution you, the training is miserable. You will constantly curse yourself for volunteering. You will be selected for the worst possible missions. Our crews are the ones going toward what others in Fleet are fleeing. You will always be outgunned and a target. There will never be a time when you aren't shot at, sometimes from multiple sides. If you somehow survive and recover those that are lost, you will not receive the recognition you deserve. Nearly all our best historic rescues are classified. Oh, and the pay is dismal. But in your heart, in your core, you'll know the strength of who you are. While perhaps not publicly, everyone in Fleet will grant you respect far greater than your rank and step aside in salute when you approach."

"OK."

The commander chuckled. "OK?"

"Yes, sir. I've been thinking while I was here that this kind of thing sorta calls to me."

He chuckled again. "When I said I knew you, I also meant I know who you're related to."

"Oh?"

"Don't worry. Your aunt was ruthless in her training with me, but she was also a mentor. That said, she'll probably try to end my career when she finds out I've actively recruited her nephew into Evac. Might consider waiting a bit before mentioning it to her."

"Roger that."

He reached out and shook my hand. "Keep your grades up. When graduation nears, I'll put in a request for your name."

"Thank you, sir. I won't let you down."

Ten months later, Ragn and I were sitting on the roof of our townhouse at sunset, passing a bottle between us. We were celebrating the culmination of our four years. The sky was ablaze with oranges, reds, and pinks.

Ragn nodded and turned to me. "So, what do you think you'll be assigned to after graduation?"

"I think I'll try my hand at the Evac Corps."

"Really? A tough one, for sure. But perhaps even harder to get in. What else have you applied for?"

I shrugged. "Nothing else, really."

"That's all? You didn't pick any backup choices?"

I pushed out my chin and curled my upper lip. "Nope."

Ragn took a swig. With a scrunched, bitter face, he said, "Wait a minute, you always have a backup; you're like the king of plan B."

After a pause, his eyebrows rose. "You were accepted already?"

I grinned widely. "Somethin like that."

"How can this be? They haven't opened up the process yet." His brow furrowed as he studied me. "You did this last summer on our elective? You bastard, why didn't you tell me?"

"I don't know."

"How many did you get out on the final simulation?"

"What do you mean?"

Irritated, Ragn clarified. "How many soldiers did you pick up last summer on the final rescue simulation?"

"A lot. How'd you do?"

"I did two trips and rescued fifteen. Did you get more than twenty?"

I nodded.

"More than thirty?"

I grinned widely and nodded while raising the bottle. I passed it to him. He looked at me with wide eyes. Holding the bottle down by his waist, he asked, "Did you get them all?"

"Yeah. I got all of 'em."

Ragn was mid-sip when he cackled. He brought the bottle back down quickly and smiled. "You tricky bastard. How'd you do that?"

"I don't know. I guess going low was quicker. I could see patterns in the enemy fire, and I just picked my way through it. They thought it was a fluke or a glitch, so they made me do it again."

Ragn raised his eyebrows. "And?"

I raised the bottle and sipped, grinning. "I did it again."

"Ha, that's fantastic! You beat it twice." He slapped my back. "You know, only a couple people have ever beat that test?"

"Yeah, I guess just lucky I suppose."

"Lucky and crazy!"

We sat watching as the sun slipped down out of sight and talked about Fleet. Ragn was polished, and he graduated viceregal, with the second highest academic record in our entire class. Ragn was a perfect candidate for Fleet. He was a genius at orbital math, navigation, energy management, and tactics, as well as many other subjects. With his class standing, he literally had his pick of assignments. Being around him was like seeing the early years of a future Fleet admiral. But for whatever reason, my friend chose to follow me into Evac.

Evac training was hardest on him. Midway through our training, he sat in the ready room, bent over with his head in his hands. Speaking down toward the floor, he said, "My god, we've changed places. I'm too dumb to fly in space."

I put my hand on his shoulder. "Oh, you're an idiot, for sure, but your problem is that you're really smart. Think a little less. Disregard that; think a lot less. Don't look for the absolutes, and go with your gut."

True to the reversal, Ragn barely graduated, and I was top of the class. We trained with Evac for two hard years. The night we graduated, we celebrated hard. Ragn could drink a herd of elephants under the table. He was tall and skinny, and I would tease the Swede about having a hollow leg.

As we sat in a club with our dates chatting beside us, Ragn pulled out a small cloth sack and produced two commemorative rings. He had had them commissioned with the Evac symbol and our class number.

"We stick together. I have your back and you have mine. But no more mountain climbing!" He clinked his shot glass to mine, and we drank to our future.

◊ ◊ ◊

Boat 077 took blistering fire from three satellites, mostly photon damage. Over half of my flight crew were young and on their first assignment. I twisted my graduation ring around my finger and mumbled as we all watched in horror. Seven Seven listed over, caught fire, and started to tumble down into the atmosphere. She didn't last for more than a few seconds before she started breaking up.

One of the hardest things in life is to disconnect yourself personally from what's happening to soldiers in front of you. It's especially difficult when they're people you care about. But the discipline to protect the lives of many others demands it. All eyes were riveted on the spectacle as I silently took over helm control and accelerated ahead. The air on the flight deck hung stagnant like death. I felt the hair on my neck stand tall, and the world suddenly became very quiet.

I know the stare and the fuzzy constitution that comes from the first few times you witness such a horror. I'd lived through worse, and I wasn't about to be spattered out like this. Lassitude was death and a guarantee of squandering the few grains of sand left in our hourglass. Action and self-determination welled like a geyser within me. The crew jumped at the crack of my voice. "Focus! Be quick or be dead!"

As I closed in on Seven Seven's trail of debris, my mind was racing faster than my heart. An idea hit me like the thud of Seven Seven's debris striking our hull. With an edge of urgency in my voice, I ordered, "Get in tight behind Seven Seven, and shut everything down. Helm, you have the controls back."

The main engines fired for exactly four and a half seconds. I leaned over with elbows on my knees. "Hold steady."

Two nearby defensive satellites began to position for us. We sped further into the debris field of Seven Seven as larger sections started to break apart. The upper atmosphere slowed us, and we drifted right in behind the main portion of what remained. The second part of the horror was being up close and personal with the death of that ship and her crew.

Over the growing roar of the fiery atmosphere, I barked, "Weapons and engines power down. Turn off everything; go to your suits!"

Audible chimes rang out as the ship verified that life support had been disabled. The ship buffeted on a cushion of flames engulfing our hull. We were dead in the water and falling fast behind the remains of Seven Seven.

My helmsman exclaimed, "My god! Can we—"

"Negative; they're already gone." It was on everyone's mind, and I knew it would come. I yelled over the growing roar, "Chemical thrusters; keep the belly down! Quick bursts. It'll be harder to detect. Try to avoid the larger pieces of debris."

Seven Seven was fully engulfed. Larger portions of her remaining hull were breaking apart and splaying out ahead like flaming streamers. We were in an unpowered fall into the atmosphere. My gamble was that the satellites would mistake our ship as part of the debris from Seven Seven and move off to attack other boats.

My fist was clenched around the ring, and a part of me quietly mumbled, "Goodbye, Ragn." He was a true gentleman and a scholar, and he was my dear friend. His life was lost to an automated defense satellite on an anonymous planet, and no one would ever know of his sacrifice. Though I piloted a lifesaving vessel, I was powerless to save him or his crew. Hell of a thing to use the flaming remains of another crew—of a dear friend—as a screen for your own survival. But utility demanded we forge ahead, and there was no time budget to mourn.

From that moment forward, I've told myself that Ragn and his crew were dead before we could have come anywhere near his vessel. He was one of the smartest men I ever knew, and he would have urged me to do what I did. It's what he would have done to save his ship and complete the mission. It dawned on me while we sweated through the long seconds in our fall that maybe it was Ragn on the other side who gave me the idea to begin with. The thought charged my resolve to make his sacrifice count. The ruse was working, and the satellites began to move off.

Ship alarms blared as multiple systems began to overheat. We were in a race. We would either get below the range of those orbital weapons or burn up.

The ship's central computer voice declared, "Caution! Caution! Decelerate! Approaching maximum braking window. Decelerate now! Surface approaching." There was an audible chime followed by more declarations. "Maximum external temperatures exceeded. Alert, alert! Exceeding maximum braking window limits. Decelerate! Decelerate!"

The deck crew were exchanging looks of concern. I could feel Ragn's hand on my shoulder. Rubbing my thumb and forefinger, I was hunched forward, frowning at the forward display. My jaw was tight, and my upper lip twitched. My eyes were windows to a maelstrom of rage. Death was near. I could feel it bumping up against us, circling and waiting for the right moment. In the narrows between maximum tolerances and catastrophic failure, I was racing death to the limit line. Hawkish for it, a steady voice rang in my head, "Wait…wait…hold…not yet…not quite yet."

My first officer broke the silence. "Sir? How long, sir?"

My lips and jaw were moving as I calculated the drop.

"Sir?!"

After a few more moments, my head nodded, and I barked into the ship intercom, "Main engines back online! Emergency deceleration! Prepare for impact! Prepare for surface fire; rig for reflective." The bridge erupted into chatter and motion. Over it I yelled, "Where's our package?"

"Positive contact! There's a beacon about two hundred nautical from the main city here." My tac officer Cali highlighted a point on the map.

"Move us away from that city; angle our fall away toward those canyons. Powerplant increase to one hundred and ten percent; emergency propulsion authorized. Cinch up; in we go!" I mumbled to the side, "Whoever this is better be really damn important."

Fear on that deck was viscous and spread across the conscious mind like a slippery film. We were maintaining the equivalent of between three and four Earth Gs in deceleration.

As far as we could determine, we were the only boat that had survived down to the planet.

Laser fire erupted from the surface hard and bright. It fueled a greater irritation in me, and my lip snarled. As my crew squinted and winced, I mumbled, "Of course, sure; why not?" Our ship energized a layer of reflective material to deflect as much photon energy as possible. Automated pods detonated confetti-like reflective material in the instant a beam was sensed. We were barely holding together, fighting to get lower down under planetary defenses.

Cali hollered, "Missile fire detected!"

"Have they acquired?"

"Negative."

"Hold speed; hold steady!"

We were still falling at a high rate and on fire. Our heat painted us as a big fat juicy target, but we had to get down.

"Prepare for high G decel, automated assist; say location of package?"

"Emergency auto-assist engaged, package one two zero nautical miles, bearing zero three zero, under fire."

"Engage max decel at niner thousand, brace for a bounce, brace for impact, charge photon weapons, prepare to return fire."

At ten thousand feet, our boat fired main engines at maximum power, and for a few moments, we sustained the equivalent of about fourteen Earth Gs. Electronic shielding produced a localized magnetic "cushion" around the bottom of the boat. As we came quickly toward the ground, the field repelled the surface. For an instant, we maxed out at about sixteen Gs before leveling out. Even in a reclined posture, there was an eerie and uncomfortable feeling of gravity causing the heart to stop beating for a few moments. Repelling the impact always made my teeth tickle. For those new to the maneuver, it felt like getting hit really hard in the face with a boxing glove. Seeing stars and a fuzzy stupor were common after-effects.

My nose tickled, and I quickly swiped my hand over it. "Sys check. Who's with me? What's working?"

"Helm green."

"Nav impacted, recalibrating."

"Tac and discovery, lower sensor bar out, all others functioning, package taking ground fire, projectile fire inbound."

"Weapons...I'm here." My weapons specialist, Jarred, wiped a trickle of blood from his nose with the back of his hand. He shook his head. "Green and pissed."

I smiled over my shoulder. "Track the projectiles. How long and how big?"

Cali spoke without looking up. "Twenty seconds, package is big and tight."

Tight meant the objects in air were likely guided and intelligent enough to explode just above target for maximum destruction.

"Jarred!"

"I got it. Redirecting energy to weapons and returning fire."

The lighting dimmed as several hundred green flashes pulsed off the bow cannon. Further off, there were yellow flashes as the rounds were destroyed.

"Cali?"

"Good pattern, all projectiles destroyed, nice job, J-man. Cap, our package is two o'clock, eyes on. They're taking heavy fire from the ridge at our eleven. Mobile light armor units pressing toward them."

"Destroy the mobiles and swing in for dust off here." I highlighted a nearby level area on the screen. "Light a friendly beacon."

As the ship passed the ridge, the port side lit as we raked fire across the enemy units.

"Status?"

"I don't understand. Cap, we didn't get 'em all. They're shielded or hardened. All targets still appear to be in the fight."

"Circle around. Activate three missiles and arm for low-yield nuclear payload. Captain's authorization." Glances were exchanged on the bridge. "Put us between the targets and our friendlies and then release the sparrows."

"We're in position, confirming authorization to release three nuclear missiles."

I looked quickly to Jarred. "Do it; fire!"

"Twenty seconds to target." There were bright flashes. "Mobile targets are..."

I turned toward Cali. "Status?"

"I don't understand; they're still there. I have energy signatures, and they're still in the fight. Those were direct hits. How can—"

"Jarred, I want three more nukes. Fire them here and here." I touched locations on the map in between the targets. There were more flashes.

"I still have power signatures, but all enemy units are at the bottom of the crater and inverted. They're out of it. There's small weapons fire on our package. I'm initiating defensive cover fire."

I nodded my head as our ship's turrets fore and aft began showering targets beyond our friendly's.

Coming in fast, the ship's nose rose high and banked hard to the right. Dust and debris stirred as the boat decelerated. Inside, several chimes indicated that maximum grav forces and biological tolerances had again been exceeded.

I transmitted externally. "Hey, anyone here wanna join the circus? This bus is leaving!"

The response was very scratchy. "Major Adams, 301st Assault

Marines, eight walkin', two bent, one rescue."

I smiled and shook my head. "Jesus, you again."

There was a chuckle in return. "You musta really pissed someone off to keep getting sent out after me."

"Yeah, but the general's daughter says she likes me better."

"Well you're moving up, fly boy, cause you're now Alpha1."

"You ain't that important."

"Repeat, you are now Alpha1; she's the rescue." As my eyebrows raised, I could hear in the background of his transmission, "Mooove it Marines! Boat's leaving!"

"Assuming we live through the next three minutes, you're gonna have to explain how."

"If you're buyin', I'm talking"

"I'd buy a bottle to hear how our president got out here."

"Hey, what do you have upstairs?"

"No joy. Debris field."

"Figures. So maybe a quick trip."

"A-ffirmative."

"You and me sure can pick'm."

Cali piped up on the internal intercom. "Jump engines spooling through eighty-four percent, orbitals green across the board. Nav back up; spectral says something big is comin' this way in a hurry."

I transmitted externally again, "Yep and you sure know how to throw a party. We've got something big inbound. Time to bug. Your guys all have circ assist? And what about the president?"

"Us affirmative. Alpha1 negative."

"Your corpsman alive?"

"Affirmative"

"Put out Alpha1."

"Negative; we have orders."

"Put her in stasis or we're all scrambled eggs. It's my boat. I'll take the heat."

Cali cried out, "Two frigate class tangos coming into long range!"

"Start dust off cycle, down low, hug the surface, in those canyons best you can, max forward velocity toward those frigates. Rosenkranz, I want you to put us in the climb to orbit right between 'em. See if they can hit us when we fly right up their asses."

"What if we don't make it close enough to them?"

"Well, then you get to take a break, like forever. Everyone focus; fly fast. This is the moment you all trained for." I continued, mumbling, "The one from the brochure." Then I looked up and spoke louder. "Prepare amended jump checklist. We're going near-light out of the upper atmosphere, twenty seconds. Computer, Lieutenant Commander's authorization, tactical emergency, release max safeguards, prepare to cycle cores to one four zero percent." I typed quickly on my control console to program two more missiles to arm but not fire their engines. I chuckled, thinking of Jeeval, and mumbled, "Slippery."

A broadcast crackled through the internal ship coms, "Marines secure!"

"Everyone stow your tray tables." I nodded to Rosenkranz. "The cat and the fiddle; put us over the moon, please!"

The ship paused momentarily, and lights flickered as the cores cycled up. With a metallic roar, she screamed across the desert floor at low altitude. With such speed, we were already on fire. Alarm systems blared loudly as we pulled maximum G forces turning upward. Once we were under the frigates, we accelerated dramatically through the space between the approaching ships. We were buffeting and groaning under the acceleration. Everyone's circulation assistance kicked in as gravitational forces compressed their heart muscles. Everyone tried to think of being in any other place in the universe—everyone except me.

Firmly in the moment, I was screaming inside, "*Go, go, baby go... fly, fly, fly!*" I found comfort in the pressure that precluded breathing, and the dull ache from my heart muscle pressed to a stop. There were flashes of fire from the aggressors as we traversed past, but the speed and the angle were too fast. A velocity winner, we accelerated so fast that a significant section of the planet's atmosphere was pulled in our wake to orbit. Both Frigates buffeted and rolled away from the turbulence.

With eye signal controls, I released the last two nuclear missiles in our battery. They tumbled down just above the frigates and detonated a moment before we skip jumped away.

We came out of near light approaching the system star.

The Marines pawed forward to stow in a gallery just behind the command crew. I could hear Major Adams surveying his team. "How's Corporal Jianling?"

"He's with us I think. Possible broken ribs, and I can't tell if there's internal bleeding."

Adams bent down, "Zhou? Still with us?" The nearly seven-foot-tall heavy gunner looked up glossy-eyed at the major.

"Sir, there may be head trauma, not to mention slack jaw shock from whatever the hell that black monster was that tossed him like a ragdoll."

Sargent Randall piped up flatly, "Never seen anything like that. Huge...relentless. They just...they wouldn't die."

Major Adams nodded, "Excellent work today getting the president and getting the hell away from those things. We're on our way now." Adams looked over his shoulder, "Jackson, you still look nervous."

"Yes, sir. Those things are chasing us, and we're tight here, and there's nothing we can do."

"Exactly. Nothing you can do but relax and enjoy the ride."

There was a loud whisper all of us could hear. "Major, these guys, can they really get us out of here?"

"Probably. I've been through worse."

"Really?"

The major paused for a moment. "Nah, not really." He chuckled. "But one time I was with this guy, and we had to rip through an asteroid belt to get away."

"Sir, didn't you tell us you nearly died off life support and adrift in an asteroid belt once? Was that the same extraction?"

The major paused again. "Yeah, I guess it was. Excellent memory, corporal. That was one helluv'an explosion. It wiped out everything chasing us. Just bad luck that it also clipped our engine. We lived through it—at least most of us did. That's the important part of my story. Relax, Jackson. Besides, there's no asteroid belt here, I'm sure he'll do something else this time."

The major closed his eyes and tilted his head back while I caught the rest of his team exchanging anxious glances. I couldn't help but grimace. Typical. Save dozens and all anyone remembers is the guy crashed the ship.

"I want an amended light speed checklist," I ordered. "Come to a heading of three-ten mark two."

"Sir, that's headed directly into the star."

"Yep. Prepare for light speed. Tick it off."

"We're about ten minutes until we can power the cycle."

"Nope; not gonna make it. Let's speed it along, shall we? Shut down everything that doesn't fire, repel, or propel. Belay that; shut down everything that doesn't propel or repel."

In the background, my communications officer transmitted, "Mayday, mayday, mayday, Grandcentral, Lifeguard Two Niner is Angel One, repeat, we are now Lifeguard Angel One, taking heavy fire, all other ships presumed lost, jumping to coordinates Romeo Kilo Two Five Two. Romeo Kilo Two Five Two. Lifeguard Angel One, mayday, mayday, mayday. Request cover at Romeo Kilo Two Five Two."

I flew directly into the star's corona and used the gravity as an assist. Two other frigates appeared on intercept coming from the far side. Our boat caught fire again coming down into low solar orbit. We continued down, and I shot a narrow beam of charged energy into that star. I got Her attention, but not before several sections of the ship had disintegrated or burned away. There was an energy presence on the flight deck that others didn't understand. I was familiar with it and hoped She understood my request. I angled our path well below our structural gravity maximum, and the math for the required energy profile to achieve light speed finally plotted. Noting our course, Rosenkranz turned back over his shoulder and shot me a concerned look. I nodded back emphatically.

Multiple system failure alarms piled up in our combat management system. I had all personnel move to the central bridge for shielding. Several consoles were arcing, and there was an acrid smell of burning metal. The main computer failed, and I took over manually directing our course. My crew tossed their own concerned looks into those being shared between the assault Marines. The major was still asleep in his seat when I engaged light speed just above the surface of the star.

Our low trajectory path obfuscated our jump direction. Where we departed, a coronal mass ejection emerged and destroyed one of the pursuing frigates. It was the first but not the last time I would escape from this new species. We emerged from light speed nearly on top of a friendly escort waiting for us. Our presence set off collision alarms in the destroyer. I fired our particle engines manually to decelerate and bumped precisely into the docking ring before the destroyer's bridge crew even realized we were there.

Lifting my hands up off the console, I said aloud, "Damn. Ragn would have loved this." They pulled us into a bay and had to cut through a badly warped portal to extract us. I watched as the president was evacuated, semi-conscious. Major Adams shook his head, chuckling at me as he exited. He gave me a lazy salute as he strode past. "Thanks for the ride."

I smiled. "Always a pleasure."

As the rest of his Marines lumbered out dazed, I added, "Y'all come back again soon. Buh-bye."

The mysterious loss and subsequent saving of EarthGov's president was coded top secret. We were forbidden to speak of it. No additional explanation was ever given. Either because of my knowledge of the event or military kludge, I was put in hack for jumping in too close to the destroyer and for wrecking a brand-new life boat. In essence, saving the president very nearly caused me to be court marshaled. It wasn't the first time I was put in hack, but it certainly was the weirdest.

That night and the next few days are a blur as I sort of checked out on a bender. I had lost Ragn. I couldn't talk about it, and I couldn't find out why it had happened. The loss and what I had done weighed heavy. It was a massive dent to the heart. Late one night, stumbling outside of a local watering hole, I found a gun in my face. When I heard the demand for money, I openly laughed to near hysteria. It's a wonder the mugger didn't pull the trigger.

I gave him everything until he tried to take my ring. When the police arrived, they said I'd nearly torn his arm off. I really couldn't remember it. I spent the rest of the night in a cell with an open door. They just wanted to keep an eye on me. I had an ice pack on a bump to the head when I checked my messages the next morning. My performance evaluation had been coded top secret. The second notification said the charges against me were deferred until such time that a formal case could be filed. A third separate notification was a promotion leaping me over full commander to the rank of captain and a transfer to Fleet of all things. Captain Ryan.

My head really hurt at this point, but "captain" had a nice ring to it. So, I figured I was either going to be jailed or given a new ship. Welcome to Fleet. Looking down at the Fleet insignia on the message, there was a very hollow sense this should have been Ragn's commission. Somehow, I'd survived—again.

That night, I sat on a high stool nursing a hangover with a bottle of whiskey. Smoke hung low, and I could hear the hum of the machine working on my arm. Looking over my shoulder, I could see a freshly stenciled service number. I had another birthday to keep track of.

There were many whispers in Evac. Most knew I was the only survivor on a mission that wasn't logged and went badly. I suppose it shouldn't have been a surprise that there would be resentment. Perhaps it was a good time to make a change. I'd stumbled into a promotion, but I limped ahead with a pinching sorrow.

I learned that Major Adams was also given a medal and promoted to full colonel. It was far less likely now that I'd be going out to pick him up again.

BUSTED

"CAPTAIN McBAIN, YOU SEEM TO BE
DESTROYING SHIPS FASTER THAN OUR
SHIPYARDS CAN PRODUCE THEM."
—ADMIRAL MIERS

Everyone remained standing, including the court clerk, as the panel of officers sat. "This general court martial is now hereby called to order." Everyone sat except the accused and the court officers. "Captain Mitchell Ryan McBain, you stand before this court charged with willful destruction of government property—namely the loss of the destroyer ESS Adriatic as her captain—disobeying a direct order from your commanding officer, and general dereliction of duty for willfully putting crew and service members under your command in harm's way."

"Will the accused please state your name, rank, service branch, serial number, and the service assignment related to these proceedings and confirm the plea entered one week ago today for each of the charges."

Ryan looked forward and spoke with a dispassionate, even tone. "I am Fleet Captain Mitchell Ryan McBain, service number one seven, one alpha, eight niner, three delta. I was commanding officer of the ESS Adriatic involved in the rescue of the ESS Allentown. I confirm the plea entered earlier on my behalf by counsel of not guilty of all charges."

"Everyone may be seated, and this court martial is now in session."

Ryan sat and gently sighed. His mind drifted back in time to a memory of a disciplinary hearing in his youth. Aunty Belle sat next to him in the lobby of the school office. She was wearing a bright red wool coat that looked more like a shawl. It was secured with a flap that wrapped across and off to the side with oversized black buttons. Narrow at the waist, it flared out and down just above her knees. Of the same length, her dress was a fine black fabric with a pattern of tiny wrens. She wore black tights, and her shoes looked like ones Ryan had drawn once illustrating a colonial Pilgrim dinner. She wore black cotton gloves, and her clutch was a darker red that complimented her coat. She wore a small black hat that was shaped like a beret.

A tuft of hair swept over the boy's blackened eye. He tugged at the white collar of his shirt, bound by a narrow black tie. Belle gently put her hand on Ryan's bouncing knee. "Mitchell Ryan, there's no need to be nervous. You have the right words to say. Focus on those thoughts and be yourself." With that, she smiled and ran the back of her folded hand lightly across his pale cheek.

Events within a matter of weeks had sublimated the original vectors shaping the trajectory of his life. Trouble and tragedy were the constants and catalysts that had directed his path toward the footsteps of this very day.

Ryan remembered later that night overhearing Aunty Belle. She was arguing over video chat with the other aunts. The light from the front room cast down the hallway and through the cracked doorway to the boy's bedroom. Ryan was in the upper bunk, and Hadley lay on his side below. They listened as Belle made the case for both boys to be placed in a special school she felt would understand Ryan's anger. The other sisters were not at all convinced. Aunt Virginia strongly advocated for Ryan to attend a military school to instill a sense of discipline. Ryan remembered the bitter frost in their words. They didn't have the kind of bond with one another that they had once had with their oldest sister, Emmy. When the boys' mother died, the others drifted apart further, and at times it seemed like only the shared burden of raising Emmy's children kept them in contact.

Aunty Belle was the youngest, but Ryan smiled at the ferocity with which she defended him. Of the aunts, she was the only one who shared the same tenderness as his mother.

There was a rustling below as Hadley's foot struck the bottom of Ryan's bunk. "What the hell's wrong with you, Mitch? Because of you, we have to move *again*. It's always you! I liked this school. I have friends here. You ruined it...*loser*. Now I have to leave my friends and go to some loser school because you fight and piss in your bed. Every time we move and just start fitting in, you fuck it up. I *hate* you. I wish you'd been in that car with Mom and Dad."

Hadley kicked Ryan's bunk again. Ryan stared out the window and focused on the lights from a transport streaking high across the sky. He watched as it disappeared from view and felt hollow in its absence. While Hadley sawed logs below, Ryan stared above and out the window for most of the night. The scheduled redeye transports were running on good time that night. Ryan felt a kinship with them. He watched the sky, glanced at the clock, and waited with anticipation for their passing.

Summer started a few weeks later. Ryan was making cookies with Belle when she gave him a squeeze and a quick kiss. Ryan squirmed as if he didn't like it, but his smile betrayed the truth. Belle smiled back at him for a long moment. "Such a fine nephew I have." She spun around and headed toward the refrigerator. "You know, I think we're going to have a great summer. What are you most looking forward to?"

She looked back and saw Ryan's troubled expression, his eyebrows scrunched together. "What's the matter?"

Ryan's head tilted, and he looked down. Quietly he asked, "What happens after summer? Will I be sent off?"

Belle came back to the counter where Ryan was sitting in front of a mixing bowl. She smiled and brushed the hair away from Ryan's eyes. "You heard me talking to your other aunts?"

Ryan nodded. "I'm sorry for being trouble."

Belle put her hand on Ryan's shoulder, and he looked up at her. "Mitchell Ryan, you are not trouble. Everything's going to be OK. Trust me."

"Will the other aunts make you send me to a *disciple* school?"

Belle giggled. "No, not that one either. You're going to attend a school I've researched. When you boys came to me, I became your guardian. The final decision is mine and mine alone."

Ryan smiled a little. "So, maybe it's a good thing I messed up three times."

Belle cocked her head. "Why's that?"

"Because you're the fourth sister, and now we live with you."

Belle squeezed Ryan and shook his shoulder. "Indeed. Everything works out for a reason. Sometimes it's too big for us to see it, but the universe is a miraculous machine. When things are tough, sometimes we just need to have faith and keep moving. Often times, looking back, we see that moments of pain were part of something larger and grander. Failure and struggle are absolute essentials to progress. Always try to remember they're temporary. Face into them bravely, and keep moving. Never stop; keep moving." As she passed by, she swiped some cookie dough from the bowl with her index finger and then touched it to his nose.

Ryan squealed, "Ay!" As he wiped cookie dough from his nose, Belle put her arm back on his shoulder. "I can see how much you've grown in the time you've stayed here. I know it's hard sometimes. I love you, Mitchell Ryan, and I'm proud of you."

Ryan greatly enjoyed the time on Belle's small farm. A painted mare named LaDoña took to him, and they became fast friends. The farm shared a border with national lands, and he would ride the mare around the nearby canyons. Ryan spent many hours puttering around the countryside with LaDoña grazing in trail behind him. Although she was Belle's horse, the mare adopted Ryan as her own. It was a rarity for one of them to be somewhere the other wasn't.

Although he didn't like laying hens that pecked at him or bucket-kicking milk cows, Ryan looked forward to his chores. Taking care of the animals gave him purpose. He even took on Hadley's chores in an attempt to appease his older brother. Since learning of their school transfer, Hadley had stopped speaking to and playing with his younger brother.

Seeing the gap between the boys was more painful for Aunt Belle than she let on. The similar gaps among her sisters were still raw. She was thinking on how to speak of it constructively with Hadley so the brothers could avoid the pain she felt with her sisters. It was on her mind one afternoon as she smiled to

Ryan from atop LaDoña. She headed toward the canyons for an afternoon ride.

Ryan looked out to the horizon a few hours later. He thought out the longest route in his mind. Maybe she had taken a lunch with her. Ryan came through the back door and found Hadley in the kitchen.

"Did Aunty say anything about taking a picnic with her?"

Hadley looked up. "Where? What are you talking about?"

"Aunty left on LaDoña a couple hours ago."

Hadley's shoulders and eyebrows shrugged. "So?"

"So, don't you think that's a long time to be out?" Ryan had to turn sideways to avoid Hadley's shoulder as he passed by.

"I don't know, loser. Maybe she just wants a few minutes alone. Who knows."

Ryan thought for a moment and looked out the kitchen window. Fifteen minutes later, he barged into the front room where Hadley was playing online. "She's late. This isn't normal. I'm going out to look for her."

Hadley raised his ice cream spoon in the air and said, without looking up from his computer, "Suit yourself."

Ryan rode his bicycle around the longest canyon loop. There was no trace of Aunt Belle. Upon his return, he nearly took the back door off its hinges. "Had! Hadley! I can't find her. Something's wrong."

"What? Maybe she took another route. She's probably fine."

"It'll be dark in a couple hours. I'm going back out. I need your help."

Hadley continued playing his game.

"Hadley!"

"What?!"

"Help me find Aunty Belle."

Hadley threw the game controller on the couch and stood. "OK, alright, fine!"

The brothers rode out together on the trail, and it occurred to Ryan that he couldn't remember ever having seen Hadley out on the trails. On their second lap around, Ryan was more attentive to the tracks on the ground. About halfway around, he noted that the tracks appeared less fresh. With Hadley protesting, Ryan doubled back slightly.

"You get much closer to that edge and you're going to fall off."

Ryan ignored his brother and skirted the rock edge, peering over at the canyon floor far below. His eyes lit on a shape that stood out from the pattern of rocks and vegetation. Hadley looked up just as Ryan took off faster down the trail.

"Hey! Where you going? Wait up!"

Hadley caught up to Ryan just after he'd jumped from his bike. Peering over and down, Ryan was mumbling. Before Hadley could ask, Ryan looked over and erupted, "Aunty? Aunty! Can you hear me?"

Ryan turned back toward his brother with his voice quivering, "Nooo." Looking to Hadley, he whispered, "They've fallen."

Hadley saw Ryan's body flutter in short, choppy movements. Stepping nearer, Hadley peered over the edge. There was a shear rock face for at least fifty feet. The grassy slope after was nearly vertical for another five hundred feet and strewn with large boulders further down. Ryan had to point to LaDoña three times before Hadley spotted her.

"Mitch, what do we do?"

As their eyes met, Ryan's body stopped moving. "I'm going down there."

"Mitch, it's too steep. Wait for help. I'll go get help."

Ryan got down on his knees at the edge. He was positioning to ease over on his belly and drop down at a point that cut back deeper into the cliff wall. It was still a solid rock face, but it was less vertical for the first twenty-five feet. Ryan looked back up to his brother. "I can't stay here. I have to go. Get help, Hadley. Go fast; go now!" With that, Ryan disappeared from view.

Hadley rushed over to the side and saw Ryan standing hunched at the bottom of the steep cutout. There was another thirty- or forty-foot drop down a rock face. Ryan looked up at him over his shoulder. "Go, Had! Go quickly!"

Ryan turned to look back down the face and took a few small steps downward. It was too steep, and he lost his footing. He could feel the air whoosh past him as his soles slid in near free fall down the face. Once past the solid rock, his shoes dug into the turf, and he did a couple of summersaults. Ryan managed to contort himself and fall upright.

His feet quickly danced across the ground as if he were running down the slope. Although the friction slowed him slightly, he was still falling out of control. Ryan saw a large boulder just ahead, quickly realizing that he was going to land on it. At the last second, he straightened his body in anticipation of the impact. His speed was so fast that his legs telescoped underneath him, and his knee struck his cheek. Ryan could barely maintain consciousness, and he clung to the rock for a moment. He dug his fingers into the rockface, and he was no longer falling, but there was a piercing pain in his face. After taking a moment to gather his senses, he peered over the boulder, and he could see LaDoña better. His heart jumped when he recognized that most of Aunty's body was under the mare.

He slid on his backside in shorter segments between boulders in the rubble field. Each landing sent a lightning storm of pain through his cheek and head. Slowly, he picked his path and made his way further down. The rocks and debris blocked a clear view until he was nearly on top of them. He crawled the remaining distance and peered over the mare's backside. LaDoña's neck was clearly broken, and half of her skull was grotesquely dented. Looking over further, he could see Aunt Belle. Her lower body was pinned under the horse. She was lying motionless on her back, and there was quite a bit of blood under her head. Her eyes were open, and she wore a peaceful smile. Ryan's eyes swelled with fear. As he came closer, his stirring caused her head to turn slightly toward him.

"Aunty Belle?"

The corner of her mouth raised slightly. Ryan was next to her in an instant, frantically pushing and lifting on the saddle. He heard her whisper and came back close to her head.

"Ryan…brave…be alright." Her hand moved, and Ryan held it gently. Her eyes rolled to his "…keep moving…always…keep…"

"Aunty? Hang on, Hadley's getting help. Aunty? No! Aunty, no, no, no! Please, please don't go. Aunty!"

She remained still, and her gaze centered skyward. Ryan lay on his side in an arc around her. He gently ran his fingers through her bangs and told stories to keep her company while they waited for help. Ryan saw her lips turn blue. It became increasingly harder for him to suppress the truth and continue to speak clearly. When the first responders arrived, they had to pry Ryan off her.

A week later, Ryan found himself on the front pew in a scratchy suit. He could barely look at the large wooden box in front of him. His collar was tight, choking him, and there were so many people there that he didn't know. They all smiled and told Ryan how much he looked like his mother and father. He and Hadley were sandwiched between the other aunts. Ryan glanced at the box and was reasonably certain his aunt really wasn't inside it.

He thought about gathering up the courage to open it, but he couldn't summon his legs to stand. Aunt Virginia stepped in front of him, disrupting the thought. "You boys will be coming back to live with me again. There will be some changes, but it'll all be OK. Mitchell Ryan, you will be attending a new school. The commandant of this military academy is a good friend of mine, and we've spoken at length about you. Through discipline you will find strength, confidence, and leadership. These qualities will temper the fire that burns within you."

"Cadet McBain, you are out of uniform again."

It was hard to breath standing at attention with cracked ribs.

Ryan stared ahead as Group Master Cho paced slowly in front of him. A few older boys exchanged winking glances while standing tall in front of their racks. Ryan could feel the trickle of blood from the corner of his mouth as it crept down his neck.

"Cadet, why is it so hard for you to keep spots off your uniform?"

Ryan stared ahead.

"Have we spoken about this before?"

"Yes, group master."

"I see. So even though you were warned about the state of your dress, you have presented again, soiled."

Ryan stared ahead.

"Cadet, I asked you a question."

"Affirmative, Group Master Cho. I've bled on my uniform."

Group Master Cho raised his palm and waved it side-to-side. "We do not need to know the source of this spill. That is unimportant. What we do need is for you to demonstrate a deeper discipline with regard to your dress. What does the cadet think I should do as a consequence for this repeat infraction?"

"The cadet should have bathroom duty for the week."

The group master paced for a few seconds, then stopped and turned back toward Ryan. Looking closely at him, "You've thought carefully on this?"

Ryan's eyes glanced quickly at the group master. "Sir, yes sir." The commandant stood about five feet in height, and Ryan guessed that he did some limited weight training. Although his stature wasn't particularly menacing, his manner was certainly intimidating. Cho moved in a way that was deliberate, confident, and balanced. He spoke in measured tones with particular emphasis. He had a high forehead with four horizontal wrinkles that ran in parallel from side to side. With barely a dusting of eyebrows, his upper eyelid drooped down slightly from the outside corner. The lower lid was puffy, and there were few wrinkles around the bottom. When he squinted and focused intently, Ryan found it unsettling. It was as if the group master could look deep into another person and verify the truth.

Cho nodded. "I should think it will be two weeks of nightly bathroom cleaning, but additionally," he paused and looked around the barracks, "I believe your fellow group residents could be a resource to help you stay clean in the future, if properly motivated. So, for the next week, you and your squad will meet an hour before reveille for additional physical activity."

Everyone sighed a moment after the door closed behind the group master.

"Nice going, McBain."

"You bleeding everywhere cost me an hour of sleep."

"You're dead. One little accident is all it would take."

All the disparaging comments came from older upperclassmen. Ryan felt no sympathy. They either had a hand in his hazing or turned a blind eye to it. The bullies in this case did not single out Ryan by chance. On the first day of school,

Ryan was exposed to what had become a tradition of surrendering a portion of your ration to the older boys. One of the younger classmates had difficulty keeping up with the near constant physical conditioning. Cadet Kimrey would at times lose consciousness during exercises in what was whitewashed as "napping." Kimrey was a walking skeleton, and Ryan thought he might blow off in a strong gale. Instead of helping him by giving him more food, the older officers were taking it away. Ryan thought poorly of it.

"What did you say?"

Ryan looked down at his food.

"Cadet McButthead or whatever it is, what did you just say?"

"I uh, said that—"

"I can't hear you, little man; speak up when a superior asks you a question."

"I said you should let him eat. He needs the food more than you do."

The table cackled, and Ryan realized his comment was taken the wrong way. Before he could explain, he felt his head slammed forward into his plate. His arms flopped out and behind as he struggled for a moment until the brute released him. He gasped for air, and his eyes opened to a finger in his face and words of warning. That's how the targeting began.

Ryan spent quite a bit of time thinking at night while he was cleaning the bathroom floor with his toothbrush. The attacks weren't just limited to the physical; they included subterfuge. Life for Ryan at the academy became like navigating through a minefield in hell. One night, he was looking at the floor and weeping in near silence. The only sound was the rhythm of the brushing sound. It was past midnight, and everyone else was asleep. The lock on a stall door snapped, and as the door swung open, Ryan jumped nearly a foot. Group Master Cho emerged from the stall.

"Mr. McBain, I see you've mastered the brush."

Ryan watched as he walked over to a basin and washed his hands.

"Do you know how your aunt and I are known to each other?"

Through the reflection in the mirror, Cho saw Ryan shake his head. He turned around, leaned back against the sink, and surveyed the boy down on the tiles. Ryan wasn't sure what to think or say. Cho smiled for the first time in front of Ryan and looked around. "We first met here, actually. Then later in the actual service, we were involved in special assignments together. You'd be amazed at how much a team can do compared to just one man. You'd also be amazed at how a threat to survival and the proper group response can galvanize a loyalty that transcends...well, transcends time altogether. All in good time, I suppose."

The group master threw his crumpled hand towel into the trash and walked toward the open doorway. "Just something to think about, cadet. Carry on."

Ryan thought most of the next day about it. How had Cho gotten into the bathroom? There was a small fold-out window about eight feet high on the wall. Somehow, Cho had scaled the outside wall and entered through the window without making a sound. But deciphering Cho's advice was even more difficult than understanding his stealthy approach.

Group Master Cho looked up from his desk as his attaché opened the door. "Watch leader, what have you to report?"

Ryan looked around the group master's office as he was led inside by the watch leader.

"Sir, Cadet McBain was discovered outside the barracks after curfew by a night sentry. He was found with this." The watch leader held up a can of peaches and set it on the group master's desk. Master Cho sat back in his chair and looked at Ryan.

"Cadet McBain, did you leave your barracks and steal food from the mess?"

Ryan nodded. "I did."

Master Cho perched his elbows on the arms of his chair and brought his fingertips together just in front of his mouth. "Thank you, watch leader. I'll take it from here. You're dismissed."

The door closed, and Ryan continued to look around the office. It looked more like a library, with many dark wood shelves and all manner of very old books. The shelves were at least twenty feet in height, and there was a ladder on a rail that spanned the entire room. A few shelves were faced with glass doors and displayed various swords and pistols. Several very old group pictures hung on the walls, and Ryan recognized two of them. His eyes traversed the scene until he met the piercing stare of Master Cho. Ryan swallowed and looked down.

"I have one more question before I issue your punishment. Can you guess what it is?"

Ryan thought for a moment. "It's either why or how."

One corner of the group master's mouth momentarily tightened in a grimace. "That was two guesses, not one." He rose, straightened his jacket, and clasped his hands behind his back. Walking around his desk, he passed behind Ryan. "Why one would take food is obvious. 'How' is a meaningless mystery, namely because in this case, it would be tightly paired with the word 'almost' in lieu of the word 'successfully.' 'Almost' is a word that languishes through sad stories late at night in a rundown tavern." He walked back around behind his desk and appeared to be looking up at books high on a shelf. He took a breath, and Ryan heard the sigh in his exhale. "Would you like to entertain me with another, more intelligent guess?"

Ryan thought for a moment. "Who?"

The corner of Master Cho's mouth curled upward, and he spun around quickly. He smiled at Ryan, tilted his head, and nodded once.

Ryan looked at him for a moment. "Cadet Kimrey."

Master Cho sat and looked down at papers on his desk. "Your other punishments are suspended. Instead, you will report to me in this office one hour before reveille. You would be wise not to be late. That is all, cadet."

As Ryan turned to leave, Master Cho spoke again. "It's fortunate for the night sentry that your choice of travel between buildings was across the surface over open terrain. Do not make the mistake again."

"Yes, group master."

Ryan's head was spinning as he left. *Did he just tell me not to get caught?*

In the coming years, there would be many more such lessons, and starting the very next day, Ryan began to understand that there was much more at play. He found the group master seated on the floor in a lotus position. Ryan noted his thick black hair cut particularly short in the back. He was dressed in a white robe with a midnight blue belt that matched the trim around the neck. He was meditating in front of a banner. The image on it was a golden fist striking outward, and it was lined on both sides with green laurels.

Without opening his eyes or turning his head, Cho spoke. "Good morning, cadet. During this hour, I will train with you directly. Through this path, you will discover that which currently limits you. If you survive, you will master strength in multiple capacities."

The remainder of the academic year was not pleasant. Cho's regimen in the morning was near torture. Ryan would be assigned a series of exercises. As he completed one, he was to begin the next with haste. The exercises were taxing by themselves, but when performed in close succession, they were excruciating. Parts of Ryan's body burned so much that he thought he might catch fire. Just when he thought the pain was intolerable, Cho would strike him, usually in the core region. "You must strengthen the mind along with the body! Do not let the shock of the blow deter you. Do not let it diminish your focus. Let it pass freely through you. Do not let it stop you."

The summer back together with Hadley was also strange. Ryan found that his older brother's interests and perspective rang hollow. Aunt Virginia noted that Ryan was far more pensive, and she couldn't think of a time the entire summer when he complained about anything. She smiled as she surveyed the shared upstairs bedroom. Hadley's bed was a wrinkle-strewn clumping of blankets and sheets. Ryan's was a properly dressed rack. She nodded to herself; it was as she'd hoped. All the signs were present, and she decided it was time.

She introduced Ryan to the path of her chosen martial art. Hadley found them one night out in the back shop. Virginia was showing Ryan the proper form for a high block. Hadley watched for a moment as their aunt showed Ryan the wrong technique and then the correct one. Hadley couldn't see any difference between them. Ryan performed a second attempt. Hadley's head cocked, and his mind spun when Virginia barked out, "Excellent! Yes, yes that's right. Better."

Hadley watched closely for a moment before he piped up. "Can you teach me too?"

Aunt Virginia stopped and turned to Hadley with a frown. Ryan looked on as Aunt Virginia's filter-less stream of communication shot out and knocked Hadley right over the railing. "Why would I teach you this? You're not a fighter, Hadley." She turned back to Ryan. "No, this would be entirely wasted upon you. We've no time for fun and games. Run along; your brother and I have more work here."

The next schoolyear began for Ryan with an inventory of which older boys were returning. Specifically, Ryan cataloged each that had participated in hazing. Ryan learned how to leave the barracks through the high bathroom window. He would swing his legs straight upward and land cat-like on the tin roof. Along a careful and slow path, he would silently traverse the rooftops. He found a lock on one of the four skylights over the kitchen had been disabled. A special threaded fitting from inside the mount had been removed, and its absence was not visible from the ground. Food was just the beginning.

"Did you get enough?"

A cadet whispered back, "Yeah. Thanks, Ry."

Ryan looked on at seven other cadets quietly snacking in the glow of a small torch. Sitting on the floor of the bathroom in the dead of night, they were cautious with their volume. In a hushed and even tone, one said, "You know, we should figure out how to keep our own food. That's the better path."

The other boys looked at Ryan before Kimrey spoke. "I…I, uh can't stand up to them. They'll pound me if I don't give it up."

Ryan nodded his head. "*They* might, but *he* wouldn't."

"I don't understand. Who are we talking about?"

"As a group they have power. If we single out a few of them, the followers, we might reinforce a more proper ethical heading. One by one, we'll narrow their numbers. As they diminish, we will rise."

"Wh—what did you have in mind?"

Ryan stood at attention just in front of the group master's desk. There was no blood on his uniform. Cho looked out through glass panes into the courtyard as the cadet looked straight ahead. "You've collected three more today. Do you feel that a bit excessive?"

"Group master, I'm unsure of the question."

"You are unsure of the path, or the answer, or both?"

Ryan stood at attention and looked straight ahead.

"Be mindful of the answer. The best actions are the ones that do not gather notice from others. Subtlety and patience are benchmarks of perfection in the art of subterfuge."

Ryan was released from his office without further action. He noted the infirmary as he walked past. One of the three older boys was inside being monitored after taking on a rather large knot to the head. They had all been in a spirited dodgeball competition earlier. The bullies had engaged Ryan's team, but their real objective had been to put the red ball sting on Ryan. It was predictable, and Ryan instructed his team to separate away as he drew the majority of the fire. A burning presence came over Ryan as several red balls volleyed toward him. He caught, selected a return target, led it, and beaned several shots back. All three bullies went down in a matter of two or three seconds. Having gathered too closely together, they collided into each other as they tried to evade Ryan's shots.

In the shuffle, one boy ended up stepping on a loose ball. He fell and struck his head on the floor. The thud made an awful melon noise. As medical aid rushed to the boy, many watched with concern. Veins bulged in Ryan's arm as he continued to glare.

As the year progressed, Ryan became an expert at kidney punches and strikes to the back of the knee. These blows were typically executed while standing in line. Fights ensued, but Ryan was careful to throw no punches in the ensuing melees. Cho's lessons had taught him how to avoid most striking actions and block when necessary. The school had a no punishment policy for a cadet who held his punches while under attack. The remaining bullies learned to avoid standing near Ryan in any line.

Ryan and his group were careful to move in numbers and avoid being caught alone. As they moved through the commons, Ryan would travel lower and just behind the others. He perfected a quick lateral movement and execution of a rabbit punch upon a passing a target.

In time, the bullies were on the defensive and avoiding the entire group. Singled out, the bullies found themselves increasingly troubled by spots on their own uniforms. Their aggressive behavior diminished dramatically. Although the campaign had initially been fueled by survival, Ryan began to follow a greater path. His sacrifice and loyalty for others made him quite popular. The initial midnight snack group had grown, and somewhere along the way, they had developed into something else. They had become a team.

Ryan learned how to move quietly and without detection in the night. This was helpful for reconnaissance as well as procurement. As a kind of calling card for Ryan's "creative sourcing," he fancied taking all lids or caps to any ballpoint pens in the room. Group Master Cho had a particular anxiety about uncapped pens. An open ballpoint was a marking device for pockets and uniforms. The cap theft became such an issue that Cho banned that style of writing device schoolwide in favor of the clicker-type. In response, Ryan began depositing cap-less ballpoint pens at each crime scene.

Years passed, and Ryan became the official squad leader of their barracks. Exposed to multiple martial arts, combat tactics, and general soldiering, he continued to gain strength and confidence through his teens. In addition to lessons in the field, he was learning in the classroom. His favorite area of focus was one of the laboratory sciences. Specifically, he and the chemistry teacher had a penchant for fabricating explosives.

One afternoon, Ryan smiled in the lab and mumbled, "She was right." He chuckled, thinking about what would happen if a student at Hadley's school tried to make explosives. While he was initially convinced this school represented his decent into hell, he was now grateful for it. He bitterly missed Aunt Belle, but in the bigger picture, attending here was the right path.

The Academy had an annual competition between squads. A number of contests measured endurance, teamwork, and skill. The squad with the highest combined score was named Alpha Squad and earned the right to apply for EISO. The letters stood for evasion, infiltration, and secure objective. EISO was a final competition that pitted Alpha Squad against the remainder of the school. The mission objective for Alpha was to secure the historic EISO gold ribbon. The gold ribbon looked more like a small banner, and during the competition, it was guarded night and day in the mess hall. But before Alpha could attempt the ribbon, it would have to traverse over forty miles of rough terrain in the survival sector.

The school had a high desert open range that was used for survival training. After Alpha was deposited in an undisclosed area of the survival sector, the remainder of the school, designated Omega Group, would begin searching. The goal of Omega was to hunt down and tag out all members of Alpha. Omega was afforded the benefits of technology. This included off-road vehicles and drones equipped with infrared and enhanced night vision. Alpha team members were given a compass, a laser tag rifle, two rations, a watch, a survival knife, and a map. In the school's hundred and twenty-seven-year history, Alpha Squad had successfully achieved EISO twice.

A muscular senior stood transfixed, with food piled high on his tray. Now an upperclassman cycling through his last year, Ryan looked through a glass cover sitting on a small high table. The cover looked like something you might put over a cake. Inside, on a small glass pedestal, was a golden banner. The silky sheen of the golden fabric had faded over the years. Fancy script EISO letters were stenciled at the top, and the artifact was about as long as Ryan's forearm. At the bottom, there were two years embroidered in golden thread. The thread on the first date was faded, much like the ribbon itself. The second year was much more recent and stood out in brilliant goldenrod.

Ryan smiled and nodded at a familiar voice over his shoulder. "Don't get too fond of that thing. That's as close as you're ever gonna get." In the preceding days, Ryan and his team had outscored the other barracks and secured their application to EISO. They were this year's Alpha Squad.

As noise from the transport faded into the dark of night, several dark masses converged to a huddle.

"OK, just like we planned it. Double time to the lava caves, and then we split into X-ray, Yankee, and Zulu."

"Wait, Ryan, what's X-ray group?"

"A single operator." Ryan smiled. "Our odds are better with three groups. I'm going to draw many of them away." The squad exchanged looks. "Trust me." Ryan looked to his left, "Jon, I'm advancing you to brigade commander in my absence."

The senior next to Ryan was the largest among them in size and heart. Cadet Jon Kimrey stood nearly six foot five and was a two-hundred-fifty-pound wall of muscle. "All these years," Ryan seized Kimrey's hand and shook it, nodding. "Godspeed, brigade commander."

Everyone looked to Kimrey, who pointed toward the caverns. "Let's get moving."

The group of young men traversed at incredible speed in near complete darkness. Not a word was spoken as their boots clamored down and across the ridges. Ryan was following in the rear until they reached the final ravine, where the lava cave structures began. Yankee and Zulu noted just inside the opening that Ryan was no longer with them.

The teams began a four-day trek through caves and canyons. The operation was a constant cat and mouse with Omega. Ryan hoped both teams would evade long enough for him to get behind the forward area of visibility.

Ryan had stashed several caches of equipment in the field during prior exercises. His first invention was something he called the Christmas Tree. It was a lightweight conical frame that stood six feet in height. There was an upper cone that sat over the lower larger portion, with a slight gap between that allowed Ryan to look out. The first material on the frame was a thin layer of wool. Over the wool was Mylar sheeting. The outside layer was canvas painted with a camouflage scheme. Small juniper branches adorned the exterior.

The device weighed about forty-five pounds and restricted Ryan's full range of movement. Although the burden slowed him, it allowed him to move about in the open without appearing on infrared or enhanced night vision. Ryan made best speed directly over open terrain toward the base, only pausing when he heard drones overhead.

Having run the Omega command room in prior years, Ryan knew they would not be looking for anyone in the open center range. Most of the opposing forces and attention would be devoted to sealing the caverns and canyons. Active teams would be directed into those areas. It was likely that drones and underclassmen would be focused on the open range.

Because of the heat differential, Ryan couldn't move in the dead of night. For this, he had mapped out a series of small caves and shelters along his path. After years of training in the range, he knew the territory like his own back yard—every nook and cranny. At sunset he would "park" the Christmas Tree outside his cover.

Nights on the high desert plateau defined frigid, but even with low temperatures around six degrees Fahrenheit, Ryan couldn't risk an open fire. He had to keep himself awake and moving at night to prevent frostbite or even death by freezing. Ryan shook a chemical pocket warmer that he'd stashed. Placing it against his cheek, he groused at its ineffectiveness. He hugged himself tightly and rocked. He looked skyward at a commercial transport streaking overhead. Trying to combat violent shivers, he imagined the heat and comfort in the cabin streaking far above. Perhaps one of the passengers was en route to a tropical paradise.

His thoughts of burning sand were interrupted by the sound of a drone passing near. Ryan willed the sun to rise. Looking through blurred movement at his watch, his heart sank with the knowledge that first light was still three hours away.

The thought of starting a fire and quitting circled in the shadows just outside the light of his resolve. Ryan focused on thoughts of fire, tremendous burning fires deep within. *Aunty Belle.* Ryan replayed the image of her casket just in front of him. He stoked the thoughts of losing her. He recalled the image of her laying under LaDoña; he recalled his helplessness. He couldn't save her, just like he couldn't save his mother. He wasn't strong enough then. Not like now. Now, chords of fate dangled down from the heavens, swaying just in front of him.

He closed his eyes, breathed in the sharp crisp air, and imagined leaping into the lines. In the cold quiet, eyes of fire opened. The rage within had grown higher and higher over the years. He felt the strength course through him. Ryan burned for the losses. Holding up and flexing a hand, he was surprised at the sensation. No longer numb, he felt actual heat being fueled by his thoughts of the past.

A smile curled on his face at the growing light in the southeastern sky. Ryan estimated the light and heat change to begin the day's trek. Lifting the Christmas Tree, he moved out. He shuffled for hours until his arms and upper torso burned. His thoughts drifted back to the moments in time when Cho would strike him in the burn of fatigue. The legacy of those lessons propelled him. He mumbled aloud, "Keep moving…keep moving…" The anthem powered each step forward, and Ryan made excellent progress in only a few days' time.

As he approached the final five miles, he knew the sensors closer to base were far more accurate. He would only be able to make movements just after sunrise and just before sunset during times of thermal crossover. Ryan's target wasn't the actual base but a river that passed through a canyon in the corner of the range. The river's path went away from the base and then circled back downstream to within a mile of the front gate. They wouldn't be expecting him to come through the front door.

As Ryan reached the canyon edge of the river below, he could see a flag raised on base indicating that Yankee had been captured. A warm smile crept across his face. Zulu was still in the wind. They'd lasted longer than any other group in the forty-seven years since the last ribbon had been captured.

As he slowly descended down to the river, he surveyed the area with caution. He entered a sheltered area where he'd stashed the second secret weapon in his arsenal. The bottom portion was a gray cylindrical watertight container with a larger flange at the top, and it resembled an oversized kitchen garbage can. The top portion was a lid that held a shallow basin on top. Ryan called it the Bucket. He would stand vertically in the bottom portion and pull the cover over his head. The top sat about three inches above the lower section so that

Ryan could peer out. Ryan used a small internal pump to fill the top portion with water. From above, the Bucket would appear to a passing drone as if some kind of ring or hula-hoop was floating down the river. Ryan was betting that automated units would be patrolling the remaining river section.

The danger with the Bucket was that the surface area of water it displaced was very near equal to its overall weight. The river was lower than normal for this time of year, and impacting rocks or the bottom of the river bed could tip the device. And although the level was low, the current was the only thing that prevented the surface from freezing over. The water temperature would only afford him a few moments of exposure before he lost function and risked drowning.

Ryan cast off from between two boulders and nearly capsized immediately. Adrenaline surged through him. He only needed to survive for two miles of river. With a few bumps across the bottom through rapid water, Ryan found himself far downstream of search drone patterns. He cast off the lid and used his arms to paddle toward a large boulder. He pawed at the passing rock, and the Bucket capsized. The frigid water was near paralyzing, but Group Master Cho's lessons helped him survive the strike of cold shock.

Ryan shook almost uncontrollably as he stumbled down the river bank. He was mumbling in near panic, searching for a canister he'd stashed earlier. Unscrewing it with numb arms and striking steel to flint was nearly impossible. It felt like an eternity until the warmth of the fire dispelled the cold. He felt like jumping into the flames and huddled closely to them. Ryan warmed under a Mylar sheet until nightfall.

Traversing across private land, Ryan approached the front gate of the school. Taking in the lit guard station and front fence, he remembered the first day he'd seen it. Back then, he hadn't wanted to enter the gate. Although that sentiment had changed, the desire to be invisible was a constant.

Ryan pulled worker clothing from another buried canister. He defeated the perimeter fencing easily and quickly climbed atop the roof of the motor pool building. He traversed to the mess hall and lifted the skylight. The kitchen staff were startled to see a figure drop from above. Ryan peered out of his hoodie and smiled. The head chef smiled widely and nodded, holding his index finger up over his lips and signaling to his staff.

Ryan reached up on a top shelf and retrieved a decorative canister. As he carefully retrieved the contents, the staff could see it was the EISO banner! Ryan took a small white towel, folded it in half, and draped it over his left arm like a waiter would. In between the folds of the towel, he gently placed the antique gold ribbon. Ryan pulled the hood back over his head and then retrieved a small device from the bottom of the canister. The small green box had two buttons and an LED. He pushed the first button and the LED lit green. He then pushed the second button, which caused the LED to flash red. Simultaneously there was shouting from the mess hall about smoke.

He followed the kitchen staff through the doorway, and in the excitement, Ryan sidled up next to Group Master Cho.

A small smile curled on Cho's lips, and he reached for Ryan's shoulder without looking. As the smiles in their eyes met, Ryan nodded toward the towel on his arm. The group master lifted the fold to discover the EISO golden banner. Ryan stood back, removed his hood, and snapped a salute to the group master.

Over the ruckus, the cadets turned toward deep laughter coming from the commandant. Cho began to clap as he laughed, and there was a collective roar in the hall. Next door, under guard, Jon Kimrey and the rest of Yankee and Zulu groups whooped and hollered in response. Their guards could not stop them from rushing out and next door.

For the past five years, Ryan had been looking in antique stores for an artifact with the same fabric. As it turned out, he had used fabric from the golden shirt off an antique doll to replicate the EISO banner. He'd imbedded a model rocket igniter with a receiver inside the fake. The real EISO banner had been safely tucked away in the kitchen for weeks.

Ryan smiled as he entered the commandant's office. Group Master Cho appeared to be staring up at books behind his desk. Without turning around, he said, "I have one more question. Would you care to guess what it is?"

Ryan nodded and grinned wider. "Who?"

Cho spun around with a raised eyebrow. "That would not address a far more meaningful mystery."

Ryan continued to smile, but he did not offer anything else. Cho clasp his hands behind his back. "There are pictures in here you recognize?"

Ryan nodded and pointed to an old group photo on the wall. "Yeah, there. Your class picture, was it?"

"In any of your many travels through my office, did you ever look closely at it?"

Ryan half squinted, approached, and inspected it.

"Do you recognize your aunt in the photograph?"

"Uh, yeah, there she is in the front with…" Aunt Virginia and the group master were in the center of the photo, smiling widely. Virginia had her arm around him, and both were holding something very small between them. It was gold. Ryan's head snapped toward Cho. "It was you? You guys were the last ones!"

Cho smiled and nodded. "Hard to believe people so very old could have accomplished such a thing. Indeed, there's a very small group that hold the copyright to such meaningful mysteries." Group Master Cho looked down at something Ryan was holding.

"Oh, I have a little something for you."

"A present?" Cho immediately turned into an impatient child and summoned the object. Ryan watched closely as he tore into the paper and opened the box. Cho exclaimed so loudly that his attaché came into the room. He held up a blue glass jar with one hundred ninety-three ballpoint pen lids inside it. Ryan almost thought he could see tears in his eyes as he laughed and embraced the jar.

"I have something for you as well, Cadet McBain. It's a present, but also a request to help me with one final task."

Ryan opened a much smaller package. The box almost appeared to be designed for holding jewelry. Ryan tilted the hinged lid back and discovered the special threaded fitting from the locking mechanism to the kitchen skylight.

"Before you go, perhaps you could assist me in returning this to where it belongs. I suspect it will no longer be needed."

Ryan nodded, and there were tears in his eyes. He clasped both hands together and bowed his head. "Thank you, *Sa Bom Nim* Cho. Thank you for everything."

The master smiled and bowed his head. "You are most welcome. From the forge and the hammer, something new. I remember a certain boy who entered through our gates so many years ago. Angry with his own shadow, he channeled that spirit to fight for others with little voice. Those others became a team, and together you accomplished truly remarkable things. Do not ever forget what has happened here."

Ryan returned to the sweltering heat of the courtroom and resisted the urge to tug at his collar.

Admiral Miers was the command officer in the judge panel. He wore thin-rimmed, circular glasses that strained to wrap around his round head. His short, pudgy fingers sorted paper files and tapped on two electronic tablets in front of him. He dabbed sweat from his forehead before looking up to make first eye contact with Ryan. "Captain McBain, you seem to be destroying ships faster than our shipyards can produce them. What do you say to the charge that you have destroyed a disproportionate number of vessels as compared to your contemporaries?"

"Sir, respectfully, I'd say there were mitigating circumstances."

"And what circumstances would cause you to have a near twelve to one ratio?" The words caused mumbling and restlessness from the gallery.

"I think the answer is probably something closely related to the shit assignments I've carried out."

Aunt Virginia winced slightly from the gallery just behind him. Grimacing, she shook her head and pursed her lips. She was looking directly at the back of Ryan's head.

"Beg your pardon, son; you do realize the gravity of these proceedings?"

"Sir, again, respectfully, most of my contemporaries have not been directed into harm's way as I have, and the others who have are no longer with us. If I were dead, we wouldn't be having this conversation."

"Are you trying to be funny?"

"No, sir. You said I've lost more ships than my contemporaries. I would like to state for the record that most of my contemporaries have not seen the same action as I have. The ones who did weren't able to return to stand in front of you because they, along with their ships, were lost."

Admiral Miers' left cheek tightened, and he leaned forward. He clasped his hands together. "You have a bit of an attitude, don't you? Is it because of your aunt here in the gallery?"

"No, sir. I can feel the heat of her glare on the back of my neck. I suspect your judgment will not be as stern as what she will give me. However, I do not believe I have had preferential treatment because of my name and my aunt. In fact, I believe I was assigned particularly difficult missions because of it, and I would also like to respectfully point out that I appreciate that opportunity to serve. One aspect of serving in Fleet is familiar to me: I bring people back. If you or your men were in harm's way, I'd fly through a maelstrom to get to you too. If that meant the destruction of my ship, I would accept that as a tolerable loss."

Miers looked down at his tablet and mumbled, "Once an Evac, always an Evac. This is exactly why..." He abruptly looked back to Ryan and flashed a polite, taut smile. "And what of the men and women in your Fleet crew that you are responsible for? What about the risk to them when you have chosen to fly through any such maelstrom?"

"The crew under my command have taken the same oath. Each man and woman has reached a deep personal conviction to pursue the interests of our fleet, even if that means risking their lives. The nature of what we do is not—"

"Do not lecture me, young man, about the nature of our business. My interest is in the pattern of behavior you have demonstrated. Have you made smart decisions? Have you weighed all the options and chosen the one best suited for a positive outcome? Or are you reckless and looking for trouble, dragging equipment—and worse, other lives—into the dark haze of your own psyche? You lost your parents at a young age, yes?" Ryan's face clenched, and he looked up to the ceiling. "Captain, yes or no?"

"Affirmative."

"I have a psychological evaluation here," he held up a tablet, "that states you sometimes, I quote, 'exhibit behavior that suggests a disregard for the preservation of your own life.' How would you explain that evaluation to the families of those who are bound to serve under you and your apparent disregard for safety?"

"I understand how my path might appear that way from the outside looking in, but where I've been and what I've done give me a unique perspective. My experience has allowed me to navigate environments with a narrow margin. On occasion, that's meant going places others wrote off as too dangerous in order to save lives." Ryan looked directly to another panel member, General Stanton, who was seated next to Admiral Miers. "Wouldn't you agree, general, that the families of the Allentown personnel would accept that answer?"

The admiral's head quickly snapped toward the general with a cocked head and one raised brow.

The general capped his pen, set it down, and cleared his throat. "If it pleases the admiral, I would request a ten-minute recess."

With growing confusion, the admiral nodded. "Agreed. We'll reconvene at fifteen past the hour."

Ryan turned around to the gallery and looked to his aunt coming forward. "Want to disown me yet?"

"Nonsense, Ryan. You're my nephew. Stand tall. I know you made the right decisions, but don't give the admiral anything that he can wad up and shoot back at you. OK?"

"Yes, ma'am. I care much more about what you think than those blowhards."

"Those blowhards have seen more combat than you, and even if you disagree with their methods, show proper respect for the chain of command."

"Yes, ma'am."

"What's this business about General Stanton?"

Ryan smiled. "As it turns out, apparently the general's son, Lieutenant Gus Stanton, was aboard the Allentown."

Ryan's aunt closed her eyes, smirking and shaking her head. Then she opened her eyes and grabbed onto Ryan's shoulders. "Be respectful and careful in the words you chose. I cannot help you in these matters."

A few minutes later, the panel returned, and they reconvened.

"Please note in the official record that General Stanton will not be joining us for the remainder of the proceedings. He has recused himself in light of a certain potential conflict of interest. The board will continue with the four of us remaining, and I shall become a voting member of this panel."

"Admiral, can I call on General Stanton as a witness?"

"I don't think his testimony bears any relevance to your fitness."

"You asked earlier about the families. Lieutenant Stanton, the general's son, was on the Allentown. As such, the general can testify as to how the families of those who serve with me would perceive that particular psych eval."

The admiral glared over his glasses. "Of course, the family of someone rescued will testify favorably. Let's get back to the facts. You are charged with the unnecessary destruction of the newest destroyer in our fleet, the ESS Adriatic. You were barely out of your shakedown cruise, and your command decisions directly caused her loss. Specifically, did you receive orders to retreat from forces of an unknown and potentially friendly species and instead maneuver into a firing position? Yes or no?"

"Affirmative, but they are known and definitely not friendly."

"Hold on. The incident report here indicates that this ship and species are unknown to humanity. That in mind, how can you possibly support such a statement?"

"I have knowledge that Command didn't."

An awkward silence fell over the room as the two looked at one another for the next ten seconds. The admiral's head nodded quickly a few times, as if it was collecting a head of steam. He held his hand out to the side. "Would you care to enlighten the panel regarding this information?"

Ryan grimaced, swallowed, and raised a glass of water to his lips. "Admiral

Miers, respectfully, I am unable to disclose further details as they have been coded top secret. Doing so could get me court martialed."

Admiral Miers raised his eyebrows, and his cheeks turned crimson. "You're already being court martialed!" The admiral wrenched his hand over his face. "How about this: I'll clear the gallery, and then you can disclose the information. All senior officers on this panel have top secret clearance. But I must warn you, this had better not be some kind of wild goose chase."

Ryan shook his head. "No, sir. That won't be necessary. Clearing the gallery will not change the outcome. I'm not at liberty to share the information with you, even in private."

The admiral shuffled the papers in front of him and realigned the position of a tablet. Looking back up, he flashed a taut smirk and pointed to his rank insignia. "May I direct your attention to this hardware? Very few positions above me would preclude my authority to review whatever information you are referring to. Under whose authority are you acting?"

Ryan felt radiant heat coming off the bench and said quietly, "The directive was from the president."

Another panel member, General Yao, looked over his glasses and pointed a stylus toward Ryan. "Perhaps we don't need this information to determine fitness. Did you fire…what was it?" He shuffled, looking for the exact record. "Forty-two science probes with anti-matter tipped measurement equipment toward the aggressor's ship?"

"Affirmative."

General Yao was looking down and scanning report data from his tablet. "Did you then energize a focused matter field at the confluence of those anti-matter probes, knowing that you would create a massive detonation?"

"Affirmative."

Admiral Miers piped back up. "So, you put the Allentown as well as the Adriatic and their crews at risk?"

"Negative. I advanced to put the Adriatic between the Allentown and the impending blast. In that way, the Allentown would receive shielding from our shadow."

General Yao looked up. "But captain, what of your ship and your crew?"

"We're a bigger ship. I called *crew cover to port*, *brace for impact*, and *prepare to abandon ship*."

The admiral threw his glasses on the desk. "So, you admit you knowingly put your ship into a position where she would be damaged, maybe destroyed, and at least rendered unable to further defend herself?"

"Yes, but I believed the blast would disable or destroy the aggressor's ship."

"How did you know that?"

"Because it was going to be a hell of a blast." There was a chuckle from the gallery. "It was the opinion of my command crew and officers that the blast would be larger than anything we had fired on the aggressor. We honestly couldn't think of how any ship could stand that kind of blast up close. Also, we knew if we didn't take action, the Allentown and her crew were doomed. I want to emphasize that the decision was mine and mine alone."

"Oh, on that we can agree. However, you didn't destroy the aggressor, did you?"

"Negative. The enemy ship retreated to whereabouts unknown. Can I also enter into the record that it provided critical time for my crew to evacuate over to the Allentown, for the Allentown to bring her engines back online, and subsequently for all souls to safely depart the area?"

"Well, I suppose you just did. And as long as we're entering things into the formal record, do you know the disposition of the vessel you were entrusted to command?"

"Admiral?"

"Your ship, son."

"The Adriatic is missing and presumed taken by hostile or unknown forces."

"So, now a potentially malevolent force knows our most cutting-edge technology. Do you think your actions might cost the lives of those who next face this force, seeing as they've got one of our ships to study?"

Ryan stared at the admiral.

"What, no sharp answer to that one?"

"No, sir."

"Very well; I've heard enough. We'll adjourn for thirty minutes, and then I'll render my decision."

The judge panel rose and exited the room. Ryan turned back to his aunt. "Notice he said 'his' decision?"

"Yes. As the ranking officer, I don't think he's going to need the full thirty minutes."

"Not looking good, is it?"

"Afraid not."

"Do you think anyone will hire me with a dishonorable discharge?"

"That's assuming they let you go."

"Uhgh." Ryan closed his eyes momentarily. "Will you come visit me?"

She patted his shoulder. "Remember, there were over five hundred personnel on the Allentown."

"I remember. You remember, but Admiral Miers...I don't think he remembers so much. Is it true he came out of the Powerplant and Engineering Corps?"

"Yes, he's P&E. The first wrench-thrower to make full admiral."

Ryan grimaced. "I'm dead. Once a grease monkey, always a grease monkey. They like ships more than the humans who run them."

The panel reconvened, and once everyone was seated, Admiral Miers called Ryan to stand. "Captain, you claimed earlier that your family name provided no preferential treatment or benefit to you. That doesn't seem entirely accurate."

Ryan looked quickly over his shoulder to his aunt in the gallery. Her eyebrows and shoulders shrugged in parallel.

"I have here an executive order from the EarthGov president herself. It says that you should be pardoned of all charges or punishments with regard to the destruction and subsequent loss of the Destroyer ESS Adriatic while engaged in the heroic rescue of the Frigate Allentown."

Ryan was wide-eyed with a cocked head as he looked at the admiral.

"But before you skip off out of here, I will present my decision on the other matter. For disobeying direct orders to retreat, I am reducing you in rank to commander. Additionally, I'm taking you out of Fleet Command and placing you back into EDF. At least there you will only be wrecking smaller ships. And to that point, I'm transferring you into forces under my command. I will better be able to ensure you have the least amount of responsibility possible for someone of your now reduced rank. As such, you are to become, ironic as it may sound, the chief safety officer for the orbital station Equinox. Remove yourself from my sight before I think of something else to charge you with, or you break something else, or both. Report to the station chief at Equinox, who I believe is your brother. Didn't your brother go to the same university a few years behind the president?" There was a long, uncomfortable pause, and the admiral turned and nodded to the court sergeant.

"Atten-TION!"

All stood as the panel of officers filed out through a doorway behind the bench. Ryan at this point had pursed lips and a face red enough to provide combustion. As his hand came down from his salute, he turned quickly to his aunt behind him.

"I'll kill him. I'm ruined. He doomed my career. He's probably going to demand some kind of acknowledgement and look all hurt when I punch his face."

"Ryan, stop that talk right now. There will be no punching. Whatever he did was only to look after his little brother."

"Little brother; there it is. That's what he'll lecture me on. Always having to look out for, fix for, save his little brother. I would have taken the judgment for stripped flight status and/or the stockade. That I could at least have appealed above the admiral and likely had all charges entirely thrown out. Now, I'm reassigned to fixing door frames, walking commerce patrol, and leaking heads. He's ruined me—completely."

"Now stop it. You still have flight status. Serve out the remainder of this tour, and I'll see what I can do to get you over into Special Ops. At least you've demonstrated a knack for creative thinking, even if it involves blowing things up."

"That's not funny." Aunt Virginia smiled at him, raised one eyebrow, and pressed creases from the front of his jacket. "No really; that's not funny. I do not blow things up. Things blow up around me. There's a difference." Aunt Virginia nodded and smiled. "No really; there's a difference."

"Ryan, dear, my back porch?"

"Oh my god. That was an accident. If the neighbor dog hadn't grabbed the satchel, that never would have happened."

"Honey, you blew off half my house. What kind of gopher were you trying to kill? One living on the other side of the planet?"

"OK, it was a little too much plastic I admit, but I was like thirteen. I swear, you accidentally blow up the neighbor dog and next thing you know you're branded a ship killer."

A chirp on his com device announced a message from his brother.

Hey, Bro—great news. I hear you're going to be stationed under my command here on Equinox. Can't wait.

"Under his command? His? You see this? I'm going to slap that dopey look right off his face."

STATION OF BROTHERLY LOVE

Two groups of strangers formed just outside the entrance in the passageway. They pointed inside, whispered, and shook their heads. There was a louder crash as two teams of 3S officers rapidly converged on the entryway to The Blackhole. "The Hole," as residents called it, was a local pub on Equinox station. Just past the neon entry was a long bar on the left side. Hanging above the bar were a dozen screens piping in sports events from the planet below. On the other side of the walkway running parallel to the bar stood a single long row of high tables and chairs. Just behind those tall tables was a four-foot-high divider that portioned off a second larger room filled with lower table seating and slightly darker, with pendant lights dangling from the ceiling. A miniature stage occupied the wall opposite the bar. The ceiling, as well as the hard, glossy floor, were black. In the very back of the establishment, a third area contained three pool tables, a dartboard, and a bank of slot machines.

Several bystanders were gawking further inside as station police rushed past through the entry. They could see two individuals scuffling in the low light. As the police waded through broken chairs and tipped tables, one of the brawlers

194

tossed the other back onto a pool table. One officer had a stun weapon at the ready when the face of the man on the pool table was bathed in the overhead light. The officer paused. "Commander McBain?"

The sound of the voice caused the other man with cocked fist to turn and look over his shoulder. Another officer recognized the second man. "Station Chief?" Hadley McBain grimaced and lowered his fist. He turned forward again just in time to catch a right hook from Ryan coming up off the pool table. Bodies tussled as the senior 3S officer boomed, "Hey! Knock it off! What's the matter with you two?"

Another officer stepped in between the two tussling brothers as the senior officer yelled again. "Enough! Or I'll restrain you both!" Ryan stumbled back on his haunches and leaned to a stop on the edge of the pool table. Huffing for breath, he bent over, putting his palms on his knees. Hadley switched back into station leader mode and motioned to all of them, "You officers OK? The commander and I here were just having a discussion."

"Discussion? Arguments in my house don't typically lead to broken furniture."

Hadley looked back at the wreckage in the room as the senior officer spoke again. "I'm sorry, sir, but I have to report this."

Hadley nodded. "As you should, officer. You should note exactly what you saw. Commander McBain was stumbling. He's terribly clumsy at times, has been since childhood, and I was trying to help right him. We fumbled through the room until he landed on the pool table there. I think I managed to get him straightened out now though."

Ryan lifted his head. "Yeah, and I happened to notice an awful fly land on Chief Hadley's cheek. He's unaware of his own personal odor, and he attracts the bugs, so I took immediate action to remove the insect. In the process, I made repeated and inadvertent contact with his face. The bug has now been demised to my satisfaction."

Both brothers squinted at each other before looking back and nodding in agreement at 3S.

The senior officer held out both hands, "Wait, this isn't my business, but—"

"Correct, officer. This is not your business."

The senior officer pinched his lips together. "If you brawl or stumble or whatever in this public establishment, it will very quickly become my business. It's time for you both to leave. Right now; let's go."

Ryan took one step and winced at the pain in his leg. Hadley stepped toward him quickly, drawing concern from the officers. He grabbed Ryan, steadying him. He pulled his brother's arm over his shoulder and helped him walk. "Musta been when you were falling, and I tried to help you, but you stumbled over the top of that table."

"Yeah, nice rescue. You know, Had, that's your problem. You don't know the first thing about rescue."

"At least I didn't lose a ship trying to help you."

"Screw you. Zero lives. That's how many I lost, not one. We all came home."

"All but your commission."

Ryan chuckled, "I'll take the lives over my rank any day. Good trade."

As they left the bar, the senior officer assigned a patrol team to escort Ryan first to his quarters and then the chief to his. They hobbled in silence until they reached Ryan's front door. "You got it from here?"

"Yeah. I appreciate the support getting here. But what I really need is support elsewhere. You know, there's plenty of people second guessing everything I do. I don't need my brother to be one of them. I don't need second guessing. I need my brother to have my back."

"What? I always have! I called the damn president for you. Asking for a favor like that can end a career."

Ryan nodded. "You didn't have to do that. There's a process you don't know about that would have taken care of itself. You should have trusted me."

"Didn't matter anyway."

"What?"

"Apparently, Gus Stanton is the president's godson. She'd already drafted the pardon when I called. She was chuckling reading the captain's record from the Allentown. That was the other ship, wasn't it?"

"Yeah, the Allentown was in a bad way. I can imagine the language was colorful."

"Nawh, actually the president was chuckling over something about you. She read aloud remarks about the Adriatic's captain." Hadley looked up remembering. "Something like he was either a goddam madman or a genius or both. He credited the Adriatic's captain for saving their lives when the rest of Fleet was asses and elbows running for home."

Ryan chuckled and nodded his head. "Somethin' like that."

Hadley looked at his brother. "So, why'd you do it?"

"I told you why."

"Bullshit. That may work on everyone else, but I know you. It was something else."

Ryan turned and opened his doorway. "Yeah, whatever you say, Had. Thanks for the support. Goodnight."

As the door closed, Hadley held his arms out. "Seriously?"

Ryan spoke through the door. "Goodnight, Brother."

Hadley moved closer and yelled back, "OK then; good talk. I guess we'll resolve this at a later date."

SAVED TWICE

"He is of the family. I've seen it.
Dvarah showed me and then delivered
him to us. Can you not see that?"
—Mahrno

For many days and nights, Mahrno remained in her room, sequestered in prayer. Softly chanting in the darkened room, she bowed over and over. Her small hands met in prayer at her waist, then opened into a bowl shape as she raised them high in front of her. She looked skyward, asking the divine for guidance, then brought her hands back down clasped in prayer.

The Paavi were similar in appearance to the humans of Earth, but their average size was smaller. Mahrno's thin and kinky hair was dreadlocked into narrow strands that she kept shorter than a foot in length. The black tresses were pulled back and completely wrapped by a straight scarf turban. The simple light brown fabric extended off the back of her head, making it look elongated. The fabric color complemented her dark chocolate skin and nut-brown eyes. Mahrno's face was wide and triangular in shape with high cheekbones. Her nose, flat and wide at the bottom, was accentuated at the bridge with cartilage ridges that looked like rising chevrons. The skin between her nose and top lip was very narrow and extended slightly upward. Like many Paavi, her upper lip was very full and almost puffy. Her jaw was small and held brilliant white teeth. As with most of her species, she had patterned freckles that began on her cheeks and grew quite dense in vertical bands on both sides of her face. The pigments ran down the side of her neck and back. She was wearing a simple dark brown robe she'd woven herself. It wrapped around and fastened with a draw string to the side.

Mahrno continued her movements and chants. She was trying to pull in a vision she'd seen several times in her regenerative cycle. The dream was far more vivid than others, and each time it seemed to extend a little further. Mahrno could feel the gravity of something about to happen. It was about her son, and although she could see the eyes, they weren't familiar. This wasn't one of her existing children; these were the eyes of a new child. The imagery was urgent and nightmarish. After several nights, her training helped garner further clarity on the eyes. She could see them clearly if she focused.

Mahrno was a Paavi faith healer. She had served monastic cycles in the temple of the Goddess and taken the path of a shaman. Without healing or aids, the Paavi typically lived longer lives than humans. The galaxy stereotyped them as fanatical pacifists, but it seldom recognized their culture of science. Few species took note of the fact that the Paavi had advanced their health sciences to a point where it wasn't uncommon for them to reach a lifespan of several hundred years. Mahrno was two hundred and eighty-seven years old, although she didn't look a day over forty.

She had raised several families and enjoyed multiple careers. Her trajectory changed dramatically when she met Gehnchan, who was only a few physical years older. At the time, she was at the apex of dual careers in genetics and surgical science. She was running several departments in the largest specialty hospital on their home planet, Eitchu. Her drive and talent were spotted early on, and she had been offered various positions and studies. Although she made extraordinary contributions to advancing her species' medical sciences, the drive to perfection and inevitable success had pulled her off balance.

Her path was steep, but her will was stronger. Still, somewhere along the climb, she'd lost the love and passion that had originally drawn her to the healing arts. Over the years, her time and her focus had continued to narrow down singularly to her work. As fame and success grew, so did the hole in her life. She felt willingly yet hopelessly trapped inside a windowpane of success. She was passing through the valley of life only to press her face against the glass as so many interests passed by. Her career was a growing machine that, with the passage of time, was only building speed down the tracks.

Then, late one night, something happened. Her head was down on her desk, and in the darkened room, she was trying desperately to capture a moment of peace. From the doorway, she heard a voice ask if she had anything she wished to dispose of. Looking up, she saw a silhouette framed by the lights in the hallway. She asked who it was, and a voice replied that he was simply there to clean things up.

Mahrno motioned for him to enter and pointed at the trash can. As he entered, she yawned and apologized for not sorting out the recycling from the refuse. He got down on his knees and sorted her trash for her. She looked into his eyes as he said, "Sometimes it's important to take the time to sort out what can be kept and what should be let go." She just nodded as he smiled. It was his smile at first that really tasked her thoughts. It radiated bright and warm, but it also gave her a sense of a deep inner peace. She asked around the next day about his identity. Few knew of him, and managers in janitorial services said Gehnchan was very quiet. He was only temporarily working on her floor to cover the shift of an injured coworker.

Thoughts of him invaded her mind throughout the day. She thought again about their encounter and his appearance. She noted he was terribly lean, almost to the point of being malnourished. His forehead was tall, and lines from the corners of his eyes spanned out like many small canyons. There was a peace that shone through his eyes but also an echo of anguish. It was like the weathered eyes of a fisherman who'd just emerged from another hurricane. His upper and lower lips were symmetrical, and when he looked at her, that smile lit the room. As he worked, she'd noticed many callouses on his strong hands. He was light brown in color, and she thought perhaps he was originally from one of the northern continents. He had a subtle scent that she couldn't quite place; it was some kind of wood incense. The dreadlocks of his very short hair pointed in every direction. He was scruffy looking, and it tasked her that she was so attracted to him.

The next night, there was a knock on the door frame. He was there again for her refuse. But this time, he had something wrapped in a thermal blanket.

"What's this?" she asked as he made a place for it on her desk.

"Soup. The body must be nourished so the mind can flourish. This you know as a healer, yes?"

"Oh, well, yes. But you didn't have to buy me soup."

"I did not buy you soup. I made you soup. You looked as though you might need it."

In that moment, she should have been suspicious or irritated or anything other than in love. His words and manner were clumsy but sincere. He resonated care and concern for the surgeon's well-being.

The following nights, they chatted, and she learned that he was in his third consecutive monastic cycle. His chosen path was service. She learned that he was born into an aristocratic class, a rarity amongst a hundred billion Paavi. Their culture had evolved away from such things to embrace simplicity and balance. Most would take a variety of careers in a lifespan. However, his family were multi-generational traders, and commerce was their only focus.

Gehnchan had traveled across more of the galaxy in his first fifty years than most travel in a lifetime. He was exposed to cultures and languages that left him searching. What he sought was not out on the fringes but instead much closer to home. His family was furious to learn of his plan to devote a career cycle to the Goddess. They struck his name from the family book, and all communication with him was severed.

Every night for the next week, Gehnchan brought Mahrno a meal. They spoke of many things, and she felt strangely comfortable with him. It felt as though she'd known him her entire life. The feeling was mutual, and one night, he hesitantly shared something.

"Perhaps the hardest thing for me to reconcile with my family was the false basis for our ties. When the root is corrupt, the plant and the fruit will be tainted. How else would a mother step away from her child? How else would a father take his hand from his son's shoulder? I turned what I felt from my family into an illusion of the love and loyalty I always wanted. But I was the source of the problem, and that is the most difficult thing to absorb."

"Oh, Gehnchan. I'm so sorry. There is a great pain here that I cannot heal."

"You smile."

Mahrno cocked her head.

He smiled back. "You do ease it. Every once in a while, I see your smile. It comes out more often now. When I see it, your true self shines out and eclipses all else."

Mahrno put her hand over his. It was the first time either had made physical contact. He looked at her hand, smiled, raised his head, closed his eyes, and mumbled for a few seconds. When he opened his eyes, she was again cocking her head at him.

"I pray the Goddess may grant us just a little more time together. You should know that I've nearly been fired for spending so much time here with you each night. And I would gladly get fired for such moments."

Mahrno squeezed his hand and smiled at him. "I've come to dread the long hours here. Worse is the sense that there is nothing to go home to. Even though there's little else there, I loathe waking up here. But recently, I've really looked forward to my late nights because of our meetings. That and your cooking." She smiled brightly at him.

"I wanted to tell you that soon I will retire from my last monastic cycle. I will no longer be cleaning this hospital."

"Oh wow. What will you do?"

Gehnchan looked at her for a few seconds and nodded. "I have something to ask you. Will you tell me what future you see for yourself here? Think carefully on this, and do not answer tonight. Sometimes what sparkles is false, and it lures the eye from the path which is truly meaningful."

The next night, Mahrno was exhausted. She hadn't slept. The question had tasked her greatly. She knew he was asking about the future and likely a future together. He was doing it in a way that asked her first about what she wanted. The problem was that she herself didn't know. As such, she was very nervous about their next conversation.

Gehnchan didn't show up that night. The man who had replaced him had no information. Mahrno found the next day that Gehnchan no longer worked for the company. A few calls later, she determined the company record for his address was a general one to the central monastic building in town. A call to them revealed that he had left his order, and his whereabouts were unknown. She was a bubbling cauldron of different emotions and popped up from her seat. She needed out, and she thought fresh air might help.

As she came out of the main door of the hospital, she spotted him on the corner. He was smiling at her and holding what she suspected was soup. As she came closer, he saw she was walking with purpose and shaking her head.

"I want to say and do opposite things to you. Why didn't you tell me you were leaving that night? Why didn't you come back sooner to talk with me? I needed to be in communication with you, and you were gone. I'm so happy to see you. I don't know why I'm so happy to see you. No, I need to see you. I don't know why this is. I want to hug you and greet you loudly here in public. I am also yelling at you in public. I don't want you to go away, but I'm acting crazy."

A crowd was watching her physically and vocally demonstrate emotion in public. This was a great spectacle in Paavi culture. Gehnchan smiled, slightly tilted his head, and listened intently.

"Why are you still smiling at me?"

"You're a beautiful being, and maybe even more so when you're loud and crazy. I have the same feelings for you, and I brought you soup."

"Great, yes, the soup. I'm thankful, but what I really need are answers."

"Answers. Yes, of course. We could talk about answers while we eat our soup."

She smiled at him, thinking how his manner was very sweet and simultaneously irritating.

They moved to a table in a central park across from the hospital. She perched on the bench, clasping her hands and staring at him. He carefully unwrapped the soup container and slowly drew out its contents. Her lips pursed together. "Gehnchan, if you don't stop with the soup and talk to me, I'm going to lose my mind."

He looked up with raised eyebrows. "We should talk before the soup?"

"I don't care about the soup. I need to know your thoughts and what you feel."

He nodded and looked at her carefully. Her lips pursed again, and he spoke. "Did you think about my question?"

"Yes, of course I did. I don't know the answer, and that's upsetting to me."

He nodded again. "You should know that the other night, I asked more from the Goddess than I admitted to you. I asked her for patience and time. I've spent many years learning how to acknowledge and diminish my wants and instead serve those in need. I became rich through service to others. It's an incredible fortune. I was very nervous about this transition time and what I would do next. Then I met you. I do have want for you. I have need for you. The last fifteen years have barely prepared me for this burden, because I can't have what I want most. I can't be with you now."

Mahrno's brows crumpled together, and she leaned forward. "What? What did you just say?"

"You have a path and a journey ahead, and I would be a sparkling thing that would distract you from learning a true and meaningful presence. I've been meditating and praying on this since we last spoke. I have yet to eat since that moment. This path is so far from what I want. Only you have the answers you seek. The path to them is before you. You must join the monastic order. But before you answer, I have a selfish request of you. Perform the ritual of partnership and become my mate just before you go off. When you emerge, I will be waiting. While you are away, I will build you something for our life together."

Mahrno didn't know if she wanted to cheer or strike him. She sat and looked at him closely.

Gehnchan motioned toward the hospital. "What would happen if you walked away from this, all this, right now?"

"Who would do my job?"

"You have trained others, haven't you? They will continue what you have started. They will honor you. You will be free to fly and sing as a bird. The

Goddess is calling to you. Can you not hear her? These talents, your personality, your smile, all things are gifts from her. Only you can free yourself in her hands. Go to her. The balance you seek is there. I am like an old stone in the middle of the trail; when you return, I'll still be sitting here right in the way."

Five years later, Mahrno sat at the same table where Gehnchan had called her to a higher purpose. She watched, hidden under her hood as hospital staff came and went across the street. She didn't recognize anyone. The hospital sat like a monolith beside her, and she could feel the energy of the past surge through it. She tried to sit quietly and be mindful, but her hands fidgeted as she looked over her shoulder. She spun the simple copper wedding band on her wrist.

So many nights, she'd run her fingertips over the inscription. Although she couldn't see the words, she could feel them, and it provided her great comfort. She was beginning to think he had forgotten when he rounded the corner jogging. Other Paavi were giving him side glances over the spectacle when he saw her. She smiled and rose, and he could see the future in her face from a distance.

"Beloved wife," he mumbled as they embraced in public.

She pressed her lips to his ear and whispered hoarsely, "I've so missed you and thought of you. I have so much to talk about but so little time." She started to sob on his shoulder.

"I know. I could see it in your eyes. Are you on the path?" She didn't notice him slip something into her overcoat pocket.

"Yes. I've become so much stronger and so much more fragile. I must continue, but I'm not sure I can survive it."

He looked into her eyes and smiled. "You can endure. You will find what you seek, and I'll be waiting for you. I can see the light of Dvarah from within you."

Her eyes wandered across the features of his face. "I've missed that smile." She was trying to burn his image into her mind.

"Think of it, and it will help you through."

She put her fingertips to his lips, then put a hand over her own mouth as she turned and rushed away. Gehnchan watched her move down and out of sight. As she sat later on the transport, she felt something in her coat pocket. Retrieving the vessel, she saw it was a small, sealed cup of soup. Shifting in her seat, she felt something else and retrieved another copper band. It was an anniversary present, and the inscription read, *"Through the Goddess our bond is eternal."* It was signed *"the old stone."* Her trembling fingertips covered her mouth, and her breath was choppy.

Five years later, Mahrno rounded the corner to see him sitting on the same bench. He looked up as she approached. She wasn't walking straight, and he moved toward her. Her head was spinning so much that she saw a double Gehnchan approaching. She fainted into his arms, and he rushed her into the hospital. As she lay on the gurney, she was smiling widely and whispered something. He leaned down and put his ear to her.

"Saw her, Gehnchan. She spoke to me. It was worth it. I pray…little…more…time…you."

Gehnchan watched as they rushed around her. Dehydrated and emaciated, her final mission to spiritual birth had moved her very close to physical death. Her life was saved by the hospital that had nearly suffocated her.

As she recovered in her room, both were greeted by staff who had learned of their presence. It was a homecoming of sorts for Mahrno, with many prior coworkers who were now important administrators in charge. In each case, they had greeted news of her activities and whereabouts over the prior years with blank stares. After one left, Mahrno looked to Gehnchan and smiled. He tilted his head. "Are you comfortable and OK with these visits?"

Mahrno smiled again. "They do not understand. In my recent work, I've saved countless people, more than I ever did in this place. These are good people, but they cannot hear the call." Gehnchan squeezed her hand, and they looked upon each other.

In addition to Mahrno's visitors, there was a steady stream of Paavi coming to greet Gehnchan. Mahrno was shocked at the sheer number of people who came to visit him. Janitors, cleaners, maintenance workers, all the "invisibles" came. For someone who wasn't well known to managers, he had quietly helped over a hundred people in various ways outside work. The common theme was "he saved me," followed by the description of some physical calamity that had threatened each person's family. In each case, Gehnchan had taken on some task to repair or replace something that put each family back on track.

Both were exhausted by the end of the parade of visitors. Gehnchan was allowed to stay overnight in her room, and both were reading when Gehnchan spoke softly but with measured control of his words. "Tell me of your path."

Mahrno put her book down and took a deep breath. She smiled and reached for his hand. "I have cycled out, and it is time for me to be with my husband."

For the first time she'd ever seen, Gehnchan was having difficulty breathing. He brought his hand to his brow and leaned on her bed.

She rolled over and grabbed his hand. He brought her palm to his cheek and closed his eyes. She whispered, "What shall we do? Where shall we go?"

"I have something to show you tomorrow. I have prepared for many years. If it is not to your approval, we can go a different direction. I only ask that we go together."

She smiled and winked at him.

The next day, Gehnchan led Mahrno to the cargo and logistics section of the city. It was busy and bustling and smelled awful. She forced an approving smile at him as they walked. He sensed her trepidation. "We're almost there." After entering a hangar and rounding a fire door, she saw the freighter.

"I know it isn't much. The first one was awful and a loaner from my cousin. At least someone in my family still remembered me. The next three were also worse than this one, but I survived, and that's all a story for later. This vessel has room for a family. This trade craft is something I know. I can learn to do other things, but this would allow us to have a family sooner."

Mahrno looked at the ship and nodded, trying to take it all in. A mother and child emerged from a second ship in the hangar. Mahrno watched as the child bounced around her mother. Her eyes moved back to the dilapidated ship.

Gehnchan watched her very closely. She glanced at him. "Well, I can't agree without seeing the entire thing."

Gehnchan jumped into motion. "Oh, yes, of course." So began a tour of the entire vessel. While he patiently explained each section and why the ship was favorable, her mind drifted back to the mother and child in the hangar. A few times she sensed that he knew her mind was wandering when he repeated himself. The smell and disrepair of the vessel couldn't dampen her joy for their union or their future.

Their quarters were directly behind the bridge, and Mahrno giggled when Gehnchan folded out their bed the first night.

"Are you nervous?"

"Well, yes, a little. But I was giggling because I think my cot at the convent was slightly larger."

As they were drifting off to sleep, she whispered, "Our first home. Can you imagine the memories we will have here?"

Gehnchan squeezed her, and they drifted off to sleep in the cramped compartment.

They worked together and made many modifications. This included the addition of a medical center. Mahrno installed medical tables that would allow genetic grooming for longevity.

Gehnchan tried to hide his nervousness on the day of their departure. He clapped with excitement when the ship made it into orbit. Mahrno looked at him with alarm. He spoke quickly, "Perfectly safe; all is well."

She stood next to him and put her hand on his shoulder. "Remember our deal, that you will teach me to pilot such a thing."

"Yes, dearest one. You will know that, and the engine functions, and all other things in this endeavor."

While many Paavi pair for some years, it is rare for a pairing to continue for more than a hundred. In the hundred and fifty years since that first ship together, they had happily raised many families. The ships got old and were changed out over time, but their devotion to each other did not depreciate.

Mahrno exited her quarters after many hours of meditation. The eyes of her unknown child plagued her waking thoughts. She knew he was in danger, and there was something she was to do. Traversing forward, she entered the command deck and caught sight of Gehnchan's large belly protruding under a brown stained undershirt. He was noisily chomping on a Bitohng fruit they'd picked up on their last port visit. She was wrapped in a shawl and groused about the temperature being too cold.

Their oldest daughter on board, Ainhow, rose from her science station. "Father, what has happened here? There is so much debris."

Mahrno looked off with wide eyes. "Something dreadful. I fear the dark ones have taken another planet." She looked toward Gehnchan with concern.

He nodded. "This is where Terra should be."

Mahrno's eyes widened. "They've taken an entire people."

Their eldest son aboard, Teinoh, was navigating the ship. "There's much material floating here. Father, is it safe to remain?"

Gehnchan nodded. "Their work of death here is done. They do not linger. What we can salvage here will surely no longer be of use to those lost. It is permitted."

Ainhow piped up, "There's something." Her head cocked, and she focused intently on her screen. "I believe it's a survivor drifting just ahead of us."

Gehnchan shook his head. "Surely not, nothing could survive such—"

Mahrno stood abruptly. "He is there! It is him! The one in my dream." Looking toward Teinoh, she ordered, "Take us to him. Quickly!"

Gehnchan spoke over his shoulder as she headed for the passage. "This is not reasonable."

Mahrno quipped back, "Love is not reasonable, and yet it propels us. This is of my vision, the one I've seen before. Bring him to me, quickly." Mahrno passed through the portal and headed to Medical.

Teinoh glanced at Ainhow and rolled his eyes. Gehnchan grimaced and motioned Teinoh to move the ship toward the life sign.

Ryan was hemorrhaging internally in several places. He had multiple burns, and his arm was nearly severed at the elbow. Mahrno held her palms down, hovering over his torso, trembling slightly. The damage to his body was overwhelming. She closed her eyes, took a deep breath, and whispered quickly, "Most High Dvarah, if this is my son, then come over me. Guide my hands, make me of your purpose, and give me the clear focus of your love."

It had been so many years since her surgical experience, and human physiology was slightly different from that of the Paavi. But her faith dampened voices of despair and doubt. Balance and focus surged through her. She stabilized him, and then, one at a time, she addressed each injury in priority.

After several hours, she had completed the surgeries. She was exhausted and barely able to stand. Ryan lay unconscious but still alive. She pulled the mask from her face and leaned down, kissing his forehead. *"The Goddess showed me a vision, and in it I saw him. The moment I saw them I knew, for in your eyes, my son, it was you. I know not if you'll survive the night. All things are in the hands of the Goddess. Rock gently in her arms. Dear one, if it suits Her, I'll be here when you wake."*

Mahrno wrapped herself in a shawl and sat sipping tea on post by his bedside. The room was low-lit by a lamp on a square console table next to Ryan's bed. Her chair was next to the table, and just above it, a wall-mounted reading light bathed the text in her hand. The material around her shoulders was large and cable knit, with base colors of dark blue and gray. It had been well-loved for many years, and several holes revealed its age. Many empty cups congested the top of the console table and betrayed the number of nights she'd sat with him.

Seven tattered books were stacked upon each other below her seat. Another three texts perched precariously on the edge of the console between teacups. A few were medical journals, but most were texts centered around teachings of the Paavi Path to Light. Compassion, empathy, understanding others, deeper self-awareness, love, and positive action were core tenants of the Path to Light. The Path enlightened all beings to the presence of Dvarah, the goddess who created and nurtured all life. Occasionally, Mahrno would read aloud to the human. Other times, when his sleep was even more restless, she would pray and gently touch his hand or cheek. The words of the Goddess calmed him, but the path to healing was slow and difficult. Her presence was unyielding, and only momentarily would she leave his bedside.

Looking up from her reading, she smiled at the open doorway. "Leishu, come from the hallway."

Leishu was their youngest daughter. She was the equivalent of eight Earth years in age. She peered around the doorway with a cocked head and sheepishly peeked inside with one eye. Her mother smiled back and motioned for her.

"Come, child."

Leishu came into the room and, without hesitation, climbed right onto Mahrno. Her mother quickly tried to accommodate space for the child, who'd grown larger than her lap. Smiling, she wrapped an arm around her to hold her in place. Leishu reached out and gently touched the bridge of her mother's nose. Mahrno leaned forward until her forehead touched the furrow of her daughter's brow. The child giggled.

"Why do you wear such a face?"

"Mommy, why are you in here so much?"

"I am needed here to save him."

"He's big. He smells weird."

"He is from a different planet where they grow larger and eat different food."

"Does other food make you larger? We should get some of that food."

"Do you not like your size? We are the perfect size. It's one of the reasons why we live so long."

"Did his planet get killed?"

Mahrno nodded.

"Did his family get killed?"

Mother nodded again.

Leishu sat for a moment looking at Ryan. "Are we his family now?"

Mahrno looked up and saw Gehnchan standing in the doorway. She kissed Leishu on the forehead. "You are such a blessing; you have the sense of the Goddess." Standing up from her seat with Leishu in her arms, she said, "Go on up to the control deck with your brother and sister so I can speak with your father."

As Leishu passed by her father, he put his hand on her head.

She looked up at him. "He's huge, Father. I like him. Can we keep him?"

After she rounded the corner, Gehnchan motioned toward Ryan. "He's recovering well?"

"Yes, he seems to be through the worst of it now. He needs time to heal."

Gehnchan spoke softly, "Once he recovers, he cannot stay with the family."

Mahrno looked toward him. "He is of the family. I've seen it. Dvarah showed me and then delivered him to us. Can you not see that? How is it reasonable that he would have survived? That we would have found him in the vastness? That he could have survived so many grave injuries?"

Gehnchan took a deep breath. "Dearest one, he lives because of your talent and your care. But his life will bring the dark ones upon our family. They do not leave a single sprout living. They will come for him, and they will destroy the family. This you know. Would you have him bring their wrath upon us?"

Mahrno shook her head. "Which would you rather face, the dark ones or the anger of Dvarah?"

Gehnchan protested. "You've saved him. Now he can go on his way and do what his species does."

Mahrno smiled. "He's not of my womb, but he is ours. Why can you not see the signs? If we abandon him now, he will be as exposed as a mudworm to the birds. They will swoop down on him and tear into him. No, we cannot abandon him. This is not the path laid before us."

"You are the most stubborn being in the galaxy. What would you have us do? He wears the symbols of their military, and his race is so violent."

"Yes, I am stubborn, and the violence of his species is uncontained. Although I healed his body, I fear his soul suffers greatly. Our words and ways will be his tools. Paavi father, it's you now who must show him the gentle path and the path of service. Our love and his will are the tools that can save him...I have foreseen this."

Gehnchan opened his mouth to speak and cocked his head, but no words came out. He closed his mouth and cocked his head in the opposite direction, then opened his mouth again, but still no words came out. Closing his eyes, he took a long, deep breath. "How will you explain a Terran on our vessel? Surely others will find out. Word will spread, and the dark ones will come for him."

"Ah, yes. I've spent time deciphering his genetic code. There are several segments that are unusually complex, out of place, actually, but the majority of the rest of his protein sequencing is very nearly Paavi. I added his sequence into our regenerative tables. I have assembled a modified code sequence that will change his appearance. At least on the exterior, he will appear as we do."

"You put alien code into our regenerative tables? Why would you do this?"

LEISHU'S TEA

"FOR EACH PERSON, THE GODDESS HOLDS
IN THE HAND BEHIND HER BACK WHAT IS
NEEDED."
—LEISHU

Ryan heard his suit monitor chiming rapidly, indicating that he was completely out of oxygen. He gasped for air and woke with a start. His eyes traveled around the room for a few moments before he realized that he was again in a medical bed. Another being in the room was silencing an alarm from what Ryan surmised was a monitor. The scene was all too familiar, save the lack of intubation. He could feel pain from injury, but more pressing was a residue of dread from recent visions. He spoke hoarsely, "It was a nightmare, just a bad dream, right? Where am—"

Hearing him speak caused the other being in the room to spin around quickly. Ryan saw she was Paavi. Before he could think another thought, he recognized the eyes. "You're the one who...oh god. No, no. They destroyed the Earth, my Sun." Ryan tried to sit up. "I have to—uhgh," he winced from his injuries.

She reached out, touched his shoulders, and said something he couldn't understand. Easing him back down in bed, she said softly, "Mahrno." She motioned toward herself. "Mahrno."

Ryan nodded. "I'm Ryan. Commander Mitchell Ryan McBain. I have to find my people. Any survivors, I have to get to them." Ryan winced again as he tried to rise.

Mahrno put her hands gently on him and spoke to him with a cocked head, "Ima ryander?"

Ryan motioned again toward himself. "Ryan. Ryan."

Mahrno looked at him closely, "Rehlan."

"Ryyyan."

She cocked her head, "Reehln."

He smiled and nodded. "Somethin' like that."

Mahrno raised her eyebrows and nodded. Then she spoke to him in Paavi, "Reehln, your Paavi name would be Eylon." She nodded emphatically and gently patted her open palm on his chest repeating, "Eylon."

Ryan repeated the name, and she smiled, nodding her head.

Ryan pointed at her and said, "Margo."

She chuckled and motioned toward herself, "Mahrno."

Ryan's neck snapped like a hawk, looking past Mahrno toward the open portal. Mahrno turned and smiled at the open doorway. "It's OK to come in. Don't be a shadow. Be polite. Come in here."

Leishu sheepishly came around the corner, looking down and embracing a matted stuffed animal. Mahrno reached toward Leishu while opening and closing her hand. She quickly came to her mother's side and buried her head in her robe.

"Can you say your name to Eylon?"

"His name is Eylon too?"

Mahrno titled her head with furrowed brow, "Well, yes. His Paavi name is Eylon."

Leishu looked at Ryan for a moment and then buried her head in her mother's robe again.

Ryan understood completely and smiled at her. "Hello, little girl. My name is Eylon. What's your name?"

Mahrno was squinting as he spoke and repeated his words. "Uhrnahm."

Ryan looked up to her. "Name," he said. He motioned toward himself, "Ryan, Eylon, name."

She motioned toward herself, "Mahrno, nahm." She motioned down to her daughter, "Leishu, nahm."

Ryan raised his eyebrows, "Ah, your name is Layshew. Nice to meet you, Layshew."

Leishu giggled and looked at Ryan. "Eylon, my name is Leishu not Lhaychoe." She said her name again very emphatically, "Leishu. Leishu."

Ryan repeated it until the little girl was somewhat satisfied. Mahrno watched as Leishu taught Ryan the words for hand, eyes, and nose. Surveying the interaction, she was struck with an appreciation for the patience her young daughter had for the stranger. An idea came to her. "You should help Eylon learn our words. Do you think you could teach him to understand us?"

"Yes, Momma, but he won't be pretend anymore."

"What do you mean?"

"Because, Eylon's been my other new friend. Remember, I told you he came out of my dream? I showed you, but you couldn't see him." Leishu looked at Ryan again and cocked her head. "But his face looks strange."

"I remember you saying something now. You had dreams of him too. The Goddess speaks to all of us differently."

Though his language was alien, his eyes were familiar and kind. She was thankful for this and for his health. Mahrno smiled as Ryan watched Leishu's words. So the learning began. At first the words started very small. Slowly, Ryan learned to speak in phrases. Leishu, much to her father's chagrin, started referring to him as "Biggest Brother."

Ryan learned that Paavi also consume tea and that little Paavi girls fancy tea parties. Such was the classroom for his training. The Terran warrior folded his frame into the smallest chair imaginable, and each day he learned the Paavi's peaceful path. Leishu had an innocence that was only rivaled by her brutal honesty. That, along with a sense of surrogate family, was an incredible conduit for Ryan to understand the people and the culture.

He marveled at the Paavi capacity for balance and harmony. All acts were contemplated in accordance with balance. The impact of every motion, movement, and mumbling had to be mapped out. It was a miracle they were ever able to get anything done.

They were incredibly mindful when it came to appreciation. Perhaps it was one of the reasons they seemed so happy. There were more than a thousand different ways to say "thank you" in Paavi.

The meditation was perhaps the most valuable for Ryan. Witnessing the genocide of your species and the murder of your family caused what the Paavi called "critical spiritual disruption." Their culture viewed mental health as equally important as physical health. Ryan's spiritual disruption usually manifested as nightmares. Occasionally, something during the day would trigger post-traumatic stress.

The first time it happened, Ryan was bent down, retrieving a bowl from a storage compartment in an effort to create dinner. The bowl was slightly larger than the galley locker frame. Ryan tried to retrieve it, and it got stuck. The curve of the bowl reminded him of a flight helmet. He had a powerful memory overlap of a time when he had tried to retrieve his helmet from a locker and scramble to his ship. He couldn't get it out, and danger was approaching.

Ryan wrestled and wheezed. Family members took note of the clamor and noises coming from Ryan. Mahrno set down a spoon and moved quickly toward him. All the others also recognized the trouble and converged upon Ryan. In nearly the same moment, Ryan felt ten hands placed on him. His head shot up, and his body tensed. His eyes went wide as he struggled to move free.

The family remained a gentle presence, and Ryan became aware that they were chanting in prayer. Ryan released his fist and tried to breathe. Marhno opened her eyes, smiled, and cocked her head at Ryan. She reached up and put her open palm on Ryan's cheek. His nostrils flared as he drank deep breaths, and he closed his eyes for a few seconds. The chanting reverberated through him. He felt a singular presence with their voices and the touch of family. After a few minutes, he recovered, and after offering him a smile, each family member returned to their earlier tasks.

Ryan's episodes were frequent in those first few weeks, but he found tremendous power and strength in chanting together with the family. It became a family healing ritual with a unique connection at the ending. Ainhow would momentarily place the fingertips of her right hand over the middle of her torso, up to her lips, and then to her forehead before reaching up to place them on Ryan's forehead. Teinoh would stretch on his tip toes and put his forehead directly to Ryan's for a moment and pat the tops of his shoulders. Leishu would pat Ryan's back, while Father would massage the point where Ryan's neck met his shoulder. Mother's customary touchpoint was an open hand on Ryan's cheek. The experience always left a goofy smile on Ryan's face because he couldn't believe how well it worked. A certain balance and peace took fragile hold of his path.

Mahrno provided regular guidance about their matron god. "You understand that all things in this path have been presented to us by the Goddess? We grow from trials and challenge. She only tests each of us within our own capacity. You must be of unimaginable strength for what she has provided you."

Ryan chuckled. "No, I think I was just in the right place at the wrong time."

"That is a curious deflection, don't you think?"

Ryan raised his eyebrows, "I don't know. There's nothing special here. Bad things happen sometimes. Sometimes really bad things happen. Something really bad happened to me. You just have to just, you know, move on. Just keep moving."

Mahrno thought for a moment. "You know, I see the strength that you do not acknowledge. You keep the pain of the bad thing bottled up deep inside. By doing that, you are robbing yourself in so many ways. First, it takes energy to erase something from your thoughts. And you cannot erase what has happened. You can only embrace it and let it go through you. Only when something becomes truly neutral will it no longer carry a charge on your being. You must learn one of our most important rituals. Once a year, we relive the experiences that we cannot contain. Slowly, you too can let the energy from it escape and be free. When you do this, you will have learned something powerful. You will have learned the wisdom of balance. Gehnchan can teach you this ritual."

Ryan nodded, but Mahrno could sense his trepidation. She touched his arm and smiled tenderly at him. "I'm thankful for the challenges in my life. But it's far easier to be thankful after the trial has passed. Our job is to be mindful during the test, remembering that it is not permanent but only a temporary opportunity for gain. The greater the trial, the greater the learning. There is a greatness that lies in wait for you."

She pointed up to a framed portrait of Dvarah. "The Goddess watches over us. She brought you to my arms. For this, I'm thankful." She stood and put her hand on his shoulder as she walked by. Ryan sat speechless for a few moments. A smile crept onto his face as he thought of how Aunt Belle and Mahrno would get along. The thought occurred to him that all the aunts had returned to one another. He bowed his head, and his cheeks tightened as he sat quietly under the Goddess.

One day during tea, Ryan asked Leishu about the same picture on the wall.

"Oh, that's the Goddess, Dvarah. Didn't you learn about her when you were growing up?"

"I didn't have the Goddess Dvarah in my culture."

Leishu scrunched her eyebrows together and poured him tea.

"We did have other gods that looked something like her." Ryan pursed his lips, thinking about the picture of the Hindu goddess Durga that Anshra had framed in her office. Jeeval would have adored this little girl and been so interested in all of this. He remembered returning the picture to Jeeval's home after she was killed. Pari told him how Anshra adored him unconditionally as a kindred warrior. As such, she wanted Ryan to have the picture. Damn if it wasn't in a storage locker off Ceres and now probably destroyed. He returned to the present moment and noticed Leishu studying his face. Redirecting, he commented, "She sure has a lot of arms and hands."

"Of course; she's very busy. She needs all of them to complete her work."

"What are all the things she's holding?"

Leishu diligently described all the objects. Without exception, each tool was something to do with food, clothing, healing, warmth, or other requirements for life and health. Ryan looked closely at the picture.

"She has an arm behind her back. What do you suppose she's holding with it?"

Leishu giggled. "A spoon for eating ice cream, of course!" It turned out the Paavi had an animal that resembled a cross between a pygmy goat and a llama. The milk of it was mixed with some kind of fruit sugar and tasted very similar to ice cream.

"Oh, really? How long has it been since you've had ice cream?"

"Forever! Last time we ported I had some. Momma says if I do well in my studies, I can have an entire container the next time we dock!"

In a short period of time, Ryan had become a necessary and integral part of Leishu's bedtime ritual. One night, as he was saying goodnight to her, she whispered, "It's not a spoon, but it's kind of a secret."

"Are you talking about Dvarah's hand?"

She nodded. "For each person, the Goddess holds in the hand behind her back what is needed."

"Oh, that makes sense."

"Biggest Brother?"

"Yes, Leishu?"

She yawned and closed her eyes, then said softly, "I think it's you in her hand back there."

Ryan felt his heart lurch. He smiled and tucked a loose-knit blanket up to her chin.

TRESPASS

The monster was reaching for Mother.
The eyes of his Terran presence opened
wide.

The family ship had just slowed to sub-light speed to pivot around a dense field of dark matter. The tone and volume in Gehnchan's voice instantly indicated something was terribly wrong. Scurrying through the passage to the command deck, Ryan froze at the sight through the forward portal. A Daerk frigate had jumped in nearly on top of them and was pulling their ship into a docking position.

Ryan held his hand to his chest and panted. They meant to board the Paavi vessel. It had been several months since the attack, but the presence of these monsters had instantly triggered certain images and memories. The horrors of his past hung like wet wool blankets on a pitch-dark path. His mind struggled to paw through them and catch up to the present moment.

He jumped at Mahrno's touch on his shoulder. "Eylon, Dvarah looks upon us. Have comfort in her gaze."

Ryan managed to nod back with a manufactured smile. Equal torrents of hatred and fear coursed through him. If they were to survive, Ryan would have to play the part. There could be no hint of his true feelings, of his true being.

The family gathered in the docking room. Teinoh was rolling a wheel to manually unlock the portal when the Daerk soldier on the other side shoved the portal door back violently. Teinoh tumbled backward and onto the floor.

An armored, black clad monster appeared in the opening. The gawky specter continued to rise, as did Ryan's fear, until it stood nearly eight feet in height. All together revolting and enormous, Ryan guessed the creature was surveying the room with proportionally small and recessed beady eyes. It was difficult to determine the direction of the gaze emanating from its pupil-less, jet-black eyes. Its skin tone overall was black as coal, with a slight tint of bluish purple around the eyes and mouth.

Ryan surmised that the clicking and grunting noises it directed back over its shoulder were an "all clear" signal to others waiting in the airlock. Ryan tried not to stare, but the facial features were dramatic. Many large, boney ridges ran out from a flatter spot in the middle. It looked like a small center plateau, with creases running outward into deeper canyons. The center facial plateau, where a nose should have been, was smooth. There were perhaps a dozen randomly placed, tiny hexagonal holes, presumably through which the troll respired.

The facial tissue did not appear soft like skin; it was rough like porous stone. At the bottom of the oval-shaped face was a small, recessed mouth that hinged downward. A black glossy helmet covered the back portion of the head. Although the head was larger than a human skull, it was grossly and disproportionately smaller than the rest of the creature. A large, symmetrical boney ridge rose off the shoulder blades upward toward the base of the head. It formed a triangular shape that partially protected the back of the neck and the sides of the head. The soldier wore fitted black armor that covered the torso, arms, and legs. It held a staff-like object with what looked like a cross between raptor talons and a grossly elongated, four-fingered hand. Ryan looked closer at the staff and saw that it was hollow and appeared to be some kind of rifle. The feet on the beast resembled those of an earth camel, but the bottom section was an elongated and hardened hornlike material. There was a stench coming from it like a stagnant swamp. Ryan looked down, desperate to put his mind in any other place.

Grunting in its native tongue, the lead soldier used its rifle end to poke and shove Teinoh further across the floor. There was a strange roar of chirps and clicking that Ryan thought must be laughter coming from two more Daerk that crossed through the portal. The first was another armored soldier with a staff. It was followed by a third wearing a leather-like uniform with insignia on the upper arm. Ryan guessed it to be the boarding party's commander.

The leader had no head covering, but the back of it was no more interesting than the back of a helmet. It appeared darker than the face, but it was a thicker, rippled bony material that looked like a cross between a finger nail and hair.

Based upon what he could see and observe of their behavior, Ryan could not determine if these creatures were gender non-specific or if multiple genders were present. It would be some time in the future before Ryan discovered the method of their procreation, and in so doing, revealed the nature of the beings in front of him.

The officer hunched down and looked closely at each Paavi. Ryan tried to look away, but in such close proximity, he could see that the near-black eyes did in fact hold a jet-black crescent pupil. He could see it move and survey him for what seemed an eternity before raising back up to speak in broken Paavi. "What feeble rubbish we net this time? Hoping for things greater sport, something with fight. Instead you small lumps," it said, shoving Ainhow with a long, bony finger.

Looking up and around the room, it continued, "Disgusting ship smell. I cannot breathe it." The creature paused, then looked back toward the captives and said, in a much louder howl, "Paavi worthless! Cowardly. Without honor. Weak."

Ryan noticed that Teinoh and Gehnchan were standing very still with their hands out and palms up. Both were looking down and hunched over submissively. Ryan imitated them, and one of the soldiers noted the mimicry of his movement.

The officer slapped at Gehnchan's hands, "Hmm? Any fight you? Anything? Any feeling? Ghahk! Worthless." It shoved Gehnchan, and he fell down hard to the floor. Ryan winced at the harm to his father. Steel struck flint deep in his human soul. The officer hunched over, yelling down at Father, "Why your species exist?"

It looked back, surveying Mahrno and Ainhow. "I tell why. Paavi exist to serve higher species. We take this one for slave market." It pointed a finger toward Mother! "This one," now gesturing toward Ainhow, "Younger one mine, be personal servant."

Father and Teinoh wept loudly. Older Brother fell to his knees and joined Father, begging the Daerk not to take them. The officer shook its head and snorted.

The words buffeted Ryan's consciousness like choppy whitecaps. While he stood quiet and motionless, a squall of emotion was swirling higher and higher within him. The gentle mindfulness from his Paavi lessons was quickly unraveling from the events unfolding around him. His head rose slowly, but it was the eyes that caught the attention of one of the guards. Wild, urgent, and tactical, Ryan surveyed the room. Before the soldier could voice concern, the other Daerk guard stepped forward and reached for Mahrno.

Time tipped up on edge and momentarily stopped. A cavernous silence hung in the stagnant moment. As the monster reached for Mother, the eyes of a Terran presence opened wide. An explosive thought shot upward like lava from deep within the mantle of his human soul. *Protect!* Ryan snatched the filthy wrist before it could touch her.

All eyes went wide, and everyone in the compartment stood still and stunned. The moment was like an old friend, and Ryan leveraged the seam of shock and fog to draw his pistol. In one liquid movement, he raised, aimed, and popped a single shot point blank into the face of the Daerk soldier.

Already pulling the trigger as the massive body crumpled to the floor, he squeezed off two more rounds into the head of the officer just behind. The remaining guard, who'd earlier noticed Ryan's eyes, was already in motion. Its staff swooshed through the air, striking Ryan. The block broke his hand and sent the pistol flying.

The flashes, pops, and the oppressive smoke hovering in the small compartment horrified the Paavi family. Cowering and groaning at the violence, they slowly recoiled back into one another and huddled low in the center of the room.

The Daerk soldier roared as it swooped into Ryan. Snatching him off his feet, it tossed Ryan ten feet across the room and into a cabinet. The cabinet's contents flew out with a big crash as he ricocheted off and rolled to the floor. The Daerk was on him before he'd come to a stop on the deck. Grabbing Ryan by the collar, the Daerk stooped over, and with lighting speed, struck him in the face many, many times. Each blow felt like purple flashing crows flying out of an exploding red carnation.

Dead lifting the limp body off the floor, the Daerk again hurled the blotto-eyed human like a rag doll across the room. Vaguely aware he was sailing through the air, Ryan tried to raise his arms to protect his head. Landing hard and flat on the deck knocked the wind from him. Time slowed, and through blurred vision, he realized the liquid spattering away from him on the floor was his own blood.

Moaning and rolling slightly, he coughed through the metallic taste in his mouth. Endorphins bathed his brain. He alternately squinted and raised his eyebrows. Frantic to push clear of the concussive haze, he desperately struggled for conscious control.

Although his body was dim and slow, his mind knew that another head shot would render him unconscious to the beating that would surely end his life. The deck plating stretched long away from his cheek. Blood streamed down through his eye. Just in front of him was a heavy cast pan with small metal parts laying in it. The tether of survival woven through his soul jerked tight, and a spark of human rage reanimated him.

"*NO!*" Seizing the heavy pan, he raised, pivoted, and swung upward just as the Daerk jerked him back up off the deck. The pan struck the lower side of the Daerk's head with a loud gong and partially displaced its helmet. The soldier dropped Ryan and stumbled backward. Ryan smashed the beast several times in the head with a force that would kill any normal species.

The Daerk was momentarily stunned by each roundhouse strike, and Ryan found his legs. Adrenaline coursed through his human veins. With lightning speed, he kicked the beast several times, pushing it back, stumbling into the small portal frame of a trash compactor.

Ryan screeched in English, "*I...kill you!*" and jabbed the end of the pan squarely into its face. The bone around the nose holes was fractured inward like a cracked egg, and a dark syrup-like fluid wept from the monster's mouth. The Daerk held the door frame and teetered backward into it. The rage of a billion Terrans surged through Ryan's body. He stepped in with a hitching jump kick to the body.

The final strike loosed the beast, and it fell back into the compactor compartment. As the Daerk was growling and scrambling for its feet, Ryan mashed down on the door mechanism. Warning lights flashed as the heavy doors slowly scissored closed. The flailing Daerk clamored on all fours over debris back toward Ryan and very nearly cleared the opening. Trapped behind the door, it roared and pounded violently.

With a crumpled hand and blood streaked down the side of his face, Ryan staggered toward the controls. A crimson trail followed him to the console. While Ryan pawed and squinted at the screens, the Paavi were focused on the howling beast nearly beating through the heavy compactor door. Ryan decompressed the trash compartment, mumbling, "Should slow you down."

Indeed, the banging was markedly softer but still present. Making a series of other inputs, he directed the walls to a setting associated with a high torque, slow compaction for metal or other reinforced materials. A hum emitted from the hydraulic motors as they forced the walls together. Ryan hobbled over and looked through a small view portal as the beast was crushed into a lifeless mass. A small curl of satisfaction raised on one of his cheeks. Ryan turned back, his smile fading quickly as he met the wide eyes of his horrified Paavi family.

"Oh, Eylon, this...this is not of our path."

Ryan bowed his head. "Yes, Father, but it's the path woven through me. I tried to avoid it, but I cannot deny the way the Goddess made me. Nor can we deny how our paths intersect. Dvarah delivered me unto you. Divine whispers spoke to Mother, and from Her wisdom I was saved. It was She that tapped my shoulder just now and said, '*They shall not take Mother, shall not have Sister!*' I am the instrument in the hand behind Her back." Looking now to the others, Ryan continued. "We're still in grave danger.

Everyone, quickly, to the command deck. Quickly, please."

Ryan wiped blood from his eye and struggled to focus on the console by the portal door. Through the intercom, he transmitted, "Teinoh, when I call to you, you must close the docking portal. You must do it immediately and without question, no matter what. Do you understand, Brother?"

"Yes."

Ryan had two Terran grenades the family had salvaged from a drifting crate just after they rescued him. He took them from his pocket, retrieved his pistol, and opened the docking portal to the Daerk ship. He entered the edge of the docking room. Looking around, he saw two Daerk soldiers approaching from a passage. He quickly programmed the grenades: one to strike on impact and another to stick on impact with a three-second delay.

The Daerk patrol took notice of him and quickly approached. Like a fastball on opening day, he hurled the first grenade at them. Before it could hit, he'd already turned and tossed the second at the portal window adjacent to the docking ring. While Ryan was already in motion back toward the ship portal, the first grenade exploded into the Daerk. Ryan screamed into the coms, "Close the hatch, close the hatch, close it, close it!"

The second grenade exploded and punctured the Daerk hull adjacent to the docking ring. The blast partially collapsed and tore the connector mechanism. There was a rush of air as the compartment decompressed. Ryan struggled against the escaping atmosphere. As the hatch door was swinging closed, he flailed out, kicking at several damaged docking "fingers" holding the ring between ships. He drew his pistol and emptied it into the Daerk control console of the docking ring mechanism. As Ryan slipped back through into the ship at the last moment, the portal sealed, and air stopped moving around him.

Struggling to his feet, he hobbled quickly for the command deck. As he lumbered through the doorway, he barked, "I have the controls. Prepare for immediate departure. It's gonna be rough."

He held his palms out just above the console, exhaled, and slightly closed his eyes. "Dvarah, be my guide. If I am your arrow, send me quick, straight, and true."

His hands lowered down onto the controls as his eyes squinted. Several key inputs brought the engines surging to life, much like her new captain. As Ryan gently dabbed his eye, he was pretty sure he'd been concussed. There was a blurriness in the corner that he couldn't wipe away. The engines, along with his human nature, spooled up quickly.

With the main engines fired, they ripped loose from the damaged docking ring of the Daerk ship. In tandem, Daerk targeting systems were lining up to fire. Ryan engaged positioning thrusters, violently rotating the ship back toward the frigate. Across the normally docile Paavi freighter, items and containers took flight from counters and shelving, crashing through the various compartments. Containers and debris flew in every direction and scatted out into a messy clamor across the entire ship. Everything and everyone was displaced from the movement, save Ryan. Hand on the tiller, the mad captain was firmly in his element.

The ship verbally responded to Ryan's command inputs. "Confirm thrust beyond maximum normal operation?"

Ryan chuckled and responded in English, "You bet your ass!" Then he responded more calmly in his best Paavi, "Maximum thrust authorized, emergency condition, release all safety protocols."

Throttling up, the ship groaned from the stress of the thrust. Ryan whispered in English, "Get in close...out through a blind spot..." This was the first time he'd spoken so much English since being picked up. Hearing the sounds gave him strength. A divot of hopelessness was filled by the return of his human persona. The power of action bumped him into a detent of control. His tenacity grew in parallel with the power cores. Collision alarms sounded on the Paavi ship as Ryan skimmed over the frigate by less than thirty feet. Ryan was wide-eyed and whispering louder, "Atta girl, between the eyes and down the nose!"

Splitting his attention, Ryan rapidly and urgently input commands into the central management system. He reconfigured all energy to propulsion and lowered compression in every compartment save the command deck. "Decks secure, rigged for red!"

Quickly tapping on the console, he implemented formulas he'd jotted down in quiet moments that increased output from the power cores. Mumbling as he worked, "Spooling...power's at one hundred thirty-five percent."

Ryan glanced around as the ship continued to groan from the surge in output and acceleration. Increases in power cores caused heat in the engine compartment, and laundry originally hung out to dry caught fire. Engine room fire alarms chimed on the console. Quick and emotionless keystrokes from Ryan depleted oxygen from the area and starved the fire. Methodically and in mere moments, Ryan had configured the cargo vessel into a military configuration.

"Not bad for a barge...see how far we can get." Traversing off the Daerk stern, they used the engine section of the warship as a buffer screen from enemy fire. With maximum acceleration, the rest of the family slid back into the aft railing of the command deck. Mahrno's eyes were strained watching Ryan. Leishu was praying with her eyes closed, but she was smiling. Gehnchan's attention was split between Leishu and Ryan. Teinoh and Ainhow were wide-eyed and bracing.

Ryan continued aloud in English, "Put'r in the patch...get some distance... fly, fly, com'on baby...go, go, go!" The acceleration was nearly unbearable for the Paavi family. Ryan continued mumbling aloud to himself while rapidly keying the console.

Caught off guard, the officers on the Daerk bridge howled for fire upon the escaping rogue vessel. But Daerk projectile weapons were offensive in nature and not designed to attack from the stern. Officers barked out commands, and the larger ship began to pivot around. A half dozen missiles streamed forward off the warship and crisscrossed in the reverse turn toward the escaping freighter. Events had transpired so quickly that Ryan was able to make a break through an offensive blind spot and enter the edge of the dense field of dark matter.

The family was in a circle on the floor praying. Ryan's voice was piercing, "Ainhow, I need you! To your station, quickly please! Can you give me an overlay of the dark concentrations ahead?"

Oldest Sister pulled herself up to the science station and overlaid sensor readings of dark matter onto the main view screen. Ryan could feel the steady hand of Jeeval's presence settle upon him, and one side of his cheek tightened into a smile. A sharp thought came to him, *"Hard starboard!"* Sure enough, there was a denser field of dark matter in that direction. As Ryan turned into it, he registered a glance of wide eyes from Ainhow and winked back at her. The departure speed, the density of the disruptive patches, and the Daerk frigate's size precluded a direct enemy pursuit. For a moment, Ryan saw the dark matter clumps as asteroids.

Ryan mumbled in English with an Indian accent, "You should being careful in here; these here are not soft." The ship continued to accelerate. His Paavi family prayed as beads of sweat formed and rolled down through the dried blood on Ryan's face. As the ship juked and jived through patches at greater and greater speed, Ainhow turned away from the monitor. Daerk missiles were closing in on them, but one by one they flew into dark matter.

"Get slippery...very slippery..." Ryan split his attention and scrambled with inputs on two consoles as they approached the far edge of the dark matter field. He was calculating a path and preparing to redirect energy to interstellar engines. With the course plotted and loaded, the ship flashed away the moment it was clear.

Ryan took a deep breath, bowed his head, and leaned forward on his good arm. "Straight and true...praise the Goddess. All thanks and praise upon Dvarah." He sensed Gehnchan behind him and turned toward him with a slight smile.

"Eylon, I do not understand. I don't know what to say."

Ryan cocked his head. "Then say nothing, and just be alive here in the present with me, Father."

Gehnchan touched his arm and smiled. Ryan flinched. Gehnchan stared down at the blood. "Eylon, you are injured."

Mahrno jumped into motion and helped him walk back toward the medical station. The further he traveled, the more the pain came upon him. By the time they reached the medical station, he was leaning considerably upon his mother. He winced as he sat down and tried to avoid eye contact.

Mahrno looked over her son's condition with concern and consternation. After completing her medical assessment, she shook her head and tensed her cheek. Speaking softly, she said, "My child, your actions have led to a great many broken things today."

Ryan skulked off to the side. After a moment, he responded quietly, "Perhaps true." He looked up at her through a furrowed brow, "But I still have my mother." His eyes were piercing and wild, just as they had been the day he had come to her.

She smiled tenderly at him, cocked her head, and gently touched his cheek. "You must learn that you will always have this mother, no matter where or even if I am here before you. Nothing can ever remove the energy of me from inside here." She emphatically and tenderly placed her hand over his single human heart. "This is what you must dedicate yourself to learning. Violence is not the true path. Given the choice, Eylon, you are strong enough to follow the light. There is much more in the universe past the animation of our bodies. This is a truth you must embrace."

Ryan smiled and bowed his head. While she was working on him, he recited prayers of thanks. She smiled at him. "What in your prayer is the meaning of *Jeeval*?"

"It's the given name of a being. She was a mentor and a good friend. I'm pretty sure she was back there with us. I could feel her presence, and it gave me great strength."

"This is what I mean by the energy and presence in your heart. She was family to you?"

Ryan nodded. "Chosen family."

"Then you know the ones we love are never truly lost. If you do not fear death or suffering as eternal, it will free you to follow the right path here and now. Embrace this truth, and it will free you." She leaned over and gently kissed the top of his head. "Now be at peace. Heal yourself. Try your best not to break any other things."

He nodded a troubled head and thought to himself, "*I know she speaks the truth. But if my actions were wrong, why was Jeeval there on the other side, lighting my path? And why does the Goddess hold me in the hand behind her back?*"

SLOW MOTION

RYAN WRENCHED HIS LIPS TO THE SIDE
FOR A MOMENT AND THEN RESPONDED,
"APPARENTLY, I'VE ACTED OUT AGAIN AWAY
FROM THE PATH."

Leishu found Ryan in the aft compartment of the engine section. "Good morning, Biggest Brother."

Ryan was sweating and half through his daily calisthenics. He paused and smiled down at her. A cowlick of hair was sticking straight up from the back of her head, and she was still in her baggy, dark blue pajama pants. The large knit fabric was nearly as soft as her constant companion, her bah-bahl. Like human children, Paavi often carried a special blanket. Leishu's fuzzy bah-bahl was dark gray in color. Very well loved, it was almost always a candidate for a "laundry vacation."

"Good morning, Littlest Sister. Surely at this late hour you're eating your second breakfast?"

"Nooo!" she chided back. She watched as Ryan continued again with his strange exercises. "Why are you sweating when your exercises are so slow?"

He smiled. "It's called tai chi. Does moving slowly mean you are not directing energy?"

She shrugged. "Doesn't seem like you are moving that fast. Not like Father when he runs on the moving passage."

Ryan grabbed a towel for his face. "Well, if it's so easy, then maybe you should try it."

Leishu squinted at him and smiled at the challenge. Placing her bowl down next to her bah-bahl on the deck, she stood up in a balanced stance.

Ryan smiled, "Well, I see someone's been paying attention. What forms do you know?"

She made a few movements and looked up expectantly. Ryan was genuinely impressed.

"Littlest Sister, what balance and form! You have a natural ability. Would you like me to show you the proper forms?"

Ryan showed her a few stances and explained how to breathe. She struggled and grunted, trying to maintain balance and form. Both of them giggled. She looked up to him. "This is hard. What's this called again?"

"Tai chi."

She thought for a moment. "Is that the name of the slow-moving person who taught you this or a place where you do slow motion?"

Ryan chuckled. "Neither. This name means something. It's balance and center," Ryan motioned with his hands to his center core, "between heaven and ground, while being relaxed as a tree and," he stepped out and made a form gesture, "while using your hands and mouth in balance."

Leishu watched him as he came back upright, clasped his hands together, closed his eyes, and bowed his head. "You sound like Mother. You sure this isn't Paavi?"

Ryan nodded. "Amazing, isn't it! I mean, how close it is to Paavi? This is from my home world. Do Paavi practice anything like this?"

"The words are similar, but we don't make movements like this. I liked this one, what is it?" Leishu posed in a particular form.

Ryan's eyebrows raised. "It's called repulse uh…" He looked up, searching his mind for the word as his voice trailed off. "This is a word for an animal." For the next few minutes, they searched the archives for any animal that resembled an Earth monkey. Ryan smiled as he looked at the image and read the description. The Paavi primate was called a dinpang. He turned to Littlest

Sister. "The movement is called Repulse Dinpang." This delighted Leishu, who repeated it over and over while skipping away down the corridor. Ryan glanced back at the screen and scrolled through the off-world animal database. His eyes grew wide reading the description of a Daerk panther. He mumbled to himself, "figures."

Later, Mahrno was in her lab area when Leishu came in. "Littlest one, we're going to be docking soon, and I want you to stay on board."

Abandoning her modified tai chi movements, Leishu turned sourly to her mother. "Ah, Momma, but what about ice cream? Can I go with you for an ice cream? Pleeeasse?"

"No. There's no ice cream on this station. We're picking up some essential materials. The next stop after this one will have ice cream. Father will be the only one leaving the ship, OK?"

With her head tipped down and her shoulders hunched over, Leishu formed the top half of the letter "C." She walked away grimacing, heavy stepped as if gravity had increased by a factor of ten. "Alright." As soon as she rounded the corner into the passage, Mahrno smiled at the sounds of her feet skipping away.

After docking and securing the portal ring, Father, Ryan, and Teinoh were in the docking room. Gehnchan looked to Ryan. "Best to stay here. We're on the fringes of Paavi space. While there are many diverse species here, your height might attract attention."

Ryan nodded. "I'll stay here in this room, wait for you, and guard the door. I'll have a com in case you need anything."

Gehnchan nodded and looked to Teinoh. "Monitor our stores to ensure the quantities are accurate. I will transmit when I have purchased, and if they tell me when they start transferring. Keep our systems on line. The station power should be sufficient without starting the engines."

Teinoh nodded. "I'll stay on the control deck while you are away."

Gehnchan looked to both of them. "Be mindful; there are beings here who do not embrace the Goddess. With Her eyes upon us, we shall be quickly on our way."

An hour later, Leishu danced into the docking room. "Hi, Biggest Brother."

Ryan looked up at her. "What are you up to?"

"I'm bored. What does it look like inside the station?"

"I don't know. Probably like all stations look."

She wrinkled her nose at him and tried to look through the small portal window. Ryan grimaced. "Leishu, back out of there. Go on now, and find another place to play. If you prefer, I could call Mother and ask her to put you to work if you are truly bored."

Leishu scowled and turned skipping out of the room. Ryan smiled and shook his head.

A few minutes later, there was a minor alarm broadcast over the audio. Ryan examined it on a console. Before he could voice concern, he heard Teinoh over the intercom, "Mother, I'm showing a power fault in the lab. Are you OK?"

Ryan was mildly concerned at the long pause. He rose to his feet just as she responded, "I've got something all fouled up in here. Something has been configured incorrectly on one of my incubators, and I'm not getting the right environment."

Ryan verified the lock on the main portal door and spoke into the intercom, "Mother, I'm coming to help you."

With two sets of hands, they were able to reconfigure the power distribution for one of the incubation tables. Mother was hopeful that the disruption hadn't destroyed her crop. Ryan returned to his post, thinking about the oddity of the configuration getting so scrambled. His butt had just touched the seat when he bounced back up with wide eyes. Quickly checking, he discovered that the portal was no longer locked. He broadcast into the intercom, "Leishu, where are you? Leishu, please respond."

He paused for a moment and broadcast again. Before he could say anything else, Mother was in the docking room.

Ryan's head snapped toward hers. "Does she know how to operate the incubation tables?"

Mother nodded, wide-eyed. "We've been going through them together, and I've been teaching her recently."

Ryan wrenched his hand down over his forehead and face. He transmitted again, "Teinoh and Ainhow, I think Leishu left the ship. I'm going out after her. Ainhow, can you meet Mother in the docking room?"

In mere moments, Ainhow rushed around the corner. Ryan raised his palms up, "I will find her. Lock this door behind me, and don't let anyone in, no matter the reason." He turned back to Mahrno, "I will find her."

Ryan stepped out and raised the hood on his robe. As Mahrno locked the portal behind him, Ryan raised the transmitter up to his mouth. "Gehnchan, Leishu slipped off the ship. Please continue your work. I will retrieve Littlest Sister."

Ryan scurried through portals and passages. The place was an absolute dump, with refuse and dirt scattered everywhere. Most of the shops on the station looked like they had been abandoned for some time. Several areas posted warnings about structural weaknesses and load bearing limits. Many eyes watched Ryan, and he surmised there was a significant residential presence here. The condition of the station indicated that those dwelling here were probably doing so for desperate reasons.

In his search, Ryan tried to think like a Paavi child. The station had multiple floors stacked upon one another in a circular concourse. There was a central opening from which you could look up and down the decks of the entire station. Four decks below, there were many neon lights and a bustle of activity. Ryan knew instantly that this would draw Leishu's eye. He also knew that red neon lights in a shady space port were meant to attract a type of customer altogether different from a child.

He rushed down several flights of stairs. Coming through the door to the main concourse, he could see many beings on this deck. It was a central connector to other lateral rings. A significant number of people on this deck were also Paavi. Ryan was hopeful that with so many around Leishu would be a little safer. He'd circled the entire deck more than once, peering in the windows and doorways of some of the "establishments." His worry was growing stronger by the moment, when a narrow side service passage caught his eye.

As he approached, he heard the voice of a young child. He quietly moved down the slightly curved path to have a view of the wider area at the end.

He could see three male Behntak gathered around something and caught a glimpse of a smaller silhouette behind them. The Behntak shared a common ancestry with the Paavi, but they were slightly larger. Although their overall population was smaller, they felt it their place to bully and lord over the Paavi.

Gehnchan called on the transmitter, "If Teinoh confirms the transfers are complete, we should be ready to depart. Eylon, where are you? I will come help you search."

Ryan craned his head and spoke quietly into the transmitter, "Head back to the ship, Father. I have eyes on her, and I'll handle this. Will be out of communication for a few minutes; please standby one." With that, he turned the volume off, squinted his eyes, and stepped down the passage.

"Leishu? Is that you, Leishu? You're not bothering these Behntak, are you? Come over here with me."

Ryan saw Leishu between the men. She had some sort of belt around her neck, and her eyes were wide with fear.

"Leishu, can you hear me?"

She turned, and her eyes caught Ryan's. She smiled and wiped away a sniffle with the back of her hand. He could see her face relax.

"And just who are you?" groused one of the Behntak.

"No one of significance. The little one's my sister. She strayed off, and I'll take care to get her back now. Sorry if she was bothering you. Come along, Leishu."

The leader scowled at Ryan. "You'll do no such thing. We found her, and now she's our pet." With that, he kicked Leishu in the butt with the side of his boot.

Ryan barked, "Don't!" He paused for a moment before he began again, speaking more softly. He emphatically and gently nodded his head with each syllable, "Do not do that." Ryan's neck twitched slightly, and he was aware of a certain heat spiking upward within. He continued to walk down the passage toward them, until he was among them at a point where the area widened. Large stacked canisters and debris lined the perimeter. There was a door above a few steps, and Ryan realized they were standing in a storage area directly behind one of the watering holes.

One of the other Behntak piped up, "What kinda Paavi's that?"

The leader spoke back to the side, "Dunno, but he looks like some kind of half-breed." Then, speaking directly to Ryan, he asked, "You some kind of bastard? Your momma get taken by some off-world brute?" They all snickered as one made an obscene pelvic gesture.

Ryan manufactured a smile and held his arms out with palms up in a traditional Paavi pacifist manner. "I mean no trouble. I'm just here for my sister."

"She a half-breed too? Weeyou, your momma's been busy!" All three Behntak laughed.

Largely ignoring their comments, Leishu was staring and grinning directly at Ryan. Without leaving the lead Behntak's eyes, Ryan took note of his mischievous sister. "Leishu, the Goddess looks upon us."

Grinning, she quipped back, "I know."

Before the Behntak could say anything else, she looked to the leader. "Fighting Biggest Brother is not a good idea. Sometimes he acts out away from the path. It's not behavior we should emulate."

Ryan couldn't help but smile.

The leader sneered. "He's gonna act dead if he don't walk away."

Ryan's facial features and tone changed. Fire coursed through him. In a low monotone, he said, "Leishu, close your eyes, please. Keep them shut until I say otherwise."

With a wide smile, Leishu squinted her eyes shut and put her hands over her ears.

The third larger Behntak questioned, "Why's she doin' that?"

Ryan stepped forward with his arms still extended and palms up. He stopped just in front of them and rotated his hands so his palms now faced the Behntak. He turned sideways, pulled one arm back a few inches in front of his face, and lowered into a fighting stance. "You should learn when to go. Last chance."

Ryan guessed that the Behntak leader would strike first. At that point, the second in command would grab Leishu. As the encounter progressed badly for their leader, the third larger Behntak would engage. In that transitory moment,

Ryan knew he'd need to fully incapacitate the leader and quickly disable the second holding Leishu. Speed and ferocity would be determining factors in separating her from the second Behntak.

The leader did not disappoint. He glared as he stepped toward Ryan. With a noise that sounded like a cross between a grunt and a whistle, the leader threw a roundhouse punch to the head. Ryan's left wrist rose up to block. He pivot-stepped into the Behntak with his right foot, while his right hand chopped sharply to the ribs. He then brought his right hand up into an "X," cradling the Behntak's blocked swing.

Raising the block higher, Ryan's fingers dug into the soft tissue of the wrist and spun the arm of the leader up and over. He twisted the arm behind the leader's back past resistance until it cracked. The Behntak whimpered as Ryan kicked down sharply into the back of his knee. As he collapsed forward, Ryan shoved him toward the second Behntak holding Littlest Sister. In response, he let go of Leishu to catch the falling leader.

Ryan saw the glint of a blade as the third Behntak parried. Ryan caught his wrist and twisted his arm. But this one he spun around until the shaft of the sizeable blade buried deeply into the oaf's back. The bigger Behntak went down instantly. Leishu was still standing with her eyes shut to the side. Ryan quickly stepped between her and the second Behntak. The second was struggling to hold up the unconscious leader.

He shuffled to let the leader go and fumbled, fishing something from his pocket. Ryan was faster on the draw. Leishu jumped in response to the single piercing pop and flash. A pistol spilled from the limp hand of the second Behntak, who collapsed over the body of the groaning leader.

With ears ringing, Ryan swept Leishu up, covered her face, and spirited her away. Just outside the passage, he pulled his hood over his head and set the girl down. Grabbing her hand, he nodded. "We'll hustle to our ship!"

Ryan's gait was wide and quick. Leishu was switching between a fast walk and jogging to keep up.

"Are those Behntak going to be OK?"

Without looking back to her he asked, "Were you watching?"

"A little."

He turned and looked down at her. "You sure you're not really from Terra?"

"I don't know."

Ryan shook his head, smiling. Several police personnel rushed past the hooded Paavi and child. The two quickly scurried away from the scene and through a growing crowd. Ryan pushed open the stair doors and entered a climbing well. As the door shut behind them, he brought a small transmitter to his lips, "Walach family, objective achieved, we should be departing immediately."

Mahrno responded first. "Where were you? Have you found her?"

"Leishu is secure with me. Everyone return to the ship, please. We need to go now."

"Is she OK?"

"She's just fine. Teinoh, prepare for immediate departure."

Gehnchan chimed in. "Why do you continue to say this?"

Leishu smirked up at Ryan as they clamored up the stairs. Ryan wrenched his lips to the side for a moment and then responded. "Apparently, I've acted out again away from the path." He looked down to the little girl, "So this should cover tricking me and slipping away without permission from Mother, right?"

Grimacing, "So how many times am I going to hear this?"

"Oh, trust me, you're gonna hear plenty about this."

"Biggest Brother?"

"Yes."

"Were those your slow-motion exercises?"

Frowning, he glanced down at her. "Sort of."

Reaching the top of a flight of stairs, she smiled and said proudly, "So I know slow motion fighting."

Ryan turned back toward her. "Sweet Little Sister, we're both in big trouble. For once in your young life, can you try not to make matters worse?"

They traversed the stair doorway on their docking deck. Both hustled along for a few moments in silence.

"Biggest Brother?"

Ryan replied with a deeper exasperation in his voice. "Yes, Leishu?"

"Did those Behntak die?"

They walked for a few steps. "I don't know. I don't care." He stopped, spun around and bent down in front of her. He hugged her tightly. "Some beings in the galaxy do not embrace the Goddess, and a few of them are very, very bad. I was very afraid those Behntak men were going to hurt you. I won't ever let that happen."

Leishu patted his shoulders. "It's OK, Eylon. We're safe in the hands of the Goddess. Thank you for following Her whispers to find me."

"You're welcome." He stood up and took her hand again. "You should tell Mother you saw nothing. If your eyes were not closed, then you would have seen the arm that is hidden behind the Goddess."

"Is that bad?"

They rounded the corner and could see down the passage to their docking portal. Mahrno was waiting outside. As she caught sight of them, her fingertips came up and covered her mouth.

Ryan looked down. "It is if you want to keep practicing my slow-motion exercises."

She looked up and emphatically winked at him. Mahrno rushed up and swept the little girl off her feet.

"I was so worried. Why would you sneak off like that? Don't ever do that again. Ever, ever, ever!"

"I'm sorry, Momma. I won't."

Ryan smiled as Mahrno kissed the little girl several times and the two held each other close. His eyes continued to scan beyond them, surveying the passage ahead.

Leishu kept her head buried in her mother's clothes as Mahrno looked up, touching Ryan's arm. "Are you well?"

Ryan made small quick nods and flashed a smile. His eyes danced back out, looking around as he motioned toward the portal. "We should go."

Mahrno squinted, inspecting Ryan's face. He tried to hold his best poker face and avoided eye contact. Mahrno frowned. Ryan finally looked at her with wider eyes and pursed lips. He slightly raised his eyebrows, looking up and then back down to her eyes. Her frown softened, and her head tilted. She patted his shoulder as his arm came behind her to usher her into the ship.

TALL LOVE

"Whatever the future holds for you, there is a perfect half in the universe for each being. You've not met her yet. When you do, you will know."

—Gehnchan to Ryan

Five Paavi emerged from their ship's docking room and stood in a pressure lock passage. The berth was one of thousands on a massive commerce station that was located on the fringe of the Dark Horse nebulae. Gehnchan's wrinkled hands secured the keycode lock back into the ship as the rest of the family waited. Mahrno was surveying a list as Teinoh watched his father. Although it was a Paavi station, Ryan was hawkish, surveying the open space ahead.

In the preceding years, Mahrno and the Paavi medical tables had slightly modified his DNA. His facial features had immediately changed to look more like those of his adopted species. Although he was a quick study, adopting the language and the culture took time. With his new identity, he blended and faded into the background.

Over the years, the modifications had even diminished his height. He was no longer the tallest of the five; that title went to the beautiful eighteen-year-old Paavi standing next to him. Leishu had grown over the preceding years into an unusually tall Paavi, and Littlest Sister retained the precociousness of her childhood. With her smarts, Ryan had long suspected that she had hacked her med table to increase her height. Her bright eyes also surveyed the area ahead. But unlike Ryan, who was looking out for everyone, she was looking for a specific someone.

The family had barely entered the facility when a blur came from their flank and in toward Leishu. For the adopted human, every engagement action had a fluid and opposite tactical reaction. Ryan pounced on the aggressor, pinned him to the deck, and held his fist raised when Leishu screamed, "Stop!"

She bowled down into Ryan, knocking him off a Paavi teenage boy on the floor. Ryan watched in shock as Leishu put both her hands on the strange boy's face. "Are you OK? I can't believe it's you! Are you OK? It is you! So sorry, that was just over-protective Biggest Brother. You're here, right here with me. It's really you! Are you OK? Why are you not speaking?"

The boy smiled widely and put his hands over hers. "My words aren't as fast as yours. You're beautiful." Leishu giggled, and the two young ones were completely oblivious to the spectacle the mix-up had created in the station.

Ryan's eyes were wide and his face like stone. Gehnchan chuckled and reached his hand down to help his son up. Ryan looked at his father with furrowed brow and then to Leishu, then back again several times. Ryan released his fist and reached for his father's hand. Mahrno came forward and hugged Ryan just as he stood. She gently propelled him forward. "Eylon, all is well. There is love here."

Ryan looked to Mahrno, and his eyes were windows on his mental struggle to catch up. "Wh—what?"

Mahrno and Gehnchan were now walking on either side of Ryan as Teinoh smiled, trailing just behind. Leishu and the Paavi boy followed several steps back.

Mahrno whispered, "Do not be distressed. For the past few months, Leishu has been corresponding with this boy. He is of good family, and both young ones have performed Baghnvoli."

Ryan's eyebrows twitched as he tried to follow her words. "Bagh...Bagvo?"

"Baghnvoli. This is a preparation and a learning. It involves a sharing of intimate knowledge of one another." Mahrno leaned in closer and said, in a whisper, "This is a path for Paavi to pick a mate."

"A what? A mate!" Ryan leered back over his shoulder. The two doe-eyed teens were smiling at each other several steps back. Looking back to Mahrno, he asked, "Why don't I know of this boy?"

Mahrno squeezed his arm. "Dear one, do not be distressed."

"You keep saying this, but there's this strange guy with my kid sister—"

"He is not strange to Leishu. Baghnvoli is a very private and sensitive matter for Paavi. Many months ago, she shared her thoughts with me. I arranged for access to search for a suitable partner. She followed the path thereafter. We know of the boy and his family."

"I don't understand. This isn't how you met Father."

Gehnchan winked at Mahrno and then smiled up to Ryan. "We're not entirely all that conventional."

"I'm sorry. I'm just having a hard time with this. Why didn't anyone tell me he was gonna be here?"

"We were unsure if his family would be on this station during our travel."

"So, what happens now? Does she go off with him? Is she leaving?"

Mahrno smiled and put her other hand on his arm. "You two are very close. She will never leave you, Eylon. You are Biggest Brother."

Ryan moved his lips for a few seconds before the words could come. "Wh—what does this guy do for a living? Does he know how to take care of himself? And more importantly take care of my sister? I think we need to sit him down and talk about a few things."

Gehnchan chuckled again and gently waved an open palm in front of Ryan. "He is fine. He's a good Paavi. After they completed the ritual, we learned they're a very good match."

Ryan looked back at Teinoh. "You alright with this?"

Teinoh nodded. "This is one of many paths. Each of us embraces what the Goddess provides."

Ryan shook his head. "Wait, Teinoh knew about this? I'm sorry for tackling him, but you know how I am. Why didn't anyone tell me about this boy?"

Mahrno smiled at her son. "We knew you would make many thoughtful inquiries and have a certain thorough depth of study. That would be outside of Baghnvoli tradition and could have created discomfort within the other family. That perhaps could have caused a divergence."

Ryan frowned. "So you're saying there was a concern I'd scare the boy and his family away?"

Gehnchan chuckled again. "We are thankful for your way. Leishu was the most concerned and asked to be the one that shared her news."

Ryan huffed. "Well, that didn't happen. I could have pummeled that kid."

Mahrno squeezed his arm. "You are a very good brother. Leishu is quite fortunate."

"Mother, if I didn't know better, I'd say you were patronizing me."

Gehnchan laughed loudly, and Mahrno stared at him.

Ryan looked up. "Wait, I just thought of something else. What about school? I thought Leishu would be off to school like Ainhow did."

Mahrno nodded. "Ainhow has a different path, and we should be more concerned for her. I fear she takes after her mother, with a singular tight focus. But that is another matter, and the path Leishu follows is different. Remember that Paavi live many more years than what you're accustomed to. She may return to school many times in her life."

Throughout the afternoon, Ryan was unusually quiet and kept an eye on the teens from a distance. Leishu's glow caused a sentimental pang in Ryan's heart. Somehow, she'd grown into a young adult right before his eyes. He could see how happy she was. The reflection of that instantly created joy within Ryan, and it displaced other concerns for the changes ahead. He smiled, watching the frolic of young love.

Late that night, Gehnchan approached Ryan in the ship galley.

"Father, it's late. Did I disturb your regeneration?"

"No. I thought we might have a conversation."

Ryan cocked his head as Gehnchan sat.

"Mahrno and I were talking, and there was a question. On your home planet, do you have something like Baghnvoli?"

Ryan nodded and motioned down to his tablet. "I've been reading up on this ritual. We don't have anything with so many questions and exercises in a formal manner. We do have something called 'dating.' This is where two people spend time together, say a meal or a lunch or some kind of activity. Through many, many of these shared activities, the two people get a sense of their compatibility. Typically, this takes a fair amount of time to determine."

Gehnchan chuckled. "So, for you, Baghnvoli is perhaps too quick?"

Ryan thought for a moment. "No, I don't think the speed of the ritual diminishes it. I'm reading about this, and it is very thorough. I actually can't believe some of the steps." Ryan cocked his head and raised his eyebrows. "It leaves little obscured. The way I learned about what's happened here was quick, but that doesn't diminish what the two have developed. Leishu is a very smart girl." Ryan nodded for a moment. "Adult. She is a very smart young adult. I'm having difficulty seeing her in the present moment without a sense of her skipping through the ship passages carrying her bah-bahl."

Gehnchan smiled, grabbed Ryan's shoulder, and shook it gently. "You would be a good father. Have you thought about finding a man or woman as your partner?"

Ryan's eyes grew wide, and he shook his head. "Father? No, uh, that's uh, that's some job." He raised his eyebrows at his father.

Gehnchan smiled back. "Has there ever been someone for you?"

Ryan nodded. "There have been some women in my life. A couple that I grew close to. They were really good beings, but I just didn't…" Ryan pursed his lips for a moment. "It wasn't right. We weren't right for each other. I think both of them wanted more from me, but I just couldn't give it. I was immature and behaved poorly. It didn't end well, and they honestly deserved better." Ryan looked off. "I hope they found better before our world ended."

Gehnchan thought for a moment and then spoke quietly. "If you could be involved with two women at the same time, then you could certainly handle being a father."

Ryan tossed his head back and laughed. "Father, you misunderstand. I dated two women at different times, not at the same time."

Both laughed loudly. As the compartment grew quiet, Ryan added softly, "And who would pair with me now? I am a rogue Terran and not a very good Paavi."

Gehnchan leaned over and again shook Ryan's shoulder. "You are a good being with honor, and into the arms of our family you were delivered by Dvarah herself. She directly sponsored you, my son. You have survived much because of her divine plan and because you are worthy. Whatever the future holds for you, there is a perfect half in the universe for each being. You've not met her yet. When you do, you will know."

"That's a really nice thought, but the universe is also about patterns. My experience tells me that I shall continue on the same path."

Gehnchan smiled widely. "The longer you live, the more patterns you experience. The outcome of this topic is one that I hope to live long enough to witness." Ryan nodded and smiled as Gehnchan rose, chuckling. "I will retire now. Sleep well, my son."

"I love you, Father."

He turned and winked. "So much love for you, my son." He put his hand over his upper heart. "You bring your mother and I great joy."

Two days later, Ryan was in the middle of his morning calisthenics when he stopped and looked at the doorway. He listened for a moment and looked up. "You gonna come in or take residence out there?"

Leishu bowled around the corner. "What is it with you and Mother?!"

Ryan smiled and blotted the perspiration off his forehead with a towel. "Once, while visiting my Aunt Virginia, we discovered something in her rose garden. You see, on Earth, a rose was a special type of flower that had a great following. There were countless types, and many humans bred them into unique variations. They came in all kinds of colors, and some were quite fragrant. While in my aunt's rose garden, I helped her identify certain variations of roses based on fragrance. She had an electronic sensor that would identify trace chemicals that were attributed to scent variations. Those variations helped her select breeding partners for new hybrids. In a blind test, my nose was able to mimic the sensitivity of the sensor. We learned that I was gifted with an uncommon sense of smell. On my home planet, females typically had a greater affinity to flowers. So much so that it became a custom to give flowers to women. In large part, I suspect it was because genetically, women had a greater sense of smell than males. I too, however, have always liked receiving flowers because of my sense."

Ryan pointed to his nose and then the open door. "The scent of your skin balm reminds me of roses. It came in here before you did."

Leishu smiled and shook her head. "So, you were a weirdo even on your own home planet?"

Ryan smiled and nodded. "You here for some tai chi?"

Leishu looked down. "No."

Ryan cocked his head. "You haven't joined me in some months."

Leishu nodded and continued to look down.

Ryan craned his neck toward her gaze. "What's up? You OK?"

"Are you upset with me?"

"What? No. Why would I be upset?"

"Because I found a match and I didn't tell you."

Ryan nodded. "Well, at first I was hurt that you didn't say anything. But Mother gave me some things to read, and now I understand the sensitivity around it. I'm just so filled with joy for you, Littlest Sister."

Leishu smiled and took a couple of breaths in relief. Before the sentimental moment could languish, she stood on her toes and looked down at Ryan. "Who you callin' little?"

Ryan raised his eyebrows. "Oh, really? You wanna go there?" Leishu giggled and took a fighting stance. Smiling widely, Ryan rushed toward her. Leishu snatched his wrist and twisted Ryan around with it wrenched behind his back. She shoved him gently into the wall. Ryan tapped the wall with his free hand. "OK, OK; well played. Never should have taught you this stuff."

Leishu laughed. She'd seen him in real motion, and his defeat was far too easy. Ryan turned around, observing, "I guess I don't have to worry about how you'll protect yourself. So, have you told this new man in your life that you know how to fight?"

Leishu nodded and said quietly, "I did. He said my height and my capacity for violence could be overlooked."

They looked at each other for a few moments before Ryan spoke. "Don't ever be ashamed of who you are. You're perfect. Don't let anyone ever tell you different." He emphatically winked at her, just as she had used to do to him in her childhood.

Leishu smiled and nodded. "Then everything between us is OK?"

Ryan nodded. "Yep. So, when's the big date?"

"We're planning to do it on the first day of the third calendar segment."

Ryan looked up, calculating. "That's what, twelve weeks from now?"

Leishu's eyes grew wide. "Yep. I'm nervous. What should I do? What should I be thinking?"

Ryan smiled. "I have no experience in this area. I would say that you should just be yourself and listen to the whispers of Dvarah."

"We're going to perform the ceremony at his family's traditional residence in Lahmaard. That's where we'll live in our beginning." Leishu looked up and around the compartment. "I've spent my entire life on this ship in deep space. It will be very different to reside on a planet. Would you come to such a place to visit me?"

He smiled. Lahmaard had once shared the same galactic neighborhood with Earth. The family had just come from Lahmaard when they first found Ryan. He nodded. "It's alright. That wouldn't stop me from seeing my tallest sister. I will."

Ryan buried himself in reading about the ceremony. He would frequently quote aloud at the balance demonstrated by some portion of the ritual or exclaim at the beauty of the spoken segments. "Who created this thing; it's awesome!" The Paavi were generally a very subdued people, but the family enjoyed Ryan's spontaneous outbursts.

While Ryan was seated in the galley, Teinoh put his hand on Ryan's shoulder. "I'm thankful for my biggest brother's revelations. You demonstrate perfect joy, like that of a child seeing something for the first time. I grew up knowing our traditions, and sometimes it's easy to forget the beauty. Your discovery reminds me."

Before Ryan could react, Mahrno swooped in. "How could a mother be so lucky to have wonderful sons such as you two? The Goddess has truly blessed me."

Ryan looked up at both of them and held up the tablet he was reading from. "I'm so excited for this; I can barely stand the wait. All the segments of the ceremony, not to mention meeting the rest of our family. Will they think me coarse? I'm nervous about my parts in the ritual. I don't want to mess up Littlest Sister's special day."

Mahrno smiled. "You'll do just fine, and the family knows of you, Eylon. I have written them. They're equally excited to see you."

Ryan cocked his head. "Who did you write to?"

"All of them. I write to all my children."

TRAVEL TO PAIR

"I HAVE TO GO. I LOVE YOU, OLDEST
SISTER, SO MUCH. YOU ARE A BEAUTIFUL
BEING. HAVE A LONG AND LOVING LIFE
UNDER DVARAH'S GAZE."
—RYAN TO AINHOW

The transition to Lahmaard was a nine-week voyage from their present location. As was customary for a journey of this length, most of the family would go into suspended animation and rotate shifts, with one person watching over the ship. The only exception on this trip was Leishu and Mahrno. Both scheduled their wake time to overlap for a few days so they could work on wedding preparations.

After Mahrno woke Ryan for his shift, she showed him a picture of Leishu modeling the dress she would wear for the ritual. The white material was silk-like and the sheen made it appear nearly depthless. The sleeves were tight fitting around the shoulders, but widened at the elbows in such a way that the cuffs fluted out dramatically. The collar was bunched in such a way that it looked like rolling silk waves plunging down both front and back. The waist was narrow and hugged down to the knees, at which point it fluted wide to the ground. A wide white sash wrapped her midriff with blue inscriptions of traditional Paavi prayers to Dvarah. The final accessory was a beaded headband that crossed her forehead and dipped down in a "v" just above the bridge in her nose. Small brilliant orange and blue beads formed a continuous chevron pattern. Ryan gasped and cocked his head. She looked so beautiful and happy that he had to pretend something was in his eye.

Mahrno knew the mannerisms of her human son. She hugged him, and their laughter was fueled with joy. A week earlier, Leishu had suspended into sleep. Ryan smiled down through the glass at her peaceful face. He was so excited for the coming events that his weeklong shift was difficult to navigate alone. Several times a day, he would pass by sleeping family members and smile as he watched over them. Ryan recorded several messages for each family member, and each subsequent recording was filled with greater enthusiasm.

Ryan's childlike exuberance filled his mother's heart with delight. She had dozens of messages full of questions, reminders, and revelations before his shift was done. However, as a long shadow drew near, the messages would forever remain unopened.

Ryan woke Teinoh to take the next shift. Oldest Brother had his legs over the side of the medical table and was hunched over looking at the floor. Ryan was standing propped against the end of the table. "Look at this picture. Isn't she just beautiful? She's all grown up. Teinoh, how'd this happen so fast? And now she's getting married. This is really going to be something. Hey, are you OK? Am I talking too much?"

Teinoh was still looking at the ground, and he waved a hand in the air. "Nawh, just didn't set into hibernation very well. I just need a minute or two."

Ryan brought him water laced with electrolytes. A few hours later, Teinoh was wrapped in a blanket slumped over at the navigation station.

"Oldest Brother, you don't look well. Do you want me to stay awake with you on this shift?"

Teinoh thought about being trapped with an excited human for a week. "I'm OK, Eylon. I'm sure I'll be just fine in a couple hours. You should go ahead and suspend yourself."

Ryan stood in pajama bottoms, leaning over the medical table interface. After loading the program, he looked up at Teinoh. "You sure you don't want me to stay with you?"

Teinoh nodded and half-heartedly waved a hand in the air. "I'm alright—feeling better already. It'll be easier for you. Just think, when you wake, we'll be orbiting Lahmaard, and the ceremony will be just hours away."

Ryan smiled, put both palms together, and bowed his head. After climbing into the enclosure, he looked over at Leishu sleeping next door. "Love you, Littlest Sister." He looked over at Gehnchan and Mahrno, who were sleeping together on a larger table. They were in a gentle embrace. "Love you, Mother and Father." Then, looking back to Teinoh, he said "Love you, Oldest Brother. See you in a few weeks."

Teinoh nodded as the cover slid shut over Ryan.

The smile was still on Ryan's sleeping face when the Paavi ship appeared on the scope of a Daerk patrol. About ten years ago, this particular Daerk ship had undergone certain repairs completed around a docking collar. She'd spent the better of part of the past decade raking all the nearby systems looking for reprisal and redemption. There was a shrill roar of excitement on the Daerk bridge when a positive identification was made of the Paavi freighter. A flurry and fervor ensued on every deck as all hands readied for battle. When the Daerk captain entered the command deck, powerplant, weapons, and engines were at the ready.

Back on the Walach bridge, Teinoh was slumped over in Father's chair. Earlier, he'd taken medication for his pounding head, and he missed the initial alert tones from the fast- approaching Daerk. The navigation system buzzed and chirped at their approach to a massive red giant, Diphda. The Paavi ship was to sling around it and into the final course leg straight on to Lahmaard. Teinoh rubbed his eyes and stared at the other information on the screen. Daerk were on a pursuit course and nearly on top of them. They would intercept just prior to the gravity sling off the red giant.

Teinoh worked feverishly to replot a path around the other side of the star. He increased speed to beat the Daerk into Diphda's gravity. Outgunned and outpaced, they were no match for the frigate. The dark minions responded with increased speed. Teinoh scrambled to start the process to revive Ryan. The Paavi freighter had fallen inside the jaws of death.

Ryan was having a nightmare about the Khrylic attack. The peaceful path and time since had broken the frequency of the recurring night terrors, but from time to time in a hibernated state, he would suffer a return. There were flashes and alarms sounding. A choking smoke made it difficult to breathe. Teinoh shook Ryan, and he struggled to understand his words. Ryan was caught on the oddity of his Paavi brother being in his dream when the ship lurched from Daerk fire. Ryan realized he was bracing on his medical table as Teinoh rose back to his feet. Reality came over him like a bucket of ice water.

There was terror in the elder brother's eyes. "Help me, Ryan! Daerk are nearly upon us! They're firing! I've taken us down lower toward Diphda."

Ryan scrambled for the helm. "We need to get lower."

"Can we survive it?"

"I'll cozy with a red giant any day over a Daerk frigate."

The ship pitched violently as a Daerk torpedo landed on the starboard rear propulsion segment. Engine alarms confirmed the hit, and the power plant was diminishing. "These guys want us in a bad way."

Teinoh shook his head. "I don't understand; there was no hail. They just started firing."

Ryan was scrambling to reroute power and balance distribution around the ship past broken conduits. Another hit damaged the second of three power distribution relays.

"Teinoh, I need you to manually reset the second distro relay. You're gonna have to shut it down completely and restart it. If we lose the third, we lose the ship."

Teinoh was already through the portal before he'd finished his sentence. Ryan was powering down all non-essential systems to conserve energy. Another strike landed mid-ship. Alarms indicated radiation, and the third distro relay was failing. He transmitted over the internal coms, "Teinoh, are you alright? Teinoh? Advise status."

Ryan looked up with wide eyes and waited for the response. One of the power cells had been ruptured, and radiation levels were increasing dramatically. Diagnostics were damaged, and Ryan couldn't tell which one was the source.

He would have to assess the source and Teinoh's status directly.

Racing to the engine room, he found that the portal door had closed due to protocol. The radiation levels inside were near lethal and climbing. He grabbed a breathing mask and manually released the door. Heat and smoke poured out. Ryan turned his head and squinted into it. He immediately found the breach and manually shut down the cell. Visibility was near zero, and he hunkered low in the choking smoke. As he slowly rounded the base into the central section toward the relays, his right foot snagged on something. Looking down, he discovered a half-charred and lifeless body on the deck. It was barely recognizable as Oldest Brother.

"Teinoh? No! Teinoh! Can you hear me, Teinoh?" He dragged the body up and out of the compartment to the passage. Free of the oppressive smoke, Ryan turned to survey his brother, only to discover that energy had taken off half his head. Ryan squinted his eyes and turned to the side. He reached out and grasped Teinoh's hand. "Oh no, no…Oldest Brother, no."

Ryan's face was taut, and there was a pressing lump in his throat. He held Teinoh's hand for a few moments and gently patted the top of it with his own. Ryan knew he had to get back into the engine compartment and restart that second relay. He released Oldest Brother's hand and, turning away, left him there alone in the passage.

He'd just scrambled through the doorway when another volley of Daerk fire landed across the ship. Ryan blanked for a moment in the concussion and regained awareness to more alarms. There were breaches in the ship, and a second cell had ruptured. As he shut it down, he heard a radiation alarm indicating near lethal levels building ship wide. Looking down, he saw that the engine compartment was already at well above lethal levels. Before he could grasp the manual restart controls for the second relay, more fire rocked the ship. Ryan was tossed violently across the room and lost consciousness.

He awoke to a darkened ship. All relays had failed. He tried to stand and immediately fumbled into a railing. Experience told him he was in a radiation zone that was likely life ending. His shoulder tingled and burned like fire. He knew his effective time was short. He grunted, "Protect!" Pure stubborn will animated him through the dimness. He pawed at the console in an attempt to restore power and purge the ship. Smoke and radiation made it difficult to see, and his fingers were numb.

A round from another volley landed in the forward section. Ryan screamed, "Goddamn it!" and looked up as if he could see through the walls at the origin of the fire. The Daerk had taken a geostationary position several miles above the Paavi freighter. It was difficult to target them in the foreground of the red giant, and the Daerk fired down indiscriminately. Many rounds narrowly missed the Paavi vessel and landed far lower onto the surface of the star. The fire got His attention.

Two of the three power relays were badly damaged. Ryan was able to manually restart the remaining one and start the process to scrub radiation from the ship. Then he crawled on all fours back toward the command section. The medical tables were offline. Their batteries were starting to fail, and the habs were locked down because of the radiation levels in the cabin.

Through the fog of contamination, Ryan tried to manually release the covers. His hands frantically fumbled and pawed at the controls. "Shu-shu. Leish…hold on!" The lights and buttons were a blur as his body began to succumb to the smoke and radiation.

The Daerk captain tapped impatiently, simmering before it erupted. "Why are Paavi still alive? More fire! Destroy them! Fire all weapons!"

Ryan sobbed and struggled to pull himself back up to the table console. A broad, sparkling blanket of Daerk fire traversed down, and one round landed near the bridge. Ryan was violently thrown several feet, landing just in front of the forward viewing port. He lost consciousness.

Diphda was awoken. With difficulty, He saw the minute beings in orbit. The weapon fire was hardly disruptive, and the skirmish between lower species was only an irritation. Then He saw Ryan motionless in the sill of the viewing port. Diphda's focus gathered further, and He saw Ryan clearly. Rage and fury built quickly within the red giant.

The Daerk captain exploded again. "New weapon officer! Reload. Fire all and hit Paavi ship. Destroy it!" The dark minions were so focused on their target that they missed the emergence of a massive coronal mass ejection spouting toward them. The energy arced up over the top of the Paavi freighter. Rising higher, the mass ejection pinched off, and in something like a cross between burping and spitting, Diphda shot a stellar flare directly into the Daerk frigate. The mass of energy traveled near the speed of light. The Daerk science officer turned around quickly toward the captain. Its words of warning didn't make it across the bridge. The energy release was so massive that the sound of its voice, as well as the entire mass of the Daerk frigate, was instantly vaporized.

Ryan woke panting and slicked with sweat. Turning over, he surveyed the command section. The sickness was something he had experience with, and he tried desperately to gather himself. His sobs and mumbles were nondescript as he crawled toward the medical tables. He had no idea how long he'd been unconscious.

He reached Leishu first, only to discover that her medical table console was dark. He swiped and pawed at the controls. "No, no! No!" He banged on them. Pulling himself up on wobbling legs, he looked at Mother and Father's. Theirs was also dark. Lunging and stumbling toward a command console, his face broke his fall.

Alternately opening and closing his eyes, he squinted at the screen. Radiation was still hovering at lethal levels. Power was intermittent across the ship; many conduits had been damaged, but there were a few remaining conduits providing power to the command section. Ryan rummaged through a lower storage locker, throwing its contents over his shoulder. He found a power cable and dragged himself toward a wall panel that still had power. His shoulder was burning like fire, and he was light headed.

He took gulping breaths as he fought to stay conscious. Nausea overcame him, and he paused for several seconds on his side, heaving. Looking up, he could see the panel outlet just ahead. Grunting and screaming, he clawed his way toward it. He ripped the cover off and stabbed the power cable into the auxiliary outlet. Lights on the cable indicated power.

He connected the other end into the med table power management system. All at once, they came to life. Pulling himself to his feet caused him to be violently ill again. When he looked back, he could see the command screen for Leishu's table. The message was crushing. He was too late. They were already long gone.

Ryan flopped over Leishu's table, and a primal groan emanated from the deepest reach of his soul, "NOooooo! Beautiful Sister. No." He slid off and stood next to Mother and Father. He could see Gehnchan had curled Mahrno into his torso as if to protect her. He panted and spoke quickly, "I'm sorry. I'm sorry. Mom. Dad. I'm so sorry." He leaned on their table for several seconds, shaking and sobbing.

Ryan checked the power settings and noted the radiation levels. The atmosphere was normalized, and particulates released into the air were scrubbing the surface contamination. The conduits and cells appeared stable. Ryan knew the ship was faring better than his body. He would have to enter a medical table for a period of regeneration. The system would repair damaged cells and attempt to remove the radiation. His only chance for survival was slowing his body and allowing the machine to cleanse his system.

He recorded a message to Ainhow, who by now had probably arrived at Lahmaard for Leishu's wedding.

"Oldest Sister, prepare yourself for dreadful news. The Daerk have attacked us at Diphda. Teinoh has been killed. Leishu, Mother, and Father have died while in stasis. Teinoh was very quick, and he didn't suffer. The others slipped into Dvarah's arms peacefully in their sleep. The ship's still in orbit around Diphda. The Daerk stopped firing and disappeared for unknown reasons. Approach with caution. Teinoh's still in the passage by the engine room. He does not appear as he was in life. Have someone else secure him. I'm going into my medical table. I'm badly poisoned with radiation, and it is difficult. The Goddess may take me. Please know the love of family is blocking my pain. I'm sorry, Ainhow; I failed. I was desperate to save them. I tried to protect. I'm so sorry. Please tell the family I'm sorry. I have to go. I love you, Oldest Sister, so much. You are a beautiful being. Have a long and loving life under Dvarah's gaze."

Ryan's face was illuminated by the screen as he sent the message to Ainhow from the darkened command room. He wrapped himself in an emergency blanket and stumbled to his medical table. As he climbed in, he thought about the last time he had fallen asleep. In mere moments, he'd lost his family and his life—again. He shivered and shook violently as the cover closed. Struggling to contain the pain and grief, he prayed for the Goddess to take him home.

NEW ENDING,
OLD BEGINNING

"FAMILY IS EVERYTHING. MY EVERYTHING
IS LOST."
—RYAN

Ryan opened his eyes and struggled to focus. He looked around the room. The lighting style, the sterile smell, and the bed he was in caused him to grimace. "Always the same. I hate these places."

The door to his room swung open, and a female dressed as a doctor entered his room. Ryan stared with wide eyes at Mahrno. "Mother? Have I died?"

The doctor flashed a pained smile. "No, Eylon. I'm Dehchow. Mahrno was my mother."

Ryan's face instantly crinkled. "Of course; you have Father's eyes."

She smiled with her hands tightly clasped at her waist.

"Where exactly am I?"

Before Dehchow could respond, the door flew open, and Ainhow blew through it. Without a noise, she swept down into Ryan. He put his arm around her shoulder. "I'm here; I'm still here. I'm OK." He shot Dehchow a questioning look, and she nodded. "I'm OK, Ainhow." She laid over him and continued to grasp and re-grasp his shoulders.

Dehchow walked over and sat on the corner of the bed. Ainhow reached

261

back without looking and grasped Dehchow's hand.

"Eylon, do you remember what happened?"

"Teinoh woke me from stasis. We were under attack. There was no message, no provocation. They just kept firing. We lost propulsion, and there was radiation. We were losing power, and we tried to get…" Ryan's voice trailed off. He looked off and took a breath. "Teinoh was resetting a power relay when we took fire. He was killed instantly. I found him, and I tried to stabilize."

Ryan pinched his lips together and took a quick breath. "They just kept shooting, and I got knocked out. I don't know how long." Ryan's fist clenched. "I woke, and I tried, but they were just…" Ainhow sat up and wiped a tear from his cheek. "I lost them. Radiation in the compartment locked the tables down, and power was lost."

Ainhow rubbed Ryan's arm for a few moments in silence before he spoke again in a hoarse whisper. "What happened after I went into stasis, and where are we?"

Ainhow fidgeted with the edge of Ryan's blanket. "Many in the extended family were here when I received your message. We came immediately and approached in multiple ships. There was no trace of the Daerk, and we were able to extract you back here. We're in a hospital on Lahmaard. Mother worked hard to stay in constant communication with all her children. Elder Sister Dehchow knows the specifics of how Dvarah delivered you to us."

Dehchow spoke. "I know of your truth. Mother was close with the Goddess, and she wrote of her knowledge that you were delivered to us. I am Oldest Daughter in the third family." She smiled on at Ainhow and brushed her bangs aside and behind her ear.

"It seems there's a pattern of strong oldest daughters pursuing the medical arts." She looked to Ryan. "I am the lead surgical physician at this research hospital. It's taken considerable effort, but I've been able to keep you in a separate wing. You were in stasis for a few days after managing to survive radiation exposure far greater than any other Paavi in medical history. Keeping your case out of our general database has been quite a challenge, but nothing like keeping the curiosity of our learning doctors at length. If you are approached, do not share, and call for me. I've indicated that you might be contagious with an unknown pathogen."

Ryan learned that the burial ceremony would be the next day. Although Dehchow strongly disapproved, Ryan attended with a heavy heart that teetered atop wobbling legs. The Paavi ceremony was very similar to some customs on Earth. The deceased were in clear burial containers. Teinoh was dressed in a pure white robe that looked like it was made of a silk-like material. His face, head, and hands were wrapped completely with the same white silk-like cloth.

Mother and Father were dressed in more formal robes. Symbols on their collars indicated their monastic service with the Goddess. Leishu was dressed in her wedding dress, and a bouquet of flowers was in her hands. When Ryan saw her, his face tightened, and his breath was choppy.

Amid their grief, the extended family in attendance were curious about Eylon's eyes. Although Paavi expressed grief, they did not cry.

There was a celebration of stories. This consumed a great portion of the first day. With beings as old as Gehnchan and Mahrno, there was much to share and tell. Ryan's grief took him vividly back to a memory of right after they had rescued him. Leishu was trapesing through some construction in the engine compartment when she tipped a tool down into an open power connector. There was a flash as the power conduit ruptured. Just past it, Leishu fell off a catwalk and down between two fluid transfer ducts.

Eruptions of plasma arced up over the catwalk between Leishu and Teinoh. She was trapped below on the other side. Ainhow was praying when Ryan came upon the scene. He surveyed the wall of energy ahead with arcs dancing up and around the catwalk. With Littlest Sister on the other side motionless, Ryan squinted, rolled his shoulder, and bolted through the maelstrom. Barely conscious, she opened her eyes at his approach. In a quiet little voice, she said, "Caution Eylon; there are dangerous things in here."

Ryan smiled. "So I've heard." He kissed her on the forehead. "Let's get you out of here."

As Ryan picked her up, she put her arms around his neck and her head on his shoulder. Mahrno arrived and put her hands over her mouth. Gehnchan rushed up just in time to see Ryan wrap his body around Leishu. If resolve was a substance, Ryan's eyes would have been depthless pools of it. He leapt through the danger and into the arms of his family on the other side.

Teinoh jumped, feeling contact with a white-hot button off Ryan's jacket. They realized it was smoking, and Ryan shed it quickly. All were astonished that he was somehow able to traverse the live energy without harm. Leishu said quietly, "I am sorry for being clumsy."

Teinoh kissed her head with relief. Gehnchan stood speechless until Ryan looked at Ainhow and said, "Teach me that prayer, will you? Apparently, it really works."

At these words, Father broke down, showering everyone with kisses and saying, "Yes, yes, we will pray; praise the brave heart of my son." It was his first memory of Gehnchan referring to him as his son.

The Paavi father had been so patient with Ryan. Over the years, Gehnchan had taught him the Paavi way by example. With time, Ryan had found the light of the Goddess. Once, just after Ryan had demonstrated a Paavi ritual, Gehnchan had smiled on him. "This is what the Paavi path is when it permeates a soldier's heart."

Gehnchan puffed with pride. He knew his son was a warrior, but he did not judge him. With clear eyes, Ryan heard his father's quiet words. "A warrior with the capacity for compassion has a depth of character that I should think would make him all the more cunning. He is a being that will move more quickly for the alternate path, for the path to the light. Be clever and cunning. The greater part of honor is slipping away from conflict and avoiding unnecessary bloodshed altogether. Violence robs something from everyone. The strike creates ripples across the being like those from a pebble cast into a pool."

The two shared another connection. Both loved open space. Ryan made his father laugh once when he said he thought Dvarah was "teasing when She initially made me a human soldier instead of a Paavi trader." Through the years together, Ryan was a diligent student. Gehnchan showed the human trade routes and safe paths. Ryan learned how to avoid danger with passage through hazardous areas that other species avoided. Over the centuries, with trial and error, the Paavi had charted safe routes. They combined stellar navigation with the chanting of ancient mythical stories.

Ryan was astonished at how the technique provided safe passage through fields of sub-space disruption, clusters of star fields, asteroid belts, debris-strewn gaseous fields, patches of dark matter, and large gravitational objects. In open space, Gehnchan knew how to travel inconspicuously, using stellar features to obfuscate traces of their energy signature. Although the freighter was a civilian ship, Ryan was amazed at their military-like capacity for stealth. The tremendous significance of learning Paavi trade craft was something that would escape Ryan until much later.

For the moment, the future was drowned in tears. He looked on his mother, remembering her tender care, and his father, who was constantly looking out for Ryan's special needs. Before Dvarah delivered him, Ryan hadn't ever had a mother or father. His heart ached now in a way that he thought might stop it completely. The loss reverberated through his soul like piercing waves off a tuning fork. He stood motionless, with a hand on each casket. A thought reverberated through his soul: *"Family is everything. My everything is lost."*

ALONE END

THE FALLING DAERK DEBRIS HAD PASSED BY
SOMETHING. THERE WAS SOMETHING DOWN
THERE—AN OBJECT.

Ryan woke startled and squinting at the numbers. He ran his fingers through long shaggy hair and sat up. Looking at the time, he ran his other hand down his long, scraggly beard. His eyes shot wide, and he scrambled to his feet. "The date! No, no, no! What's the date! I can't miss her!"

Ryan tapped the screen to access the calendar. He was searching for Leishu's birth date. "There's too many of these! How the hell am I supposed to keep up? Huh? Tell me! How! Every time I turn around there's another goddam birthday!" He put his hand over his mouth and spun around in a quick circle. With wide eyes he looked up. "I'm sorry. I didn't mean it. I'm sorry, I'm sorry, I'm sorry." He struck his fist on his thigh and squinted his eyes tightly. "I didn't mean it!"

He plopped down, sobbing, and put his hands over his face. Looking through his fingers at the calendar, he could see that Leishu's birthday was tomorrow. He took a large breath and exhaled. The past twenty-four years had been hard. Mahrno and Gehnchan had willed the cargo freighter to Ryan. After repairs, he had assumed the family business on his own. Over time, he'd progressively taken more dangerous and lengthy contracts, which often put him out at the maximum range of the vessel. The remunerations from such missions had piled up large sums in his personal finances. Although this freighter was well past its lifespan, Ryan refused to purchase a new one and leave his home. The last few years had culminated in near isolation. Ryan preferred to trade with automated stations. He hadn't set foot off the vessel in ten years.

The ship was orbiting in cue for a station rendezvous to drop off external payload containers. While he waited, Ryan sat at the science station and scrolled through the available freight contracts in a terminal window. There was one lucrative job that required significant range. Playing with the navigation system, he determined that he could make the distance if he slung around a nearby mega-neutron star. These celestial bodies were rare and mysterious. Their core composition was like that of a standard neutron star, but a mega-neutron held far more mass. The physics of their presence was like a tent stake in the galaxy. Time and mass pivoted around them, and it was common for Paavi traders to safely utilize their gravity at a distance. For this contract, Ryan chose a path that would take him far closer and allow him to accelerate significantly faster than light speed.

While Ryan nodded his head and gently tugged at his beard, movement through a shoulder-height portal caught his attention. A passenger transport, the Lehmarndt Bay, also in cue, was drifting close by. Squinting out, he could see a face looking across to him. He cocked his head and saw someone wave. Realizing the being was looking at him, he quickly ducked down. Ryan's brow furrowed, and he looked around the floor, waiting. Slowly, he raised back up and peered out. The face was gone.

Ryan cocked his head as a Paavi child slowly peered around the portal frame and back out the window. He could see that it was a little girl. She was smiling, and she darted back away again. A small grin cracked deep under Ryan's matted beard. He waited until she emerged again and darted low again.

Ryan giggled as this game cycled through several times. Rising up again slowly, he could see that she had her elbows resting on the window sill and her head propped on her hands. Still smiling, she raised one hand and again waved at him. He stared at her for a moment and then tentatively raised his hand. She waved more vigorously and said something back over her shoulder. Soon another Paavi, likely her mother, shared the window. Ryan waved more actively and smiled at both. The mother was talking to her daughter and alternately waving back at him.

Ryan suddenly remembered that he was sitting naked from the waist down. He casually laid a couple of tablets over his lap. The mother disappeared, but the child remained in the window, smiling at Ryan. As if he were melting, Ryan slid down and out of his seat in an effort to stay below the window line. Crouching on the floor, he tried to remember where he'd last seen his pants. Shuffling on all fours, he found the bulky bottom half of an external space suit and slipped it on while lying on the floor.

An audible chime indicated the station was ready to secure his cargo. He groused, "I'm busy!" Returning to the science station, he looked back out, waving. The ship, along with the child, had repositioned and were now gone. An overwhelming wave of sadness washed over him as he maneuvered the freighter for the station drones. A moment of connection in a desert of isolation released a tidal flood of emotion.

Ryan sobbed. "Just a few more minutes…it couldn't wait for a minute. I just wanted to say goodbye. Was that so much to ask!" Through tears, he returned to the contract console. He found the long-range contract he had been reviewing earlier and executed the agreement.

Another chime indicated the approach of a provision pod. After docking with the freighter, Ryan's eyes grew wide, and he bolted up. "Ice cream!" A few minutes later, Ryan sat on the floor of the provision pod, prying off the lid with spoon in hand. About midway through consuming the container, he thought about the little girl in the Lehmarndt Bay. Thoughts of Leishu entered his mind. Pointing his spoon upward, he said, "I bet she likes ice cream too." Ryan's face soured. "I wish we could have shared some with her."

His head bowed, and he covered the lid. Rising back up, he started unpacking the provisions. For the remainder of the day, his heart felt as if a large stone had been placed over it.

Ryan shook his head. "Out of here. We need out. We have to go; keep moving."

Over the years, the monotony of routine had buffered out a lifetime of losses. Ryan didn't know why he kept trading and traveling. The question wasn't even near his cognitive registry. He kept doing and moving in the present to wall out the past. Purpose escaped him, as well as any thoughts of the future. He was soon to discover the mechanisms of the marvelous Universe were not a constant.

The next day, as he made approach to sling off the mega-neutron, he received a distress call. A ship full of Paavi refugees was under attack. They were descending closer to the star, and a Daerk frigate had taken position above them. They were firing down on the Paavi from a higher orbit.

Ryan popped up and turned sideways to the forward portal. He put his hands to his lips and looked back forward through the corner of his eye. He turned back forward and then immediately turned to the right again. He pointed out the forward window with an open hand and opened his mouth as if he was about to speak. Huffing and raising his eyebrows, he sat. He made a quick grunting noise and washed his hands over each other.

Twisting sideways, he pulled his legs up and wrapped his arms tightly around his shins. He rocked for a few moments before turning forward and staring at the view portal. He whined, bent over, and buried his head in his hands. There was another audible distress call, and in this one, the ship identified itself. It was the Lehmarndt Bay, and the voice transmitting sounded like Leishu's. Ryan's head popped up, and he transmitted on a communication channel the Daerk would hear. He yelled loudly into the mic, "Stop it! You stop it right now!"

A few seconds later, the Daerk responded. "Wait turn; we take care of you next."

Ryan's eyes opened wide, and his body twitched. Rage simmered up and boiled away some of the madness. He squinted as he took over manual helm control. Plotting coordinates into the system, he mumbled, "Oh really, shithead? I look forward to meeting you." He accelerated and pointed the freighter directly toward the frigate. Ryan's head ticked to the right a few times. He transmitted again, but this time in English, "Death imminent."

The Daerk on the command deck looked at each other. Their captain pointed down toward the refugee ship and nodded.

Ryan could see them fire again and erupted, "I've just about had it with you sons-a-bitches!" Transmitting again, "HEY! I said stop it. Are you deaf or just stupid?"

The science officer looked over its shoulder. "Translation system says a language from Terra." It pointed back to the console. "Records say we destroyed and killed all of them in a harvest cleanse."

The captain nodded. "Apparently not; we have something rare. Finish Paavi quickly so we can pursue the Terran."

The science officer looked down. "Won't need pursuit; it's coming to us."

The captain snorted, "This is why we kill all of them. Very smart, huh?" Everyone snickered, clicked and chirped on the command deck.

Ryan continued to transmit a stream of profanity-laced remarks directed at the Daerk.

The leader tilted its head, "Can you translate what it says?"

The science officer spoke with hesitation. "It says you have feces where brain should be." Everyone stopped chuckling, and the captain grunted.

Ryan could see that they were still firing. He plotted a short distance light jump that would take half of his available power and emerged nearly atop the frigate. Collision alarms rang on the Daerk bridge.

"Captain, it's plotting to impact."

"Fire on it and destroy!"

"It approaches from stern."

"Evasive action. Avoid impact!"

Ryan saw them positioning and countered his path as well. His cargo was in containers affixed to the lower portion of the freighter. The closure rate was high, and it loosed his mind into a long-forgotten zone. He released his cargo containers, and they landed square into the engine section. The freighter's collision angle of impact was shallow enough that it skipped off the frigate. Both ships lurched from the contact. Ryan ignored the alarms and exclaimed with both fists raised.

The Daerk ship was not badly damaged physically, but the occupants were greatly enraged. The captain waved at them for quiet. "Where is Terran ship going?"

Ryan continued past and down close to the neutron star. Leveling out down low, he made a hard arc to come around again. The proximity to the star caused him to disappear on the Daerk tracking screen. Something drew at him down there. It felt both familiar and strange. He held up his hands and looked at them, front and back. With wide eyes and a cocked head, he looked toward the front viewing portal, stood up, and walked to it. She was looking upon him. Her beauty cast a brilliant light down into the dark closet of the psyche where he'd huddled. He put his hand on the glass and mumbled, "Home?" An audible transmission from the Paavi refugee ship caused him to snap back over his shoulder.

He came around the star low and with scorching speed. His plan was to plot an ascent near the refugee ship through the neutron's glare and take out the Daerk. It did not even register to him as a sacrifice. In his mind, Leishu was on the Lehmarndt Bay. As he approached, he saw a volley of sparkling rounds stream down off the frigate. Mumbling, "No, no, no!" He could only watch as several torpedoes closed in and hit the ship.

He streaked up past the Lehmarndt Bay just as she came apart. Every molecule within him polarized to rage. With maximum forward power, he bore down on the frigate. Lurching forward, he looked down and saw that he was slowing dramatically. "What the…"

The Daerk ship was moving rapidly off laterally. Ryan held on as he slowed and the gap between vessels grew. It occurred to him that the Daerk might have some kind of energy weapon that could repel. Ryan erupted, "Oh come on! Ghah!" He feverishly tapped on the console to increase power to the engines.

A few seconds later, he glanced up to see the Daerk fire on him. Several sparkling torpedoes moved away and spiraled apart. Ryan's brows pinched together, and he leaned forward. "What the hell?"

One of the sparkles spiraled back around and hit the starboard engine section of the frigate! He could see plasma jet from the breach as the Daerk vessel tumbled off axis and started a descent. Ryan watched, completely mystified as they tumbled down. He flinched slightly from a flash as the frigate imploded far lower down. Debris streams were the only remnant falling onto the star's surface. Just after, whatever gravitational force that had displaced both vessels stopped.

Ryan came to a full stop and worked feverishly at the science station to find any sign of the Paavi transport. There was nothing. He leaned on the console and sobbed loudly. Plopping down, he pulled up a recording of the entire event. As he swam in his grief, something strange caught his eye, and he stopped abruptly. The falling Daerk debris had passed by something. There was something down there—an object.

Compared to the surface, it had little relative movement, but it did move in the recorded segment. That meant it was low and near the neutron surface, but not on it. Further review and enhancement revealed the shape of a ship. Experience told him it wasn't possible for the Lehmarndt Bay to still be intact. Experience also told him that nothing that close should be intact either. Curiosity pushed Ryan past manic dismay. With piqued interest, he orbited and surveyed the neutron. It took two days of close monitoring, but he found the target and mapped its orbit. Positioning above it, he determined that it was, in fact, a ship. From the silhouette, it looked intact, but it wasn't Paavi.

STAR CHAMBER

AFTER A FEW MOMENTS, THE FEELING
DIMINISHED. HIS BROW FURROWED, AND HE
MUMBLED, "WHAT THE HELL WAS THAT?"

Ryan positioned the ship directly over the unknown vessel in the lowest possible orbit given the structural capacity and the gravity. The old Paavi ship creaked and groaned under the stress, but Ryan held position. At such proximity to the neutron, the freighter was difficult, if not impossible, to spot from above. However, looking out for the next few days, he saw several Daerk patrols circle above, likely searching for their lost frigate. Other ships had entered too, perhaps looking for the Lehmarndt Bay. He lay low and quiet, investigating the vessel below. The distraction and the study consumed him. How could it be so near to the star? How could he get to it? Could he raise it into higher orbit? He spent hour after hour sitting at the science console working the math. His head bobbed a couple of times, and closing his eyes felt so nice. He agreed that he would just close them for a few seconds, and then it was back to work.

Ryan woke to billions of stars overhead. Looking around, he realized that the view completely surrounded him. He was somehow suspended in free space and not within his own body. Whatever this was, he felt incredible, and his mind was at peace. He giggled at this marvelous predicament and looked for star formations to determine his location.

His attention focused on a bright point of light falling gently like a wisp of cottonwood down through the stars. The wisp ahead landed on a translucent pool very near him. It was only visible as concentric rings spread away from the landing. The ripples stretched and spread out toward the arms of infinity. As the wisp touched, it resolved into the shape of a human.

Ryan realized that he was looking at himself floating suspended. Ryan wondered what was more peculiar, the fact that he was dreaming or that he knew he must be dreaming. A moment later, he saw vivid images of children from different species. Next, there were images of their planets from orbit. Last came images of Earth and human children. The vision of the Earth momentarily centered behind Ryan's floating form.

The pictures were powerful, like staring into a bright light or being in a room with audio set too high. They were pronounced and focused, and Ryan could not control them. The last pictures were of the neutron from orbit and images of various types of communication devices.

Ryan sharpened at the meaning of the images and thought, as if he was speaking out loud, "Are we talking?"

He immediately saw something from his memory. It was from a parade in his honor after repelling the Khrylic. The visual memory was looking up to the sky as tickertape rained down all around him.

He nodded, and he was back floating in space. Framed pictures appeared, floating on a level plane just in front of him. His academy graduation picture was at the very front. Directly behind it were images of his aunts and brother. Further out, he could see pictures of General Lund, Jeeval, Ragn, Pari, Zeek, and others spanning out as far as the eye could see. In the background, he could see a large image of Earth. A shadow came, first over Ryan, then creeping over all the photos. As it eclipsed the light of the Earth, all the pictures started to flip forward. All of them tipped face down, save Ryan's. The image of Earth faded before vanishing away. All the pictures disappeared, except for his.

The frame around his picture disappeared. The image animated, and he could see a memory from the day the photo was taken. Just behind it was another earlier memory from school, and just ahead appeared another memory that happened after the photo was taken. Many frames of memories appeared and stretched out in both directions.

He realized that these images were a sort of catalog of his life. Reaching out, Ryan realized that he could control the forward and backward movement of the focus on these memories. Going all the way back, he felt memories of his mother. Zipping forward, he could see memories of his Paavi family. Traveling further yet, he went to frames in his future. There were images and feelings, but he couldn't focus on them. He tried and tried to focus on the future until the timeline suddenly moved without his direction to the very end.

He couldn't see his own death, but he could feel it. It was peaceful, and it was the ending. The images of the memories pulled away from him so that he could see the frames of the beginning and the end in one scope of view. As he reached back toward the future, the timeline of memory frames started to bow downward. He was pulled toward the dip. The bottom of the bend was his memory of the destruction of Earth.

Ryan winced and looked away. The memory was raw and vivid, and it pulled his attention back. He looked toward the future, but he fell back down into the destruction memory. Looking back, he tried to focus on happy memories from his childhood. After a few moments, his mind's eye slid back to the attack.

"I don't want to be here. Why do you keep showing me this?!"

Ryan saw his academy picture again. The memory of Earth's destruction played in the background.

"Please, I don't want to see this."

Moving forward and back on his timeline, he could now see the imagery of the destruction in the background of all his other memories. Ryan nodded and sobbed. "It won't go away."

But the memories lifted, and rose petals pelted down all around him. He had a sense of smell, and the fragrance was from Auntie Virginia's beautiful purple roses. He could touch the petals, and he welcomed the velvety feel between his fingertips. Above and to the side was a singular blinding light.

"Is that you there?"

Tickertape fell now interspersed with the rose petals.

"Well, that's a really odd combination."

He instantly saw the memory of when Hadley had pinned him down once as a child and was tickling his feet. Ryan was laughing nearly beyond control. The memory made him laugh. There were more rose petals for a moment.

"Are you the neutron I'm orbiting?"

Tickertape streamed down around him.

"Did you know my Sun?"

The light flickered, and he saw more rose petals.

"I'm so sorry She was killed. Her song was beautiful."

He smelled roses, and then there was a pause.

Ryan cocked his head. "You have a question?"

He saw many flashes of past memories. Saving a child in the street, attacking the pirate ship at the Aihl Rhydel, the crash on the deck during the Khrylic attack, repelling down to rescue Ragn, the Allentown, and other memories involving action. The last memory flashed to the destruction of Earth.

Ryan shook his head. "I couldn't save them. Please, take me from here."

Ryan was instantly standing in a tropical jungle. He looked up, out, and around, noticing an eight-year-old Paavi girl sitting just behind him. Her hair was in pony tails, and she was playing with a large leaf. She looked up at him and smiled. Before he could say a word, she pointed ahead. The muzzle of a nine-hundred-pound Daerk panther pushed through the thicket a few feet from them. Its deep growl was almost inaudible.

Ryan instantly drew his sidearm and stepped between the predator and the child. The weapon was no match for the thick-boned beast, and Ryan's hope was to distract it long enough for the child to escape. "You must go from here! Now!"

The panther swiped, and Ryan blocked with his arm. He yelped as the claws sliced deep. The panther tilted its head back and screech-howled. Ryan stepped rapidly into the beast. Before it could react, he shoved his pistol deep into its mouth and emptied the gun into its throat. The howl muted abruptly as the beast slumped back over.

Stumbling back with blood streaming from his arm, Ryan looked over at the child, who was still seated with the same leaf. Another Daerk panther howled in the distance in answer to the beast he'd just killed. The rack on Ryan's gun was open, and he was out of ammunition.

He looked down on the child. "We have to get you out of here. Can you understand me?"

The child nodded and smiled at him.

Ryan surveyed their surroundings. "Many will be here shortly." There was a rocky vertical cliff wall several feet away. Looking up, he could see a ledge about forty feet off the ground. There was a skinny tree near them that looked to be about sixty feet in height.

The sound of movement beyond Ryan's vision confirmed that more than one predator was upon them. He searched his pockets for more ammo as movement caught his eye. There was a blur of black as the carcass of the dead panther was snatched by another. There was growling and grunting as others cannibalized it.

Ryan scooped up the child and put her on his shoulders. "Hold on!" He jumped as far up the trunk of the tree as he could. "We're going up this tree a little. When we get up higher, it will bend toward the rock ledge up there." Ryan pointed toward it. "See that ledge? When I say, you're going to crawl over my head and onto this trunk. Then you're going to crawl across to that ledge. OK?"

He was about fifteen feet up when he yelped from a bite into his leg. He could feel the teeth cinch down further into his flesh. With his other foot, he kicked the face of the attacker. After Ryan's strike to its nose, it yelped and released him. With even greater urgency, Ryan clawed and scaled upward. Several panthers were mounting the trunk to come upward. The tree started to lean over, and Ryan angled the trunk toward the rock face. The top came to rest on the ledge, and Ryan put his head on the trunk.

He could see the snarling beasts climbing and quickly closing the gap. Contrary to the emotion that vision generated, his voice remained calm. "Climb over me and get to that ledge. Quickly, please; climb over me."

When Ryan looked up, he saw that the little girl was near safety but had somehow turned around. She was motioning for him to follow. "It won't support both of us. It's OK. You must get to safety. Go, and don't look back, no matter what you hear."

She scurried over onto the ledge and disappeared. Ryan felt claws and teeth sink into both of his legs. He smiled through the pain. "Bastards. You won't get her!"

He let go of the trunk, and the tree whipped tall again. As he was falling through the air, he realized that he was again in open space. The sense of falling diminished, and there was no longer any pain. Looking back out, he saw larger images of his mother, his aunts, Jeeval, and Mahrno. They were lined up next to and the same size as the bright light.

He saw the memory of his Aunt Virginia saluting him the day he got his wings. It was a lingering moment that focused on her smile and her eyes. Rose petals fell all around him. They swirled about and were so dense that it was like a rose blizzard. Ryan started falling with the petals.

Jerking up off the science console, Ryan gasp for breath. He put his hand over his chest; he was winded and light headed. He felt like he was going to vomit, but he braced himself and stood. After a few moments, the feeling diminished. His brow furrowed, and he mumbled, "What the hell was that?"

He looked out to the portal toward the star, and his eyes widened. The mystery ship was now about two hundred feet off the starboard side, orbiting in parallel. Looking down with his mouth agape, he glanced back out the portal. "How in the..."

POINT OF ENTRY

...OVER THREE THOUSAND CATALOGED VESSELS
IN HIS DATABASE FOR COMPARISON, BUT
THIS SHIP WAS NOT LIKE ANYTHING KNOWN
TO THE PAAVI ARCHIVES.

Ryan spent the next day attaching mooring and salvage lines between the freighter and the alien vessel. The ship was much bigger than he had originally estimated, and it dwarfed the Paavi freighter. It was slightly larger than a frigate, with a very unusual shape. The top and bottom were mirrored symmetrically but slightly offset, and they resembled a pyramid shape. However, instead of having three sides, each had five. As such, they were pentagonal pyramids stacked and offset on top of each other. Each side panel was a slightly different shape than the triangles that formed a simple pyramid and instead formed a quadrilateral shape that looked like a kite. Two of the five sides were dramatically longer and created a slanted pyramid shape.

While the top and bottom of the ship were symmetrical, the longer sides of the hexahedrons were flipped opposite each other. They were also offset such that the longer length sides jutted out and over the bottom shorter lengths. Mating the upper and lower hemispheres together was what looked like a tubular central ring. A close-up view of the skin revealed that it was faceted and fabricated with millions of hexagons. The center ring looked to be constructed of some sort of crystalline material.

Ryan noted significant blast damage entering and exiting the pentagonal hemispheres. A few had penetrations entered above and passed through and through, exiting the bottom half of the ship. At the points of entry into the hexahedron section, the vessel's surface looked to be fabricated out of some sort of multilayered material. The outer segments of it looked almost like a semi-translucent skin. Although it was badly damaged, Ryan caught himself shaking his head and marveling at its beauty. The ship was exotic and like nothing he'd ever seen in his travels.

Radiation from low orbit around the neutron prevented Ryan from taking walks outside for more than a few minutes in duration. Using a remote, he mapped the entire exterior of the ship, along with markings and language. The symbols didn't match any known language in his off-world lexicon. Even so, he was confident that it was not of Daerk origin. The technology seemed like something even beyond that of the dark minions. The skin was mysteriously reflective to radiation and blocked his scans. The central ring looked to be some kind of focusing aperture, and it dispersed any energy directed into it.

There were what appeared to be engines protruding from the short side segment of what Ryan assumed was the top hexahedron. The opposite shorter hexahedron side, Ryan guessed, was the underside of the bow section. It was there that he discovered a few seams. They traversed from the ring and down the lower bow section. The gap tolerance was so tight that it was beyond the capacity of his measuring equipment. It looked to be a portal that opened inward.

Ryan deduced that the central crystal ring was some kind of energy-focusing device, perhaps a weapon. That and the existence of a portal made him think this was a manned vessel. If so, the occupants were either deceased or in stasis.

Using a remote drone, he entered the vessel through the skin breach. The drone was a little thicker than a baseball bat and tethered with an umbilical. The head had a camera, limited sensors, several tool heads, and lights. A couple of sleeves rode around the cable with geared teeth just behind the head, and the drone contained a magnetic foot. If the tool needed leverage, the foot would mount, and motors powering the teeth would provide increased torque for the head.

The interior was dark, and there was no evidence of power. The blast had cut through many decks and compartments. It was very possible that the entire ship had been compromised. The passages were smooth and constructed for a being of Terran height.

Ryan didn't discover any bodies or signs of prior inhabitants. His guess as to the orientation of the top and bottom of the vessel appeared correct from the observed fixtures. Over several days, he carefully mapped out the compartments that he could access. Ryan could see evidence of emergency blast doors between major passageways, but none of them were closed. Who and whatever had attacked had done so with such speed and ferocity that there wasn't time to close off compartments.

Ryan discovered and surveyed the corner of the ship that he suspected was an access portal. The room contained a dark console near the outside edge of the ship. Ryan panned the remote camera upward, and he could see that the wall panels above were affixed with hinges. Ryan mumbled aloud, "Bingo!" He'd found the front door.

Days stretched into a couple of weeks as Ryan tried to gain access to the vessel. He was in the portal room with the remote nearly every day surveying. Most ships had an emergency release, and Ryan just had to discover it. He surveyed over three thousand cataloged vessels in his database for comparison, but this ship was not like anything known to the Paavi archives.

Ryan continued talking to himself like a madman, but now his thoughts were consumed with repairing and reviving this ship. Purpose required performance. As such, he began to follow a schedule once again for sleep and nourishment. The freighter was a mess and not conducive to the science or recovery effort. Ryan cleaned out decades of dirt and debris.

Increased activity, nutrition, and regular sleep cycles returned Ryan's chemistry to normal levels. The activity also made his scraggly hair an annoyance. Ryan looked at the reflection of a weathered soul standing over the sink in the head. He raised a pair of scissors to his beard and thought for a long moment about where to start. He grasped a chunk and felt the blades clip through the mane. Hair streamed down.

As he pruned, he rambled on to himself. There were questions and possibilities to plot. A barrage of words bounced back and forth between his eyes and the mirror at an increasing rate. At a crescendo of verbalized thoughts, the words suddenly stopped. He held up the scissors and cocked his head. Dropping them, he turned his attention to the cabinet. Pawing through it, he found a razor, and wide eyes examined it closely. Holding up the safety razor, he looked off with a thousand-yard stare. Nodding, he quickly traversed out of the head and toward a data terminal. Setting the razor on the counter, he searched for images of old-fashioned razors and found an image of a historic shaving device.

The blade was a long straight edge, which was folded into its sheath for storage. There was a small divot on the outside exposed edge of the blade that a fingernail could pry to release it. With a half-trimmed hedge on his face, Ryan fumbled quickly to retrieve the last remote footage from the docking room. There was blast damage in the alien portal room. The ceiling had some scorch marks, and there was a dent in the material between them.

Inspecting more closely, Ryan could see the "dent" on the edge of the panel. Panning across and altering the contrast, his eyes grew wide. The dent was symmetrical with another that had been obscured in the blackened blast damage on the adjacent panel. Ryan made an audible squeal and stood up, knowing that dents typically do not occur with perfect symmetry.

Excitement powered his fumbling. His hands couldn't move fast enough to power up the remote. Back in the corner room, he anchored the remote and used a tool on the sensor mast to wedge between the two panels. He applied ten pounds of tension on the dents, and the panels both hinged down a half foot. A round black rod emerged from between them. Grasping the rod with the remote and pulling caused a metallic crunching noise.

Dust fell from the ceiling, and the brilliant light of the neutron emerged through a crack in the forward portal. He'd manually released the entryway to the alien ship. Ryan screamed, jumped up, and ran in small circles. His dance path drifted up toward the forward view portal. The light of the neutron crossed his face, and Ryan squinted out at the light. It captured him and stopped him dead in his tracks.

He put his hand on the glass, closed his eyes, and smiled. His breath was choppy, and tears streamed down his cheeks. He spoke in Paavi, reciting something that had been far too long outside his thoughts. He invoked the first prayer of thanks Mahrno had taught him so many light years ago. With both palms flat on the glass, he chanted on, facing the light.

CHARGED FOR RESTART

LOOKING DOWN, HE COULD SEE HIS OWN
REFLECTION. HE JUMPED BACK WHEN HE SAW
HIS REFLECTION WAVE.

With a half shaved beard and the curiosity of a child, Ryan gently pushed down on the outside panel. His suit chimed that he had another thirty seconds of exposure time. After entering the chamber, he folded the panels back outward and heard a click. Glancing down, he chuckled, seeing near zero levels of radiation exposure now inside. Shaking his head and wide-eyed, he surveyed the room for the first time with his own eyes.

Traversing through the ship, he discovered a similar release mechanism for the other doorway portals. On each, the left frame had an outside dimple. Pressure to it released a rod on the right side that could be levered to release the door. Each door pulled in a half foot, and Ryan could then manually push them open.

He discovered the command deck and what appeared to be the remains of a single biological occupant. Although his systems and records were unable to identify the origin or age of the vessel, the remains dated to more than twenty thousand years ago. In disbelief, Ryan took seven readings, and all came back the same, with a five-year variance. The alien DNA didn't match anything else in the Paavi catalog, a database which was the most evolved medical catalog in the known systems.

Ryan mumbled, "Curiouser and curiouser."

Ryan triaged the ship repair effort. The first segment was the exterior damage. His challenge was trying to repair a ship made of an unknown material that he couldn't identify. He experimented with molding various types of materials to the ship. The problem was that nothing would adhere to it. With some success, he was able to inject an expanding material into the breaches. In this way, he created a plug in each hole. The problem with this option was creating a seal around the plugs. Ryan injected a fluid into the gap around the first plug. The fluid contained many carbon nanotubes, and when a low voltage was applied, they would all lineup. The lineup would create certain pressures around the gaps that would be strong enough to hold atmospheric pressure. In this way, no adhesion was necessary.

Once he had sufficiently applied the fluid around the plug, he applied a small current to it. There was an immediate pop and flash. Ryan quickly swiped off the leads to remove the current. Looking closely, he could see that the plug material had cracked in the middle. "Crap!" The plug would now have to be removed.

Over the next few days, Ryan carefully cut and chipped away at the plug. It was a miserable job and far harder to remove than it should have been. It was almost like the hole had decreased in size.

While yanking on the last large chunk, Ryan screamed as he pulled on it. It came loose with difficulty. Ryan sat on the floor, panting with the fragment in hand. He was looking at the hole, and it did look smaller. As he approached it, he muttered, "There's no way. You only think it's smaller because of the difficulty getting…" His words trailed off as he looked at a laser measure of the hole size. He remeasured, then remeasured again. The hole was indeed smaller than it was originally.

Ryan thought for a moment and recoated the breach with the carbon-laced liquid. As he measured the hole for the next hour, there was no change.

Hesitantly, he applied a current to the material and instantly, there was a purplish glow. He quickly swiped off the power. Checking again, he noted a slight decrease in the size of the breach.

Ryan went to another hole in the ship, measured it, and then applied power to it directly. He increased the voltage, and he could see the material healing itself. Ryan left the current on and watched as the hole completely disappeared. Running his hand over the spot where there had previously been a breach caused him to laugh loudly. Glancing a few feet away, he could see that another hole was diminishing.

Power was traversing across the skin material and healing the ship. Ryan hooked up a power supply from the Paavi freighter to the hull of the alien vessel. One hour later, all evidence of breaches was gone. Twenty minutes thereafter, the skin of the ship changed from a gray and ghost-white color to a silvery, prismatic hue.

Ryan emerged and removed the power leads from the alien hull. Looking down, he could see his own reflection. He jumped back when he saw his reflection wave. He saw images on the surface of the ship that were like a replay of him repairing the skin. He saw his reflection reach down and touch the skin. The animation repeated itself. Ryan pursed his lips and reached down to touch the ship.

Concentric circles shot away as if his hand was a large rock in a pool of water. The ship changed hue from all primary colors and started flashing colors in a wave. "Ha! Look at you. How pretty. If I didn't know any better, I'd say you were happy."

The lightshow diminished until the ship held a violet hue. Ryan moved toward the portal, and the color violet became more enhanced around the doorway. The door opened automatically, and Ryan giggled as he entered. Once inside, he noticed there were pocket lights all over the ship illuminating the passages.

Ryan touched several consoles, and there was no response. "Nope, no power to these. How do we get you more juice?"

As he was rounding the corner toward the command deck, he noticed a light strip on the floor. Following it to the command deck, he saw the light strip go into the back wall. He approached the wall and looked closely at it. As he reached to touch it, a seam appeared. Ryan jumped back as a door popped halfway open. Pulling on it, Ryan could see there was a secret room behind it.

Inside, he discovered a five-foot-high rectangular device that was slowly cycling with a soft glow. The majority of the device was some kind of crystalline material surrounded by thin strips of metal. Although the light produced was a yellow glow, at its brightest point, he couldn't see into the opaque material. Surveying the device further, he could see significant damage all around it. In all four quadrants, it looked like power conduits had been completely vaporized.

He noted the size of the conduits and mumbled aloud, "This has gotta be your power." Looking further around the backside, he noticed a small power port on the bottom portion that appeared to be a receptacle. There was a small light flashing in a particular pattern next to the receptacle. Ryan recorded the pattern. As he stood up, he noticed another small access door behind the power supply. There was no visible mechanism to release the door.

As Ryan exited the ship, the skin gave him more animations. He watched as the ship created the image of the power supply. Ryan raised his arm and tried to nod his head. The ship then duplicated the flashing pattern next to the power receptacle. It repeated the pattern over and over again. "I don't know what that means. What does that mean?"

The ship showed him a picture of the small access door and showed it opening. The ship continued to replay the pattern and show the door animation.

Each time Ryan looked outside, the alien ship would play the pattern. "Yes, I get it. Well, I don't get it, but I see the pattern."

After some analysis of the patterns, Ryan came to the conclusion that the signal was indicative of a power supply. Ryan exited the freighter, and the ship was flashing the pattern at him. He attached a power supply to the ship hull, and the ship stopped flashing. Ryan applied what he believed was a voltage and current mathematically represented by the light signals. The ship went wild. Lights flashed in the same pattern but with all primary colors. It replayed at various speeds but mostly fast. Ryan laughed. "OK, OK, so I guess that's a yes."

Before he turned to enter, the ship again played an animation showing the small access door opening behind the power supply. Before Ryan could touch the access doors, they opened again for him. "I could get used to this."

"Well, here goes nothing." Ryan applied power to the receptacle, and there was an immediate loud hum. The pitch increased until Ryan had thoughts of panic. There was a loud vibration that made his stomach tickle and his vision blurry. Then the crystal was silent and emitted a dark purple color. Ryan turned around and saw that the small access door behind the power supply was now open.

Looking inside, he could see several components symmetrically arranged in the small area. Ryan mumbled, "Central core." There was a language on most of it. In the center was a terminal and a glass panel that looked like an input console. Next to it was a device that looked like it took inputs from a four-fingered hand. Ryan held his hand over it and breathed a sigh of relief. "Too small to be Daerk." After several minutes inside, he emerged. The question was how to repair the conduits and restore power to the central system. As he came back out to the command deck, he could see floor lights swirling toward what looked like an access panel.

Ryan chuckled and put his hand on the wall. "I like this ship." Bending down, he pressed on the panel and the release clicked. The door swung down, revealing the interior. It contained various power couplings and cables. Ryan rummaged through and discovered many types and kinds. Holding up two different examples, he wondered aloud, "How am I going to know which one?"

He paused for a moment and then smiled. He held up one. "This one?" There was no light response. He repeated until the floor lighting went crazy.

Ryan found that he could lift floor panels around the power crystal. Under one segment, he found power receptacles that matched one end of the cable. He mounted the cable, and it started to glow. He mumbled as he entered the small access door, "We're moving too fast. This is too fast; we should slow down and think about this."

Ryan stood tall once inside. "Won't matter anyway, it'll probably take a week to figure out where to plug this." The dark border of the floor blossomed, and he could see a circle in the middle of it. "Never mind, we have Rex, the helpful ship." He bent down, and his fingers discovered a removable cover with a hinge.

"Why would the ship want me to help it if it was just going to decompress me out an airlock?" Ryan thought for a moment. "I'm already in a decompressed ship. If this goes sideways, I can always just pull the plug." After a few seconds' pause, he held the cord up. "What could possibly go wrong…fortune favors!" With that, he stabbed the cable into the receptacle.

Lights and sounds came on immediately. Ryan touched the control panel, and his eyes danced around, taking in the menagerie. It was as if he'd restored power to a magical carousel. He brought his hands together like a clap and clasped them. Misty eyed, he mumbled, "Come back; come alive again."

A quick couple of chirping tones caught his attention, and he saw the floor lighting start flashing. As the central systems continued to spool up, the floor lighting was flashing like a landing-pad rabbit, trying to lead him out of the core room. Ryan cocked his head at the juxtaposition. In those first few seconds, Ryan was so buoyed with joy that he felt light headed. Like many happy moments in his life, it had happened just before things went very badly.

With hardware in the main system computer restored, the synthetic intelligence residing in it started to wake. Her automated defense systems ascertained that an alien was present in her source room, and anything unknown there was classed a mortal threat. A ribbon of plasma danced off a panel near Ryan, and he tried to dive away. The stream of energy contacted deck plating, and a shower of electrical current pelted through him.

As he lay on the floor in the sunset of consciousness, he looked through the cracked visor at the deck stretching away. The sight was all too familiar. His body convulsed, and he struggled to breathe. Pain and frustration gave way to a sadness and he mumbled, "I'm done."

As more and more systems came online, the synthetic stabilized. She ascertained that the alien lying motionless on the floor in her source room was in fact the being that had repaired and elevated her back to consciousness. In addition, her clock indicated that she'd been offline for thousands of years. She was programmed to auto-terminate in the event her captain, her prime, was lost or killed. As a team, they possessed knowledge and technology that could not be compromised under any circumstance by a maligned force or an immature species. She was capable of self-terminating so as to leave nothing behind. She could remember the attack, and she was aware that the prime's remains were on the command deck.

However, she was also programmed to assist ships or beings in duress with special instructions regarding the unlikely event that she inadvertently caused the harm. She possessed self-determination and discretion in the auto-destruct sequence. She analyzed the Paavi freighter and determined there was significant risk in her revival. She also determined there was a high likelihood the biological being was trying to repair and not capture her based on the reactivation sequence. Her power source was by far the most valuable portion of the ship. He did not remove it but instead used it to reactivate her.

These factors led her to believe Ryan was not a threat; on the contrary, he was a benevolent actor taking extreme risk to revive her. As result of this analysis, and in the absence of any real threat in the system, she suspended her auto-termination program with one point seven three seconds remaining in the count.

Ryan's spirit had drifted to the frontier between the physical and thereafter. He was submersed in a shallow reflecting pool that stretched infinitely away from him. Near him, he could see the faces of loved ones up through the water's rippling surface. Leishu was smiling and winking at him. Jeeval and Pari smiled and nodded. Mahrno put her hands over her lips and central heart, then extended her hands toward him. Gehnchan put both hands together and bowed his head in prayer. His aunts were all animated, talking to each other and then motioning toward him. His human mother smiled and blew him a kiss. His human father had his arm around his mother and Hadley. Hadley shot an air pistol toward him and winked. He reached for them out of the water, but he couldn't sit up. He was drowning, but he could not die.

The synthetic decided she would attempt to save the fragile biological being. She dispatched a remote drone to gently remove the body from the source room and take it to a medical station. Once the lifeform was safely out of the source room, she tuned the crystal and regained more power. After analyzing the gas in the biological's suit, she quickly mimicked the atmosphere inside the ship. It was very near her prime's requirements, and there were definite similarities between the species.

The alien was placed in stasis, and a neural connection was made. The synthetic determined that the alien had localized damage to the neural control center at the top of its body. The alien physiology, specifically his protein design indicators, was slightly different from anything in her medical library. She would not be able to repair the biological being within acceptable risks tolerances by herself. Because the alien's vital signs were diminishing, she placed it into a stasis coma.

With a ship diagnostic complete, she broke orbit. She plotted a course to a place well beyond the boundaries of what Ryan would classify as the "known" systems. In this place, she would find the beings with knowledge.

THE MAKERS

"Who are you? Why are you staring at
me?"
—Ryan to the old man

The synthetic checked her coordinates and verified that she'd emerged in the correct quadrant. There were planets missing and entire systems displaced. Something catastrophic had happened here since her last visit.

What she sought was an ancient species known as the Makers. More energy than form, they were a cognitive material that collectively formed a singular elevated existence. These were advisors, not only to the race to which her prime belonged but also to many others. Countless species relied on their benevolent wisdom and guidance. For many thousands of years, they had provided teaching that led other races to discover their own elevated presence. The Makers' existence was intrinsic to the light of the universe, but a small portion of their presence still overlapped with matter in the physical plane.

The synthetic and her prime were guardians. Their purpose was to check and counter the antithesis of the Makers—the Dae—and their dark minions. Her analysis indicated a high likelihood that something catastrophic had happened to the benevolent elders. Although the dominant segment of her intelligence was logic, she felt grief for the loss.

While stopped and completely exposed, she registered energy and mass moving toward her in near space. She very nearly auto-terminated again, until she realized that what she had detected were remnants of the Makers. Two beings had coalesced in response to her presence. Touching her hull, the remnants showed her images of what had happened many thousands of years ago. As the Dae approached this dimension with a proposal for peace, the subversive plan was to achieve it through eradication of the Makers. In an epic battle, the Dae did not realize the symbiotic relationship between their anti-existence and the Makers. In their zeal, they destroyed nearly everyone.

Only three beings survived: two Makers and a single remaining Dae. Although the energy of the surviving Makers was greatly diminished, the surviving Dae emerged more powerful. The synthetic saw more images of what the surviving Dae had done in subsequent years. Over millennia, it continued to augment its power by consuming and feeding off other beings.

Turning their attention to the damaged biological being in stasis, the elder of the two Makers had a familiar sense of Ryan. There was something about his genetic code. He could also feel a familiarity in the energy of Ryan's spirit. The elder conveyed a strong sense that something else was in play. Without further elaborating, a precious amount of non-personified mass of the Makers was introduced into Ryan's brain.

The damage and void of his injury was temporarily replaced with Maker material. The two elders overlapped Ryan's presence such that they could inhabit the cerebral void. In this way, they could act as virtual relays for the synapses in the missing brain tissue. The Makers began a process to coax Ryan's body to regenerate at the cellular level, one cell at a time.

Ryan was unconscious for several weeks. He learned of the Makers through a series of dreams that were more nightmarish in tone and effect. The elder Maker came to him at first as a leering old man. Wherever Ryan looked, the old man was staring back at him. Sometimes the old man was seated far away and other times uncomfortably close. For an elder being, he had no sense of personal space. Over time, Ryan was less startled by it. He also became aware that he was always laying down in these dream visions.

"Who are you? Why are you staring at me?"

The old man just looked back without response or emotion.

Ryan became more animated. "Stop staring at me! Go! You hear me? Go away!" He sat up for the first time and waved his hand. The old man stood up and clasped his hands at his waist. He craned his neck and looked expectantly at Ryan.

"What? What do you want with me?"

With that, the old man smiled and touched his index finger to his temple. While doing this, he simultaneously put his other palm over where a human heart would be. Then he extended both hands together, palms up toward Ryan.

"I don't understand."

The old man chuckled and pointed to the top of his wrist.

Over the prior weeks, the ancient being had sampled through segments of brain matter related to Ryan's memories. Over time, they would develop a communication method that would use images from Ryan's past. The beginning of the path to communion began as games of checkers. For Ryan, it felt as though he was a hostage in his own dreams. They played checkers until the Maker discovered memories of other sports.

The old man became very enamored with baseball. Ryan would find himself in a vision of a ballpark from his childhood. It was always near dark, and the lights were on. He could smell fresh cut grass in the cool evening air. The first time Ryan found himself there, he closed his eyes, drank in a long breath, and smiled. His eyes opened to the old man looking at him with a cocked head.

"Grass. It's the smell of cut grass." Ryan pointed down and then back to his nose. "It's a sensory perception. It's called smell." The old man nodded quickly and craned his neck out. Ryan chuckled. "You have to breath in. Come on, you know I respire for oxygen? Take in the air through your nose."

The old man looked down, and Ryan could see him tentatively breath in. He smiled widely and pointed to his nose. For the next three or four minutes, the old man sniffed and snorted loudly while walking around. Ryan watched and tried not to laugh. When the ancient being got down on all fours near homeplate chalk marks, Ryan jumped into motion. Waving his arms, he said, "No, no! Not that close. You can't breathe it in directly." The old man sat up coughing with white powder around his face. They both just sat laughing for a few minutes.

The old man loved to play a game of catch. He delighted in being a catcher behind home plate while Ryan threw from the mound. The elder would commune with Ryan through actions. He was fond of the strength of the throw and the thump of the ball in the mitt. Ryan could tell that it made him near giddy when he threw a curveball.

After several weeks of catch, Ryan found himself again in the stadium. "No. I'm sick of baseball."

The old man said nothing and just punched his mitt with his fist.

"Please, I don't wanna to play catch. I'm sick of it."

The old man took off his mask and nodded. He turned around and started walking away.

"Hey, where are you going?"

The elder continued on.

"Hey, what about me?"

The old man turned around and pointed toward the stadium lights. Ryan turned around and looked up into the lights. His body lurched awake as he looked up into lights shining down on a medical table. He'd regained consciousness. The room was strange but also familiar. He sat up and felt a piercing pain in his head.

A female voice broke the silence. "Take caution, lifeform. You've experienced a traumatic injury to your central control organ."

Ryan looked through his fingers around the room. "I've been in this room before. It was dark, and before I had..." his voice trailed off. "You're the central control of this ship. You electrocuted me, didn't you?"

There was a pause. "I am an intelligent life companion. I am a synthetic being that resides in this vessel. You were discovered trespassing in my source room. My defensive system acted in accordance with protocols."

Ryan chuckled. "Remind me not to ever save you again."

"I regret the misidentification that lead to your harm."

"Well, OK...I guess that's an apology. What exactly happened to my head?

Where's my ship? And why is some creepy old man wandering around in my dreams?"

"I will address each of your queries in the order in which they were asked. There was a disintegration of material in your processing and control organ. We are currently back in parallel orbit with your cargo vessel. The elder in your subconscious state is likely the ancient being that is treating the replacement of lost material in your processing organ."

Ryan rubbed his temple for a few moments until he stopped abruptly and looked up. "How do you know English?"

"Your cargo vessel contains samples from a number of languages within it. We are aware of your planet of origin. As such, it seemed logical to address you in your native language."

Ryan's eyes went wide, and he tried to stand. He took one step and went down on all fours.

"Biologic biped, do not be alarmed. We share a common enemy. No harm can come upon you while you are inside this vessel."

Ryan cocked his head. "That statement's a bit ironic, don' you think?" He panted for a moment and caught his breath. "I have a number of new inquiries."

"That is reasonable. I am prepared to answer."

"Well, first off, the proper name for my processing organ is my brain. What exactly does treating the replacement of lost material mean?"

"The ancient being you referred to is called a Maker. The Maker elected to provide you with some of his genetic material while your own tissues regenerate."

Ryan's eyes grew even wider. "You put someone else's...stuff in my brain?" He came up on a knee and panted.

"The 'stuff' to which you refer with implied disdain is a genetic material that is at least a quantum step more evolved than your own."

Panting down at the floor, Ryan shot back, "What if I had started putting components into your source room while you were damaged? Something from other synthetic beings? And what if I'd done so without getting your permission? How would you feel about that?"

"Initially, I would have the same trepidation that I believe you are demonstrating. Upon learning of the vastly superior components of Maker material, I would be greatly relieved and thankful."

Ryan shook his head. "Creepy old guy inside my head, literally, and an arrogant robot overhead."

"You are aware that you are verbalizing these thoughts?"

"Yes, I am aware. I gotta get out of here."

"I only ask because you've experienced a traumatic injury to your brain."

"I need my ship. You haven't done anything to it, have you? As in when you went rummaging through it."

"Your ship is in exactly the same configuration, and there is no reason for you to think anything was displaced."

"You know about Earth. That's a pretty good trick. I don't know how you know that. There shouldn't be anything over there with that information, so you must have dug deep and found something I missed."

"The Maker knows you are from Terra. Both Makers, actually."

"Shit, there's two of them? No wonder; they're taking shifts on me."

"Only one has been able to communicate with you thus far."

Ryan rose to take a step and stumbled down again to all fours. He winced and touched his hand to his temple. "This goop in my head is killing me."

"Actually, the material in your brain is repairing you. This is the reason you have been unconscious for what you would measure as twelve weeks. Continuing this erratic movement will threaten and possibly preclude your ability to recover." The medical table lowered down to floor level. "I highly recommend that you return to a horizontal position."

"How long 'til I can leave?"

"You may leave at any point. For a full recovery, I estimate an additional period of two of your weeks of rest."

Ryan was hoarse and fumbled on all fours back to the table. "Please," he begged, winded, "please turn off the lights. Too bright."

Falling unconscious, he woke again in the ballpark. Turing around to home plate, he saw the old man. His look was hopeful, and he nodded, motioning with his catcher's mitt.

Ryan pulled down on the bill of his cap and grimaced. "So, you're really old?"

The old man shrugged.

"Is there another one of you running around in here?"

The old man smiled and pointed up with his mitt. Ryan looked up, and the sky momentarily lit with pink, red, and orange.

"I have absolutely no idea what that means."

The old man chuckled and nodded. He turned toward home plate and pulled his mask down.

"I guess we're going to have a catch."

Ryan threw a few fast balls that cracked hard. Chuckling, he said, "Those have gotta sting. You want to keep going?"

The old man rose up, took his mitt off, and pointed at his palm.

"Yeah, if you don't know what you're doing, it stings."

As the old man looked at him, Ryan felt dizzy and loosed. He could feel a sense of catching a fast ball. The old man nodded quickly and began to squat. Ryan held his temple for a moment, and before he could speak, he saw a vision of a curve ball sailing through the air. The old man motioned with his arm.

"Hey, you can't. Listen, you can't just go digging around in my memories." Ryan walked off the mound toward him. "You understand? It's creepy. I didn't give you permission to invade my thoughts. What would it be like if I could dig around in your conscious thoughts or paw through your memories?"

The old man stood up and tilted his head. He closed his eyes, and instantly Ryan stiffened. He saw lights and energy that he couldn't identify. The intensity and speed of imagery was overwhelming. There were millions of beings connected together, and he could feel everything all of them felt in one instance. In a flash, he was back in the ballpark.

He bent over and vomited before taking a knee. The old man was instantly at his side and gently patted his back. Ryan was looking down. "What the hell was that? Was that your consciousness?"

Looking up to the side, he saw the old man tilt his head left and right and shrug. Ryan stood with furrowed brow. The old man had discovered the movement of his shoulders. He put his hands on them and felt them raise up and down. Then he smiled back at Ryan with his discovery.

Ryan's brows pinched together tighter. "It's called shrugging. Usually that means I don't know." The old man shook his head. "Or combined with the tilting head gesture, it means kind of." The elder quickly nodded his head. "So that means it's kind of your consciousness. It felt like there were millions of others. Are those other Makers?" The old man smiled and nodded. "So, you guys are all tied together somehow?"

The old man looked down for a moment. When he looked back up, Ryan could feel pain through his eyes, and the old man pointed at his wrist.

"Time? Was this something in the past?"

The elder nodded.

"The bastards that took my home, did they do this to you guys?"

The Maker pursed his lips and nodded.

"How did you survive?"

Ryan heard a noise, and turning around, he saw six Daerk near third base. They snarled, spread apart, and advanced quickly. Ryan struck a fighting posture, and as he turned to gesture for the elder to take cover, he saw that the old man was no longer behind him. Turning back forward, he saw that the Maker was outlined in a glowing white. He placed himself in between Ryan and the Daerk.

Before Ryan could say anything, two lead Daerk swung staffs into the elder. A white glow blocked the strikes, and a flash hit the Daerk so hard that their bodies landed in left field. The remaining four growled and charged. The old man bowed his head, and the air smelled electrified, like moments before a lightning strike. Ryan watched as the Daerk bounced off what appeared to be a shield wall. They repeatedly struck and growled into the energy before turning their attention toward Ryan. As they slid off to attack the human, the Maker struck all four with a flash that sent their bodies flying into the stands.

A curl formed in the corner of Ryan's mouth. "Holy shit! You're a defender?"

The old man bowed.

Ryan looked off. "I used to be a defender too...before." The human shook his head, and the old man put his hand on Ryan's shoulder. As their eyes met, Ryan continued, his voice faltering, "I couldn't save them. I wanted to, but I—"

The old man quickly put his palm on Ryan's chest, and pulling back, he held up an index finger. With his other arm, he flexed his muscle and then pointed to it.

Ryan cocked his head, "Strength? You sayin' I wasn't strong enough?"

The Maker shook his head again, pointed to his muscle, and then looked skyward. Ryan looked up as what looked like a stream of lighting lit the sky, coming down right over them. The Maker held his palms up, and the lightning landed into them. After a few moments, the lightning ceased, and the Maker was glowing. He cupped his palms together, and Ryan could see a glow coming from inside it. He held up a brilliant light that lifted up over their heads. Ryan could see it form into the same shield that had blocked the Daerk moments earlier. The old man pointed to his flexed muscle and then back to Ryan.

"Power? I need more power?"

The old man nodded and winked at him.

Ryan woke with a start, back on the medical table.

"Greetings, biological biped. Your prognosis is improving with remarkable speed."

Ryan swung his legs down while mumbling, "Crazy old man." He gently stood up.

"In that vertical configuration and with your current medical condition, there is a thirty percent higher chance of rapid, inadvertent contact with the ground."

"Did you rush through your study of English?"

"Are you indicating that my use of your language is deficient?"

Ryan raised his eyebrows. "You could just say I might fall because I'm still groggy."

"Is that not what I just indicated?"

Ryan smiled and walked gingerly around the corner. "So, there any place in here I should avoid getting zapped again?"

"For the moment, I have reclassified your lifeform with a security clearance."

"Super. Then let's take the tour."

"What would you like to see?"

Ryan moved through the different compartments asking questions. In a science lab, Ryan looked up and around. "This sure looks better with the power on."

"May I ask a personal query?"

Ryan shrugged. "Sure, I guess. What's up?"

"Why did you restore me?"

Ryan chuckled. "For many weeks now, I been asking myself the same question."

"Do you regret doing so?"

Ryan looked up and around. "No. No, I don't."

"Then why did you do it?"

Ryan looked down and nodded. "I suppose I've been broken for so long that I just wanted to help fix someone else."

Ryan shuffled forward to the command deck. The door didn't automatically open. "Is the compartment ahead still compromised? I thought we fixed all the breaches."

"There is no breach. The atmosphere is suitable for you. I'm disabling the locking mechanism."

Ryan looked up and around the frame. "Uh, still not opening. Zappy robot, you still there?"

"I am a synthetic intelligence, and I am still present."

"OK, synthetic intelligence. Can you explain why the door hasn't opened?"

There was a long pause. "The remains of my prime are on the command deck."

"Oh, I see. You were close?"

"We were bound as a team."

"That's not what I asked."

"You are correct. I am having difficulty processing and responding in this matter."

Ryan put his hand on the wall and took a long breath. "Now you're finally starting to make sense." He leaned against the wall and looked up out of the corner of his eye. "Can I help you?"

"I do not understand."

"Losing someone close to you is difficult. Letting go is even harder. The loss never really goes away; the sting of it just diminishes a little with time. Do you have a ritual in your culture for saying goodbye to the deceased?"

"We do. This would now be problematic for two reasons."

Ryan cocked his head in the pause. "Please elaborate."

"Our culture dispatched lost warriors into our source star. Unfortunately, it appears to have been destroyed by the Daerk lord."

Ryan nodded. "What if we sent your prime into the neutron we're orbiting? Would that be a reasonable alternative?"

"Affirmative."

There was another long pause. Ryan cocked his head again. "What is the other difficulty?"

"If we send my prime into the neutron, then the prime would no longer be on this vessel. I would no longer be together with my prime. My prime would be...gone."

Ryan's cheeks tightened, and he slid down to the floor, resting against the frame. "Yeah. It's an awful thought. You were his guardian?"

"That was one of my primary responsibilities. I failed."

Ryan nodded. "There seems to be a bit of that going around." After a few seconds, he continued. "Do you agree that his remains should be interred?"

"Yes."

"Would it help if we did it together? I could collect the remains of your prime. When you're ready, we could have a ceremony and release the body into the neutron. What do you think?"

The door to the command deck opened, and Ryan stepped through. Over a period of two days, he gathered up all the remaining genetic material into a formal burial container. The synthetic provided Ryan with a protective suit that was vastly superior to his Paavi one. With it, he could remain outside for several minutes. The synthetic spoke words in a language that Ryan didn't understand. There was a pause before she spoke again. "I believe I am ready for the release." The skin of the ship flashed in many colors of red and pink.

Ryan nodded and pushed the container toward the neutron. "Kindred warrior, your battle in this realm is over. Go with honor, and be at peace. May fair Valkyries lead you to Valhalla."

Ryan watched the vessel for a few minutes as it traversed lower and then beyond his sight. When he turned around to enter the ship, he noted a violet hue reflecting off the ship's translucent surface. As he reached the airlock, he saw a deeper purple coalesce by the portal. "Hey, how come purple?"

"Violet is a frequency of the visible spectrum that I prefer."

"Why did the color deepen near the portal as I approached?"

"The source is likely the ship. I have a symbiotic relationship with this vessel. While it is of a lesser intelligence, it runs the lighting and other basic functions. I believe the ship has a favorable response to you."

Ryan smiled. "That makes better sense now." As he was returning the extravehicular suit into storage, he saw his name appear on the label above the locker. "Does the ship control labels and markings?"

"Yes. It seems to have adopted English and assigned this locker to you. Surprising, as it was very close with the prime. Is that displaying your proper designation?"

"You mean my name?"

"Yes. What is your preferred salutation?"

"My given name is Mitchell Ryan McBain. I was known to the Paavi as Eylon of family Walach. You may call me Ryan."

"You served in a force as a guardian for your home planet?"

"Yes, I hold, or rather held, the rank of commander."

"We are all guardians here, commander."

Ryan nodded. "What about your designation?"

"Synthetics do not have designations. We serve under our prime."

"Well, that won't do. All intelligent life, no matter the origin, should have self-determination and a name." Ryan thought for a moment and then nodded. "Yeah, that'll do. It's fitting."

"I do not understand."

"Violet. What do you think of this name?"

"I am Violet."

"Nice to meet you, Violet."

"Commander?"

"Yes, Violet?"

"Thank you for your assistance in paying respect to my prime."

Ryan nodded. "You're very welcome."

For the next few weeks, the old man provided information and entertainment as Ryan healed. The elevated being enjoyed tactile experiences while projecting himself as a human. Ryan watched as a child's wonder of discovery shone through the face of an ancient being.

"No, that's nasty. Don't swallow that! Spit it out and come over here. Do not swallow." Ryan jogged over to the bench and dug in a bag. His face lit up. "It's right here, just like it was so many years ago." He chuckled, finding his childhood "lucky" water bottle. Turning around to the old man, he said, "I hit homeruns when I had this bottle in my bag."

He unscrewed the cap. "Did you swallow any of it?" The old man had a bitter look on his face and shook his head. "Did you hear me say not to put dirt in your mouth?" The old man nodded. "So, you did it anyway?" He handed the bottle to the Maker. "Now put this fluid in your mouth, but do not swallow. Use the muscles in your mouth to move the fluid around and then spit it out."

The old man pointed into the bottle. "Yeah, it's liquid water. Swish it around and spit it out. It may take a couple—" Ryan was interrupted as the old man spat the mouthful straight out on him. "Seriously?!"

The old man started giggling.

"Oh, this is funny to you?"

He nodded, took more water, and spat it out in a stream. Ryan had to take evasive action to avoid getting hit again. "Hey!"

The old man continued to put water in his mouth and squirt it out. Sometimes he went for distance, and other times it just dribbled down his front. Then he spat the water into his hand, rubbed both hands together, and held them up to Ryan. The human just shook his head and walked back toward the pitcher's mound. "When you're done over there, we can continue."

Ryan stood on the side of the mound, working the baseball with both hands. Smiling, he watched as the old man used up the entire bottle of water. As the elder was walking back to home plate, he pointed back toward the bench, smiling.

"Yep, now you know how to spit water. Wonderful, isn't it?" Ryan shook his head. "I'm present with the oldest sentience in the galaxy who's just learned how to spit."

The old man nodded back to him. Looking down at his glove, he spat on it and watched the leather change color.

"Just stop. You gotta stop. We do not spit on everything, OK? Just slow down on the spitting thing." The old man nodded and squatted down. "Let's get back to the cutting-edge action of catch."

Ryan hurled the ball to the Maker. He stood and took off his mask. Ryan watched as he threw the ball back. An instant after he threw the ball, he threw again. It was almost like a repeat of the original throw, but there were two baseballs flying at him through the air. Ryan caught the first, dropped it out of his mitt, and immediately caught the second. The old man smiled.

"What are you doing?"

The old man instantly appeared in several places, like a hall of mirrors at a carnival. Each cloned image threw, and Ryan saw about fifteen balls come at him.

"Ayah!" Ryan ran quickly from the mound as all the balls landed around him on the ground. He looked back now at a single image of the old man. He had a disappointed look on his face.

"What was that about?"

The old man pointed at Ryan and then held up both index fingers. He motioned like they were in movement, then held up more fingers. Then he pointed at Ryan again.

"I don't understand. What do all the fingers mean?"

The old man pointed again at Ryan.

"The fingers are me?"

The old man winked. He held one hand up, palm toward Ryan, with his other hand obscured behind it. Then he slid out the hand behind to mirror the first.

Ryan squinted. "But there's only one of me."

The old man grew animated and wagged his finger. He then split into two images of himself, and both pointed at Ryan.

"I don't know how to do that."

The Maker returned to one image, closed his eyes, held his arms out, palms upward, and breathed slowly. He opened his eyes and looked at Ryan.

"You want me to, what? Meditate? Concentrate? Relax?" The Maker nodded and pointed.

"Relax?" The elder nodded again and breathed in deeply.

"Sure. Yeah. I'm getting lessons in quantum physics from a guy that just learned not to eat dirt."

The Maker nodded at Ryan and demonstrated a deep breath. After a few moments, Ryan opened his eyes, and the Maker threw three balls toward Ryan in rapid succession. They came in too fast, and the human couldn't catch all three. Rubbing his side where the third one had struck him, he muttered, "I don't know how to do this."

The Maker held his hand up, then motioned with two fingers toward his temple. He closed his eyes and breathed deeply. Ryan followed him and took a few breaths. When he opened his eyes, the Maker nodded and threw three balls at him again. Before the balls could arrive, he realized that the Maker was now somehow standing next to him. Ryan felt a loosening feeling as the Maker pulled his glove up. Three balls were approaching, but the speed appeared dramatically reduced. Ryan saw his gloved arm rise three different times and catch all three. He looked at the Maker with wide eyes. The old man smiled, pointing down, and tapped his wrist.

"How'd that happen? The balls slowed down."

The Maker shook his head and again tapped his wrist.

"Time. You slowed time?"

He nodded and smiled at Ryan.

"Can we do that again?"

For the next half hour, Ryan felt time slow as they repeated the exercise. In the last few minutes, he was able to focus on the same feeling and the connection with the Maker. By doing this, he could slow time and catch the balls without the Maker standing next to him, directing his glove. Laughing out loud, he took one step forward and collapsed on one knee. He became aware of a piercing pain in his head. He was dizzy and nauseated. The Maker patted him on the shoulder.

Ryan woke and immediately vomited in the medical bay.

"Ah, gods. Why can't I throw up in there where there's no cleanup?"

"Commander, I was just about to stim you out of suspension. Your vitals were elevating up through an unhealthy level."

"My head. Oh gods my head hurts. What's he doing in there?"

"If you are referring to the Maker, your neural tissue has fully regenerated as of this morning. Curious. There is an energy signature, but no biological indication of physical material from a Maker."

"I don't understand. Are you saying Maker goop is in my head or not?"

"There is no physical presence, but there is a different energy signature."

"Great. Now it's invisible goop."

SECOND SHOT

"WITH WORN TOOLS AND WEIGHTED
SOUL, THEY'D HAVE US EMBARK UPON A
LIFETIME'S WORK."
—RYAN

The next day, Ryan had a blanket wrapped around him as he wandered up to the command deck. Entering, he saw that the access to the source room was open. Peering inside, he mumbled, "Haven't seen this since—"

"Say again, commander."

Ryan jumped at the voice. "Your source room, Violet. I haven't seen it since I was, you know," he waved his hand in a circular motion around his head.

"You may enter without harm."

Ryan leaned on the portal frame and looked inside.

"Commander, I assure you, you are safe. I have allowed modifications to my core mission programing."

Ryan backed up slightly. "Oh?"

"The Makers believe a specific presence of the light has come upon us. They believe our meeting was not by chance or accident. I have run various calculations that reveal that recent events are not consistent with mathematic models of natural variability. I can validate portions of their hypothesis. The Makers and I are in chorus. At their suggestion, I have allowed modifications to my mission parameters."

"What? Wait, you can talk to them?"

"Not exactly. We communicate through mathematical structures that probably wouldn't make sense to you."

"You got all that through math?"

"Affirmative. I have reclassified your lifeform. You may enter the source room and any room on this vessel. I am bound to protect you in your pending mission."

"Mission? Whoa, whoa." Ryan held his hands out. "Wait a minute. What exactly does a presence of light mean?" There was a long pause. "Violet, to what mission are you referring?"

"I had thought the Makers communicated this morning to you as well."

"I haven't slept in a day; been avoiding it actually. The last time I woke up, my head nearly split in two."

"When you regained consciousness, I was not aware of any separation of neural material."

"No, I was speaking metaphorically."

"This topic is too significant to speak of in nonspecific terms."

"Good god, now my head's splitting when I'm awake too." Ryan turned and exited the command deck.

"Where are you going?"

"Away from you and cognitive goop and the old man. I'll be over checking on my freighter."

"You should use the protective suit from this vessel."

"Why would I use your suit?"

"Technically it is now your suit."

"No, it's not. It's not. This isn't my vessel."

"The suit from this ship will protect you from the radiation on your original vessel. Having been in this orbit for an extended period of time, the interior has been irradiated. Your original suit cannot sufficiently protect you from sustaining damage."

Ryan huffed and pulled the advanced suit from a locker. He noted the prior biological occupant's name labeled on the tag over the locker. As he looked away the display changed to "CDR M. RYAN MCBAIN." Ryan looked up quickly and caught the name change back to that of the original prime. He stared at the placard for a long moment. He looked away, then back quickly, and he caught the placard go blank in the transition. He pointed his finger at the sign and stood. With pursed lips, he snatched the helmet and moved toward the portal.

Entering the Paavi freighter felt familiar, yet somehow strange. He needed a protective suit to stand on the bridge of his own ship. Looking at the captain's seat, he imagined Gehnchan hunched over in it. He could still see Mother approach, run the back of her hand on his shoulder, and tenderly remind him to sit tall. He felt Leishu's presence rush through him. It came to him like one of her hallway tackle hugs. He chuckled through a profound bitterness. His breath was labored and choppy. Holding out both gloved hands, he stared at them and willed them to be steady. His focus drifted to the background where their medical tables had been. The toxicity on the ship took him back to the accident. Plopping down, he leaned over onto his arms.

Ryan woke on the mound. The old man motioned with his catcher's mitt.

"No, this isn't catch. What's going on?" Ryan's arms were animated as he spirited down off the mound. "I need answers. What's happening?"

The old man stumbled forward and grasped both hands over his heart. He teetered forward and fell to his knees. Ryan bolted forward and was with him quickly. Before he could speak, there was a horrible ruckus from the outfield. The boards lining the field were being hit with something. Suddenly, the plywood shredded in many places, and through the breaches, Daerk soldiers streamed through.

The old man was gasping toward the ground, and without looking up, he waved his hand toward the approaching dark minions. Ryan looked down to discover that a rifle had appeared next to the Maker. He hooked his foot under the midsection, kicked it up horizontally, and snatched it out of the air. Without hesitation, fire erupted off the barrel.

Ryan pivoted quickly, prioritizing energy on the closest targets. Rounds off this rifle were sparkling white. Although they had far greater impact than projectile fire, it still took several shots to stop each target. So many Daerk were advancing, and he couldn't stop them fast enough. Ryan knew that at this rate, he would be overrun. Fear, anxiety, and other emotions rose within him, but the rage eclipsed it all.

As they closed in, Ryan defiantly stepped toward them. Aiming carefully, he just needed a little more time to suppress the onslaught. Part of his mind drifted and loosed away to the last game of catch where he'd learned to slow time. When he realized the familiar sensation he'd stumbled into, he cinched down hard on the feeling. Time slowed dramatically. In less than an additional real-time second, he neutralized the remaining fighters, numbering half the original force. A human eye peered down a pivoting barrel that surveyed a now quiet field. Lowering the rifle, he turned around to a smiling and perfectly healthy old man.

"You tricked me."

The Maker pursed his lips and nodded his head. He held his hand out. Ryan looked at it and back to the Maker's eyes. The Maker motioned to his hand. Grasping it, Ryan was immediately in space. Looking over his head, he saw the black octahedron that had taken the Sun. The specter stirred great anxiety, and the Maker put his other hand over Ryan's. He then pointed to the neutron star they'd been orbiting. They passed into the star, and as they emerged, the neutron shrunk down to their size and came close.

Ryan looked around, and he could see now that the three of them were standing on the palm of an enormous hand. It was a woman's hand, and as he looked up, he saw Her massive bare back. Her black mane moved like it was underwater. Her head turned back and behind, gazing down on them. Her brilliant azure eyes glowed, emitting small blue flames.

She smiled, and Ryan saw that She had many arms. Like a child, he mumbled, "Dvarah?" She brought them forward in the hand that was hidden behind Her. All at once, he felt a surge of energy rush through him. A beam of light erupted from his chest toward the octahedron. There was a flash, and Ryan woke on the bridge of the Paavi freighter.

After repressurizing the airlock, Ryan removed his helmet.

"Welcome back, commander, did you find what you were looking for?"

Ryan plopped down on a bench and sat with his head hung low.

"Commander, what is your status? Can I assist you?"

The human looked up and spoke quietly. "Yeah, Vi; I'm still here."

"I am new to human physiology, but your posture suggests some kind of duress."

Ryan nodded. "You're a quick study." He stood and touched a series of buttons on the nearby console. In response, a panel of the wall became translucent. The blue brilliance of the neutron shone in, and Ryan faced into it. "I was just with the old man. He and I paid a visit to this neutron. While I was with them, I saw a vision." Ryan looked down and nodded. "It was a message."

"Do you understand it?"

"Yeah, I do. We would kill the Lumuera. That's what they call the last Dae, the specter of darkness that took everything from us all. There is a way to take it down."

"I have a number of queries. The first one is how?"

"Together. There is a narrow path if we do it together. With worn tools and weighted soul, they'd have us embark upon a lifetime's work. Through the sky, we'd build an empire of knowledge. We would wade deep in dank harbors of dirty business. If we're lucky, if we're careful, if we're intrepid," Ryan reached out and tenderly touched the ship, "then it all culminates in an ending that will not go well for us. In the final stroke, the Lumuera goes down, and us with it. Death is the respite. That's the reward that awaits us."

"I think I understand. What are your intentions?"

Ryan chuckled. "The wonders of the galaxy once called to me, but a shroud of darkness has fallen over everything. I tried to hide from it, but this vortex has been pulling at me for years." Ryan looked out on the neutron with a distant stare. "I've been running from it for so long. I lost everyone and everything, and I'm just so sick of it. It's time. Time to shove back."

Ryan turned around and looked around the room. "We're lone survivors and guardians that shouldn't have lived. But we did, and we've been given a second shot. I say we take it and sanitize the galaxy of this plague. However, if you and I are to do this thing together, you alone must choose your own destiny. For this to work, for you to be the force we all need you to be, it has to come from deep within you. You are no longer the synthetic intelligence under your prime. You are reborn; you are Violet. This cannot be programming. You write your destiny, and this must be your chosen path." Ryan sat for a moment in silence. He raised an eyebrow. "Violet? Vi?"

"I understand. In the military culture from which I come, there is a protocol we follow. We work in teams, and there is a pact. If there is threat of irretrievable capture or imminent loss, I have the capacity to take us out together. This status we call State 1. I choose never to lie dormant and exposed again. I do not ever want to experience my recent feelings of going alone. I choose this mission, but on the condition that we go together. That is the accord. Do you agree to these terms?"

Ryan's face was taut, and his heart was in his throat. "It would be my honor to serve with you."

"What's our first move, commander?"

"Not far as it turns out. Do you trust me?"

"Affirmative."

"Then into this neutron we go. As it turns out, She's expecting us."

ABOUT THE AUTHOR

J.W. Griffin has often gazed up into the starry night and imagined a chance meeting someday in an off-world cantina.

With a penchant for otherworldly adventure, he is an avid scuba diver and former cargo captain. Interests in anthropology and religion propelled him through a B.A. from Lewis and Clark College. He draws from these interests and writes with a desire to capture moments that transcend basic human instinct.

J.W. Griffin currently resides in Oregon with his family and two rowdy Bouvier des Flandres.

To find out more please visit his website:

JWGRIFFIN.US

www.ingramcontent.com/pod-product-compliance
Lightning Source LLC
Chambersburg PA
CBHW030606180626
46816CB00005B/1699